RECIPES FOR ROMANCE

& You Anthologies

Another Chance to Get It Right: A New Year's Eve Anthology

As the Snow Drifts: A Cozy Winter Anthology

Craving You: A Spicy Valentine's Day Anthology

Recipes for Romance: A Sweet Valentine's Day Anthology

RECIPES FOR ROMANCE

A Sweet Valentine's Day Anthology

Edited by Nicole Frail

www.andyoupress.com

Trigger Warnings: Terminal illness,* Death of a sibling,° Death of a spouse,¤ Infant loss§

To order in bulk or to sell this book in your retail brick-and-mortar or online store, contact sales@nicolefrailbooks.com.

Cover design by Kerri Odell
Arranged, edited, and typeset by Nicole Frail/Nicole Frail Edits, LLC
Proofread by Constance Renfrow/Renfrow Editorial

First publication: January 2025

www.nicolefrailbooks.com | @nicolefrailbooks | www.andyoupress.com | @andyoupress

Print ISBN: 978-1-965852-12-5
Ebook ISBN: 978-1-965852-11-8

Contents

"The Missing Cupcake" **209**
by Megan D. Wood

Lucy, with her dreams of opening her own bakery one day, accepts the opportunity to bake cupcakes for a corporate event. However, this means giving up the perfect Valentine's evening she had planned with her boyfriend, Ian, which potentially puts their relationship on the rocks.

"A Note to Remember" **232**
by Bjarne Borresen

Charlie Nunley, following the death of his wife, has been walking through life in a daze, just going through the motions. A note passed to him from a friendly bartender could be just the spark Charlie needs to start living again.

"Sweet As Pie" **235**
by Krista Renee

After a run-in with her daughter's girlfriend's mother, Georgia Lynn feels the most alive she's felt in years. Will spending time with Jill put the fragile relationship she has with her daughter at risk? Is the chance of something new worth it?

"Brownie Points" **244**
by Aimee Maineaux

Cordelia is having the worst Valentine's Day ever, so she decides to do what any self-respecting college freshman would: she plans to eat her feelings. The brownies she tries to make in her dorm kitchen are inedible, but she is rescued by David, an upperclassman who knows his way around the kitchen.

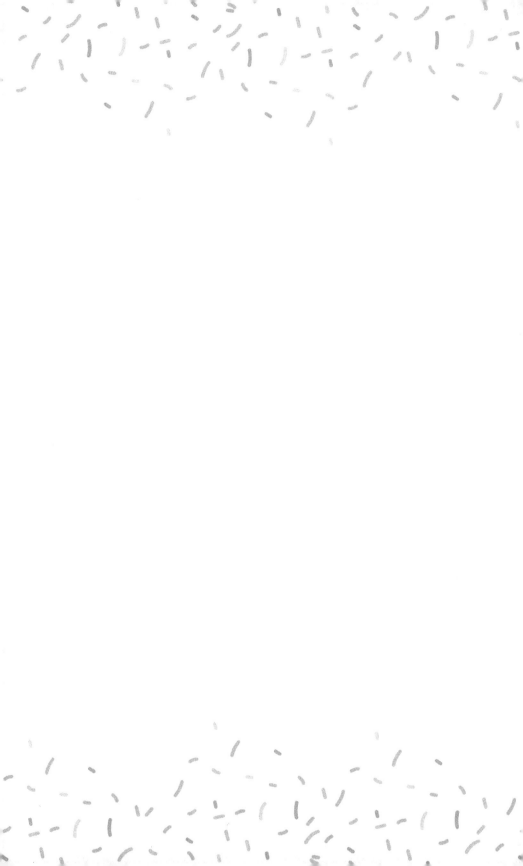

Introduction

Nicole Frail

"Food is symbolic of love when words are inadequate."
—Alan D. Wolfelt

Thank you for choosing to celebrate this day of all-things love with *Recipes for Romance: A Sweet Valentine's Day Anthology*. Within these pages, you'll be treated to nineteen courses that will introduce you to both debut and established authors who have prepared for you a collection of fictional stories ranging in length from bite-sized but satisfying morsels to larger portions that may require you to take a breather between chapters.

The stories in this anthology aim to demonstrate how powerful the experience of sharing a meal can be when getting to know another person and how much thought, effort, and care goes into cooking or baking for those that we love and cherish. Whether someone is treating you or you're treating yourself, food can be a real comfort and perhaps even proof of true love.

In these short stories, the characters you will meet are all brought together leading up to or on Valentine's Day in kitchens, bakeries, restaurants, bars, or other establishments where food and drink may be served—unless, of course, they snuck in their own snacks (I'm looking at you, "MJ's Jersey"). You'll spend time with the host of a matchmaking cruise and her unconventional ways of matching singles over their drink orders in "Misery on the

Bounty," a witch who travels to the mortal realm and just so happens to pick up a Valentine's Day date (and a head cold) in "Comfort Food and Covert Magic," a mother from the Midwest as she teaches her children about the true meaning of Valentine's Day while baking cookies in "Love Through a Cookie," and two hilarious undergrads who prove that opposites attract and depression brownies can actually be quite delicious when made from scratch in "Brownie Points."

Grab your soft blanket and warm beverage, cuddle up beside your real-life Valentine, and prepare to be smitten with this cute collection of sweet stories. Enjoy!

ANOTHER FISH IN THE SEA

Another Fish in the Sea

Amy Kelly

"I LOVE YOU," I COOED as I woke to a gentle face. The face's mouth twitched into a knowing smile.

I turned to the woman at the foot of my bed who was adjusting my catheter. I loved her, too.

"I love all of you."

I felt deeply confident that these women were going to be my best friends.

"You guys are *so* awesome."

A wrinkled face with a tight schoolmarm bun rolled her eyes to the other, exchanging a look that said: "Oh great, the Cheech of the postanesthetic recovery room."

I was unfazed by this, because, as much as I knew I loved my new best friends/nurses, I also knew I was Ethel Merman. Or maybe I was the greatest Broadway showstopper of all time.

"Isn't it a lovely day to be caught in the rain . . ."

I was really singing to the back of the room now. I felt the heat of the spotlight and the roar of the audience amidst the beeps of my pulse oximeter and the burning smell of urine and disinfectant.

"Miss Smith." The schoolmarm nurse interrupted my solo. "Marie, you just had surgery," she said in exasperated blurts over my singing. "Take it easy."

I was vaguely aware that I answered to Marie, but the audience needed me, so I sang even louder.

"You are disrupting the other patients." Marm-nurse had switched gears to guilt.

Behind the curtain, a man cleared his throat. *Here we go, another hater for my performance.*

To my delight, however, he began singing the next line of the song.

"As long as I can be with you, it's a lovely day," he continued in a baritone voice. Was he the Louis Armstrong to my Ella Fitzgerald?

"Heaven, I'm in heaven . . ." He matched my melody and tune.

The nurses performed their perfunctory checks and threw their hands up in disbelief as we crooned.

"Just keep it down," schoolmarm said, enamored by our obvious musical talent.

Drugs are funny beasts. You ride them and feel so strong and certain to your core, but then they gradually recede, your confidence trickling out as the cracks of life break through.

As reality emerged from the anesthesia, I realized maybe I was just Marie, the substitute teacher who was a Broadway fanatic but who rarely sang except for "Happy Birthday" and only then for an audience of children.

Details flooded back.

Suddenly self-conscious after our last duet of "Let's Call the Whole Thing Off," I mustered up the courage to talk to my costar. Maybe he was just as gooned as me.

"Hello?" I peeped.

"Hello, Marie," the voice behind the curtain said. "What is a nice girl like you doing in a place like this?"

His voice was light, flirtatious, and playful, like he was a fisherman dancing a fly across the surface of a river. Not what I expected from someone with an IV. Not a typical swimmer in my dating pool.

"Original," I said, picking up on his humor but wanting to tease him.

"What are you in for?" he asked.

"Bad date, spilled shrimp, car accident. I think."

I remembered biting into the oily, crunchy coating, tasting the savory flesh of fried shrimp. The flavor was a quilt wrapped around me by an affectionate parent. *It will be all right*, the carbs and fat had signaled to my brain. After such a bad date, the comfort permeated my body so completely that I almost closed my eyes, forgetting I was behind the wheel.

I had swerved in time to miss the person exiting the drive-thru next door, only to spill hot, oily shrimp all over my lap and floor. A moment passed where I was unsure of whether I was more upset about my burning lap or that I had to go back for more shrimp.

I must have been reaching for a shrimp on the floor when the truck hit. Flashes of a brown purse, long hair, shrimp, and wrappers rolled past my face as my car flipped into a ditch.

"You still there?" he popped me out of the slideshow of my night—titled "Bad Times at the Corner of Sad and Sadder"—playing in my mind.

I shook my head.

"Sorry. What about you?"

"Bad date, appendectomy," he said.

"I win."

"Hey, I lost an organ," he said playfully.

"Sorry, broken leg and head injury trumps your useless organ," I teased. My cheeks lifted and I could feel my eyes crease at the corners.

"I guess you have me there. What was your bad date? And on Valentine's?" I heard the smile in his voice.

"Dating has led me to believe that someone has a penchant for kidnapping monkeys from the zoo and dipping them in noxious hair-removal agents to pass them off as bachelors." I felt the dark, cold space of my heart in my chest as I spoke.

"Tonight was no exception?" he asked.

"Tonight's date put both my patience and Darwin to task. Missing-Link, as I will refer to him, was a beautiful, muscular specimen." I wet my lips with an ice chip from a Dixie cup marm-nurse had just handed me.

"Must be the great ape family."

I chuckled at how far from great anything that guy had been.

"He checked out his reflection, hair, and teeth in his spoon before ordering. That was my first red flag. When he thought he was picking his nose covertly behind the menu before flicking it into the potted plant beside us, I should have run. My stomach opposed my better instincts. I was at least going to get fed tonight."

"Girl's gotta eat."

"Missing-Link had smoothed his oily hair and pulled at his collared shirt, buttoned just above a lowly tuft of chest hair where his gold chain nuzzled in his little monkey bosom."

"They missed a spot," he said. "Bad form for monkey converts."

"It gets better. He proceeded to order for us. No pause for consent or input. It was like he had never been told no in his entire monkey life. Even my stomach gave up at that point." I could feel him listening through the curtain. "When he excused himself to 'powder his nose,' I grabbed my clutch and busted out of there."

"And you ended up here," he prompted.

"Close. I ended up face-deep in a cup of fried shrimp at the drive-thru on Fifth. Then a car accident. Then here." The details still felt clouded. The drugs were like a fog lifting on a midnight drive. The visibility on the night's events was still poor.

I was suddenly aware of how much I was talking. "What about your bad date?"

"No-show. I was on my way home when the pain hit. Came in hoping I was overreacting to maybe gas."

"Not the deep-rooted pain of rejection?"

He laughed.

"Hey, can I tell you something?" He was switching gears.

"Sure." I fiddled with my sheet, worried he was going to pause, to need to rest. My heart thudded, hoping that we would keep talking. There was a sprout of something green and new and hopeful germinating in the dank cave of my chest.

"I am really enjoying this . . . you," he said coyly.

"Me too." I flushed and fumbled for another ice chip, my fingers feeling less like overstuffed sausages each time I moved them.

I heard the nurses shuffle in behind the curtain. The mechanical drone of a bed being lowered before the foot brake is released. They were going to roll him away. I wanted to leap out of my bed, but my movements had been slowed by the melting-marshmallow effects of the drugs on my muscles, and my body was skirting the edge of pain. My chest was tight with the thought of never actually seeing the man who belonged to the voice behind the curtain.

"Maybe sometime when we both get out of here, we can get you a redo on that shrimp. I'm the chef at Dockside. You should come in sometime."

"I would really like that."

Through the fog, the sound of the wheels squeaking away, the pain, and all that was broken, I felt a small tendril of warmth unfurl in my heart.

About the Author

Amy Kelly is a former midwife, current therapist, mother of two neurodivergent teens, and farmer on Vancouver Island. Her nonfiction has appeared in the *Yummy Mummy Club*, her fiction in *805 lit + art*, and *As the Snow Drifts: A Cozy Winter Anthology*, and her poetry in *Tiger Leaping Review*. She has been accepted to the Yale Writers' Workshop, as a McLoughlin Gardens Artist in Residence, and into the SFU Writer's Studio. One of her YA manuscripts, *Little Acts of Useless Rebellion*, was a finalist for the Leapfrog Global Fiction Prize. Her last great adventure was hiking to Everest Base Camp at forty; she hopes that publishing her books will be her next.

You can find Amy on:

Instagram: @amykellywrites

You can visit her website at:

www.amykellyauthor.com

BATTER TOGETHER

Batter Together

Katie Fitzgerald

"NATALIE!" KAITLYN MORGAN STOOD IN the kitchen holding her daughter's stinky backpack and wondering what on Earth a twelve-year-old could be carrying around to create such a stench. A moment later, she found out when her hand descended into the depths of the main compartment and landed on a forgotten orange covered in mold and oozing rot.

"Ew, ew, ew, ew!" chanted Kaitlyn as she carefully extricated the furry fruit. Attached to the sticky rind was a crumpled piece of paper that floated to the floor as Kaitlyn dumped the orange into the trash. Before she could bend down to investigate the document, Natalie appeared.

"Mom, did you remember to—" She came to a halt midsentence. "Oh, you found it!"

"The orange?" Kaitlyn hoped she hadn't just destroyed a science project.

"Not that." Natalie wrinkled her nose. "The bake sale note! I just remembered you're supposed to have twelve dozen brownies ready to sell at my concert on Friday night."

Kaitlyn instinctively glanced at the calendar hanging above the kitchen island. Friday night was Natalie's Valentine's Day choir concert: An Evening of Love. Kaitlyn had been dreading it, as she imagined any single mom dreaded anything that required her to think about love on Valentine's Day.

"I've got the concert on the calendar," she said, happy to note that she had not forgotten, "but nothing about any baking."

Natalie stomped over, picked up the paper on the floor, and shoved the wet, slightly browned notice under Kaitlyn's nose. "It says it right here! Thank God you have this. I thought I forgot to give it to you."

"You *didn't* give it to me!" Kaitlyn protested, feeling a headache forming behind her eyes. "It was attached to your disgusting, rotten orange!"

Quickly, Kaitlyn scanned the document. Her eyes popped when she saw that the requested number of brownies was, indeed, a whopping twelve dozen. "No way," she said, shaking her head. "Do you realize today is Wednesday?" She smacked the note down on the counter. "I can't do that amount of baking on this short notice. You'll have to tell your teacher we'll bring napkins or something instead."

Natalie shook her head right back. "She said no napkins. I heard her say sixteen moms signed up for napkins last time. Now the school will have them out."

"Then you're bringing nothing, Nat. I'm sorry."

Kaitlyn sighed as Natalie frowned and hung her head. She hated letting her daughter down, but she would have needed this information weeks ago to be able to pull off this task. She would have taken a day off, or asked her mother and sister to help, or used any of the other fail-safe methods she had developed over the past eight years since Natalie's dad had walked out. But she didn't have a time machine, and that seemed like the only thing that could help at this point.

"Mrs. Bentley is going to be mad at me, Mom," Natalie said. "She specifically said that the same five moms do all the work, and she wants to see other families participating. *We're* other families!" She paused, still frowning, then lifted her head to meet her mom's eyes with a sudden pleading look. "Could you get in touch with Eric?"

Kaitlyn's head snapped up and she eyed her daughter. *Not this again.* She pinched the bridge of her nose. "We have talked about this. Things with Eric are complicated right now."

Kaitlyn's history with Eric was fraught, to say the least. First they were across-the-street neighbors. Then they were friends. Then he was at her house most nights, helping with the dishes, assisting with science homework, changing light bulbs in locations that triggered Kaitlyn's fear of heights. He had essentially become part of their family. Now, though . . . was there a word for a man you both loved and never wanted to see again at the same time? Whatever that word was, that was the situation with Eric these days.

But try explaining that to a very black-and-white-thinking twelve-year-old who loved and missed the only father figure she had ever really known.

"We haven't talked about it at all, Mom!" protested Natalie. "I didn't forget to give you the note on purpose. But he has big ovens at the bakery, right? You could help me and make up with him at the same time."

Kaitlyn watched the light of hope rise in her daughter's eyes, and her heart went out to her. She had not meant to hurt Natalie with her behavior toward Eric, but it was clear she had anyway. Would it be so bad to reach out and see how he responded? The ovens at Eric's bakery typically weren't in use between 4 p.m. and 5 a.m., when he baked the morning bread loaves. For Eric, twelve dozen brownies wouldn't take that much longer than one dozen.

Kaitlyn looked at the clock, then glanced over at her phone.

"Please, Mom? I miss him."

Natalie was all but pouting, but Kaitlyn had already made up her mind. She really didn't want Natalie to be singled out at school because her mom never participated in anything, and she knew she owed it to Natalie to get closure on her relationship with Eric one way or another. Her daughter was right; this was the perfect excuse to make that happen.

Please don't let me regret this. "Okay," she said, exhaling slowly, still fighting that inkling of a headache. "No promises, but I will text Eric and see what he says." She picked up her daughter's backpack. "And in exchange, you will go hose this down."

"Thanks, Mom," said Natalie, kissing Kaitlyn's cheek as she took her soiled bag. "You're the best."

Ha. The best. Eric used to say that, too. As she picked up the phone and selected his name in her contacts, Kaitlyn wondered what he thought of her now.

The next evening, Natalie had a dress rehearsal, so Kaitlyn was entirely on her own when she parallel parked in front of the bakery and popped open the back of the SUV to grab her baking supplies. Eric's text message had simply said, "Come on down!" in a much warmer tone than she'd expected given the way she'd been ignoring him since back in the fall.

Actually, *ignoring* wasn't the right word. She was avoiding him, yes, but she was paying more attention than ever to the details of his life. She knew which nights he went to the gym, because she saw him get into the car in his sweatpants with a water bottle in hand. She knew when he went grocery shopping, when he got the mail, when packages were delivered to his porch. When it snowed, she peered out the window to make sure she wouldn't run into him while he was shoveling. During the most recent storm, Kaitlyn had found herself mesmerized by the sight of him effortlessly lifting and tossing scoopfuls of snow. Around the same time, she had also noticed with great pleasure that the car belonging to his girlfriend, Angie, had stopped coming around. She really wanted that to mean something.

Kaitlyn set down her supplies on the sidewalk, shut the SUV, carefully stepped over a snowbank, picked up her stuff again, and then ducked between the bakery and the Chinese restaurant next door, heading for the employee entrance around back. Angie. She knew how pathetic it was to hate a woman for liking the same man she liked, and it was worse because Kaitlyn had specifically told Eric to move on. Correction. First, she had almost kissed him, then he had said he wanted a relationship, and then she had told him it was a mistake and he was free to date anyone he wanted from now on without thinking about her. What kind of hypocrite was angry with someone for doing exactly what she told him to do? *This one right here.*

"It's me!" Kaitlyn called. Her hands were full, so she gave an awkward knock with the toe of her boot. The click of a lock sounded from inside, and then the door opened, and there was Eric. Kaitlyn was surprised when he grinned from ear to ear and immediately relieved her of her box of ingredients. His grin faded after a few seconds, though, as he set the box on a nearby counter and began to unpack its contents. Holding up a box of dollar-store brownie mix as though it were the corpse of a rodent, he said, "I'm sorry, did you bring a box mix to my bakery?"

"What's wrong with that?" Kaitlyn shut the door against the February chill and rubbed her hands together, enjoying the snug warmth of this neat, yet cozy, kitchen. "It's just a school thing. Kids don't care."

"Are you trying to kill me right now?" Eric shook his head. "I'm not putting that abomination in my oven. You had to know when you asked for my help that I'd want to do it right."

"I don't need a whole involved thing," Kaitlyn said. The last thing she wanted was to be more of a burden to Eric than she already had been. "I just need Natalie to feel like her teacher doesn't hate her."

"You're allergic to involvement," Eric said pointedly, and Kaitlyn felt her cheeks flush. "This has been noted. But I'm allergic to baked goods made from garbage. My kitchen, my rules." Then he began to move around the space, opening cabinets and pulling out various items.

As with shoveling snow, Eric's baking preparations seemed effortlessly choreographed. For a few moments, Kaitlyn stood watching the way she might watch a ballet recital or Broadway performance, losing herself in the efficient and natural way he could pull together a recipe without even thinking about it. She only snapped out of it when she found Eric standing in front of her, blinking.

"You're gonna want to take that coat off. You should know by now how hot three ovens can get."

"Right," Kaitlyn said, loosening her scarf. She willed herself not to remember past evenings spent together in the kitchen, talking and hanging out while Eric worked. They felt like scenes from another life. "Sorry. I'm just—sorry."

Eric's gaze lingered on hers for a moment, but when she broke eye contact, he moved away again. Had he thought she was apologizing? Would an apology even be welcome? She shed the coat but immediately started to sweat anyway.

Eric stood at the counter, surveying everything he had pulled from the cabinets. "Okay," he said. "We're going to make four varieties, a double batch of each. We'll do one plain, add a little cherry to one, some chocolate chips to another one, and some cream cheese to the last one for a marble effect."

Kaitlyn turned to smile at him, so impressed by his magic in the kitchen that she temporarily forgot to feel awkward. Eric was completely focused on the task at hand and didn't even notice. She hoped that just meant he was in the zone and not that he was completely shutting her out. It would be hard to make up with him if he wasn't willing.

For the next few minutes, Eric called out the names of ingredients, and Kaitlyn dutifully handed them over, keeping pace with him as best she could. It was hard not to remember the times they had cooked together at his house, or hers, or the times they had worked together on other projects, like building Natalie's bookcase or planting Kaitlyn's front garden. She would be lying to herself if she tried to say she didn't miss those things. What if she just broke the ice and said so? As she stood by with the chocolate chips, her mind wandered, trying to come up with the words for what she wanted to say to make things right.

When Eric turned around and they were suddenly face-to-face, as close as they had been the night on his patio when Kaitlyn had leaned in for a kiss and then bailed at the last second, she startled back to attention, the open bag of chocolate chips falling to the floor and losing some of its contents.

"Sorry!" she gasped.

"You keep saying that," Eric muttered as he instantly bent to clean up the mess.

"Sorry," she said again, then laughed at herself. "It's a nervous habit."

"Why are you nervous?" he asked, tossing the escaped chocolate chips into the trash. "We're just baking. It's not like we've never done this before."

"But we haven't done it since . . ." She didn't know how to describe the whole kissing debacle, so she just repeated her last word. "Since."

"Since you kissed me, then threw me at Angie, who then broke up with me because I talked too much about you? Since then, you mean?" Eric shook his head. "Again, why are you nervous? You know exactly how you feel about me. I'm the one who's all over the place."

Well, that showed how much he knew. Kaitlyn had never known exactly how she felt about him, and she still didn't. When they were in separate homes, in their separate orbits, it was easy to convince herself all the warmth she felt toward him was just admiration and friendship. When she caught him shoveling, or in gym attire, it was equally easy to convince herself she was just lonely and would feel the pull of any halfway-attractive male. Here in the kitchen, though, nothing seemed clear, and everything seemed possible.

"All over Angie you mean," blurted Kaitlyn.

Eric laughed sardonically. "You don't get to be mad about that," he scolded. "I don't stick around where I'm not wanted. You made your position clear. It's not my fault you didn't like her. I couldn't just wait for you until the end of time, Kaitlyn. I had to see where things with her could go."

He turned his back to Kaitlyn and finished mixing the batter for the first batch of brownies, then poured it into a pan and popped it into the oven. Meanwhile Kaitlyn tried to come up with the best way to explain herself.

"I freaked out, okay?" She followed Eric from the oven to the fridge, where he pulled out the maraschino cherries and cream cheese but kept his back to her. "I relied on you so much, and we make such a great team. On paper, it makes so much sense. But then I just thought . . ." She sighed. "I thought about what it would be like if we made that leap and it fell apart."

Silently, Eric began to mix the next batch of brownies. Kaitlyn wondered if she was saying too much, but she also couldn't seem to stop herself. She needed him to understand that she liked depending on him for companionship and emotional support, but that she also worried that her messy, disorganized life was a burden that would eventually crush him and, by extension, her and her daughter.

"Natalie would be heartbroken," she went on. "*I* would be heartbroken. I couldn't risk it. Angie has no kids, and she's really pretty, and it seemed like you guys would get along so well, and I just wanted you to be happy. I want you to love someone who isn't such a needy mess all the time."

After a moment, Eric finally turned to face her, batter-covered wooden spoon in hand. He brought it to Kaitlyn's mouth. "Taste this, will you?" he said gently, and Kaitlyn opened her mouth to accept the chocolate-covered spoon, then took the handle from him as well.

"There," said Eric. "Now let me talk for a second." He wiped his hands on his apron and leaned back against the counter. "Angie is the most annoying woman on the planet. She's so perfect. Coasters under every glass. Hospital corners on the bed. She vacuums four times a day. There is not a LEGO set or a headless Barbie doll in that house. Her life is utterly sterile." The second oven beeped to signal it was preheated. Eric took the tray of marble brownies and shoved it into the oven before turning back to Kaitlyn. "Basically, she's everything I want in an employee but absolutely nothing I want in a girlfriend. I need more personality. More unpredictability. Somebody who needs me sometimes."

Kaitlyn savored the chocolate in her mouth and swallowed, trying to take in everything Eric was saying to her. "Well, I'm sorry," she said. "The truth is, I do know exactly how I feel about you, and it's terrifying." She finished off the chocolate on the spoon, then tossed it into the sink. "I thought seeing you with someone else would snap me out of it."

Eric laughed. "How's that working out for you?"

"Not great, to be honest." Kaitlyn exhaled shakily. "Many regrets. If I could do things differently . . ."

"It's not too late, you know," Eric said. "I'm a free man. Back on the market. Yours for the kissing."

It was already warm in here, but now Kaitlyn's cheeks flamed. "That's what got us into this mess in the first place," she pointed out.

"*Almost* kissing got us here," Eric corrected. "We don't know where *actually* kissing leads until we try it." He raised his eyebrows.

Kaitlyn took a tentative step toward Eric. She knew she could not get this wrong a second time. But what was she afraid of? Eric had never been anything but supportive. Even when he had dated someone else, he had done so mostly to please her. She'd been telling herself she was angry at him, but really, she was frustrated with herself for refusing to pursue her own happiness. This was her second chance, and she would not squander it.

Meeting Eric's warm, brown eyes with her own steady gaze, Kaitlyn took another step. Then, reaching up to cup his cheek, she guided his face toward her own. They kissed, and instantly his fingers were in her hair, his other arm at her waist, pulling her in closer until the front of her sweatshirt brushed his apron. Kaitlyn was entirely swept away on a stream of all the swoony, giddy, and foolish feelings associated with Valentine's Day.

The kiss continued for a long moment until the timer announced that the first batch of brownies was done. Kaitlyn stood back, finding it impossible to suppress a grin as Eric retrieved the brownies, set them on the cooling rack, and then immediately returned his attention to Kaitlyn.

"Now *that* was a kiss," he said playfully, toying with a lock of Kaitlyn's hair, then placing it behind her ear. "That's what I want, Kait," he said. "I want this with you."

Kaitlyn fully expected her fight-or-flight response to kick in and send her screaming into the night with her dollar-store brownie mix. But Eric's words soothed her fears. Kaitlyn could no longer think of a single good reason why they couldn't be across-the-street-neighbors, best friends, family, and something more.

"It's what I want too, Eric," she whispered. "I think it's what I've always wanted."

It should have taken no time at all to finish baking the last of the brownies, but with all the kissing, they weren't done until right before Kaitlyn had to leave to pick up Natalie.

"Eric's brownies are definitely the best ones," Natalie told Kaitlyn as they stood together in the lobby before the concert the following night, surveying card tables laden with baked goods for sale. Kaitlyn had to hand it to Mrs. Bentley. Threatening the parents had apparently been a great success. There were tons of treats. "Too bad none of them are orange flavored." Natalie smirked, and Kaitlyn frowned.

"Sorry, kid, I'm never eating anything orange again." She shuddered. "That was gross."

"Well, these aren't gross. Make sure you tell him Mrs. Bentley said they were beautiful. I think she might buy the entire batch of the marble ones herself."

Kaitlyn was about to take her phone out to text Eric this compliment when she looked across the room to the glass double doors and saw that she didn't need to. She nudged her daughter in the side. "I think you can tell him yourself, Nat."

As Eric made his way through the gathering crowd of tweens and parents, Natalie launched herself at him. "Eric! You're here!" A flutter of joy rose in Kaitlyn's chest as she understood the full implications of his presence. They could really do this. They could be a family.

"Where else would I be?" Eric grinned broadly, locking eyes with Kaitlyn even as he spoke to her daughter. Twice last night, Kaitlyn had woken up and become convinced that the events of the evening had been nothing but a dream. He was here, though, and that meant it was all real.

Natalie looked back and forth between Kaitlyn and Eric. "Does this mean you guys finally made up?" That hopeful, optimistic look was back in her eyes again, and Kaitlyn was so glad she didn't have to disappoint her.

Reaching for Eric's hand, Kaitlyn laced their fingers together, savoring the look on Natalie's face as her jaw slowly dropped. "It means," she said, "the three of us are sticking together from now on."

Natalie's eyes widened as the news sank in. Suddenly, she pumped a fist. "Yes!"

She was still doing a victory dance when the choir director appeared to ask the singers to follow her to the choral room.

Natalie clung to Eric's arm. "I don't want to let you go!" she said.

"I'll be here after," Eric said, lifting his eyes to meet Kaitlyn's, apparently letting her know this promise was for her, as well. "I'm not going anywhere."

Satisfied, Natalie ran off to join her classmates.

"She's thrilled," Kaitlyn told Eric as they stepped toward the auditorium entrance.

"And what about you?" he asked with a sly grin.

"I couldn't be happier," she assured him, squeezing his hand.

Eric held the door, and Kaitlyn walked through, ready to enjoy An Evening of Love with her own sweet valentine.

About the Author

Katie Fitzgerald is a 2024 Sparkie Award recipient for Best Romantic Suspense and a Pushcart Prize nominee whose short stories and flash fiction appear online at Spark Flash Fiction and Micromance Magazine, as well as in various print anthologies. She is also the author of *Library Lovebirds*, an ebook collection of bookish romances, and a novel in flash, *The Bennetts Bloom*. A trained children's librarian, Katie lives with her academic librarian husband in the Maryland suburbs of Washington, DC, where she homeschools her son and four daughters.

You can find Katie on:

Instagram: @katiefitzstories

You can visit her website at:

https://bio.site/katiefitzgerald

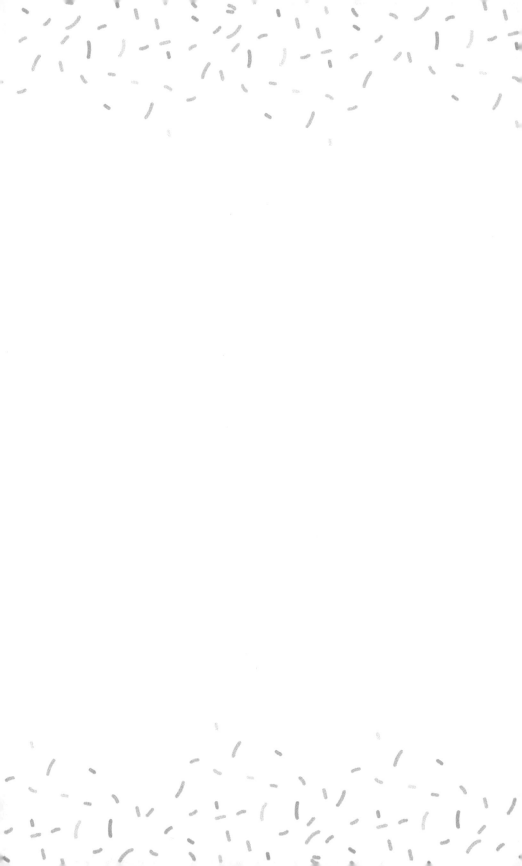

STRAWBERRY MACARONS

Strawberry Macarons

Jessica Daniliuk

Noah
February 12, 2025

NOAH HAD NEVER CARED FOR macarons. She believed each only had a whisper of flavor and didn't like that, after two bites, it was finished. When it came to desserts originating in Italy, she much preferred tiramisu. But, her potential employer, Mrs. Arison, wanted to see her make a macaron, and she needed this job, all her preferences aside.

She began crushing up dragon fruit, hoping to turn the mush into a beautiful pink cookie. Her mother always said that a messy kitchen made for a beautiful dessert, and Noah's kitchen was a disaster. She continued pressing the berries, preparing to dry them out and add them to her flour. She paused for a moment and turned to see her competition. He was already tapping the baking sheet against the counter, ensuring there were no bubbles in his perfectly circular shells. Being two steps and what appeared to be many years behind, Noah was hoping for a miracle. She needed divine intervention, or at the very least, an innovative take on the played-out dessert.

Even though she was nowhere near a romantic, she would have to come up with the perfect Valentine's Day treat. Suddenly, it hit her. A macaron with chocolate filling and a dash of strawberry jam: her take on a chocolate-covered strawberry. It wasn't the most inspired idea, but it would do.

For what seemed like only a moment, Noah blacked out, and when she came to, she was plating her macarons. This happened a lot when she was baking; the activity would take her, and she wouldn't return until there was a finished product. She looked down at her cookies, noting the few bubbles and cracks. She still cared about presentation, but Noah's favorite part of baking was always seeing the looks on people's faces when they ate what she made. She'd watch the person do a little dance as a wave of deliciousness washed over them. Noah peaked over at the competition to see a variety of macarons: chocolate, vanilla, and strawberry, all adorned with a tiny fondant heart. Noah convinced herself this man was a practicing witch because magic could be the only explanation for whipping out that many macarons in such a short amount of time. In a panic, she rearranged her macarons into a smiley face, hoping that she would get some more recognition for creativity and that Mrs. Arison had a sense of humor.

Mrs. Arison walked up to Noah's station, a smile plastered across her face after trying Fancy Chef's macarons. Noah could feel her heart clawing its way to the surface. She needed this job, and she knew a decision would be made soon. Mrs. Arison looked Noah up and down; Noah knew this dress had been a mistake. With a perfectly manicured hand, Mrs. Arison grabbed a macaron and took a bite. Noah waited for a smile, but it never came. Instead, Mrs. Arison placed the rest of the macaron back on the plate and looked at Noah with what could only be described as pity. Turns out she didn't have a sense of humor.

"I'm sorry, Ms. Finch, but we are going in another direction. Thank you for your time."

Noah couldn't help but laugh at the way Mrs. Arison spoke like she was sending an email and Noah couldn't turn to her right and see this "other direction." Noah began packing up her equipment and tried her best not to cry. After having four interviews, she'd thought this job was guaranteed. It was only when she'd arrived at the house that she realized it was between her and someone else, and of course, now they'd gone with that someone. Noah folded up the apron that once belonged to her mother and left the house as Mrs. Arison discussed plans for her party.

Noah's car sat in the shadow of the mansion. She opened her door carefully; the hinges were old, and Noah feared the day they would finally give out. The seat creaked as she sat down. She looked at her phone: ten missed calls from Kelly. She turned the key in the ignition, giving her Toyota a second to roar to life. Without calling her friend back, she traveled down the long, windy driveway and drove in the direction of Kelly's.

Henry
February 12, 2025

HENRY HEARD WHAT HE THOUGHT was a cat being slaughtered but looked outside to find a beat-up old car. He recoiled as the sun bounced from the monstrosity to his hazel eyes. He quickly pulled the curtains in and trudged back over to his bed, hoping the comfort of his cotton sheets would relieve the hangover. Drinking eight shots of tequila with some of Hollywood's greatest stars seemed like a wonderful idea at the time, but as Henry's brain pounded against his skull, he realized it had been a mistake. He closed his eyes, basking in slight alleviation for a few seconds. Suddenly, his entire stomach leapt toward his throat, and he ran to the bathroom.

His sweaty, hot hands grabbed around the toilet bowl as he regretted the drinking, going out, and even meeting the guys that "forced" shots down his throat.

"Rough night?" Henry turned to see his older brother, Ryan. Even though no other words came out of his mouth, Henry knew Ryan was judging him; he had a great angle from his high horse.

Henry slowly collected himself and got off the floor. He pushed past Ryan and sat back down on his bed. "This is what fun looks like; I know a married square like you wouldn't get that."

"Square? You've been spending too much time with Dad." Ryan laughed and sat on the bed next to Henry. Ryan turned to the right, and Henry followed his older brother's line of vision: on Henry's nightstand sat a protein bar wrapper, empty Fireball nip, and crumbled-up contract. He saw the chill that ran up Ryan's spine.

Ryan pointed to the nightstand. "I see you're ready for married life yourself."

Henry turned toward Ryan and tried not to show his emotions but could feel the anger bubbling to the surface. "I wouldn't call it a marriage. More like a business deal."

Henry tried to inch back under his comforter, but Ryan stopped him, putting a hand on his back.

"You know you don't have to go through with this, right?" Ryan's eyes narrowed, and his lips thinned, a sign Henry categorized as Ryan being serious.

"Tell that to dad."

Ryan paused. "Well, if you aren't ready, you don't have to do it *now*."

"Wait, crap, what time is it?"

Ryan checked his Rolex. "Nine twenty-seven, why?"

Henry ran over to his closet and started chaotically shuffling through clothes. A blazer would be too formal, but a sweater would be too casual; Dad always hated the way Henry looked in sweaters. He'd have to wear a button-up shirt; it was the best fit for the occasion.

"Turn around."

Ryan turned, and Henry began changing, almost putting his leg in the shirt sleeve. After getting everything on, Henry started combing through his hair while fixing his collar. He paused for a moment before tapping Ryan on the shoulder.

"You got engaged on Valentine's Day, and now it's my turn. I want to, I promise."

Henry looked into his brother's eyes, hoping Ryan couldn't hear the insincerity in his voice. Ryan seemed to believe him, and if he didn't, he wasn't obvious about it. Henry smiled at his brother and then ran down the stairs to the first-floor study.

He pushed the door open, the slam echoing through an otherwise quiet room. His father, George Arison, sat at the desk in front of two chairs: one already occupied by Hollywood's latest bombshell, Christine Paxton. Henry could smell lavender and vanilla from the doorway, Christine's signature scent. He took the empty chair, noting how Christine was shaking her leg and, ultimately, the entire area around them.

George cleared his throat. "Glad you could join us, Henry, even if you are late."

Henry looked at the big clock behind his father to see it was ten seconds past nine-thirty. His shoulders relaxed against the cushioned chair until he realized his father was still looking at him. He made his back completely straight and sat tall.

Christine gave him a small smile that seemed to be a mix of annoyance at his "lateness" and pity for his father calling it out. George stood up slightly and pushed a piece of paper toward each chair. Christine picked hers up, but Henry was too scared. Taking the paper was acceptance, and even though he'd spoken the words out loud to his brother, making an agreement like this in front of his father was different. It was law.

Henry looked over at Christine, who appeared to be engrossed in the paper. Her eyes would widen at some parts while a slight grin made an appearance at others.

"You have to read it, son. You should both know what you're getting into."

Henry picked the paper up like it was covered in molasses and infused to the table. He read the title: *Marriage Contract*. He had always heard that getting married was like entering a contract but seeing the words right next to each other in Times New Roman felt all sorts of wrong. He continued reading:

"This agreement between Party A (Henry Arison) and Party B (Christine Paxton) shall take place from February 14th, 2025, until at least February 14th, 2027, or longer, if both parties agree . . . Party A hereby agrees to maintain a faithful image with Party B, meaning the party will not be seen with any other females in a romantic and/or non-platonic setting performing a romantic and/or non-platonic activity. . . . Both parties agree not to have any offspring in the duration of the agreement, and . . . Party B shall appear in seven Arison Studios productions within the duration of the agreement. . . . After the minimum two years, Party A shall assume the position of Vice President of Arison Studios, assuming the parameters of the agreement are met. . . ."

Henry couldn't help but throw up slightly in his mouth. He attributed part of it to the previous night, but most to how all of the romance had been sucked out of one of the most romantic endeavors there is. He'd seen his father conduct hundreds of deals over the years, and this was no different. He wore the same unwavering expression, where he hoped his clients would agree to the terms and the case would be closed.

Christine pushed the paper back on the desk. Henry hoped Christine had more of a backbone than him and would speak on how insane this whole deal felt.

"So, the proposal will happen at the Valentine's party on Friday?"

Christine being so unnerved made Henry deflate in his seat.

George smiled. "Yes, this Friday."

"And I get to keep my last name?"

"If you so choose."

Christine turned to Henry, looking through him. "I'm keeping my last name."

Henry just nodded. Christine grabbed a pen from the holder and scribbled her signature on the contract. George clapped quietly, seeming to be the happiest he'd been in a while. Henry hated disappointing his father, even though he proved to be so good at it, but the feeling of discomfort gnawed at him, willing him to speak up.

"Henry?"

Both George and Christine glared at Henry. He wondered if they could see how much he was sweating.

"Can I have some time to think about it?"

Henry's potential wife rolled her eyes, but George remained calm, like he'd been expecting this kind of reaction from his son.

"Of course. You just need to sign before the big toast at the party."

Without saying another word, Henry rose from his chair and rushed out of the room. He ripped away at the buttons on his shirt as heat spread across his chest. With slightly blurry vision, he reached for the chair at the island but couldn't grab onto it. He kept pawing at it until, eventually, he was able to pull himself around and into the chair. His heart was beating almost as violently as his head while thoughts of his father never forgiving him flooded in. A wave of pure fear took him over to the point where he didn't even hear his mother enter the kitchen.

"Henry, are you okay, darling?"

Henry's face contorted as he tried his best to appear okay. Patricia walked over and placed one hand on her son's shoulder while she used the other to present a professional chef. Henry was never one for fine dining; he always preferred a fast-food burger over a Michelin-star steak, but he knew how much his mother loved that level of sophistication, so he went along with her whims.

"Meet Chef Gravateau; he will be making the pastries for the party on Friday."

"Nice to meet you, sir." Henry leaned over the counter and attempted to keep his hand steady while he greeted the chef, but he knew he'd delivered a clammy, shaky handshake.

Patricia walked over to the chef and took him to the side to assumingly talk about party details. The shaking moved from Henry's hands to his legs, almost throwing him off the chair.

He looked around for something to eat, hoping that the chewing would distract his body and eventually stop the shaking. There was nothing on the island, but on the counter right next to the stove and near the trash was a plate of little macarons in the shape of a smiley face. Henry couldn't help but match the expression of the dessert as he walked over to grab one. He took one of the eyes and bit into half of it.

The fluffy texture of the cookie mixed with the tartness of the strawberries and the richness of the chocolate transported Henry to a new place where he forgot about his problems for a second. As he finished the cookie, Henry noticed that he wasn't shaking nearly as much. There was a slight twitch in his eye, but somehow, the cookie had done what breathing exercises couldn't.

Patricia and the chef walked back over as Henry was finishing up his second cookie.

He pointed to the plate. "These are excellent, by the way!"

Patricia looked down with horror and disbelief, an expression Henry had only seen when he was a kid and had been particularly bad. She rushed over, picked up the plate, and threw it in the trash, giving Henry a dirty look the entire time. She walked back over to the chef, said something about seeing him tomorrow, and then rushed him out the door. When she returned, she looked a new shade of red.

"Hey, I was still eating those."

"Those weren't Chef Gravateau's. I hope you know how much you just embarrassed me."

Patricia walked over to the dining room and started going over options for table settings.

Henry followed her and sat in one of the seats, causing her to look less embarrassed and more aggravated.

"So, what's on the menu for Friday?"

The headache was still there, but Henry was forcing himself to think of a plan because, for some reason, he needed more of those chocolate-strawberry macarons. His body begged for more.

Patricia looked over doily options, each with unique places where they were cut. "Chef Marge is doing seared scallops and a citrus salad to start, and the entrée is going to be either a spaghetti carbonara, coconut curry chicken, or baked lobster tails."

"Delicious, delicious, you know I love carbonara."

Patricia began to warm, her scowl melting into indifference.

"What about dessert? What's Chef Gravoo cooking up?"

The scowl returned. "It's Gravateau, darling, and I think he's going to do some eclairs and a variety of madeleines."

Henry began to perform. He sighed deeply and looked around like he didn't know what to do. "Bad news, Mom, Christine's like, deathly allergic to almonds. She can't have madeleines. And she told me recently that she's trying to stay away from custard. Some weird fad diet where she can't eat custard but can eat other desserts. It's some actress thing."

Henry looked at his mom, hoping she'd taken the bait. She was a very smart woman, but over the years, Henry had learned exactly which buttons to push. And at the end of the day, she always wanted to make her baby happy.

"I'll never understand the diets these actresses are on. I'll call Chef Gravateau right now to revise the menu. Better yet, he may still be outside."

Patricia began walking toward the exit, but Henry shot up from his seat to block her path. "But there is one thing Christine does love. She loves chocolate-covered strawberries but hates the texture of strawberries. I don't know why. Again, she's weird. Anyways, I think she'd love those macarons in the kitchen."

"You mean the ones I threw away?" Patricia didn't seem to be buying it.

"Not those exact ones, but maybe if the chef made a fresh batch . . . and also catered the party."

Patricia's eyes grew wide. "But we have Chef Gravateau; he's the best pastry chef in the state."

Henry got closer, putting his arm around his mom, hoping to achieve his goal. "I'm just trying to be a good future husband and look out for my partner's needs. Something I learned from you."

Every ounce of anger or upset from Patricia subsided. She hugged her son and rubbed his back, the biggest indicator of her love.

"I guess I could call Ms. Finch and see if she's still available."

Henry dragged his mother into a hug and practically jumped up and down. Maybe now his body would stop screaming for sweets.

"Thank you, Mom. Christine will be so excited."

Patricia began walking away. "But if Chef Gravateau comes here in an angry fit, you're dealing with that."

"Of course."

Patricia gave her son a quick kiss on the cheek and walked away. Henry celebrated quietly.

Noah
February 12, 2025

NOAH ARRIVED AT KELLY'S TO find the front door wide open. She slammed the brakes, put the car in park, and ran out of her car, hoping she'd find her best friend in one piece. When Noah got into the apartment, she found Kelly to be perfectly alive and well, staring at her computer screen.

"What the hell, Kel?"

Kelly closed her laptop slightly and looked at Noah with annoyance. "Took you long enough."

Noah put her hand on her hip, trying to catch her breath. "I thought you were dead or something."

"Why would you think that?" The complete lack of awareness from Kelly replaced the fear in Noah's heart with anger.

"Why would I think that?! You called me a thousand times, and when I got here, your front door was open."

Kelly chuckled to herself with slight contention. "Yeah, you weren't answering me, and I was trying to get your attention, and I thought, 'Hey, I'll be nice and open the door so she doesn't have to knock.'"

"Never do that again." Noah began to catch her breath as she plopped down on the couch next to Kelly.

Kelly opened her laptop and showed her a picture of Mrs. Arison and people who Noah guessed were her family, as the title of the article read "The Arison Empire."

After that large occupational heartbreak, the last thing Noah wanted to do was look at the person who'd rejected her. She started to close the laptop.

Kelly pushed the screen back up. "I know you don't care about celebrity drama, but you need to hear about who you're potentially going to work for."

"I didn't get the job."

Kelly looked at Noah with empathy but no remorse. "I'm so sorry, Noah. Okay then, let me tell you about the family you aren't gonna work for."

Noah thought about arguing, but there was no use. After a decade of friendship, she knew there was no stopping Kelly when she was set on something.

"So, you already know Mrs. No Taste, Patricia Arison. Well, she's married to George Arison, who is the founder of Arison Studios. They produced that movie we liked about the cowboy traveling through space and time."

Noah's face was stone.

"But I hate it now, that movie is dead to me. Anyway, George has two sons: Ryan and the oh-so-yummy Henry. Ryan is a philanthropist; he's started a bunch of charities with Daddy's money and is married to Senator Beatrice Arison, the one whose platform is mainly about the green initiative. We love her." Noah nodded to show she was still sort of listening. "Henry, although I wish he was, is not single. He's dating upcoming actress Christine Paxton. She's dated a bunch of big names, and the two met at the Emmys or the Oscars or whatever. They started dating right after Henry went through a bit of a rebellious phase, if you know what I mean, and have been dating for around a year. Now my theory is that they're gonna get engaged at that Valentine's party, because five years ago, Ryan and Beatrice got engaged at the same party also after dating for a year."

Kelly paused to take a deep breath.

Noah tried to wrap her brain around all she just heard but was having trouble. "And you told me all of this, why?"

"You said you were interviewing for an Arison, so I did a deep dive and got really invested. Someone had to hear my findings."

Noah couldn't help but lovingly laugh. "Good thing I didn't get the job. It seems like a lot of drama. Want something to eat?"

"I knew I became friends with you for a reason."

Noah smiled with fake irritation and went back to the kitchen. She looked through Kelly's tiny pantry to find a half-full box of Ritz crackers, some salt, and a box of Kraft Mac and Cheese. She grabbed all of the ingredients and put them down on the counter. Looking at everything, she was taken back to many Sundays shared with her mom. After cooking all week, the last thing Noah's mom wanted to do was cook another big meal, but with Noah's dad in the living room watching football all day and a hungry mouth to feed, she had to improvise. Even at a young age, Noah had a pretty sophisticated palate, so she would ask for stuffed chicken and mushroom ravioli, but her mom would say that Sundays were for something simple, like mac and cheese. They ate mac and cheese on what they lovingly called Simple Sundays. A box of Kraft, a dash of milk, a bit of butter, topped with Ritz cracker breadcrumbs. Noah's mom had the innate ability to make something as small as Sunday night dinner seem fun. Noah hadn't eaten mac and cheese since her mom passed, but after the day she had, she needed a little reminder of home.

Noah whipped up the mac and cheese and brought it back over to Kelly.

"Mac and cheese at 10 a.m., yum."

Noah rolled her eyes. "I think the phrase you're looking for is *thank you*."

"Thank you, Noah."

Noah placed both bowls down as Kelly started to search for something to watch. The entire table shook when Noah's phone started vibrating. She lifted it to see "Patricia Arison" appear across the screen. Noah turned the phone over to show Kelly, both of their expressions puzzled.

"Does she want to reject me for a second time?"

"Well, if she does, I'm going over there, and not just because I want to see her son shirtless."

Noah laughed as she answered the phone. "Hello?"

"Hello! Ms. Finch?"

"This is she." Noah tried to remember if she'd accidentally stolen something or maybe left her whisk behind.

"Thank goodness. It appears I made a mistake. I hope you will still consider my offer and come work the party."

Noah lit up as she realized the proposition. "Wait, are you saying I have the job?"

"Yes, if you will take it."

"Yes, yes, I will!"

"Great. I have many things to do today, so you will have to come in tomorrow. We will work all day, maybe even all night, so you can stay in one of the guest bedrooms."

"Stay over?" Noah repeated.

Kelly snapped her head up to look at Noah, interest finally piqued.

"Yes, it'll be an early morning on the fourteenth, so you might as well stay here to avoid the commute."

"That sounds good. Thank you so much."

"No, thank you. See you tomorrow, goodbye."

Noah hung up the phone, feeling pleasantly surprised and stressed. Kelly waited for a debrief that never came.

"She just like, offered you the job?"

"Yeah, I guess something happened to the other guy."

"Or, she realized you're clearly the better choice, and she's an idiot. I feel like you could have made her work for it more."

"That would insinuate I don't need the job, and I desperately do."

Noah couldn't hold back her giddy, joy-filled scream. Kelly joined her, and they both got off the couch to jump around, exuding pure excitement.

Noah
February 13, 2025

NOAH STOOD OUTSIDE THE GRAND front door with the same amount of anxiety as the day before, even though she felt far more secure this time. As she went to knock, someone opened the door. Her hand slid forward, almost hitting Patricia Arison in the face.

"Oh god, I'm so sorry." Noah dragged her hand back, wanting to punish it.

"It's fine. I'll show you to the kitchen."

Noah followed Patricia inside. She had already been in this house three times before, but each time, her vision had been clouded by the panic of wanting to perform well and be awarded the job. This time, she was trying to allow herself a moment to take everything in. There was a large table under an even larger chandelier in the foyer, a word Noah never thought to use before because she'd never seen one in person. The table was adorned with a vase of flowers and a bowl of fake apples.

Noah was at the point in her life where she couldn't even afford real apples, never mind having ones just for decoration. She continued walking through the dining room, even though Noah half-remembered them having another dining room on the other side of the kitchen, but it didn't seem impossible that they could have two. This dining room had a gorgeous china cabinet along the wall filled with beautiful glasses. Noah had a mantra that as long as it held liquids, you could drink wine out of it, but the Arison family had specific glasses for the different kinds of wine as well as every alcoholic beverage you could imagine. There was one piece in the middle that was not made of glass. It was a pot that seemed homemade and possibly from a middle school art class. Noah didn't know Mrs. Arison very well, but she did not seem like the type to let something that did not match the fine china stay in the cabinet. Noah was glad to be wrong.

The pair continued walking until they reached the stunning white-tiled kitchen. Noah felt this would be too easily stained, but it looked very expensive, which appeared to be the theme of the house. On the counter were supplies to make more macarons.

"My son loved your macarons, so you'll be making more of those, around two hundred. As for the two other desserts you'll be making, I need something with coconut, one hundred of those, and a sort of fruit tarte, fifty of those. Can you do that?"

"Um, yes. Yes, ma'am."

"Good. I'll leave you to it. I'll be running around all day, so if you have any questions, pick up that walkie there, and you'll be talking to the party planner, Miranda."

"Sounds good."

Mrs. Arison smiled without showing any teeth or moving her lips much and walked away. Noah instantly regretted agreeing to make that many pastries. She'd never done something this big, and the weight of the pressure and the desserts began to weigh on her chest. Her feet started vibrating, sending a shock wave up to her hips. Her hips locked, and she suddenly felt frozen in time even though her jaw was uncontrollably shaking. There was a string around her heart, and it kept tightening the more she thought about how she wouldn't succeed at this job and would be blacklisted from the industry and would never write the cookbook in memory of her mom. Her entire future, her mom's entire future, would be buried under a pile of cookies and pie.

"Breathe in for seven and out for five."

Noah looked up to see a tall man with reddish-brown hair and hazel eyes. Even though most of his features were a blur, Noah could make out his eyes and a cheek dimple that popped out as he spoke.

She spoke with a clear vibrato. "What?"

"It can help with the anxiety attack."

"Breathing doesn't help me."

The man looked around the room for a moment. Suddenly, Noah felt a small and direct thud against her arm; the stranger had flicked her. As the anger flooded her cheeks, she could make out more of his features, including the freckles on his nose.

"What the hell, man?"

"By flicking you, I gave you something else to pay attention to. And some of your anxiety got replaced with the anger at some guy flicking you."

Noah hated how much it worked. "You had no other ideas?"

"Have you ever tried eating one of your pastries? That macaron helped my anxiety attack the other day."

This must have been Patricia's son. Noah was taken aback by how candid he was; she hadn't seen this level of honesty from anyone else their age besides Kelly. It was refreshing but also suspicious; she decided a long time ago not to trust people with money—they'd just try to buy you off—and this guy had enough money to buy twelve of her.

"So, you're the one who got me the job?"

"Nope, that was all you. I may have just provided a little nudge."

The sunlight peaked in through the back door, casting a light on his eyes, making them a slightly lighter shade of brown. Noah appreciated the opportunity but didn't want him to think that meant she owed him anything. She'd play it cool.

"Thank you, it means a lot. I really needed this job." So much for playing it cool. If he weren't around, she'd slap her palm on her forehead.

"Make ten macarons for me, and we'll call it even."

Two hundred and ten—that wouldn't be hard at all.

"Well, I have to get going. I'll see you later tonight with, hopefully, some delicious cookies," he said, clearly trying to get a response from her.

"I'll do my best."

His face lit up. He winked and exited through the side dining room. Noah would have to work extra hard if she wanted to impress Patricia and her apparent number-one fan.

Henry
February 13, 2025

HENRY WAS SURPRISED BY HOW pretty the pastry chef was. Usually, the professionals his mom brought around the house were older guys with sideburns and a few missing teeth—not exactly his type. He was even more excited about his intervening; now he'd have delicious food to eat and a pretty face to look at. It all only slightly took the edge off what he had to do that day.

Henry was dreading having to go ring shopping with his older brother. The paparazzi would be there at noon, and he would have to be there at eleven thirty so it didn't look like he was just there to get his picture taken, which of course, he was. Henry's dad had already picked out the ring, per Christine's request, five months earlier when the idea of getting married first entered the conversation. Henry never really saw himself getting married at all, never mind in his twenties, but now he was twenty-six and was about to get engaged to America's sweetheart.

His dad said he'd fall in love with Christine eventually, or at least he'd enjoy spending time with her, which would begin to feel like the same thing. There was nothing wrong with Christine; she had long legs, kind eyes, and was a literal model, but Henry couldn't help but feel like something was missing. He didn't want to go back to his life of dating a new girl each week and running away the second they wanted something more concrete, but he also thought he'd feel different when he was about to get married. Maybe *he* would be different.

Henry walked into the jewelry shop at 11:58. He thought maybe if he walked around the block a few times, he'd either feel better about his decision or get the courage to call it all off. Neither happened. He walked in to find his brother browsing rings, shooting him a look that said, "Dad's gonna kill you," without saying a word. Henry took a lap around the store, stopping for a second at the most expensive rings to show no sum was too big for the woman he loved. The paparazzi pretended to be discreet while "secretly" taking pictures of the excursion, but the longer they were there, the sloppier and more obvious they got. Henry knew it was all staged, but he would've eventually come to that conclusion even if he didn't. Hopefully, it would be convincing enough to please his dad.

Afterward, he went to lunch with his brother and was trained in the perfect way to propose. Henry always thought it was pretty simple: you get down on one knee and ask a question, but Ryan made it seem much more complicated than that. They were in the public eye, and having people vested in your lives meant that they would dissect every aspect of the proposal for years to come. People were still talking about the fact that Ryan switched knees halfway through his, even though it was five years ago. Henry could feel the heat start to return to his chest but extinguished it with lots of water; his brother couldn't know exactly how all of this was affecting him.

At the end of lunch, Ryan hugged his brother, something he hadn't done since they were boys. Maybe Henry wasn't as convincing as he thought he was.

Noah
February 13, 2025

MAMA HAD THE SAME ROLLING pin for twenty years. When that one inevitably broke, she'd been devastated, so Noah bought her a new one and didn't understand when she didn't use it right away. Mama explained that she'd gotten hers from her mother, and even though the handles were loose and she had to put in extra elbow grease to get anything flat, every time she used it, she could still feel her mom in the kitchen with her. Noah could see tears trailing down her mom's cheeks, hitting the pile of dough. The only thing she could think to do was gently push Mama out of the way and start rolling out the dough herself. All she said was, "Now you and I can share this rolling pin." Noah hadn't thought anything of her comment; she was just trying to make her mom feel better. When Mama started crying harder, Noah had been even more confused. But Mama just said, "That's beautiful," kissed Noah on the forehead, and took over with the rolling pin.

Noah had had that rolling pin for twenty years and feared the day when it would break. Even though it squeaked every time it rolled and had a hard time flattening most materials, it always helped her when she needed it most. It had helped her make all the macarons and her "something coconut," which was another layered cookie with coconut cream filling in the middle. The top had a cutout in the shape of a heart that Noah filled with pink sugar, so each guest was able to literally taste the love. She'd created the fruit concoction for the fruit tarts, so all she had left to do was roll out the dough to make the crust, put it in tins, and bake them. She'd fill everything in the morning. She checked her watch to see it was eleven at night. Most of the time, Noah went somewhere else entirely when she was baking, but this was new. The anxiety and drive to accomplish her dreams kept her going through the entire process, even if she did miss dinner.

The front door swung open, colliding with the wall through a loud bang followed by the hushed whispers of whoever opened it. Noah peeked around the corner to see the tall guy from before tiptoeing toward the kitchen. He kept calling behind him to tell people to stop making noise, completely unaware that he was the one causing a disturbance. Noah could smell the beer on him even from six feet away.

Somehow, not seeing her entirely, he walked to the fridge and started rummaging through it. He grabbed the large bowl housing the filling for the tarts.

"Mmmm, fruit."

Noah ran over, gently grabbed the bowl from his hands, and slid it back into the fridge. "Sorry, that's not for you, buddy." She closed the door and stepped away from him.

"Hey, it's you, cute pastry lady."

Noah wanted to smile but knew better. She hoped he'd eventually give up and leave her kitchen. She went back to rolling.

"I'm so hungry, and there's like, nothing to eat."

He flopped onto the counter behind her and started groaning. Noah walked over to the corner of the counter next to the fridge and pulled out a plate of exactly ten macarons, as requested. She put it next to him and pushed it further into his arm when she realized he was unaware anything was near him.

"No way! You remembered. Thank you, pastry lady."

Noah couldn't help but laugh. "My name is Noah."

He started shoveling macarons into his mouth but spoke between chews. "I'm Henry."

"Well, bon appetite, Henry."

Noah felt satisfied. She saw the smile and little dance she was craving, and hopefully now Henry would leave her alone so she could get back to her fruit tarts and, in time, get some rest.

"Whatcha doing?" Henry walked up behind Noah so he was talking in her ear. She felt a chill on her neck.

"I'm rolling out the dough for the fruit tarts."

"Can I help? I'm not a baker, but I'm like, super strong." As he spoke, he hit a pose that made Noah smile. He was drunk—there was no denying that—but he could roll out some dough. There was no way he could mess that up.

"Okay, you can roll out the dough. I'm gonna put the tops on these cookies."

Henry saluted to her and immediately started rolling. Noah walked over to another table where the coconut cookies were being held. She began placing the heart tops onto the cream, making them into small sandwiches. As she worked, she heard the sound she'd been dreading: a prominent snap. She turned around to see Henry holding one of the handles of the rolling pin in one hand and the rest of it in the other.

"Whoops, I think I broke this."

Noah felt like she was going to collapse. She usually felt a warmth in the kitchen, one she could have sworn was her mom. Suddenly, the entire place felt cold, and she was being consumed by it. A sob started climbing up her throat as tears filled her eyes. Henry must have seen all of the emotions seizing Noah's face because he tried his best to put the roller back together but failed. After a few attempts, he walked over to Noah and tried to speak with her.

"I'm so sorry, I'll uh, I'll buy you a new one. I'll buy like, a million of them." This interaction somehow sobered him up.

Noah wanted to respond, but she couldn't get the words out. Her sob was occupying too much space. Henry seemed to be able to tell Noah was having a really hard time, so he didn't try speaking with her again. Instead, he got on the floor with her and wrapped her up in a hug. Noah melted into his body for a moment before realizing and pushing away.

"I'm so sorry, I should have asked if you were a hug person, I—"

Noah threw herself into his body, fully embracing the hug. Her hot tears fell on his shoulder, but he didn't move her. He just let it happen. After a few minutes, Noah separated from him and finally looked him in the eyes. She wiped the tears from her cheeks and under her eyes; her mascara was definitely running. She got up, which prompted Henry to join her.

There was a slight alleviation in her throat, and she was able to get a few words out. "That rolling pin was uh—it was my mom's, and it just meant a lot to me."

Henry looked mortified. "Oh my—I'm so sorry, I don't know what to say or do."

Noah could tell he meant it, and that made her feel better. "It's okay. I've had it for like, twenty years. I was waiting for the day. If it wasn't you and today, it would be me and tomorrow. Don't sweat it."

"At least let me help you finish this. I was the one to break your tool."

Noah's breathing began to settle.

"Do you have any empty wine bottles?"

Henry cackled. "In this house? Yes, yes, we do."

Henry disappeared for a minute and then returned with two empty wine bottles. He shrugged his shoulders to ask if the bottles would work. Noah nodded and motioned for him to follow her behind the island to start rolling out some dough. She showed him how to use the bottle, even though it was very similar to how you use a rolling pin and not complicated, she still felt slightly excited to teach him something new.

"There you go, you got the hang of it." Noah loved showing one of her mom's techniques to someone new, and for a minute, she forgot about the rolling pin.

"Honestly, your mom is a visionary. This is way more fun than the rolling pin. I'm sorry again."

Noah laughed. She didn't hate talking about her mom; she always wanted to. She just hated the way her heart tightened and she felt like she couldn't breathe afterward. She could never find the words to describe how amazing her mom was, especially to people who didn't know her, meaning everyone but Kelly and Noah's dad. There was no proper way to talk about someone who was your whole world without taking up a week.

"She must have loved cooking to come up with stuff like this. 'Cause anyone could do this, it's uh, what's the word?"

Noah couldn't stop herself from chiming in. "Accessible."

"Accessible, yes, exactly!"

Noah didn't feel any weight on her chest, and her breathing was perfectly fine. Somehow, the concept of talking about her mom's dreams was easier than talking about her reality.

"That was what she wanted to do. She wanted to make this cookbook of easy recipes and kitchen hacks so that you looked like a five-star chef but didn't actually need much. She started making it, but then . . ." Noah could feel the words start to slip away.

"That's so cool. I don't even know how to boil water."

"Don't you have people to do that?" Noah regretted the words the second they left her lips. She looked at Henry, trying to gauge his reaction.

Henry stopped rolling and started laughing. Noah joined in, afraid he might change his reaction if she didn't.

"Yeah, well, maybe the people that do that for me need a book like this."

Noah could feel her cheeks growing flushed and hoped they wouldn't get too pink and stand out to Henry. The next words were being pulled from Noah; she didn't consciously want to say them, but every bone in her body felt comfortable around this boy.

"It's my dream, too. That's why I said I really needed this job. I'm grateful, but I also hope this will earn me enough money to finally find someone to help me make this book."

His smile slowly faded. Noah's heart rate increased.

"I know some people in the publishing industry if you need help."

Regret crept in once again as Noah realized how grossly misunderstood her statement was.

"I appreciate that, but that's not why I said it. I, um, I've never told anyone, actually, not even my best friend. I don't know why, but it's late . . . I mean, it's 12:50, oh god, that's the time already? Well, it's 12:50, I feel like being honest."

Noah was praying she'd see that smile again.

Henry
February 14, 2025

SHE PASSED THE TEST.

Henry completely processed the rest of what she said. “Wait, what time is it?”

She looked at her watch again. “Now it’s 12:51.”

A tangible feeling of dread washed over Henry as he imagined the next two years of his life, possibly more. Pretending to be someone he’s not while pretending to be in love with someone he’s not and eventually taking over a job he doesn’t even want. He’d never allowed that thought to push its way to the surface before. Somehow, this girl made him want to be open. She’d shared personal stuff with him; it was only fair he returned the favor. And he’d destroyed the rolling pin that belonged to her mom; he was a monster, and it was a wonder she was still talking to him.

He felt his smile turn into a frown as these thoughts infiltrated his head.

“Is everything okay?” Noah looked up at him with big doe eyes. He wouldn’t be able to lie to those eyes, and he didn’t want to.

“I’m supposed to get engaged today.”

Her eyes seemed far less curious. “Oh, wow.”

Henry scrambled, trying to explain. “I mean, not really. Well, yes, I would be, but it wouldn’t be real. It’s under contract, and my dad is making me because it makes the company look good, and I alone don’t make the company look good right now, but by marrying America’s Sweetheart, I will.”

"Christine Paxton." She spoke with pity in her voice.

"So, you've heard." Henry started putting his guard back up.

"My best friend, Kelly, did some research when I was applying for this job. She told me about your relationship, but it seemed off to me. I'm so sorry you're going through this."

Noah put her hand on his arm, causing it to tingle slightly. Henry took a sledgehammer to his wall; he felt more comfortable, if that was even possible.

"My dad wants me—*needs* me to do this for him, but it all feels so wrong. I used to never think I was going to get married, but now I want it to be for love. Christine is nice, but we don't connect."

Henry continued rolling out the dough as the vulnerability took more and more of a toll on him. He saw how Noah put the dough into the tin and followed suit. Noah sighed like she was trying to figure out what to say next.

"That's a hard one. Is your dad the kind of guy you can say this to? Will he understand?"

Henry shook his head. "He's not big on emotions. He understands everything in terms of business. There's a certain hierarchy, and everyone holds a certain power. I'm at the bottom of that hierarchy, so I have no say."

"Wow, I didn't know the wealthy had so many problems."

Henry couldn't help but laugh, relieved Noah was there to lighten the mood. He felt his smile return.

"My advice would be to tell him your decision. He can't dictate your life, so just say it how it is. If he's all about power, he might respect your honesty and how you're taking control of your own life."

For the first time in a while, Henry had achieved a new level of clarity, like mountains of dirt had been removed and he was no longer buried. All she'd done was remind him that *he* should have control of *his* life, and it'd made him feel like he did.

Noah stopped touching the dough for a moment. "You know what, both of us are going to take control of our destinies. I'm going to finally write the cookbook because I keep waiting to do it with my mom, but she's . . . she's not coming back. But I will do this for her. And you are going to choose who you want to love and not marry someone just because your dad told you to. Deal?"

Noah held out her hand like she wanted Henry to shake it. She spoke with so much passion that he believed he could make that promise. He could do anything if she was there cheering him on. He reached out his hand, and they shook.

Noah started smiling, showing some of her top teeth. Henry was mesmerized by her beautiful smile and wondered what her lips felt like. Still holding hands, he pulled her in and kissed her.

He pushed away, though, unsure if she'd wanted the kiss or if he'd misread the entire situation and would have to avoid her the next day. Her large eyes grew even bigger, and her mouth opened slightly. Henry braced himself, expecting to be met with a string of profanities and unwell wishes.

She got on her toes, put her hand behind his head, and pulled him in for another kiss. She ran her fingers through his hair, and he pulled her waist in closer. Suddenly, the oven timer went off.

"The oven's preheated." Noah sounded lost. Henry laughed, and Noah eventually joined him.

He went in for another kiss, but she stopped him this time.

"I would love to do that again, trust me, but I need to get this done, and you're gonna distract me even more now than you were already. Go to bed, and I'll see you in the morning."

Henry was disappointed to hear those words but knew they were for the best. He wanted to see Noah succeed and knew he wouldn't be able to keep his hands off her. She pulled him in for one last kiss and then pushed him away and sent him off to bed.

Henry walked up the stairs toward his bedroom, really glad he'd eaten that macaron.

Noah
February 14, 2025

NOAH WOKE UP THE NEXT morning feeling like she had been hit by several trucks but couldn't be happier about it. She'd finished all the work she needed to do the previous night and had slept on a mattress better than any hotel's. Not to mention, she'd kissed a beautiful man with emotional intelligence, which she used to think was impossible. She popped out of bed and went straight to the bathroom mirror. She frantically pawed at her hair, hoping eventually she would find a pretty style within the mess.

She heard a knock at the door, and expecting it to be Henry, Noah tugged at her clothing and checked her breath before opening it. There was no one outside, but there was a garment bag on the door with the tag: *Noah, Make sure to join us for the party —Patricia.*

Noah was glowing. She would be able to spend the day with Henry and was going to wear a dress hand-selected by Patricia Arison. Maybe she was already accepting her as a daughter-in-law. But Noah did not want to get ahead of herself. She had just met Henry, and one amazing, dreamy night did not mean forever. He still had a promise to keep, and they still had a lot more to learn about each other, but she was excited to do so.

She opened the bag to reveal a sparkly red long-sleeved cocktail dress. Noah was taken aback by the way the dress was taking in the light. She would draw attention to herself for sure. Noah slipped into the dress and continued getting ready before going downstairs.

She threw on her mother's apron and filled all of the tarts. After everything was chilled and defrosted, she put them on tiered heart displays. She even formed some of the cookies into a heart on the table. She filled in gaps with different fruits and some garnishes found in an article called "Make Anything Look Fancier" that she'd read online. She even put fake pearls and diamonds around the table, which was something she would never do before, but she was hoping to impress Patricia. She wanted to make Patricia's dreams come true even though she knew she was nowhere near her first choice.

As Noah put the last pearl on the display, Patricia walked over. "Wow, it looks . . . amazing."

Noah turned around, trying to hide her excitement at that comment. "Thank you so much."

"I have to admit, I didn't have that high of expectations when you first started, but you surprised me."

"That means a lot, Mrs. Arison." Noah tried not to think of Mrs. Arison choking on one of the pearls.

"Call me Patricia. So, your job is done, the servers are going to give out the desserts. Here is your check. And you got the dress I sent—good! Feel free to join us." An actual smile started to spread across Patricia's face.

"I'd love to. Thank you . . . Patricia."

Patricia walked away. Noah stopped herself from celebrating too much. She felt warmth back in the kitchen; she just hoped her mom was proud of her.

Noah followed the decorations to the main ballroom. She pulled open the door when she noticed Henry and his father. George put a small black box in Henry's hand, and Henry let him. He didn't fight back, he didn't throw it in his face, he took the box.

Noah's breath caught, and her vision was blurry; she couldn't believe she had allowed herself to be so stupid, her judgment clouded by one night and a couple kisses. Of course he wouldn't keep his promise; he'd given her no reason to believe he would. She didn't know him. Noah let the door slam behind her as she ran out of the hallway. She made one quick stop in the bedroom upstairs for her things and then fled the house.

Henry
February 14, 2025

HENRY'S DAD PUT THE RING in his hand, and suddenly Henry found he couldn't move.

"After my toast, you'll make one of your own. You'll get down on one knee, show the ring, ask the question, and we'll all celebrate your engagement."

The pit in Henry's stomach grew with each word from his father. His hand got tighter around the box until he could feel his hand getting red.

"No." Henry was pleasantly surprised by the word.

"What do you mean, no?" His father was not as impressed. He stepped closer, and his face grew redder.

"I'm not doing it. You've controlled every part of my life, and I'm not letting you decide who I marry, too." He started to walk away but turned back. "And while we're at it, I don't want to be vice president of the company. I don't exactly know what I want to do, but I do know I don't want to be drunk every night with guys I don't like. And I also don't want to be your lap dog. So I won't be signing your contract."

Henry shoved the ring back into his dad's hand. His dad looked down and then back up, seemingly caught off guard.

"Where are you going?" There was a slight crack to his voice while he spoke.

"I'm going to talk to a girl."

Henry walked away, not even staying to hear his father's argument. He passionately pushed through the doors and walked straight to the kitchen. There was no sign of Noah. He walked to the front door and looked for her car but did not see it. As he looked, his brother's car pulled up. He ran outside and got in the passenger's seat before his brother was able to step out of the car.

"Henry, what are you doing?"

Henry started chaotically typing on his phone. "I need you to drive me somewhere right now."

Ryan made a few noises, showing he was confused, before putting the car into drive and heading down the driveway.

A few minutes later, Henry asked Ryan to make a quick stop and ran into a store, emerging with a large bag. Ryan tried to ask questions, but Henry stopped him before he could say anything and motioned for him to keep driving.

They kept going until they finally made it to an apartment complex across town. Henry wrapped his gift up quickly and tumbled out of the car. He knocked on the door, hoping she'd answer.

A shorter blonde girl opened instead. "I'm looking for Noah. Is she here?"

"Oh, it's you." The girl seemed unimpressed.

"Can I please talk to her?"

"I don't want to talk to you." A familiar voice chimed from further in the house.

Henry pushed past the blonde girl, who made it known she was offended. He pulled his gift out from behind his back: a bouquet of rolling pins.

"I owed you a few of these."

He watched as a slight smile appeared on Noah's face but could tell she didn't want it there.

"How'd you find her?"

"You aren't the only one who can online stalk, Kelly. I assume you're Kelly."

Kelly seemed intrigued. "Point, cute but stupid boy."

"You broke your promise." The heartache in Noah's voice made Henry want to fall to his knees. At first, he couldn't understand what she meant, but then it all clicked.

"I told him I make my own decisions and don't want to marry the girl he chose or take his job." Henry timidly moved closer, but Noah turned her head, trying not to look at him.

"But I saw you holding the ring."

"My dad gave me the ring, yes. And I paused. I thought about how easy it would be to go along with my dad's plan. But then, a wise person's voice popped in my head saying, 'He can't dictate your life.' And I gave it back."

She smiled shyly.

Henry continued. "Look, I know we only spent one night together, but you understand me more than practically everyone else in my life. I just started making my own decisions like twenty minutes ago, and the first thing I wanted to do was come here and kiss you again . . . if you'll have me."

Henry was starting to get scared of the vulnerability, but instead of pushing it away, he leaned into it. He was going to be a new person; he wanted to be better for Noah. He looked to Kelly, who was staring at Noah. Eventually, Noah turned her head back and met Henry's eyes. She got off the couch, walked over, took the rolling pins from his hands, and placed them on the coffee table.

Noah & Henry
February 14, 2025

She kissed him.

About the Author

Jessica Daniliuk is excited to participate in another anthology with Nicole Frail Books. Her story "Dancing Queen" was seen in *Another Chance to Get It Right: A New Year's Eve Anthology*. She has also recently published with The Offering and KayTell Ink Publishing. She wants to thank her family and friends for always reading her work and being her greatest cheerleaders.

You can find Jessica on:

Instagram: @jmdaniliuk

You can visit her website at:

www.jessicadaniliuk.com

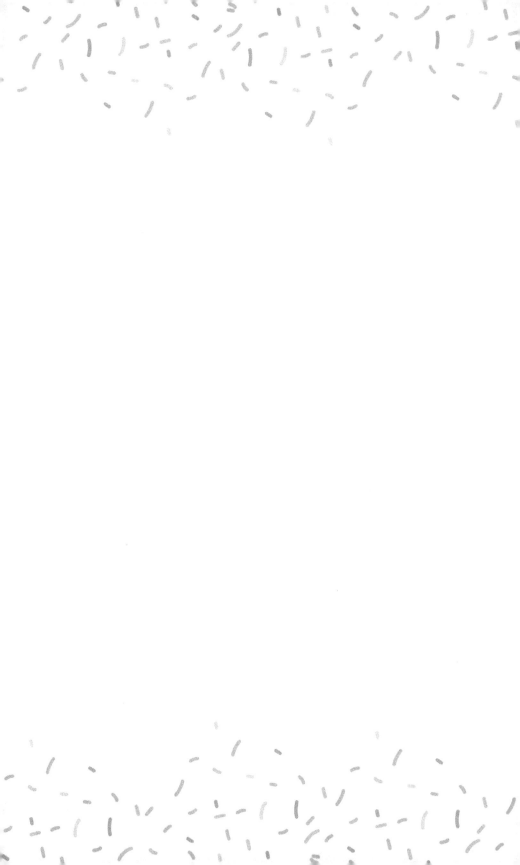

BETTER IN BLACK

Better in Black

MK Edgley

JASMINE KEPT TRYING TO MOVE, but the heated seat in her car kept her glued to the spot. She didn't *have* to go into the restaurant; she could drive away. Takeout from the Thai place near her apartment sounded appealing. With a heavy sigh, Jasmine eventually unbuckled. Cold air hit her face as she stepped out of the car and into the gloomy shadows.

At the front door, she scoffed, having forgotten the ludicrous name of the place. Ovine and Avian was painted in white script against a darkly stained wood door. *What plaid-wearing, craft-brewing, lumberjack wannabe thought that up?* Jasmine grunted as she pulled on the cast-iron handle, finding that she needed to use two hands to force it open.

Inside, the place matched Jasmine's idea of a hoity-toity eatery. She spotted a violinist going from table to table and someone else selling roses. Everything was either lit by lamps, a few subtle light fixtures, or table candles. The tablecloths, fixtures, everything that could be black was. Chairs, tables, the host podium. The trim and walls consisted of black on black. The candles themselves, even. Occasional pops of silver or white stood out, creating a visual divider for some objects and providing a slight contrast throughout such a dreary setting.

At the host podium, a young woman greeted Jasmine. "Hello, welcome to Ovine and Avian. Do you have a reservation?" The woman wore heavy makeup and was dressed in black, silver hoops dangling from her ears. She couldn't have been older than twenty-two. The amount of vocal fry in her voice was predictable, even if it made Jasmine's teeth itch.

"Oh, hello. I'm here for the singles event?"

"Absolutely. If you would follow Rosa here, she will show you the way." The host motioned to a young woman behind her wearing the same amount of eyeliner.

"Thank you."

Rosa stepped up to lead Jasmine through the restaurant and down a hallway. They stopped in front of the entry to a private room before Rosa vanished.

Jasmine didn't cross the threshold yet, but she could see inside. It was the sort of place companies would rent for their holiday functions. People were already milling about, most lined up at a small table to check in, but she barely took notice of them. The room itself kept with the dark theme of the restaurant, with a long table in the center covered in candles, but red, white, and pink streamers hung on the walls. Hearts adorned *everything*. As she eyed the confetti-sized ones strewn about the table, she determined that someone had obviously let Cupid vomit in there. To top it off, instrumental music played quietly in the background, the kind of bland soft rock with saxophone meant to set a romantic tone. It didn't.

Instead of joining the crimson and rose-colored fray, Jasmine turned and made a dash for the bathroom she'd passed on the way to the room. She leaned on the black granite countertop, breathing heavily. A pang of sadness gripped her chest while her stomach felt as though it contained an army of frogs.

She looked up in the mirror. Instead of confidence, the brown eyes staring back at her showed only fear. "Come on, it's been almost a year. You can do this."

After taking a minute to catch her breath, she checked the mirror one more time. Her makeup was still impeccable, and her smoky lids certainly matched her mood. Her hair was flawless, too. She left it mostly down that evening, pulling back only a few dark, wavy strands into her favorite hairpin. Duncan had given it to her, but she kept it because she loved the style. The dark walnut accessory blended in with her own brown hair; the grain of the wood looked like just another strand. Understated and elegant.

As she walked down the hallway back toward her own personal hell, Jasmine gazed at the floor, the color reminiscent of her hairpin. She decided then that the color scheme of the place was comforting, even if it had been a tad overwhelming at first. She appreciated the lack of holiday decorations in the rest of the restaurant, and that fact alone helped her reconsider the black everywhere. The black didn't accost her senses like several other businesses had the last month. Things like red bagels at the coffee shop and heart stickers on takeout bags had been commonplace since January. She swore if she heard that song that spelled out "love" one more time, she would scream.

Inside the room, she joined the line of people leading to the check-in table. She tried to ignore the obnoxious sights and sounds and instead examined the people already in the room. Jasmine counted about two dozen of them and a veritable cacophony of bright outfits, all centered around the made-up holiday. She felt even better about her decision to wear a mainly dark outfit, but her dress had pops of blue and green, unlike the rest of the restaurant.

Jasmine heard people chatting with each other already, some laughing, most holding drinks. Some people stood off to the side, glancing nervously at the others. The people themselves were less offensive-looking than their outfits, though hot people usually opened their mouths at some point and negated their looks.

"Hello and welcome! I'm Glenn. What's your name?" a soft-spoken man asked her. He was tall, fit, and very well groomed.

"Hello, I'm Jasmine."

"Great! Let's see . . ." He looked at the table full of stickers. "Ah! Here you are. This is your nametag." He handed her one. "Please take a moment to look it over. Is everything on there accurate? Is there anything you would like to change?"

She read over her name, pronouns, and sexual preferences. "This is fine."

"Wonderful." Glenn wore a nametag, too. His pronouns were he/him and she was unsurprised to see he preferred men, though she felt bad for having unintentionally stereotyped him. "Here's a wristband. Please wear this and the nametag for the duration of the evening. We are just mingling while everyone arrives. Grab a drink, talk to some people, and we will make an announcement when it's time to start. Eveline will explain all the logistics then."

"Thank you."

She put on the wristband and name badge, then went straight for the small, portable bar in the corner. It surprised Jasmine that she could see it, since it camouflaged against the walls so nicely. Its only decorations were small, black vases with short-stemmed red roses sticking out sitting on the black granite countertop that matched the bathroom's.

The menu showed a variety of craft cocktails, all with a Valentine's theme. It listed regular drinks, like Sex on the Beach and Pink Lady, but she rolled her eyes at the outrageously named ones. Things like Heart on Fire and Cupid's Arrow.

"What'll it be?" a woman with short hair shaved on the sides asked. Jasmine saw her onyx lapel pin read *Cam* in embossed black letters. The person worked at the restaurant, so their nametag had no pronouns listed, and like with Glenn a few minutes earlier, Jasmine inwardly scolded herself for having assumed.

"Um, do you have wine? If you have a cab, that'd be great, but I'll take whatever red you brought back here."

Cam chuckled. "Of course."

A tall, muscular man approached the bar as well. He ordered the Love Potion. She wasn't sure which was more sickening: the name of the drink or the peach schnapps it contained.

Cam got the drinks and then scanned their wristbands. Jasmine held up her arm to glance at the QR code. "Huh. Easier than drink tickets, I suppose."

"Yeah, pretty clever." The man next to her sipped his nauseating drink. "Hope you won't judge me for my drink order. I just love a fruity drink. I'm Anthony, by the way."

"Jasmine." They shook hands. "And no, doesn't the judgment come later?"

They both laughed. The man was handsome enough, his square face and prominent jawline were points in his favor. His name tag indicated he/him pronouns and that he liked men and women.

"So, what's your story? I mean, forgive me, not that anyone here is unattractive, but you're probably the hottest one."

"Um, thank you. That is very kind. I'm just trying to get back out there, you know?"

"Ah, bad break up?"

"You could say that." Jasmine took a sip of her wine, finally. Thankfully, the bold, full-bodied flavor of cabernet sauvignon hit her tongue rather than some generic blend. The taste of licorice and black currant lingered. She smiled and took a second sip.

"I'm doing something similar, I guess." Anthony kept talking. "I figured out the bi thing recently and some of the women I've tried to date have not appreciated that."

"Ah, thought you couldn't go wrong here?"

"Exactly." Anthony flashed a smile. "Cheers." They clinked glasses. "Cheers," she copied.

Anthony kept smiling wide, his unnaturally white teeth on display. Jasmine scanned the rest of him in earnest now. He had a spray tan, and she tried to decide if he'd had any Botox done. Was Anthony one of those guys who told people he was thirty-something when he was really pushing fifty? His dirty-blonde hair looked expertly styled and dyed, but a bit of his roots were showing and those had strands of gray. Anthony wore nipple rings that protruded under his skintight, pink V-neck. Jasmine fought the urge to ask him if he'd bought a sports car with his midlife crisis, too.

He took a sip of his fruity drink while she sipped her wine. "So, what do you do?"

"Oh, nothing too exciting. I work for a biotech firm."

"Uh, cool. Not exactly sure what that means."

"Don't worry about it." Jasmine waved it off. "What do you do?"

"I'm a personal trainer. I've always liked using my body."

She wasn't sure if it was an inadvertent twitch or not, but his pecs kind of moved as he said it. Then Anthony casually changed position, so his arms flexed, and she knew that had not been a coincidence.

"Got it. Well, it was nice to meet you. Perhaps we'll get paired later."

"Yeah, looking forward to it." Anthony's teeth practically blinded her.

Jasmine walked away from the bar and went to stand near a table along the wall that held hors d'oeuvres. She caught several people around the room checking her out. Her skin felt clammy, but the taste of the exquisite wine kept her from fleeing again. For now, she would stay, though her conversation with Anthony had reminded her of what she hated about dating in the first place.

As Jasmine finished reading a cheesy love poem carved on a wooden placard sitting on the table, a woman approached. Actually, she noticed the pronouns on the person's nametag were they/them as they got closer. Jasmine really needed to check nametags before starting any conversation the rest of the evening.

"Hey, I'm Sam." The person wore a white button-up shirt, red suspenders, and a red bow tie with pink and white hearts. They had buzzed, chestnut hair and plugs in their ears but not those large ones where you could see through them, at least. They were a little short and pudgy, but cute. Jasmine thought they were better looking than Anthony by quite a lot.

"Jasmine. Nice bow tie." Jasmine couldn't decide if she meant it sarcastically or not, but her tone remained even.

"Thank you. If you don't mind me saying, you're quite beautiful."

"Thank you, that's flattering." *Will it be like this all night?* Jasmine wondered.

"So, what do you—"

But Sam never finished. The clink of a glass resounded throughout the room, and everyone stopped talking. Jasmine looked toward the head of the table at a woman holding an empty wineglass and a fork, waiting for everyone's attention to focus on her. Her all-red pantsuit with shoulder pads and heavy, pageant-style makeup appeared out of place compared to everyone else, but Jasmine figured she at least matched the decorations.

"Welcome, everyone! I am so pleased with the turnout! My name is Eveline. I am with Queer City, your local 2SLGBTQIA+ community center. Please check our website for our calendar and sign up for our newsletter. We often host free events, as well as family-friendly ones—not all of them are about dating. We also offer a variety of other services, though, including free HIV testing seven days a week.

"But tonight is Queer Speed Dating. This event revolves around a six-course meal. Seven with the appetizers! The portions are adjusted to be smaller so that you can enjoy a bit of everything without feeling bloated, but don't worry! You'll still be satisfied at the end, and I don't just mean with the food!"

Everyone laughed while Jasmine held in her groan by sipping her wine.

"Now, each course will last fifteen minutes and then you will switch partners. We will take a bathroom break after course three. Based on everyone's questionnaires and their preferences, we have already predetermined whom you will sit with for each round. Each seat is numbered clearly, so find your name card and sit there. Keep it with you for each course, as it tells you where to sit. When I clink my glass, it is time to switch places.

"If the conversation lulls, the back of your name card has various topics and questions to assist you. There is no shame in needing this! After the evening is over, you will go online and indicate if there was anyone you felt you clicked with. If that person said they were interested in you, too, then you will receive each other's contact information.

"The last thing I want to remind you of is that we do not differentiate between how you identify now and your assigned gender at birth. For instance, if your pronouns are she/her and you indicate you are only interested in women, it is possible you might be paired with someone assigned male at birth, as we do not ask that. If you are not comfortable with this, then this is not the event for you. If you are paired with someone that you are not compatible with in this way, we ask that you simply continue making polite conversation for the remainder of the course. You have no obligation to select anyone online later. Anyone who engages in rude or disrespectful behavior will be asked to leave.

"With that out of the way, please find your seats and we will begin!" Eveline clapped her hands excitedly.

Jasmine's name card was in the middle of the table. She was wedged between two men, but seated across from her was a woman. She had long, straight, blonde hair she wore down and had on a low-cut, pink dress that accentuated her ample cleavage. A slight blush tinged her cheeks as she smiled at Jasmine and a pair of darling dimples appeared. Maybe the night wouldn't be horrible.

"Hi. I'm Jasmine."

"T-Tricia. Sorry, I'm a little nervous to be here." Tricia's voice quavered.

"That's all right. If it makes you feel better, I've already thought about bolting three times."

"Well, I'm glad you stayed."

She felt herself smile. "Yeah, me too." She was about to ask Tricia what she did for a living, but a waiter put a square plate down in front of her. Of course the plate was black. It had a single slice of baguette with an indiscernible black-and-white topping neatly piled on the bread. "Oh. What is this?"

"The menu card here says it's goat cheese crostini with fig olive tapenade." Tricia picked up another piece of paper from the table.

Jasmine looked down at her own. "Ah, yes, and the snacks from earlier were zucchini fritters. I didn't have any, did you?"

"I did. They were good, so this should be, too."

She took a bite. All thoughts of leaving vanished. "Wow."

Jasmine could taste the fig and olive equally in the tapenade, the perfect blend of savory and sweet. The goat cheese provided that salty taste. The bread part was slightly warm, which enhanced it all and provided the perfect crunch. Jasmine should have taken a photo before she ate it, but she typically abhorred *those* people.

"Mmm. Yeah, these are even better."

"So, what do you do?" Jasmine forced herself to make small talk.

"I'm an elementary school teacher."

"Ah, better you than me."

They both laughed. "Not a big fan of kids?" Tricia tilted her head.

"They're all right. I want them someday, but it's still an abstract concept at the moment." Jasmine shrugged.

"I don't have any yet, but it's hard to say what the future holds." Tricia flashed another coy smile at her.

Jasmine felt her breath catch in her throat. Tricia's smile really was something else. "Y-Yeah."

"And what do you do?"

"I work at a biotech firm. It's not very interesting. What do you do for fun?" Jasmine took another bite of the delicious food. It held an estimated three bites, so she wanted to savor it.

"No real hobbies in particular. I like going out with friends, though. I'm not a homebody. I'm usually up for anything."

Tricia said the last words slowly and her smile changed. It wasn't seductive, but her mouth had turned into a bit of a smirk. Something in the way Tricia said it made Jasmine's hair stand on end coupled with a sinking feeling in her stomach. Maybe it was just the crostini mixing with the wine, though. At least the frogs had settled down.

Jasmine coughed. "Uh, great. I'm big into the outdoors. Kayaking, biking, that sorta thing, and I'm a big reader. Oh, and I go to a lot of yoga."

"I can tell." Maybe it was a trick of the light, but she thought the woman licked her lips.

"Um, thank you." Jasmine decided to just push past it. Benefit of the doubt in this type of setting. "Well, are you from the area or—" Jasmine felt a foot sliding up her leg. "What are you doing?"

"You know, we don't have to wait until later to get to know each other better. . . ."

"I-I would like you to stop doing that." Jasmine pushed her chair out from the table slightly.

The woman's expression turned sour. She pulled her foot away as she rolled her eyes and scoffed. Jasmine sighed. They sat there in silence for the rest of the round. Jasmine read the menu card a few times, as well as fiddled with the edges of her place card, ruining the edges of the crisp, black paper. A waiter took their empty plates at some point. At long last, she heard the wineglass clink.

She got up and went to her next seat. This time it was a man with a chiseled jawline. His dark hair was cut short with a fade on the sides, and his facial hair framed his mouth in a square. His red V-neck shirt clung to his pecs. Jasmine wondered if the same person dressed this man and Anthony. At least his tan complexion looked natural.

"Hey, I'm Esteban." He waved.

"I'm Jasmine." The waiter set the next course in front of her then. She looked down. "So, what is it, you think? It doesn't quite look like tomato bisque." The tiny cup of orange soup was the color of Anthony's skin. It wasn't even a cup; it was a shot glass. It stood in the middle of the plate with a small salad around it, just a few leaves and vegetables, which made a ring around the soup. No, it made a heart, she realized upon further inspection. A few croutons placed evenly around.

"Pumpkin sage bisque, according to the card."

"Ah, yes." Jasmine saw the sprig of sage sitting on top of the orange liquid. She found her own menu card again. "And the salad is just a garden salad with aged parmesan croutons and a raspberry vinaigarette. Hm, seems basic after everything else."

"I guess. I mean, how many types of salad are there? It's like, side salad or Caesar."

"Uh, yeah." She feigned a smile. Maybe he was just a steak-and-potatoes kind of guy. Who knew? There was no reason to judge, she tried to tell herself.

She took a bite of her salad then. It was amazing how fresh it was. Everything was crisp and the vinaigarette paired perfectly with it. The croutons were equally delectable and obviously made from scratch. Her *mmm* was audible as she ate, but he just smiled politely. He gave no indication of enjoyment nor disgust as he took a few bites.

"So, tell me about yourself."

For what felt like the millionth time, Jasmine fought the urge to roll her eyes. If she slipped at any point, she was sure they wouldn't come down the rest of the night. "I'm a big outdoors and fitness person. I love to kayak and go to a lot of yoga. I'm looking to get certified to teach it, actually. How about you?"

"Oh, I mean, outdoors aren't totally my thing, but I like the gym." He kept eating his salad and said nothing else, letting silence fall for a beat too long for her comfort.

"Right, well, to each their own."

"Yeah. So, what do you do? I'm an investment banker."

"Neat. I work at a biotech firm."

"Biotech?" Esteban's face scrunched.

"Biological technology."

"So, robots?" He tilted his head.

"That's not really what it's about. Um, what do you do for fun then? Other than the gym?"

"Well, I go out with friends some, but otherwise, I play a lot of video games. My mom said I needed to get out more, especially after my last breakup. I saw this advertised. Can't hurt, right?"

"Right. So, you're close with your mom then?"

"She's my best friend."

"That's sweet." She took another bite to avoid scoffing. The tomatoes! Now, those were sweet.

"Yeah, she's been texting me nonstop since I got here, though. I had to turn my phone off."

Jasmine laughed awkwardly. She chastised herself, but what was she supposed to say to that, really?

"Well, it's nice she cares about you," was what she landed on.

Jasmine took the shot glass of soup in her hand then and she motioned for him to do the same. He picked it up with a feigned smile but clinked shot glasses with her anyway. They both downed the soup, and it left her dumbfounded, just like everything else so far.

Maybe I need to be dating the chef, she joked inside her head.

"Wow. That's just . . . I've never liked pumpkin *that* much." Jasmine stared at the shot glass in her hand, willing it to refill.

"Ah, so not a PSL kind of girl?"

"Not usually, no. And I don't even think that's really pumpkin. It's just cloves and cinnamon and stuff, right?"

He furrowed his brows. "Uh, I mean, it has pumpkin in the name."

"It's . . . sure." Jasmine forced her own smile.

"Well, I love them. My mom and I make them year-round at home. We don't wait for fall. But when it does come around, we always go on the first day to—"

"Oh. So, do you . . . live with your mom?" Jasmine already knew the answer, though.

"Well, yeah. I moved out for a while when I lived with my ex, Todd. But he got mad that I always wanted to have dinner with her still. She's lonely, you know? I just up and left her and . . ."

Jasmine couldn't do it anymore. She could not listen to Esteban speak about his mother in this way and not judge him. Maybe she shouldn't date, if this was how she would treat everyone. Her brain would find some way to tear them down and use it as evidence not to even try and get to know a person.

Jasmine's second glass of wine arrived, and she took a sip just as Esteban pulled out his phone. He turned it back on to show her some of his Christmas card pictures. After about three photos, Jasmine took another long drink and closed her eyes briefly, trying to block out Esteban's voice.

Mercifully, Eveline's wineglass clinked a few minutes later.

The next four courses contained four equally excruciating conversations while Jasmine ate the finest meal she had ever tasted in her life. The first main course was a piece of roasted duck with orange-ginger glaze and a few coins of tricolor roasted carrots. She wanted to weep at how wonderful the tangy sauce complemented the rich and tender meat. It was ironic, considering the person across from her, Blake, was practically in tears as they launched into a story about their ex.

After the bathroom break, Jasmine listened to Sam go on about themself next. Waiters brought each person a shot glass full of lemon water to drink first as a palate cleanser before the second main course. It was grilled flat iron steak with rosemary garlic mashed potatoes. It was the best thing yet. The two-bite steak was cooked to perfection and the tablespoon of mashed potatoes were creamy and seasoned perfectly. Then Sam suggested they have sex in a far less subtle way than Tricia had, implying they do so in the bathroom of the restaurant.

Then there was the cheese plate. Three tiny cubes of cheese paired with a thin cracker and an equally thin slice of fruit served on an ebony cutting board. She barely listened as a curly-haired woman named Monique read her the specific ingredients of each. There was also a bite-sized piece of baked brie, with a brandied jelly of apple and pear, topped with a pistachio crumble.

Nothing could compete with that, but it wasn't much of a competition, considering how dull Monique was. She might as well read more of the menu instead of speaking about hobbies as dull as hers. Or maybe they would have been interesting if she managed any inflection in her voice. Monique was a receptionist who hadn't gone to college. Jasmine cursed herself for being so elitist, but what on Earth would they talk about if the round was even another five minutes?

Lastly, she was paired with a man who spoke to the man next to him instead of her.

Jasmine spoke some with the man at her side, Kwame, but his nametag indicated he was gay.

Dessert looked like a chocolate-covered strawberry, but when she bit into it, it was like a turducken of chocolate and fruit. The outside chocolate tasted dark but not bitter. It was encrusted with peanuts with a hint of caramel and salt. Underneath was just a slice of strawberry, shaved thinly to wrap around another chocolate layer. This was white chocolate with pieces of macadamia. Underneath that was a layer of fig paste with coconut shavings. The last layer of chocolate was much sweeter than the outside and had pieces of hazelnut. Inside that was a pocket of some sort of goo that tasted of citrus.

She was unable to stop herself from making an audible noise of pleasure. Kwame snickered but then he took a bite of his dessert and made the same sound. "I guess that serves me right for laughing at you."

"You said it, not me." They both chuckled some more.

Before they could say anything else, noise erupted at the other end of the table.

". . . told you, *I* would pick up the woman tonight!" Tricia yelled suddenly, standing up.

Jasmine noticed Anthony sat across from Tricia's now empty seat, a pained smile plastered on his face. "Come on, sit back down. Let's not make a scene—"

"Oh! This is so typical of you! I cannot believe you would pull this after last summer—"

"Hey! That's not fair! You said you weren't gonna throw that in my face anymore!"

He stood now, too, both shouting. A few minutes later, a couple of bigger guys appeared and escorted the couple out.

"I guess they knew each other then?" Kwame turned back to her.

"Must have. Think it was some sort of, like, roleplay thing?"

Kwame sucked in his lips, trying to suppress a laugh. "That is one way to say it."

"So, did you actually meet anyone you like here?"

"Yeah, but he started talking to your guy."

"Ah. Sorry."

Kwame waved it off. "I told my friends this would just be a glorified meat market."

"Yeah, I'm beginning to see that."

"What about you?"

"This is honestly the most normal conversation I've had all night. So, here's to that."

They clinked glasses. "Oof. I'm sorry. You're cute and all, but believe me, I have tried to like women, and I just do *not* understand."

Jasmine laughed. "That's fine. I think I'm gonna go back to not dating for another year though. Spend some more time on myself."

"I think I would rather die. Call me when you're thinking of getting a bonded pair of cats from the shelter, though. I'll talk you down."

"How do you know I don't already have cats?"

Kwame nodded his head in the direction of Monique a few chairs down. "She's wearing a designer dress, like you, but lint rollers cannot get all that cat hair."

Jasmine looked and he was right. Even at a distance, she had not managed to clean the garment properly. "Just to be clear, are you judging her for being single with a cat, for not being able to get all the cat hair off her clothes, or the fact that she has sullied that Versace with said cat hair?"

"Why would I choose just one reason to judge people?"

They both cackled for a few seconds, earning them a raised eyebrow or two from the others. The host, Eveline, clinked her glass for a final time. Jasmine breathed a sigh of relief.

"What a fun evening! I saw several sparks flying! Please, do not forget to go online and select anyone you would like to get to know more. We would also love it if you left us a review, please. We hope to see you at another event, hopefully one of our couples' nights! Good night, everyone, thank you for coming, and drive safely!"

"They realize that we could just exchange numbers if we wanted, right?" Jasmine muttered to Kwame.

"I think they expect some of it, but they're kicking us out."

Glenn and Eveline started taking things down from the walls. The waitstaff smiled at people, offering to take their glasses. Employees emptied the tables while others gently herded Jasmine and her fellow singles toward the door. With a sigh, she handed over her empty wine glass and then followed everyone else out into the lobby as she braced herself for the cold winter air.

Sam had waited for her on the curb. "Hey, I really liked talking to you. I wondered if—"

"You are a very sweet person, but I think I've decided I'm not ready to date again after all. Have a good night." Jasmine started to walk past.

"Is that a complete no? You're done dating but maybe you would wanna . . . ?"

She did not turn back to give her answer. "No, thank you, to all things."

Jasmine heard their grumble of irritation, but the conversation with Sam just hadn't been stimulating. Sam was all-right-looking, but Jasmine had other things she looked for in a potential partner. If she could find someone to talk to with a single brain cell that wasn't centered on shallow things, then it honestly didn't matter to her what they looked like.

Jasmine continued to her car and, once inside, she put her head on the steering wheel and cried. She started berating herself for the judgments she made about these people—and for going there in the first place. She felt stupid for thinking she would find anyone there, but like Esteban, other people had pushed her to try dating again. Although, unlike Esteban, it had just been her friends and not a codependent parent.

After a few minutes of questioning all of her life decisions, she decided she wanted another drink and walked back into the restaurant. She waved to the host and then pointed toward the bar. The woman nodded and smiled.

At the bar, she found Cam. "Ah, didn't work out too well?"

Jasmine sighed and took a seat. "No."

"You driving?"

"I just decided that I'm not. Tomorrow's Sunday, so I can leave my car where it is."

"Great. You want something stronger?"

"Please. Just not anything red or pink. Or heart shaped."

"So, a shot of Jäger then?"

They both chuckled at that. "No, I think a double Jameson, neat."

"Coming right up."

Once Cam turned to start fixing the drink, a woman walked behind the bar and spoke to Cam. They both laughed and exchanged a brief hug. Cam came back to Jasmine then.

"Hey, actually, looks like I'm off the clock. My boss is getting that for ya. I hope you have a better night."

"Thanks, you have a good one."

A minute later, the other woman brought Jasmine her whiskey. The sleeves of her black button-down shirt were rolled up, and she had suspenders and a bow tie, like Sam, but hers were both black. She wasn't wearing a name tag at all. Jasmine took a good look at the person again. As with Cam, Jasmine left the pronouns open-ended in her mind for the moment.

"Hey, sorry 'bout that. She was already here longer than she shoulda been on Valentine's Day. Her and her wife have a new baby at home, and they got a sitter, but someone called out."

"No worries. Thank you." At least that settled her internal debate regarding Cam's pronouns.

"She said you were at the speed-dating thing? Do you mind me asking how it was?"

"Well, I'm back here, drinking a double scotch. I'm guessing my mascara is running. So, what do you think?" As soon as the words left Jasmine, she gasped and covered her mouth. "I'm so sorry, I didn't mean to be so . . ."

The person chuckled. "No, no. My bad, I didn't mean it like that. I shoulda been more specific with my question. I'm sorry it didn't go well for you, though."

"It's fine. Just tells me I'm not ready to be out there again. What were you asking then?"

"I wanted to know how the event ran. Did you like the organizers? The setup of the thing?"

"Oh, I hadn't thought about all that yet."

"I'm sorry, you're upset and I'm asking you weird questions. Just go about your brooding. Let me know when you want a cab, all right?" They pushed the glass toward Jasmine.

Jasmine waved it off. "It's fine. You're . . . fine." She realized then just how fine. Their auburn, sideswept bangs fell over their blue eyes adorably. Their smile was charming, dazzling even, in a way Anthony's artificially whitened teeth could never hope to emulate. "It's hard to think about the logistics of it when I'm trying to decide if there could be a six-way tie for worst."

"Oof," they winced. "That bad?"

"I just . . ." She sighed. She finally took a drink of the whiskey. It burned her throat in just the right way. "I broke off an engagement about a year ago. Caught him with someone else."

"I'm so sorry. You don't deserve that."

"Thanks. This was the first time I've tried dating since."

"Ah. That sucks."

"Yeah. I'm mostly recovered from it all. The whole thing was awful, but it was for the best in the end. There were a lot of other things. Things I ignored. I'm not certain we would have lasted for other reasons, basically. The salt in the wound was just that he didn't want me . . . Oh. You're a stranger. I'm sorry, I . . ."

Their lightly tattooed forearm waved it off. "Go ahead. I see you have your sticker on still, so I'm gonna take a wild guess it might have something to do with monogamy and scratching a certain sapphic itch?"

Jasmine chuckled as she nodded. "I would have been fine not doing that for the rest of my life. We both agreed on monogamy. Little did I know he was cheating the *whole* time. And I mean the whole time."

"That's awful. Well, I think it's very brave of you to try again." Their expression was reassuring. That same, odd sort of comfort Jasmine felt when she looked around the black restaurant.

"Thanks." She took another drink. "Tonight really was a disaster. How could I possibly choose between the man who still lives with his mother, showing me their Christmas card pictures, while they wore matching pajamas, by the way, and the woman that tried to use me in some weird sex game with her husband? Or the woman who could not hold a conversation and the man who talked to the man next to him instead of me?"

They bobbed their head a few times. "That does sound rough."

"I'm sorry, you probably have more important things to do. Your boss might get mad if you're—"

"Oh, yeah." They snickered, then spoke sarcastically. "She's a real hard-ass."

"Uh, right." Jasmine tilted her head. "Well, regardless, I'm not sure how many people were interested in actually dating. The ones looking for something besides sex were just complete . . . ugh. The food was honestly the only reason I stayed."

"Yeah?" Their already captivating smile split into a wide grin. Jasmine felt something stir in her chest.

"Yeah, I mean, I don't know how much of the food you get to eat since you work here."

They chuckled. "The chef lets us sample. Wants us to know what everything tastes like. We do give the vegans and vegetarians a script, though. I mean, not that they have to lie, they're allowed to say their diets if they want, but they just get . . . I'm rambling. You were talking about the food?"

They blushed slightly, accentuating their already prominent cheekbones.

Jasmine pursed her lips and narrowed her eyes. The gears in her brain spun rapidly. Then she remembered the baked brie and she closed her eyes, willing the food to magically appear on her tongue again as all other thoughts faded.

"I would devour an entire plate of that brie if I could. I thought 'How good could a simple salad be?' and I could not believe it. Every leaf was—and then the duck! And that soup was heavenly."

"Ah, yes. The bisque is good."

"I honestly didn't think anything would top that steak. It was one of the best things I've ever had. But dessert was on a whole new level. I mean, who could even think of that?"

They smiled their widest yet. "Thank you so much. That took a lot of experimenting, and even then, I only made a few trays. I made enough for the speed dating and the couples that had paid for the private booths and the VIP experience. They all had the same menu, too."

"Wait, are you . . . ? You're the chef?"

They blushed even harder, as bright red as Sam's bow tie. "Uh, yeah. Sorry, at first it was a bit of a joke, you talking about my boss, but then you went on about the food, and it was . . . Thank you for such a great review. I can't take all the credit, though. I mean, they are my recipes, but my sous chef did all the cooking tonight. I pretty much let him run the show. Still, I'm really glad at least part of your evening was good."

"Y-Yeah." Jasmine thought she felt her cheeks burn. "So, you're the boss, you said?"

"Yup. This is my place. I'm Amelia, by the way."

"Jasmine."

"I know. You've still got your name tag on, remember?"

She tittered, tucking her hair behind her ear. "R-Right. Um, speaking of, can I ask your pronouns?"

"Oh! Yeah, of course. She/her. Sorry. Maybe we should put those on our nametags, too?"

"It couldn't hurt. I like that the bathrooms are separated as urinals or toilets, though."

"Thanks. That was a whole thing to get approved during the remodel."

"Good for you for pushing for it. So, if you didn't cook, what did you do all evening?"

"I did cook, just at home, for my girl—I guess ex-girlfriend." Amelia sighed. Her smile faded as she looked at the bar. "I spent all week making her this complicated, gourmet vegan meal. At least that was worth it. One dish is getting added to the menu permanently, maybe two. But she didn't show up."

"I'm so sorry. Did she call at least? What happened?"

"I just got a text that said she was done and that she left a box of my things on the porch. She had grabbed her stuff from my place earlier in the week." Amelia looked down at the bar, leaning one arm against it and running her other hand through her hair.

"That sucks. You don't deserve that either."

"Thanks. Apparently, she started seeing someone else. Friend sent me a screenshot of her Insta, and it shows her on a date. She blocked me now, too, which I get, but I didn't cheat or anything. She just . . . said she was done."

"Ugh. How long were you together?"

"Just a few months. How about you and your ex?"

"It was a little over three years."

"Well, whenever you're ready, I'm sure you'll find someone better. Pretty thing like you? Easy to talk to? You'll be fine."

Jasmine felt her cheeks burn again, wishing she could cover them up. "Thanks."

Amelia blushed too. "I should uh . . . probably do a few things to start cleaning up here."

"Right, of course. Sorry to keep you."

"No worries, Jasmine. I'm always happy to hear how good my food is."

Amelia walked off. Jasmine drank her whiskey while she looked around at all the happy couples. Not all of them as jovial as others, but she saw a few older people, married couples, and even a proposal. She saw a glass of water thrown in someone's face, too, so at least she wasn't the only person having a bad night.

But Amelia didn't have a good night either, Jasmine told herself. She shook her head. The woman just got dumped that evening and Jasmine had already declared another break from dating herself. Plus, all they had really done was talk about their exes and how good of a chef Amelia was. Hardly a real conversation.

It was still better than any other conversation you had tonight, aside from Kwame, she thought.

As more and more people left the restaurant, though, she figured she should do the same. Jasmine tried to decide whether to leave without saying goodbye when Amelia came back to the bar, carrying a small food box. She set it down on the bar in front of Jasmine and then poured a drink.

Instead of disappearing again, the adorable chef walked out from behind the bar and stood in front of her. "May I sit here?" Amelia pointed at the barstool next to Jasmine.

"You may." Jasmine pointed to the box. "What is that?"

"Well," Amelia set the drink next to the box as she sat down. They faced each other. The woman's undone bow tie hung loosely around her neck. Jasmine's breath caught in her throat again. Her heart beat faster. She was glad her glass was on the bar and not in her hand, as she probably would have dropped it. "Before I tell you, I want you to know, this is not to be thought of as regifting."

Jasmine laughed. "All right. Color me intrigued."

"Technically, it is a regift, but I hope you understand the spirit of this, rather than getting hung up on technicalities. I don't think you're the type of person to judge me, but I also don't know you and I . . . just realized I'm rambling again. Sorry."

She giggled now. "It's fine. It's . . . fine." She had almost said *cute*.

"Well, you raved about the dessert. Said you liked it more than the steak. So, I have here with me the last two."

Amelia opened the lid. There they were, a deceptively simple concoction, but Jasmine knew better.

"Ah. I understand. These were for you and your ex."

Amelia nodded.

"Wait, you brought them back with you?"

“They were going to be a peace offering to Cam and her wife, but I’ve been informed that my debt is larger than some measly dessert, apparently.” They both laughed again.

“I would never describe these as ‘measly.’”

Amelia blushed once more. “Thanks. That makes me even more optimistic you will understand these are meant to cheer you up. Still, if you are displeased with the regifting situation, I don’t have to continue sitting here and eating one with you. I’ll leave you and let you have both. I’ll even pay for your drink. Though, I was gonna do that anyway.” Amelia had used a playful and rehearsed tone, similar to giving a presentation. Which, in a way, she had.

Jasmine smiled wider. “You may stay. Though I’m not sure about sharing.”

“That good?” Amelia smirked now.

“You know they are.”

Amelia waggled her eyebrows. “Maybe. But I don’t like to brag.”

“If I cooked like you, I absolutely would.” Jasmine picked up the dessert. She tried to eat it in small bites so that it would last longer. “It’s . . . beyond words.”

Thankfully, Jasmine kept her noises under control.

Amelia bit into hers and closed her eyes. “Okay, yeah. I might have outdone myself with these. Plus, they’re vegan, which most people cannot believe.”

“That is impressive. You know, cooking aside, I don’t think you’ll be single for long either.”

Jasmine hadn’t meant to say it. She thought she could almost see her words crossing the space between them, flying through the air like some awkward paper airplane about to nosedive and poke the woman in the eye. The white of the paper was comically out of place against their darker surroundings, like the hearts had been in the other room.

The woman smiled, her eyes turned soft. “Y-Yeah?” Her cheeks were red again. Now, *that* was a red Jasmine could get used to. “You think so?”

“Yeah.” Jasmine nodded.

“Thank you. That means a lot coming from you. I’m sure you’re sick of people telling you you’re beautiful all the time.”

“I mean, it can get old, sure, but it also depends on who is saying it.”

“Ah.” Amelia was silent for a second. “So, what if, what if . . .” She coughed and shifted in her seat, then spoke again in a quieter voice. “I mean, what if, and forgive me if this is too—I’m . . . I just, you know what, I need to clean.”

Amelia stood up suddenly, but Jasmine reached out to stop her from leaving. She clasped the woman's hand in her own before whispering, "I think you're beautiful, too."

Amelia didn't say anything for a second. Once she looked over, Jasmine was sure she saw a small tear. "Yeah?"

"Yeah."

Amelia heaved a big sigh. "I'm sorry. I-I'm probably not ready either. I don't want you thinking I'm like, on the rebound or something."

"I don't." She found she meant it.

"All right. Um, I don't, I'm . . ."

They were still holding hands, and Jasmine gently stroked the woman's thumb with her own. "Do you actually need to go clean, or did you wanna talk more?"

Amelia nodded. "Uh, I mean, yeah." She turned around, then sat back on the barstool.

"Do you want someone to listen? About the breakup? I mean, might be weird, we don't know each other but . . ."

Amelia stroked Jasmine's hand now. "Thank you, that's sweet of you. It's definitely upsetting. Dumped on Valentine's Day after I did . . ." Amelia sighed and looked down. She pulled her hand away. "I'm sorry. I just thought things were better than they were. There were probably red flags that I ignored. Like you said with your ex."

"Of course. It's easy to overlook stuff. But I like to think it's also, like, no one will be perfect, you know? What can I live with or not live with?"

"Hm. Yeah. That's . . . there were things I knew I couldn't live with."

"I'm sorry you put up with that."

Amelia nodded, still looking down. "I-I do want to keep talking, but I feel like I'm just bringing you down."

"After the night I had? You're the highlight."

Amelia finally looked up at her and the grin was back. "That's . . . thank you. Even if you're just placating me."

"I'm not."

"Still." Amelia took a long sip of her drink. "Um, yeah, so you think the event was okay, even if you didn't meet anyone you like?"

Jasmine thought about it. "It was organized, well thought out, and I think other people had fun. But because it was open to anyone queer, it made it a bit difficult to really match people based on compatibility. Seemed like the pairings were based on sexual preferences only."

"Should I have them back? My friend Glenn asked to have it here, and he works for them. We had a wine pairing night that was geared toward queer singles last month, but it was informal. People could mingle with whoever they wanted to, not speed dating like this."

"That might be better. But honestly, the food was really what made me stay, and I swear I'm not just trying to flatter you."

They both giggled. Amelia grabbed her hand again. "Thanks."

The woman blushed again, looking like the tomatoes from the salad earlier. Jasmine knew she looked the same.

"Can I ask you something?"

"Sure."

"The name? Ovine and Avian?"

Amelia tilted her head back and let out a single laugh. "Well, see, I don't know if you noticed, everything here is black, or, at least, dark."

"I had. What does that have to do with the name?"

"Well, I wanted it to be Black Sheep or Blackbird, but both of those are overdone for restaurant or business names. So, I decided to find a different way to say it."

"Um, say what exactly?"

"Dark can be misunderstood. Take a blackbird—what is your first thought? Something with a crow or death, right?"

"I . . . yes."

"But that's not really what blackbirds are about, any of them, crow or raven or thrush. Crows are intelligent. They get a bad reputation. And that dessert you liked so much? Looks like a chocolate-covered strawberry, right?"

Jasmine nodded. "It was so much more."

"Which is how I feel about the term *black sheep*. It's easy to take the reputation of a thing, the label, and let that be its definition. That's how I feel about my food. So, you get the name, and then you walk in, and you get the true meaning."

"Huh." Then she chuckled. "I really like that."

"Thank you. Wow, it's . . . never mind." Amelia ran her free hand through her hair again, a soft smile on her face.

"No, no. Come on."

"I just, Tiff, my ex, she never understood it. Thought it was weird."

Amelia looked at her then. Jasmine felt her chest constrict. They just stared at each other, and she felt that delicious tension, that spark, she had searched for the entire night. Gone were the frogs; they had finally changed into butterflies. She had been worried that she was no longer capable of feeling that way after Duncan.

Amelia cleared her throat and looked away, though, down at the ground again. "Sorry, I'm probably gonna be a bit of a mess for a while."

"That's okay. I know I was until just recently. It takes time, and it was only, what? An hour ago?"

"I know, you're right." Amelia took another sip.

Jasmine followed suit. "People don't understand the things I love about my job either." She sighed.

"What do you do?"

Jasmine smiled. "I work at a biotech firm."

Amelia nodded. "Uh huh. That doesn't tell me what you *do*, though."

"Oh, right. Well, I head up research and development. It's a lot of extra paperwork, but this way I know things get done right."

"So, you're a scientist?"

"Microbiologist."

"That is so cool." Amelia smiled widely.

Jasmine knew she was blushing once more. "Thank you."

"So, what are you working on, exactly? Medicines or, like, manufacturing? Biotech is a big field."

"I'm surprised you even know any of that. Well, right now, my pet project is figuring out how to get those bacteria that eat plastic to be useful. We aren't even sure if they have actually evolved or if . . . sorry, I'm probably boring you."

"Nah. It's nice to see someone passionate about what they do. I know I am." Amelia shrugged.

"I can tell."

They were still holding hands loosely, propped up on the granite countertop bar. Jasmine felt herself reposition slightly. Her mouth watered as she looked at Amelia's lips, curved into that heartwarming smile.

She couldn't help herself as she leaned forward maybe just an inch. Jasmine thought she saw Amelia do the same. So, she leaned slightly again. Amelia nudged closer, too. They both laughed awkwardly, and Amelia ran her free hand through her hair again, but she didn't break eye contact this time.

They were both leaning forward now, closing the gap between them. Two feet of space between, then one. The paper airplane from before soared, not made of boring white paper this time. Jasmine thought it looked better in black anyway. Maybe that helped it fly.

"Hey, Chef, Stella said you were here, I was hoping you could—oh, uh, sorry."

Jasmine snapped her torso upright. She turned to see who had interrupted them. It was a man in an all-black chef's uniform. He looked between them and tilted his head, a grimace on his face.

"It's fine, Oliver. Give me a sec?"

He nodded and left. Amelia then turned to Jasmine.

"Sorry. I, uh, give me five minutes, okay? I'll be right back."

"Of course." Jasmine watched the woman go, admiring the powerful-looking thighs in black slacks that carried her away.

Five minutes turned into ten. Then thirty. Her drink was long gone. The restaurant was showing signs of closing, but Jasmine did not see Amelia. The waitstaff were cleaning the dining room while the last Valentine's Day patrons finished their meals.

She wanted to wait, but her eyes were drooping. No bartender had come to replace Amelia, so Jasmine couldn't pay for her drink. She got some money out of her black leather Coach clutch and left it on the bar. With a slight ache in her chest, she ordered a ride on her app.

Jasmine donned her coat and stepped out into the frigid air. At least it wasn't raining.

When a car pulled up, she double-checked the license plate matched the app and that the driver looked like his picture. She stepped off the curb and grabbed the door handle.

"Wait!" Jasmine heard someone yell.

She turned then to see Amelia walking quickly toward her, not quite running. Warmth filled her extremities despite the cold, along with a hum of excitement. With a wide smile, she held up a finger as Amelia reached her on the sidewalk.

Jasmine turned and opened the car door. "Hey, sorry, give me a sec, please?"

"No worries." The driver waved it off.

She closed the car door again and faced Amelia. "Hi."

"Hi." Amelia smiled back. "Um, so, you, uh, I'm sorry that took so long. I really didn't mean for it to." She ran her hand through her hair again and shifted on her feet.

"It's fine. I would have waited but the alcohol caught up to me."

"Well, here." Amelia handed Jasmine's money back. "I already told you I was paying for the drink."

"I can still—"

Amelia shook her head. "No. Take it, please."

She put the money back into her clutch. "Thank you. That's sweet of you."

"I'm really glad I met you. I know that I might not—but we had such a—ugh!" Amelia looked at the ground and then groaned. "Why is this so hard?"

Jasmine grabbed both of Amelia's hands, letting her clutch dangle from her wrist. "I'm glad I met you, too. I completely understand that you're not ready for anything. I'm probably not either. I won't pressure you."

"Yeah. But I didn't want to . . . I didn't want you to leave without giving you my number." She let go of one of Jasmine's hands to fish around in her pocket. She pulled out a black cocktail napkin. "Maybe you can text me yours, and I could call you in a few weeks or something?" Her pained, vulnerable expression was so endearing as she held up her offering.

Jasmine took it from her. "You can call me before that, if you want. We can get to know each other. No worries either way, though, and I mean that."

"Right, yeah. I was . . . um, I think we had a moment back there."

Jasmine swallowed. Her mouth had filled with saliva again. "Uh huh."

"I wanted . . . is it . . . ugh!" Amelia tried to pull her hand away, but Jasmine held fast.

"I want to kiss you, too." Jasmine grabbed Amelia's free hand again, the napkin squished between their palms.

Amelia looked at her and took a deep breath. "Yeah?"

"Yeah."

A smile finally replaced the frown and then they both leaned in again. The kiss was brief but tender. Jasmine breathed heavily when they parted. She was dizzy and her lips tingled. Like the small portions earlier, every one of Jasmine's senses screamed for more.

"That was . . ." Amelia started.

"Wow," Jasmine whispered.

"Y-Yeah."

They stared at each other, smiling awkwardly and giggling.

"Listen, I'll text you, all right? I don't want to leave the driver waiting much longer."

Amelia just nodded. Jasmine leaned in and gave her another kiss on the cheek before getting in the car. Amelia stood there, clutching her red-tinged cheek with a dazed look, and waved as the car drove off. Jasmine waved back.

Immediately, she pulled out her phone and texted the number scrawled on the napkin in silver Sharpie.

I really did have fun tonight.

She watched the city through the window as they drove. "Good Valentine's then? That your girlfriend?" the driver asked.

"Hm? Oh. Yes, it was good. She's not my girlfriend, though."

"Coulda fooled me."

"I just met her tonight."

"That explains why I'm driving you home alone then."

"Yeah."

Jasmine's phone buzzed, and she looked at the screen. *Sure it wasn't just the dessert?*

Your lips were better than any dessert. Even if they were taking it slow, she could still flirt.

I liked it too. The response made Jasmine giddy. *Coffee sometime soon? Get to know each other?*

Sounds perfect but I'm buying. Jasmine just hoped her favorite coffee shop would put up St. Patrick's decorations soon.

Deal.

Jasmine spent the rest of the car ride home with a smile on her face, remembering the way Amelia's black outfit hugged her athletic frame and her smile, which lit up the dark restaurant. The hints of chocolate and whiskey on Amelia's breath were subtle reminders that true delight was often found in the unlikeliest of places.

About the Author

MK Edgley always has something to say. She took her love of storytelling and channeled it into a passion for writing sapphic romance. MK's works center on women loving women and other queer identities. From modern-day witch tales to simple meet-cutes, her stories showcase the magic of love and the things that unite us as humans. Originally from the suburbs of Portland, Oregon, MK now resides in Seattle, Washington, with her wife, cat, and dog.

You can find MK on:

Instagram: @mkedgleyauthor

You can visit her website at:

www.mkedgley.com

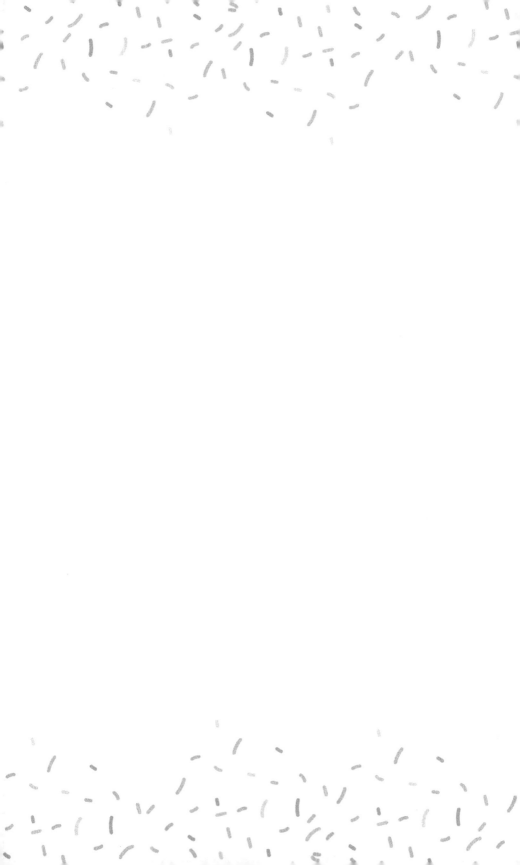

TRUFFLE AND TRUTH

Truffle and Truth

Elise Gilmore

Olivia

"WELCOME TO DON'T TRUFFLE WITH Me!" I called out when the bells on the door jingled a few minutes before closing. I continued transferring the few remaining truffles from the front case onto a tray.

"What can I get for you?" I asked from my crouched position behind the counter. When the customer didn't say anything, I peered through the glass case. All I caught was a glimpse of leather work boots and dark wash jeans, which narrowed it down to . . . any man in town. "Did you have a question about any of the flavors?"

I stood up, and my heart fluttered, but I pushed the feeling away and rolled my eyes. It wasn't a customer at all. It was Heath Bonnie, the owner of Bonnie's Blooms, the shop next-door to mine. A man who had perfectly wavy auburn hair and a matching beard. A man who made flannel look just as sexy as a well-cut suit. A man who just happened to be my best friend.

"Hey, Olivia." He moved his finger in a circle before dropping it down on the top of the glass case. "Could you tell me about this one?" he asked without even looking.

I shot a playful glare into his hazel eyes as his lips slid into a sideways smirk. "Very funny, Heath. You probably know the flavors better than I do at this point." His weakness for sweets had made him my taste-tester back in high school when I had first started working with chocolate. It was a title he still held today. "Are you ready?" I cocked my eyebrow at him.

"I am *always* ready for Truffle and Truth." He matched my challenging expression with an eyebrow waggle of his own.

As usual, I didn't last long into the stare down before breaking and heading back to the kitchen. "Let me grab the rest of the chocolates that are left over," I called over my shoulder.

Truffle and Truth was a game Heath had come up with the first Valentine's Day our shops had both been open. Neither of us had dates that year, so we settled in together at my shop with a pile of leftover truffles. There was only one rule to the game: when you ate a truffle, the other person got to ask you a personal question. Over the years I had learned that Heath was a closet heavy-metal music fan, had had his appendix removed in middle school, and that he was afraid of geese. That last one had led to me purchasing a yard goose and secretly placing it outside his shop. The look of sheer terror he had as he exited his truck that first day is one I will never forget nor let him live down. Thankfully, Adam the Goose eventually won him over and is currently standing outside his shop dressed like Cupid.

This game Heath created became a yearly tradition since Valentine's Day is exhausting for us, two small business owners providing the two things this holiday relies on: chocolate and flowers. I sighed. All day, I had found myself wishing I had someone who would buy *me* chocolate or flowers. But I was pretty sure the person I had in mind wasn't interested.

When I came back out front, Heath, in all his flannel-clad glory, was still leaning against the counter. He smiled when our eyes met. I looked down as I came around the counter with the chocolate-laden tray, hoping he hadn't seen the heat I felt overtaking my cheeks. I plopped into my usual chair at the lone table in my tiny shop and waited until Heath sat down in his. Then, I held out my hand.

"Rock, paper, scissors, shoot," we said in unison.

Heath

I GRINNED AS I COVERED Olivia's rock with my paper. She snatched her hand back quickly, and I found that mine was left tingling where it had been touching hers. These feelings had slowly started creeping up . . . again.

When I first met Olivia in algebra class back when we were high school freshmen, I had definitely had a crush on her. I couldn't think whenever she laughed, her brown eyes sparkling, and on more than one occasion, I had found myself visually tracing each wild brown curl that had escaped her regular top knot instead of listening to the math lesson. But she had been dating Tanner at the time. Then, when they broke up, I was dating Leah. By the time we were both single, I had been in the friendzone for so long, it felt comfortable there. Besides, I had always been pretty sure Olivia wasn't interested in me.

That was, until a few months ago. I had mentioned that I might ask Christie, the blonde who lived in the townhouse two down from me, out on a date. Olivia had pasted on as big a smile as she could, but I could tell from her eyes that her heart wasn't in it. Since then, I'd been paying closer attention to the smaller things, hoping my assumptions all these years were wrong. Like how she'd blushed a second ago when I smiled at her. She tried to hide it, but that wasn't the first time I'd noticed her responding to me that way.

"Earth to Heath." Olivia waved a truffle in front of my face. Right. I'd won, so I got to ask the first question. She popped the chocolate in her mouth.

"Cinnuhmuhn," she mumbled.

I smiled at her as I contemplated what question to start with. Should I start with the one I wanted to ask, or something a little less dangerous?

"Which of your flavors do you like the best?" I asked, like a coward.

"Hmm . . . that's like picking a favorite kid." She thought for a moment. "Cookies and cream. It's the first one that won a ribbon at the state fair and the one that made me go to culinary school."

I nodded in agreement. It was my favorite, too. I closed my eyes and reached out my hand over the tray. I moved it down and picked up the first chocolate I touched. I took a bite without looking.

"Red Velvet." I opened my eyes and showed her the deep red inside.

"Did you ever go on that date with Christie?" she blurted out. Her cheeks flushed, and her eyes grew wide like she was surprised she had said the question out loud.

After taking a breath, I looked into her eyes and held her gaze. "Nope." I watched as something like relief flashed across her face. She seemed to recover and put on a more neutral expression. She opened her mouth to speak.

"No follow-up questions until my next truffle," I reminded her.

She rolled her eyes and gave me her best pouty face. I chuckled, sure she didn't realize just how irresistible she looked. It took all my self-control not to walk around the table and kiss her bottom lip right then and there. Instead, I pointed toward the tray of chocolates. She sighed but plucked a truffle off the pile.

"Peanut butter cup," she said with a wrinkled nose. I shook my head. Peanut butter was not her favorite flavor; however, it was very popular among her customers. She laid the other half of the truffle to the side of the tray. She walked over to the counter and came back with two water bottles. She handed me one and opened the other before taking a big swig.

I looked down for a moment, readying myself to walk through the door the last question opened. When I looked back up, I caught her brown eyes once more and didn't break my stare. After this question, there was no going back.

"Do you wish we were more than friends?"

Olivia's flushed cheeks deepened to a bright red and her mouth dropped open. Her eyes flitted nervously around the room landing on anything *but* me.

"Of course not . . ." Her voice came out high-pitched.

I stifled a laugh. Olivia had always been a terrible liar. Those words squeaked out a few decibels higher than usual, that's her tell. I'm not sure exactly why she isn't telling me the truth, but hopefully my answer to her next question will clear things up.

She took a sip of water and managed to continue in a more normal tone. "I wouldn't have been able to stay your friend for all these years if I were pining for something more."

I shook my head at the irony of her words. Being friends with someone you like is definitely *not* easy to do.

When Olivia's gaze finally landed on me, I offered her a soft smile, hoping it would settle her nerves. Then I reached out and took another chocolate.

"Cookies and cream!" I shoved the rest of the truffle into my mouth.

"I got peanut butter, and you got my favorite." Olivia pointed her finger at me. "Lucky you."

A slow smile spread over my face as I swallowed and waited for her question.

Olivia

I TRIED TO BREATHE AS Heath stared at me. It had felt like all the oxygen had been sucked out of the room when he asked that question, and I was still trying to catch my breath. For a moment, I had wondered if I'd even heard him correctly. I had never considered the fact that Heath might be interested in me, too.

Then, I'd lied. Because what if the only reason he hadn't gone out with Christie was because he'd met someone else and it had nothing to do with me. If only I could have asked my follow-up question first; but that's not how the game worked. I kept my eyes away from him and stared at the chocolates instead as I shifted uncomfortably in my seat, regret churning in my stomach.

I had never felt nervous when we played this game before. But now, my heart was pounding, and I was having trouble focusing. Were these kinds of questions, the ones we had always avoided, going to lead to one of us walking away with hurt feelings? Had it happened already? I forced myself to look at Heath's face, trying to gauge from his expression if I'd just crushed him. That's the last thing I would want to do. But all I saw there was a patient smile and eyes glimmering with something . . . amusement maybe. I guess there was only one way to find out.

"Why didn't you go out with Christie?" I tried to ask the question without giving away anything, but it came out in a breathy whisper.

Instead of answering immediately, Heath pulled his chair around to my side of the table. I turned to face him and our eyes locked. As he sat down, his knee bumped mine. I expected him to pull his leg away once he was settled, but he didn't. Neither did I. He let out a breath of air and leaned toward me. He moved his hand over mine, then hesitated before finally taking my hand in his. If I had felt like my thoughts were jumbled before, they were long gone now. Adios. Au Revoir. Now all I could think about were the flecks of green and gold sparkling in Heath's eyes and the warmth that was spreading all over my body from where our knees and hands were touching.

"Is this okay?" he asked.

I nodded, not trusting that words would come out if I opened my mouth.

He squeezed my hand in reply. "I didn't go out with Christie . . ."

I took a few deep breaths as I waited for him to continue. Everything he had done in the last few moments led me to think that we were on the same page. Heath, my best friend, would never be this close to me or hold my hand. I mean, we had always been affectionate—a hug when we said goodbye, a shoulder bump when we were teasing each other, high-fives and fist bumps galore—but this was the first time he'd crossed that invisible line separating friendly contact from something more intimate. My eyes dipped to his lips as I wondered if his next words would be the ones I'd been wishing for. I lifted my gaze back to his hazel eyes and found they were lit up with excitement.

"I didn't go out with Christie . . . because I would rather go out with you."

Heath

I SAID IT. OLIVIA SEEMED as frozen as her truffles were when they first came out of the blast chiller. I wasn't surprised. We were now in a place this game had never been. I rubbed the back of Olivia's hand in a slow circle with my thumb, reminding her that I was still here. She looked down at our clasped hands and back up at me. She opened her mouth, but nothing came out. Her eyes flicked back and forth over my face like her brain was trying to put together the pieces of a jigsaw puzzle.

"Take your time," I said softly. "I'm not going anywhere."

I squeezed her hand and smiled at her. The twinkle lights strung across the awnings of our shops blinked on and illuminated Olivia's hair. Curls poked out from her bun in all directions. I reached out to tuck one that had escaped back behind her ear. Her eyes stilled as my hand brushed her cheek. She tilted her head toward my hand and rested it there for a moment. Her eyes relaxed, and a small smile graced her lips. She reached over the table without breaking eye contact and grabbed a truffle.

"Maybe you should ask that last question again," she said shyly before taking a small bite. She showed me the truffle's light green inside. Chocolate mint.

"So, Olivia Reese, do you wish we were more than friends?" I asked.

Her eyes remained glued to mine. "Yes." She smiled as her cheeks turned a lovely shade of pink.

I scooted my chair closer to her, shifting our legs slightly so that her knees were tucked between mine.

"When you mentioned going on a date with Christie, I realized that my feelings for you had grown beyond friendship."

"It's been going on a bit longer for me." I raked my free hand through my hair. Her eyes followed the movement and slowly dragged back down to my face. "I've actually had a crush on you since the first day we sat beside each other in algebra."

Her mouth dropped open. "What? Why didn't you tell me?"

"The timing just never felt right. But when I mentioned going on a date recently, your response gave me hope. You tried to act happy, but you weren't."

"Ugh, I wanted to be happy for you!" She stood up suddenly and walked over to the counter. "But I actually felt . . . jealous."

I followed her and spun her around to face me. Her eyes went wide and a gasp escaped her lips. "I only have eyes for you, Livey."

Olivia

A TINGLE RAN UP MY spine when Heath used the nickname he gave me in high school. When we graduated, I had asked him to stop using it. Now I didn't want him to ever call me anything else.

"Heath . . ." I leaned forward, my head resting comfortably on his chest. He pulled me close and gently ran his hands up and down my spine, causing a fury of tingles to course through me. I pulled back and moved one of my hands up to his beard. It was softer than I thought it would be.

"Is it weird that I've been wondering what this felt like?" I half whispered.

"My beard?" One of his eyebrows rose when I nodded. "For you, I'll allow it."

He winked, and I felt like I would dissolve into a pool of melted chocolate right at his feet. I ran my hand up along his jawline around to the back of his neck. His eyes darkened as my fingers played in the loose waves there. He stepped in closer, pushing me back against the counter. Then, I allowed my eyes to freely roam over his face, something I hadn't been able to do until now. I was delighted by the longing I found in his eyes. I knew it matched my own. I dropped my eyes to his lips and then pulled them back up to his eyes.

After that, it felt like everything was happening in slow-motion. His hands were cupping my face. I was tugging on his neck, pulling him closer. He tilted my face up with one hand. He moved the other up into my hair. Our faces inched closer and closer until my eyelids fluttered closed at the last moment. Then Heath's lips brushed gently against mine, tender and searching. As we lost ourselves in the moment, our kisses became deeper. Heath groaned and then kissed me softly one more time before pulling back. I was breathless. Everything I had imagined paled in comparison to actually kissing Heath.

I watched as he walked to the table, investigated the truffles, and picked up one. He came back over and held it out to me.

"I need to ask you one more question." He grinned at me, hazel eyes sparkling.

I rolled my eyes at him before taking a bite. I looked up expectantly.

"Livey, will you go on a date with me tomorrow?"

I broke out in a big smile. "I would love to." I held the rest of the truffle out to him. "I have something I want to ask you."

His eyes locked on mine as he popped it in his mouth.

"When are you going to kiss me again?"

Spoiler alert. He didn't answer. Instead, he let his lips do the talking.

About the Author

Elise Gilmore writes flash fiction and short stories in the sweet romance genre. She has had her work published by Micromance Magazine and Spark Flash Fiction, as well as in a sweet romance anthology, *Summer Sweethearts.* She currently lives in South Carolina with her husband and two boys. When she isn't writing or reading, you might find her drinking tea or kombucha, obsessing about Pride and Prejudice, or singing and dancing around her house.

You can find Elise on:

Instagram: @lifebwthepages

You can visit her website at:

https://campsite.bio/lifebwthepages

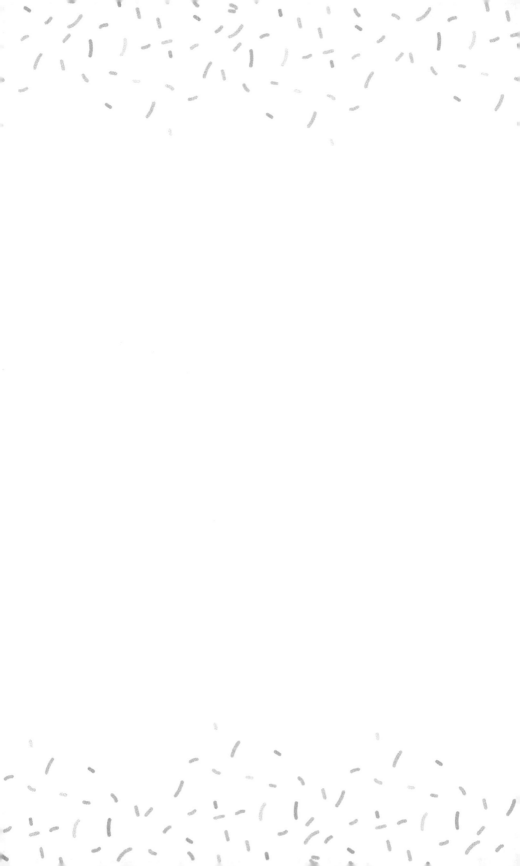

COMFORT FOOD AND COVERT MAGIC

Comfort Food and Covert Magic

S.B. Rizk

"WITCHES BRITCHES, PENNY, MOVE OVER! I can't feel my leg," said Aurora.

"Sorry, I wasn't looking where I *sat*." Penny giggled and floated three inches to the right.

When Aurora's leg was free from her ghostly friend, the blood flow returned at full force, a sensation like sharp, icy needles shooting through every nerve ending.

She shivered and rubbed her leg. "Ugh, I hate it when that happens."

Penny drifted even farther to the end of Aurora's floating four-poster bed—enough for the shimmering drapes wrapped around the frame to cut straight through the back of her head. Aurora vigorously ruffled her short, black hair, resembling a mix between a bob and a pixie cut, before concentrating on the center of the bed. Her emerald eyes glowed to a bright yellow and then an unevenly rounded cherrywood tray with a black, three-wick candle appeared.

She lightly blew on the candle, and one by one flames sprung from the wicks and combined into one rather large flame. In the small, dancing fire was the scene of a television show from the mortal realm. Penny squealed and moved her hands in a clapping motion.

Still recovering from the trauma to her leg, Aurora didn't notice the silence in her dorm.

"You know, it would be nice if we could actually hear what they were saying." Penny crossed her arms.

"Oh, right." Aurora's eyes glowed again.

This time a smooth, black stone with a mouth carved on the top appeared next to the candle. Before she activated it, she performed a quick barrier spell on her room so they wouldn't be caught watching forbidden channels.

"I meant to ask, how did your mom take the news that your murmur-rock can't be used for communication anymore?" Penny twirled her finger by the end of her ponytail. The hair didn't wrap around it, but the movement always seemed to comfort her.

"I told her a spell backfired, so she's sending me a new one—oh, I love this show!"

The flames now portrayed a woman taking pictures of herself by monuments in a place called Paris.

After hours snapping through different shows, they landed on one with women wearing ball gowns in every color Aurora could imagine, except black, in a large room, twirling with men to the most upbeat music they had ever heard.

"Can you imagine being somewhere so bright with so many colors?" Aurora rested her head in her hand.

"Never mind the colors—would you take a look at those men!"

"They don't look that different from the warlocks here, aside from their hair and the funny clothes."

Penny's jaw dropped and she brought her hand up to her chest. "It's not about their physical appearance; it's their attitude. Come on, don't tell me you can't see it!"

"I suppose warlocks tend to be a bit cocky, and I can't imagine seeing one pull out a chair for me without using their magic."

"Precisely!"

Aurora sighed. "I can't wait for graduation. The equinox is so close, and then I'm out of here."

"Why not travel now?"

Aurora quirked an eyebrow and pulled open the shimmering drapes. On her ceiling, which was a physical representation of the sky outside, the black sky and constellations were gone, replaced by a purple glow coming from the rising sun. "Um, how about because we stayed up all night and class is about to start?"

Penny swatted her hand. "I don't mean right this second. I just mean why wait until graduation?"

"My broom only flies so fast, not to mention I've had my license for what, a few weeks now? By the time I got anywhere worth going, I'd have to turn around and fly right back for class."

Penny glided over to the window. The vine curtains, sensing the movement, parted for her. She held her palm out. "Not necessarily."

"You've got to be hexing me," Aurora gasped.

"Your broom can make it to the top of the Witches Tower in no time." Penny smiled.

Aurora shook head. "There's no frogging way."

"Don't be such a wobbly wraith!"

"If you think it's such a great idea, why don't you float up there and go yourself?"

"I won't be able to fit in. They'll see right through me. Literally!" Penny waved her hands up and down her *body*.

"Yeah, but you're already dead, so it's not like they can burn you at the stake when they find out you aren't human."

"Just don't use any magic and they won't know you're a witch," said Penny. She put her hands together as if she were praying. "Please, go for the both of us."

Aurora chewed on the inside of her cheek while she looked out the window before saying, "I'll think about it."

"I can't go. I have nothing to wear," Aurora whined from inside her wardrobe.

"What's wrong with what you have on?"

Aurora stepped back and frowned. "Really?"

She had on black leggings and a purple shirt that said *Cauldron & Quill College* in a fancy script that had a quill attached to the last letter inside of a cauldron.

"Hmm. Good point. Your shirt might as well say *witch university* on it."

Aurora grumbled something under her breath about Penny being no help, and with the snap of her fingers, her purple shirt was replaced with a plain black one.

"Much better."

"I'm so happy you decided to go." Penny lay on her back, floating above Aurora's head.

"I didn't exactly have a choice with you haunting me about it all day."

Penny giggled.

"But if I get found out by the High Priestess and put on magical probation, I will have someone bind you to me. There's no way in hell that I'm getting stuck with Rufus on my own." Aurora fake gagged.

"That's fine. It's not like I can smell him anyways. Besides, what's that filthy, old busy bodygoing to do, tell on you again? Or annoy you to death with all of his snide comments? At that point you would have already been caught and in trouble anyways."

Aurora scowled, grabbed her broom, and said, "Well, this is as good as it's getting."

She straddled her broom and zoomed out of the window before she could change her mind.

"Be careful!" Penny screamed from inside her dorm.

The wind whipped at Aurora's short hair, and she closed her eyes, savoring the moment. In just the matter of a few breaths, she reached the Witches Tower.

The towering structure made of gnarled, rune-covered wood was where all of the covens converged. Aurora had never been inside; only fully certified witches were allowed entrance after graduation. But, no matter, the thing she needed was located at the top of the building—a giant, black cauldron, constantly self-stirred by a magicked wooden spoon, that overflowed with a light-blue smoke and was said to be older than the realm of Whimsica itself.

She hovered by the base of it, inhaling deeply. The roiling in her stomach felt like she'd swallowed a bucket of maggots that were now gnawing away at her insides. The doors to the tower swung open.

Not now!

Aurora angled her broom and shot up in a blur, spiraling around the tower until she reached the top. She landed on the rim of the cauldron, struggling to find her balance. The witches who exited the tower were reduced to specks on the ground below her. Aurora turned to face the bubbling, blue goo inside the cauldron as she teetered on the rim. One strong wind would push her right over. Aurora wasn't sure which way she would rather fall.

For a few moments, she contemplated just hanging out up there and telling Penny she went through with it, but she hated the thought of lying to her best friend. That and it would be extremely difficult to come up with a story that would take up the appropriate amount of time considering the time difference between the realms.

"Stop being such a wobbly wraith, Aurora," she said to herself in a mocking voice. "I hope this doesn't hurt."

Aurora held her breath and stepped forward, free-falling into the cauldron.

Her skin didn't burn like she'd expected. The blue liquid was freezing, though. She kept her eyes closed as she twisted and turned until finally her feet landed on solid ground and the freezing liquid was only up to her knees.

Water sprayed at Aurora's face, and she opened her eyes. She was standing inside of a large stone fountain surrounded by grass. People passed by on the smooth walkways that cut through the grass in all directions. The fountain was lined with red, orange, and white flowers while purple, green, and yellow were arranged along the walkways. Above Aurora were trees bursting with brilliant, pink flowers. Life radiated off of the plants, giving her magic an intoxicating boost and, if she concentrated, she could feel them calling out to her.

Mesmerized by the garden, Aurora took too long to notice that people were starting to stare.

Crap, I should probably get out of here.

When she stepped out of the fountain, the onlookers continued on their way, only one or two occasionally glancing back over their shoulder at her. Once she felt satisfied they were no longer looking, she blew a gust of wind at her lower half, instantly drying her pants.

Excess magic from the spell bounced off her and sent the pink flowers on the ground around her up, swirling through the air. But Aurora hadn't been paying close enough attention. A tall man wearing gray sweatpants and a white T-shirt with a black drawstring backpack over one shoulder jogging by had been watching. He was so transfixed by the odd scene with the flowers that he ran right into the ledge of the fountain, flipping over into the water.

"No. No. No. No. No," Aurora chanted to herself as she ran back over to the fountain. Traveling to the mortal realm was bad enough, but if she accidentally sent a mortal back to Whimsica, then magical probation would be the least of her problems.

As she approached the fountain, the man sat up, wiped the water from his eyes, and spat out a steady stream. Aurora let her head fall back and said a silent thanks to the great witch. When she lifted her head to look at him, she found golden eyes watching her, and when she raised her eyes a little more, she giggled at the sight of a tiny, green frog resting in his curly, brown hair.

"Usually I try for a smoother entrance the first time I meet a beautiful woman. I guess this was more of a splash, but hey, at least I made you laugh," he said, making no move to stand up.

Her cheeks heated. "No, it's not that."

Aurora walked over to him, bending slightly, and gently scooped up the frog, holding it out for him to see.

He laughed and rubbed at the back of his neck. "Well, this just keeps getting better and better."

She released the frog next to a nearby bed of flowers and turned around to see him climbing out of the fountain. His white shirt was see-through and the gray sweatpants clung to him, leaving little to the imagination. He stood easily a foot taller than her.

"I'm James," he said, holding his hand out to her.

"Aurora," she said. Excitement bubbled in her stomach as she took in the sight of him.

Momentarily forgetting where she was, she puckered her lips to blow a gust of wind to dry him but caught herself.

"Are you from—sorry, were you about to say something?" he asked.

Think. Think. Think.

"Would you like to take a walk with me?"

That was close. Do mortals know enough about witches to recognize a drying spell?

"I'd love to, on one condition."

Aurora arched an eyebrow.

"Let me buy you a drink."

She smiled. "Okay."

"Just give me a few minutes to get out of these wet clothes," he said, looking down at himself. "Now where did I drop my backpack?" James looked around the fountain with Aurora not far behind.

"Found it!" she said, pointing at a statue on the side of the fountain of a woman holding hands with her small child.

His backpack hung from the free arm of the child.

"Thanks for holding this," he said to the statue while he grabbed it.

After changing into his dry clothes, James led her to a nearby lemonade stand, his sneakers making a wet, squishy noise with each step, ordered two large cups, and handed her one. He laughed when Aurora sniffed hers.

"What, you've never had pink lemonade?"

"Don't be silly! Of course I have." She took a tiny sip and pulled the cup back to look at it before bringing it back to her lips and sucking down nearly half of it.

"It's good, right? Jenny has the best lemonade in town," he said between sips of his own.

They walked six laps around the park, laughing as they talked about shows they liked, hobbies, and their pets. Each food stand they passed smelled more delicious than the last. Aurora's mouth practically watered, and by the second lap, James had noticed and convinced her to indulge in a hot dog with ketchup and mustard. Midway through the fourth lap, they stopped at a bench to share a plate-sized piece of fried dough covered in a mountain of powdered sugar. It was a lot easier than Aurora had expected to keep her secret. She did have to be pretty vague about some things and to pretend like she knew what he was talking about with others, but surprisingly, witches and mortals actually had a lot in common.

The black band on James's wrist glowed red and started beeping.

"Damn it," he said, clicking a button on the side to stop it. "I have to get going."

"Oh, okay."

"I can't believe we just walked around the park talking for, like, what, three hours?"

"I guess." Aurora shrugged. "Well, it was nice meeting you, James."

She turned to leave, but he put a hand on her arm.

"Will you go out with me this Friday?"

Aurora opened her mouth to answer, but he put his hand up to stop her and rambled on. "I know it'll be Valentine's Day and we just met, but I swear I'm not trying to be weird. I really enjoyed hanging out with you and that's the only night I have off this weekend. There's no strings attached, I would just like to get to know you better. And I—"

She put a finger to his lips, stopping him. "I would love to go out with you."

"Yeah?" He smiled.

"Yes."

"Okay then, I'll see you Friday. Meet back here?" he said as he backed up, stepping on a rogue tennis ball that made him nearly topple over.

Aurora covered her mouth to hide her giggle and nodded. She waited until James was well out of view to walk back to the fountain.

"Now how do I get this thing to send me back home?" She reached down to run her fingers through the water, and the minute her hand broke the surface, she was sucked into the fountain, tumbling through freezing liquid again.

Aurora sucked in large gulps of air when she resurfaced in the large cauldron of bubbling, blue goo. The goo clung to her on this side of the portal. She swiped at the strands of hair sticking to her eyelids and very slowly clawed her way to the side of the cauldron. It took Aurora a lot longer than she would like to admit for her to realize there were steps carved into the giant wooden spoon that slowly spun in wide circles around the inside of the cauldron.

Exhausted from the energy the added weight of the goo cost her, Aurora sluggishly climbed the steps on the rim of the cauldron and whistled for her broom. Leaning over slightly to check if the coast was clear before her broom arrived, she lost her footing and slipped, falling twenty feet down the side of the cauldron. Her broom swooped in and caught her just before she crashed into the wooden tower below.

As she zoomed off into the sky, Aurora looked back, checking for any possible witnesses. Dissolving into hysterics, she managed to get out, "That was cutting it close."

Penny had been hovering back and forth across Aurora's room, but she suddenly halted when Aurora landed with a small thud.

"Aurora Hazel Arcana, tell me you did not bat out—" Her jaw dropped when she turned to face Aurora and found her to be aggressively ripping her soggy clothes off, her magic having refused to clean the goo for her.

Penny cackled, spinning in the air around the room before coming to an abrupt stop in front of Aurora. The corners of her mouth lowered, and in a soft voice she asked, "What happened? You were gone for, like, five minutes."

Aurora took a deep breath and ardently spilled the tea about James. In her excitement, she spoke faster and faster until her words became a tangled mess, but Penny hovered silently, seeming to have clung to every word.

"AH CHOO." Aurora wiped her nose and threw the used tissue at the overflowing barrel across the room from where she lay in her bed.

"I thought that thing was supposed to be bottomless," Penny said as she glided through the wall into Aurora's dorm.

"Tell me about it. I feel awful."

"Oh my goblins, isn't your date tomorrow?"

"It's supposed to be, but there's no way I'm going to be able to go now."

Penny tilted her head. "But how are you going to contact James to cancel?"

Aurora shot upright in bed and smacked her hand to her forehead. "I hadn't even thought of that. He'll think I stood him up if I don't go."

They sat in silence until seemingly out of nowhere Penny squealed, causing Aurora to jump, and then Penny disappeared from the room.

Aurora sat up and pulled open the shimmering drapes around her bed. Her door groaned, and she turned to see Penny entering the room.

"Since when do you use the—" she started to say.

Penny was carrying an armful of glass bottles of colorful liquids. "It's been a long time since I was corporeal, and I wasn't sure which medicine you needed, so I got everything. I forgot how long it takes to get anywhere when you have to use the doors!"

Aurora smiled. "Thank you, but I still don't think I'll be able to go tomorrow. I don't have anything to wear, and I haven't had any time to prepare."

"Since when are you such a quitter? Here's what we are going to do. You are going to take as much medicine as you need until we find one that gets your illness under control, and in the meantime, we will watch all the Valentine's Day films we can find to see what it's all about. And enough with you complaining about having nothing to wear. You are a ghoul-damn witch. Conjure yourself something!"

"Yes, ma'am," Aurora said with a blank face and a sniffle, and they got to work.

Valentine's Day

Aurora waited by the fountain where she'd first met James, tugging at the black lace sleeve attached to the knee-length, maroon dress clinging to her body.

Did I mess up the time conversions?

She watched couples stroll through the park close together with their fingers intertwined—some laughed, others kissed, and almost one half of every couple held a bouquet of flowers.

How did I miss that?

She rubbed at her throat, willing the tickle to go away. When it didn't, she conjured a vial of thick, brown liquid—the only thing they'd found that seemed to get her symptoms under control—and quickly swallowed the contents. The vial disappeared with the last drop. Aurora hoped it would get her through the entire date, but the effects seemed to wear off quicker each time she took it, and she had to wait at least eight hours for the next dose.

Her eyes swept over the area until they landed on the nearest flower bed. Aurora bent low to pick red chrysanthemums, yellow gerberas, and black dahlias and conjured a black silk ribbon to wrap them in.

"There you are," said a husky voice behind her.

Aurora stood and turned around, holding the flowers out to a very confused-looking James, who was holding a bouquet of red roses and white alstroemeria.

He chuckled as they exchanged flowers. "Thank you. I can honestly say this is a first for me."

"That makes two of us," Aurora said as she sniffed her flowers.

"Are you kidding me? No one has ever given you a bouquet of flowers?"

She shook her head.

"Is it because you don't like them?"

"No, of course not. I love flowers. Actually I love all plants. Most wi—" She coughed. "Women do."

"I'll be sure to keep that in mind." He winked at her. "Shall we be on our way?"

"Yes. After you." She admired the way his butt looked in his form-fitting black pants as he walked ahead of her.

They chatted about their week as they walked to the restaurant. Aurora made sure to carry her flowers in the hand furthest away from James. As both of their free hands hung between them, she couldn't help but wonder why he didn't try to hold hers.

Maybe I'm supposed to make the first move?

She swung her hand farther out so it brushed against his. James didn't acknowledge it or move away. Feeling brave, she took his hand and interlaced their fingers. Aurora was happy when he didn't pull away, and when he lifted her hand to his lips to place a gentle kiss on the back of it, lightning bugs danced in her stomach.

James held the glass door open for her when they approached a brick building. "After you, madam."

Aurora stepped into the restaurant and gaped at the scene before her. Glass jars with flickering candles lined the brick walls, and golden chandeliers with candles that didn't look quite right hung from the ceiling—the flames were made of plastic? She was most surprised to find not a single spiderweb in sight!

An older blonde woman wearing a white shirt and black skirt escorted them through the crowded dining room to a small, round table by one of the giant, arched windows. James pulled the oak chair out for Aurora to take her seat.

"Thank you."

She kept her hands in her lap, afraid of dirtying the pristine, white tablecloth if she touched anything.

Why in the cauldron would they use white at mealtimes?

"What are you in the mood for?" James asked behind his menu.

Without even a glance at hers she said, "I'm not picky. I'll probably just get whatever you're having."

He put down his menu and rubbed his hands together. "You're in for a real treat."

While James ordered what sounded like half of the menu, Aurora idly fingered the miniature display of roses and baby's breath wrapped around a single, white taper candle in the center of the table in an attempt to distract herself from the annoying tickle in her throat that was starting to resurface.

"So, what do you do for work?"

"I'm actually still in school." Aurora grabbed a hot bun from the basket the waitress had just placed on the table but quickly dropped it on her plate to shake the sting out of her hand.

"That's awesome! What for?"

"You know, a little of this, a little of that. Basically anything I thought my parents wouldn't approve of," she said with a laugh.

James's face split in a smile.

"How about you?"

"I was just recently hired at the Oakridge Police Department and am hoping to work my way up to detective one day."

Aurora choked on her bread.

"Are you okay?" James touched her arm.

"I swallowed wrong." She took a sip of her water.

He's going to find out.

The knot in her stomach at the thought of him sniffing her out like Rufus or the detectives in the shows she and Penny watched last month only grew when the waitress brought their plates to the table. Clearing her throat to hide her gasp, Aurora picked up her napkin to wipe her mouth and excused herself. Her nose started to feel stuffy, making it hard for her to breathe as she rushed to the restroom.

As she caught her breath, she checked for any feet under the stall doors. When she was sure the restroom was empty, she muttered a barrier spell over the door and pulled a small, black stone out of her bra.

"Thank you, Mom."

Luckily for Aurora, her mother had sent her not one, but two murmur-rocks.

"Penny, are you there?"

"Duh, where else would I be? How is it going?"

"Awful. I need to cough and my nose is starting to run. It's becoming impossible to keep it all in. I just found out James is a detective—I mean, he will be eventually." Aurora wiped at her nose.

"Detectives are hot."

"Which is precisely what I'll be when I burn at the stake after he discovers I'm a witch!"

"You need to calm down and get your magic together. All you have to do is make it through the date and then you never have to see him again."

"That's not all. I wasn't sure what to order, so I said I would have whatever is he having. The first plates just arrived and it's awful. Its leaves covered with a thick white liquid and topped with some kind of meat. I left as soon as the plates arrived, but I could not feel its life force. What kind of monsters eat innocent plants?" Aurora covered her mouth.

"Oh, oh, oh, I know this! I saw it on a show the other day. Mortals call them, *sall-adds*, and it's commonly eaten in their realm."

"I don't care what they call it. I will not eat a plant."

"What are you going to tell James?"

"Ugh, I don't know. I'll think of something."

"Be careful."

Aurora tucked the murmur-rock safely back in her bra and walked to the door. The moment she disarmed the barrier spell, the door started shaking as someone hammered on the other side. She pulled the door open and found James standing there with a man in a white shirt and black pants.

"Thank god, you're okay." James gently touched her cheek with one hand and placed the other on her arm.

"Of course I'm okay. Why wouldn't I be?" She cleared her throat, trying not to cough.

"You were gone for a while, so I came to check on you, but you weren't responding and we couldn't get the door open. I was afraid you passed out or something."

"Sorry, the door must have been locked. I didn't hear you."

She brushed past the two men and sat back down at their table. James took his seat and began eating his salad. Aurora grimaced at hers.

"Is something wrong with your salad?"

She hesitated before saying in a low voice, "I can't eat it."

James put his fork down. "I'm sorry. I should have asked if you had any food allergies before I ordered."

He waved the waitress down to remove her plate. The waitress asked if she could bring her something else, but Aurora assured them she was fine with the no-longer-hot bread until their entrees arrived.

"I swear I'm usually better at this." James picked up his fork.

Aurora couldn't hold it in any longer, she covered her face with the napkin and sneezed.

"Bless you."

She looked up at James, who jabbed at his salad with his utensil, but when he brought it to his mouth, there was nothing on it.

He frowned at the spoon in his hand. "That's what I get for not paying attention," he said with a chuckle.

James placed the spoon on the table, next to another spoon. He moved plates as he looked and even bent over the side of the table, checking to see if his fork had fallen on the floor.

Oh no, did I do that?

The waitress delivered two plates covered with metal lids. "Can I get you anything else?"

"Yes, I seem to have misplaced my fork," James said while he scratched his head.

Aurora sneezed as James lifted the lid covering his food.

"Waitress!"

A live lobster snapped its claw on the plate before him. With James momentarily distracted by the lobster and not paying attention to her eyes, Aurora magicked one of the spoons back into a fork. She looked up to find an old woman at the next table over staring at her. Aurora gave a sheepish smile, and the woman rubbed at her eyes before giving an awkward smile back.

"I think my lobster ravioli is a little undercooked."

"I'm so sorry about that, sir. We are at full capacity today and one of the cooks called out with the flu. I will take these back immediately and I'll send the manager over." The waitress grabbed both dishes and ran to the kitchen.

Aurora cleared her throat and took a sip of water. James furrowed his eyebrows as he picked up the fork that now sat on the table next to him.

"Hey, you found your fork. So, do you have any family nearby?" she asked in a forced cheerful voice, trying to divert his attention.

"Yeah, my parents live right down the street from me and my two sisters live on opposite ends of town with their spouses. What about you?"

"My parents live pretty far away. I was eager to leave home when I was old enough."

"Do you not get along with your parents?" James asked as he took his new fork from the waitress and placed it on the table beside the one that had reappeared.

"We get along well enough. I've just always wanted to travel."

Within minutes, the waitress returned with two uncovered plates of lobster ravioli. "Again, I am so sorry for our mistake earlier. Your meals will be comped and the manager will be by shortly."

"Thank you," said James.

Aurora coughed. "This looks interesting."

"Lobster ravioli is my favorite." James closed his eyes with his first bite.

"AH CHOO." Aurora sneezed three times and grabbed a napkin to wipe her nose.

When she looked up at James, he seemed taller. She frowned as his body rose inch by inch. It struck her as odd, since he was still seated and enjoying his food. Aurora nudged a spoon off the edge of the table.

"Whoops, I'll get that." She bent over to pick it up and beheld James's chair floating five inches off the ground. Aurora gasped, which quickly spawned a coughing fit.

With a hand over her mouth and one to her chest, she stomped her foot down while she coughed, her magic bringing his chair down with it at the same time a waiter walked by. The waiter howled as James's chair crushed his foot. He shoved the chair forward and James fell out of it, grabbing on to the tablecloth to right himself. The tablecloth slid off the table as he went down, and the candle, plates, and glasses all shattered when they hit the floor.

Aurora remained in her chair with her hand covering her mouth, feeling like she would die of embarrassment if she wasn't found out first. People from the other tables stood up to try to see what happened. Half of the restaurant staff crowded them in an attempt to help James and quickly clean up all of the broken glass.

James stood with the help of the manager, who profusely apologized for everything that had happened this evening and wiped off his pant legs. He picked up his chair and plopped next to Aurora.

"I'm starting to think coming here wasn't a good idea."

"I'm sorry." Aurora sniffled and wiped her nose.

"You didn't do anything wrong. It's just bad luck or bad timing. I was wondering if you would want to come back to my place and watch a movie? I have a roommate, but he usually does his own thing. If you are uncomfortable with that and would like to end the evening, I completely understand."

"I'd love to come over and watch a movie."

They smiled at each other.

"Let me just go speak to the manager and then we can get out of here," James said.

The walk from the restaurant to his apartment took less than ten minutes, and James grabbed her hand first as they walked this time. The cold air worsened Aurora's runny nose. She tried to sniffle softly, hoping James wouldn't hear it.

James's roommate Zach walked down the front steps as they approached the house.

"Aww, are those for me?" Zach asked, eyeing the two bouquets of flowers James carried.

"Har har, real funny. You heading out?"

"Yeah, I'm going to grab something to eat real quick and I needed the fresh air. You must be Aurora. I'm Zach," he said, holding his hand out to her.

"Nice to meet you," she said, taking his hand.

"This one has been talking about you nonstop all week." He gestured to James.

Aurora blushed and cleared her throat to try and stop herself from coughing.

"He's exaggerating," James said and nudged Zach as he walked by, tugging on Aurora's hand to keep walking.

Zach laughed right up until they walked in the house and closed the door behind them.

Once inside, they took a left into a small room with a large, navy couch in front of an extremely large television. Aurora let out a squeak; she couldn't believe she was about to watch movies on a real-life television.

"You okay?"

"I thought I saw something."

"Was it a spider? Where was it? I'll kill it." James pulled off one of his shoes.

"I'm not afraid of spiders. It was nothing."

"You sure?"

She nodded.

"I'm going to put these in some water. Make yourself at home." James dropped his shoe, kicked off his other, and walked toward the kitchen.

Being alone with the television made it impossible for Aurora to contain her excitement. She poked at the wobbly black screen.

I thought that would feel more like a mirror.

Her fingers traced along the edge of the top and down the side, stopping only when she felt a small protrusion near the bottom. During her inspection of it, Aurora pressed a little too hard and the black screen lit up. She jumped back, terrified that she'd broken it, and James walked in the room.

"Did you pick something without me?"

With a hand on her chest, she eyed the stack of pillows and neatly folded blanket in his arms and said, "No, of course not. What's all that?"

James tossed two pillows on separate ends of the couch and then held out a fuzzy blanket to her. "I figured we should get comfortable."

Aurora arched an eyebrow.

James chuckled. "On our own ends. This blanket is for you and this one's for me."

Aurora took the one he held out and saw a second fuzzy blanket in his other hand, as well as a little cardboard box.

"I know you aren't trying to make a big deal about it, but I couldn't help but notice you have a cold, so I thought these would help."

When Aurora realized the small box held tissues, warmth spread through her chest before she let out the biggest sigh and immediately took one out to wipe her nose. "Oh my goblins, thank you."

"Did you just say goblins?"

"What? No. I—" Aurora cleared her throat. For the first time tonight, she was grateful for the tickle.

"I like that. It's different. Now let's get this party started." James plopped on the couch and leaned over to pat the seat on the opposite end.

Aurora sat, ramrod straight at first, but by the second movie, she had kicked off her shoes and was curled up on the couch with the tissues. During what seemed to be the quietest part of the movie, her stomach rumbled and her cheeks heated. *Great timing.*

"I'm starting to get kind of hungry. How about you?" James asked.

Aurora's heart flickered like a candle at the gesture.

"I'm starving." She chuckled.

"I have just the thing. I'll be right back." He placed the remote on the couch next to her.

She waited until he was out of sight and then gingerly picked up the remote, taking care not to push any of the buttons.

How am I supposed to know what show each number puts on?

Aurora placed the remote back on the couch and grabbed a tissue to wipe her runny nose.

"AH CHOO." She clamped her eyes shut.

Oh no.

When she opened one eye and saw a familiar sight on the television, her stomach plummeted and the room began to spin. She would simply have to push all of the buttons on the remote until the channel changed, but before she could grab it, James walked into the room carrying two steaming, oversized mugs with metal spoons. He handed her one and took his seat.

What do I do now?

Aurora stirred the golden liquid in the cup and watched as the bobbing chunks of white, green, and orange swirled around with each turn of her spoon. "What is it?"

"My grandmother's famous homemade chicken noodle soup. It's perfect for this time of the year, especially when you have a cold," he said with a wink.

Aurora smiled, brought a spoonful to her lips, and gently blew on it before taking a bite.

"Mmm. This is delicious!"

"I'm glad you think so."

James turned his attention to the scene on the television. The cobblestones that made up the street lightly glowed in contrast to the dark sky. Floating lanterns followed people around. The brick buildings in this town had chimneys smoking in various shades of dark purples, blues, and grays. A group of girls stood outside of a caldron shop, admiring the newest model that was encrusted with black diamonds, and four or five guys flew around performing tricks on their brooms—some stood as it hovered, while others performed dangerous maneuvers.

Life in the town on the screen was in full swing. A short, bald man shouted at people to buy floating fruit from his stand. Music played in the background by instruments that were magicked by a tall, slender man wearing all black. But what worried Aurora most was the large, chipped sign front and center of the screen. It read, *Welcome to Whimsica. Where gravity is more of a suggestion. Population: More than you can see.*

"Huh, okay, I guess Christmas in July isn't enough. Now they're playing Halloween specials on Valentine's Day."

"Right." Aurora forced a small laugh and ended up making herself cough.

"Are you cool with that? Halloween is my favorite holiday, so I'm always down for this kind of stuff."

"Really? Me too."

They sat back enjoying the soup but entered a very animated discussion about things that should or shouldn't be possible with magic and soon forgot about the *show* in front of them. Not once during the entire discussion did James suggest magic folk should be burned at the stake. In fact, he seemed to think magic wasn't even real. Aurora's chest felt light and some of the anxiety about him discovering her secret floated away.

Maybe I could be safe with him.

They stretched out on their ends of the couch, their feet meeting in the middle. James tapped his foot against hers and she rubbed the side of his ankle with hers in response. This went on back and forth for a while, and when James stopped responding to her playful nudge, she knew he was asleep.

Aurora carefully slid off the couch, walked over to James, and waved her hand in front of his face, testing if he was really asleep even though she heard him lightly snoring. She pulled her shoes on and conjured a small piece of paper and a pen to scribble him a quick note that she left. She placed it on the table next to his empty soup mug.

Aurora gave James a whisper of a kiss on his cheek and said, "Happy Valentine's Day."

Aurora heard James's sleepy voice when she crept toward the kitchen to retrieve her flowers, and she paused with her back to him.

"When can I see you again?" he asked.

Her face split into a huge smile. She bit her lip in an effort to compose herself and turned around with a straight face. "When would you like to see me again?"

"My birthday is next week," James mumbled, with half-open eyes, losing his battle against sleep.

"Okay."

His eyes popped all the way open. "Wait, how am I supposed to call you? I still don't have your number."

Aurora sighed and walked back over to James. She straightened the top of his blanket and leaned in so their lips were a breath away from one another. "I'll see you next week."

While she said the words, she gently stroked her pointer and middle finger down the side of his face, using her magic to send him into a deep sleep.

Even though she knew the park with the fountain was a short distance, Aurora murmured a direction spell to find her way back. She felt a twinge of guilt using her magic on him to end their conversation even though he had already been falling asleep, but he had been asking questions she didn't have the answers to—yet. In front of the fountain, she looked down at the bouquet of flowers from James.

What should I do with these?

Aurora smiled as what she thought was a brilliant idea came to her. Her eyes glowed as she traced her fingers along the edges of the soft petals and down the thorny edges while chanting a spell. The bouquet separated into dust and swirled around her wrist until it solidified into a bracelet that looked like delicate vines wrapped around her with rose and alstroemeria charms.

Now I can keep them forever.

When Aurora's head broke the surface of the blue, a prickling sensation went down her spine. Something felt off, and then a putrid death-like odor assaulted her nostrils.

"I'm telling you someone has been making unsanctioned trips using the cauldron. I can *smell* it," a snakelike voice hissed.

Rufus.

"The matter will be looked into, and the witch or witches responsible and anyone associated with these treasonous crimes will be dealt with swiftly."

"Oh goodie, it's been so long since the last public display of your unmerciful greatness. This generation of creatures gets away with far too much."

The high priestess murmured, "Perhaps."

Aurora could not see where they were, but she knew they were close. She held her breath and tried not to move, silently praying to the great witch that they would not notice her.

Aurora found Penny floating cross-legged above her bed, flicking stations on the candle.

"You're back! Tell me everything! How did the rest of your date go?" Penny asked, flying toward Aurora.

"There's not much to tell. It was a disaster. Every time I sneezed, worse things kept happening," she said as she stripped and began scrubbing the goo off her body.

"Bummer, but at least you dodged a bullet with him being a detective and all. Imagine if the date had gone well and you still had to end it so that he doesn't find out you're a witch. That would suck so much worse."

Aurora stayed silent for a while as she worked at cleaning herself. She was dying to tell Penny that she was pretty sure he didn't think magic was real, and even if he did, Aurora's gut was telling her he would be okay with it.

When exactly was the last witch burned at the stake again? she thought and made a mental note to dig out her old textbooks.

It pained Aurora not to tell Penny that the night ended wonderfully and that she felt light as a feather around James. But telling her could put her in danger, and that's why, for the first time in all the years they had known one another, Aurora lied to her best friend.

"He's not a detective yet, he just hopes to be one day. You're right—it's better that things end now. It was stupid of me to sneak off to the mortal realm to begin with. It's been a long night. I'm exhausted and I feel like I flew broom-first into a brick wall. Do you mind if we drop this for now so I can head to bed?" she asked as she conjured a tissue and dramatically blew her nose.

"Of course. Do you need anything before I head out?"

"No, I still have a bunch of stuff from the stockpile you brought me the other day," Aurora said as she picked up a vial of thick, brown liquid and tossed it back in one gulp.

"Okay. Feel better," Penny said as she floated out of the room.

Finally alone in her room, Aurora put up a barrier spell, just in case her friend tried to pop back in, dimmed the lights, and made sure the vines were closed.

She moaned as she got comfortable on her bed and called a black leather journal and a textbook titled *From Salem to Safety: The Evolution of Witch Concealment* from her bookshelf. The books lazily glided over to her as if she had woken them.

Aurora pulled her favorite inkwand from inside the spine of her journal. The stars and moon had disappeared from her ceiling by the time she finished writing. As she looked down at the page with the words *Observations from the mortal realm* scribbled at the top of the page, she felt alive with excitement. If she was going to keep going to see James, then she would need to keep track of what she had learned.

The most important aspect of all of this was making sure Penny never found out. Penny knowing about her sneaking off to the mortal realm once was one thing, but the amount of time Aurora hoped she would be spending there in the future spelled out far worse than probation if she got caught, and she would not let Penny be culpable. Even if Sweet Penny could no longer remember her human life, which had been cut short, Aurora would not ruin her afterlife. So she spelled the journal to look blank to anyone who wasn't her before placing it back on the shelf.

Aurora tried once again to ignore the guilt swirling around in her stomach as she lay in bed playing with her new charm bracelet and planned her next secret trip to the mortal realm in search of somewhere nice she could bring James for his birthday dinner. Her magic, and maybe a little something else inside her, hummed in anticipation.

About the Author

S.B. Rizk lives in Medford, Massachusetts, with her husband and their two sons. In her free time, she loves to draw, cook, and read. While her background is in culinary arts, her true passion has alway been with books. Most of her teenage years were spent inside with her nose in a book. As an adult, she spends as much time weaving her own stories as she does reading others. S.B. Rizk has short stories published in *As the Snow Drifts* and *All the Promises We Cannot Keep*.

You can find SB on:

Instagram: @author.sarahrizk

You can visit her website at:

https://linktr.ee/author.sarahrizk

THE DAY BEFORE LIFE GOES ON

The Day Before Life Goes On

Annabel den Dekker

JESSICA INHALED DEEPLY, TAKING IN the delicious scents from all the Valentine's Day pies, heart-shaped cookies, and other baked goods around her. They were fresh out of the oven. She'd just arranged them on the display shelves by the window, hoping their warm, inviting aroma would lure in passersby.

She beamed as she glanced around her little bakery. She had recently held her grand opening, finally fulfilling a dream she'd nurtured since childhood. She'd never taken the leap until both her now-girlfriend and best friend had inspired her, having both taken *her* advice and made their own bold, life-altering decisions, confirming her belief that sometimes the scariest steps are the ones most worth taking.

From behind the counter, Jess watched as a few people slowed down to peek through her window. She grinned when she spotted Meg among them holding a pink balloon. It wasn't a surprise that her girlfriend would show up on Valentine's Day, but she was earlier than Jess had expected. There hadn't been much reason for her Meg to smile this past year, not until Jess had finally admitted her feelings for her. Now, here Meg stood, beaming as she waved through the glass.

Seconds later, the bell above the door jingled. Meg walked past the small, cozy tables and headed straight to Jess, pulling her into a hug. She clung to her, as if afraid Jess might vanish if she let go. Meg was slowly returning to her old self, but her time away from their small town, living with her abusive ex in the big city, had left her feeling insecure and a bit clingy. Jess understood;

she knew her girlfriend had been through a lot. Besides, she loved taking care of people—especially Meg. That's why she hoped she could make today special for her girlfriend. To help her forget about all the anxieties that awaited her outside the shop.

"It smells amazing in here," Meg remarked when she finally let go, gazing around the bakery. "And it looks amazing too."

Jess bit her lower lip, a grin tugging at the corner of her mouth. Her heart danced every time someone complimented her work, but even more so when it came from her girlfriend. "Thank you, Megs."

Meg lowered her gaze to the ground, her fingers fumbling with the balloon's string. When she finally looked up again, Jess recognized a flicker of uncertainty in her eyes. "For you," she said in a small voice as she handed her the balloon. It was heart-shaped with *I love you* on it. "I hope it's not too cheesy?"

Jess felt a pang in her heart, knowing why Meg was so insecure about it. Meg's ex had never appreciated her romantic gestures, claiming she didn't try hard enough, even though Jess didn't know many people who tried as hard as Meg.

"Of course it isn't. I love it," she answered gently, her eyes locking with Meg's. "It's perfect."

"You're perfect," Meg whispered shyly as she tucked a strand of blonde hair behind her ear. She looked like she was about to say more but stopped when the soft jingle of the bell over the door broke the moment.

Jess looked over to see an elderly woman eyeing the freshly baked Valentine's treats on the shelves. She greeted the customer, her voice light and friendly. "Good morning. How can I help you?"

The woman smiled, her eyes crinkling. "Everything looks and smells so lovely in here. I couldn't resist stopping by."

Meg watched quietly as Jess helped the woman choose her treats.

"I'm looking for something sweet for my grandchildren. People often think of romance when they talk about Valentine's Day, but to me, it's about love in all its beautiful forms. And there's no one I love more than the little ones."

"I couldn't agree more," Jess replied, her thoughts drifting to all the times she'd given Valentine's gifts to her friends and family. "How about a few of these heart-shaped cookies?" Jess held them up for the woman to see.

"Oh, they look lovely! And maybe a small cherry pie as well," she answered, nodding in approval.

"Great choice." Jess carefully wrapped the cookies and slid them into a brown paper bag, folding the top and sealing it with a small label. She then placed the pie in a kraft box with a window on top, allowing a glimpse of the delicious pastry. "These will stay fresh for a couple of days, but they probably won't last that long," she added with a wink.

The woman chuckled. "You're probably right."

Jess slid the bag over the counter. "Here you go. I hope they enjoy it."

After the woman left with a friendly wave, Meg turned to Jess, a shy smile on her face. "Can I help today? I know you have to work, but . . ." She nervously fidgeted with her fingers. "I'd rather not be alone. And I'd love to spend Valentine's Day with you, of course."

Jess's heart squeezed. She knew Meg often grew anxious when she was by herself for too long. Jess and Meg's lives had been tangled ever since they became best friends in grade school. They'd gone to high school together, shared secrets and made memories in their little town. Even when Meg left for the city to study, they'd stayed in touch. It wasn't until her best friend started dating that Jess realized she had feelings for Meg beyond friendship. She ached every time she remembered how awful he had treated Meg, especially seeing how it had changed her. Growing up, Meg had always been the more adventurous one. She used to be so full of life, unafraid of anything or anyone. Nowadays, there wasn't much left of that person, and it hurt Jess to her very core.

Things were starting to look up. Meg laughed more often, and there were moments when her old self—bold and silly—would suddenly shine through. Still, Jess often worried about her. She sometimes felt afraid everything might go south again and that there was nothing she could do to prevent it. But maybe they could pretend that everything was all right, that the recent past was ancient history and held no bearing on the future, even if just for a day? They could live as if time had stopped and exist in their own bubble for a while. Life could go on after that.

And what better day to pretend than on Valentine's Day?

"I always love having you around," Jess responded. "But you don't have to work if you don't want to. You can just be here and hang out with me."

"That's okay." Meg looked at her sweetly, her eyes sparkling as a soft grin spread across her lips. "I'd love to help out."

The rest of the morning passed by pleasantly, with one or two customers trickling in every half hour. Meg helped out as promised, mostly handing over bags or ringing up small orders, while Jess did most of the talking.

As they moved behind the counter, taking orders and wrapping up pastries, Jess couldn't help but glance over at Meg every now and then. Each time, her girlfriend would give a little wave or a wink, sending a rush of endearment through her.

Around lunchtime, the bakery filled up, the bell above the door jingling more frequently. Soon all tables were occupied, and a small line started to form by the counter. Jess peeked over at Meg, who was already stepping up to help the next customer.

"I think a lot of people need to buy some last-minute sweets for their sweethearts," Jess joked.

Meg grinned back. "I think so, too."

As they worked, they fell into a smooth rhythm—Jess packing up pastries, wrapping cookies, serving customers at the tables and explaining the day's specials, while Meg managed the register and handed out orders.

When the stream of customers eventually slowed, they tidied the counter, wiped down tables, and put away some of the remaining baked goods. When the last customer left and Jess turned the sign to *Closed*, she grabbed two cookies from a plate and leaned against the counter, handing one to Meg. "Thank you for your help. You were incredible."

"You are very welcome," Meg replied sweetly before taking a small bite of the cookie, her face lighting up with pleasure. "It's delightful."

Jess's stomach seemed to flutter and churn, a gentle warmth spreading through her as if she'd swallowed sunlight. The sensation spread through her chest and rose all the way to her cheeks. She reached across the counter, taking Meg's hand in hers. "I'm glad you're here with me."

Meg squeezed her hand, her eyes soft. "I wouldn't want to be anywhere else."

For a few moments, they stood in comfortable silence, simply gazing lovingly into each other's eyes. After a little while, Meg said hesitantly, "I was thinking . . . You know I'm pretty bad at baking, while you're amazing at it. I was wondering if you could teach me how to bake one of your delicious pies after we finish for today? As a Valentine's date?"

Meg clearly didn't want this day to be over yet. Jess certainly didn't either. She needed more time if she wanted to make today perfect for Meg. The bakery felt like their own little bubble, a warm, quiet world where time seemed to slow down, and everything outside felt distant. Jess wanted to stay there as long as possible and keep Meg safe from her worries. She leaned forward across the counter and pressed a soft kiss to Meg's cheek. "I'd love to."

After they finished cleaning the tables and stowed away the last of the baked goods, Meg followed Jess into the kitchen. They opened a few cabinets, gathering all the baking tools and ingredients they needed, before laying them out on the counters.

Jess pulled on her apron and handed a spare to Meg. "How about we make the pie extra special?"

Meg raised an eyebrow, intrigued. "Extra special? How?"

"Since it's Valentine's Day, maybe we can make a strawberry heart-shaped pie—with strawberries mixed into the filling, a layer of chocolate inside and out, and fresh strawberries on top." Jess pulled out a heart-shaped pie tin and set it on the counter. "Do you like that idea?"

Meg nodded eagerly. "It sounds great."

With their aprons tied and the ingredients ready, they started with the crust. Jess carefully explained how to measure out the flour, confectioners' sugar, cocoa powder, and butter.

Meg nodded, her brows furrowed slightly in concentration as she followed Jess's instructions. "Like this?" she asked when she'd put the correct amounts in the bowl, together with salt and an egg.

"Exactly." Jess grinned. "Now, go ahead and add one teaspoon of vanilla extract."

As Meg mixed the ingredients, her hands a little tentative, Jess watched closely. "All right," she said once the batter was ready. "Let me show you how to knead it properly."

Meg smiled, biting her lip as Jess moved behind her, resting her hands over Meg's to show her how to work the dough. "I always thought baking was so complicated," she admitted with a laugh. "I can't believe you do this all the time now."

Jess chuckled softly, her breath brushing against Meg's ear as she leaned closer. "It's not so bad once you get the hang of it. You're doing great."

Meg turned and nuzzled her nose gently against Jess's. "I do have a pretty great teacher."

"Flattery will get you everywhere," Jess teased before pressing a tender kiss on her lips.

Jess's hands still guiding Meg's, they continued kneading the dough together until it reached just the right texture. "How's that?" Meg asked, glancing up at Jess, her big, green eyes longing for approval.

Jess was all too eager to give it to her. She wiped a stray bit of flour off Meg's cheek with her thumb. "It's perfect."

Her words had the desired effect. A smile grew on Meg's face, one so radiant it melted Jess from the inside out. To keep from staring at her endearing expression for too long, Jess grabbed the rolling pin and handed it to her girlfriend. "Now, let's roll it out."

Meg raised an eyebrow. "This might be where it all goes downhill."

"Don't worry. I've got you," Jess chuckled. She watched as Meg carefully spread the dough across the counter, fully concentrated, her brow furrowed in adorable determination. But when Meg tried to roll out the dough, it stuck stubbornly to the rolling pin, bunching up into uneven patches.

Frustration flashed across her face and she let out a groan. "Ugh, why is this so hard?"

Tenderly caressing her back, Jess pressed a kiss to Meg's cheek just beside her earlobe and said softly, "Don't worry, that happens to everyone at first. You could add a little extra flour to keep it from sticking."

Meg leaned into her, her back pressed snugly against Jess's chest as she dusted more flour over the dough. Jess gently placed her hands back over Meg's, guiding her movements. "Just like this," she whispered, her voice soft in Meg's ear as they rolled the dough together. "Even pressure, from the center out."

Their hands worked in sync, the dough slowly spreading into a smooth, even circle. "See? You're getting the hang of it," Jess complimented, her tone filled with quiet pride.

With the dough now rolled out perfectly, they carefully lifted it and pressed it gently into the heart-shaped tin. With Jess's hands still over Meg's, they molded the edges with care, making sure the crust fit just right.

Meg tilted her head back slightly, smiling. "What's next?"

"Let's put it in the oven," Jess replied. Holding the tin together, they slid the pie into the preheated oven. Then Jess turned to Meg. "We can make the filling while it's baking. Let's start by melting the chocolate."

She poured chocolate chips into a saucepan, watching as they began to melt. "We'll mix this into the filling," she explained, glancing at Meg, who was watching her intently. "Could you slice the strawberries into quarters for me?"

"Sure thing!" Meg replied quickly, picking up a sharp knife and a cutting board, her focus shifting as she carefully began slicing the bright red strawberries. She concentrated, her tongue peeking out adorably. It made Jess want to wrap her tight in her arms and keep her close forever. Safe from any harm that might come her way. She didn't, of course. Instead, she kept watching her, enjoying the fluttery feeling in her chest.

Once Meg finished slicing, she looked up hesitantly. "How do they look?"

"Perfect!" Jess beamed at her, wanting Meg to feel the encouragement she so desperately needed. "Now, let's get those strawberries into the bowl." She tossed them in with a sprinkle of sugar and a bit of cornstarch to thicken the filling. "Now you need to stir it," she instructed, handing Meg a wooden spoon.

As Jess poured in the melted chocolate, Meg stirred, carefully folding all ingredients together until they formed a creamy filling. Jess grabbed a spoon, scooped up a bit of the mixture, and held it out toward Meg with a sweet smile. "Want to find out if it's good?"

Meg leaned forward, tasting it. Her eyes grew wide as the heavenly chocolate and fresh strawberries melted on her tongue. "Mmm, that's delicious! I think we nailed it." She leaned against the counter, wiping her hands on her apron. "I have to admit that baking is a lot more fun than I expected."

Jess tilted her head. "Even with flour all over your face?" she teased.

Meg's eyes widened. She immediately reached up to touch her cheek. "Wait, do I really have—?"

Jess chuckled. "No, I'm just messing with you."

Meg tried to playfully swat her shoulder, but Jess caught her hand midair, bringing it to her lips and pressing a soft kiss on her knuckles. The simple gesture must've made an impact, because Meg's cheeks flushed pink right before Jess pulled her into a warm hug. "I'm so glad you're here," Jess whispered into her hair, breathing in the comforting scent of flour and chocolate that clung to Meg.

"I'm glad, too," Meg replied, sinking into the embrace. "I never knew baking could feel so special."

Jess pulled back slightly, looking into Meg's eyes. "It's not just the baking; it's who you're sharing it with that makes it special." She chuckled at her own words. "See? It's completely okay to be cheesy on Valentine's Day. It's required even." She kissed her cheek. "Do you know what else is required to make today a success?"

Meg shook her head, staring into Jess's eyes as if searching for the answer. "No?"

"Dancing!" With a bright grin, Jess reached for her phone to put on some upbeat music. She couldn't help but sway a little as the first few notes filled the air. "While we clean," she added. "We can do it as we wait for the pie to bake."

Meg immediately joined in. They danced around the kitchen, twirling and laughing as they rinsed bowls and wiped down counters. Jess playfully pulled Meg closer, guiding her into a spin. Meg giggled, her long blonde hair flying around her like a halo.

"Watch out for the flour!" Meg warned, narrowly avoiding knocking the bag off the counter.

"But it's part of the experience!" Jess declared, giving a little shimmy as she tossed a small handful into the air, sending a cloud of white floating down around them.

Meg laughed, brushing some flour off her clothes. "Well, now I'm covered in flour."

Jess playfully rubbed Meg's face with a cloth, gently wiping it away. "Now you look like a true baker."

They continued to dance while cleaning, stealing kisses between washing cutlery and wiping down surfaces.

"Okay, your turn!" Jess said, pushing Meg playfully toward the center of the kitchen. "Show me your best move!"

With a mock-serious expression, Meg struck a pose, hands on her hips, then suddenly broke into a goofy dance, her arms flailing as she spun around in a whirlwind of energy. Jess burst into laughter, her heart dancing with joy. This was something the old Meg would have done without hesitation. She joined in quickly, mimicking Meg's exaggerated moves.

When the song ended, a slower one started playing. Jess instinctively wrapped her arms around Meg's waist, pulling her close. Gradually, their silliness transformed into something more intimate.

Jess brushed a stray lock of hair behind Meg's ear, her fingers lingering against her cheek, savoring the softness of her skin. "Have I already told you today how beautiful you are?"

Meg smiled shyly, a hint of color blooming on her cheeks. She looked down for a moment, flustered yet delighted. She surprised Jess when she leaned in closer, their foreheads almost touching. "Let's make a promise," she said, her expression turning serious. "No matter what happens, we'll always find moments like this. Just us."

Jess nodded, her heart swelling with emotion. "I promise. Always."

The timer rang out, interrupting their moment. Jess sighed softly, pressing a tender kiss to Meg's forehead before reluctantly untangling herself from their embrace. Already, she missed the warmth of Meg's touch and their closeness. She smiled faintly as she slipped on her mitts and opened the oven door. Carefully, she pulled out the heart-shaped pie crust and set it on the counter to cool.

They fell into a comfortable silence for a moment, both of them admiring their creation. After the pie crust had cooled just enough, they poured the strawberry-chocolate filling into it.

"Now," Jess said, grabbing a bowl of leftover sliced strawberries, "let's arrange these on top."

Together, they placed the red slices, their fingers brushing occasionally as they worked.

Once they were done, Jess melted a few handfuls of chocolate chips until they became a glossy sauce. "I'm going to drizzle this across the top of the filling and let it set as a chocolate layer." She carefully poured it over the filling, making sure it spread evenly. The chocolate cascaded down in silky ribbons, pooling beautifully over the strawberries.

Meg gazed down at the result. "It's almost too pretty to eat. I can't believe I actually helped make this," she said, her voice filled with wonder.

"I'm very happy with our pie, too, but it would be a shame to miss out on its taste," Jess said. She grabbed two forks from the drawer, handing one to her girlfriend. She cut into the pie and scooped up a generous forkful, holding it up to Meg's lips. "Here, let me feed you."

Meg opened her mouth. Her eyes sparkled as she took the bite. "Oh my gosh, this is amazing! We actually did it!"

Jess chuckled, loading her fork with more pie and taking a bite herself. As the rich chocolate and sweet strawberries melted in her mouth, she was pretty sure her face matched the bliss she'd just seen on Meg's. "Wait until the chocolate has hardened again; it's even more delicious that way," she noted after she'd swallowed her bite.

"Then I guess . . . I'll have to stay even longer?" Meg replied tentatively, her voice wavering slightly as she looked down, seemingly unsure if she was overstaying her welcome.

"You can stay as long as you want," Jess answered, her voice gentle but clear. "Today is perfect, and I have no intention of ending it already."

Meg smiled gratefully, wrapping an arm around Jess's waist. "Happy Valentine's Day, Jess."

Jess beamed, her heart swelling with love. "Happy Valentine's Day, Megs."

Eyes sparkling with affection, Meg leaned in for a kiss. It was sweet and romantic. The kind that made time stand still for a while.

Jess savored the moment, the delicious taste of the pie still lingering on their tongues. She knew tomorrow life would continue the way it always had, with all its complications and messiness. For now, in Jess's bakery, their world was perfect, and everything was just right.

And who knew? Maybe it still would be the next day.

About the Author

Annabel den Dekker (she/her) is a queer author from the Netherlands. When she's not writing, she can be found strolling through nature, daydreaming about her favorite characters, or conjuring up new stories. She's also an avid admirer of books, music, and TV series and delights in sharing them with others.

After years of creating numerous short stories, novels, and fanfiction, she self-published her debut novel, *Ailene. Purpose*, and *Just Like Christmas* followed only a year later. Now she is eager to add many more books to her repertoire.

You can find Annabel on:

Instagram: @bellsbooksandwritings

You can visit her website at:

annabeldendekker.com

SECOND TIME'S SWEETER

Second Time's Sweeter

Melissa Mastro

Charming Chocolate Company Holding Valentine's Day Contest

Brussels, Belgium – *Charming Chocolate Company, the world's leading supplier of semisweet chocolate chips, just announced a Valentine's Day competition that challenges contestants to celebrate the love of chocolate by creating a unique recipe using the brand's flagship product. Two finalists will be selected to visit the Charming Chocolate headquarters in Brussels, Belgium, for the Sweet Showdown, where they will work with chocolatiers to bring their chocolate creation to life. Charming Chocolate's tasting panel will then choose their favorite of the two recipes and the winner will be awarded $25,000. It's sure to be the sweetest competition of the season! Enter now on the Charming Chocolate website!*

OPHELIA WATSON COCKED HER HEAD as she read the news article. When she finished, her lips curled up into a triumphant smile. "We're going to Europe!" she announced to her cat, Teddy.

The orange feline stared at her blankly. He'd been her only companion as of late. Teddy didn't know about "the incident," so he couldn't judge her, or take sides, or decide if she was a crappy human being or not. Teddy was happy as long as Ophelia was feeding him, and Ophelia was happy as long as Teddy was keeping her company.

On the other side of the country—Seattle, Washington, to be exact—Tate Ripley was reading the same article. "Does anyone actually enter these stupid contests?" he asked his best friend, Neil.

Neil peered over Tate's shoulder to see what he was talking about. "Maybe you should," he replied. "You could use a vacation after everything that happened. Plus, that chocolate-peanut-butter-covered bacon you make would probably win."

Tate scoffed. He was the head chef at one of the most popular restaurants in the area. He didn't need to seek validation from a silly recipe contest.

"I'm being serious," Neil continued, "you've been so . . . bitter . . . since the, uh, you know. It might be good to distract yourself. Take your mind off the animosity."

"I'm not bitter," Tate retorted.

"Mhmm," Neil hummed. "Just think about it, okay?"

Tate knew that his friend was just looking out for him. "Okay, I'll think about it," he agreed.

In her small New York City kitchen, Ophelia combined ingredients. She wasn't much of a cook or a baker, but she was a foodie, and she loved chocolate. *This'll be easy*, she thought. A few hours and many f-bombs later, she made something that could actually contend for the win.

"These are incredible," she said to Teddy as she bit into a chocolate balsamic fig truffle. "Pack your bags, Teddy bear, because you and I—we're Belgium bound!"

Her furry friend looked as unenthused as ever. Ophelia expected nothing less.

I can't believe I'm actually doing this, Tate thought as he pressed the big SUBMIT RECIPE button on the Charming Chocolate Company's contest page. The screen froze, and Tate wasn't sure if he was concerned or relieved. *Is this a sign? I knew this was a bad idea. . . .* It was too late, though. A pop-up message appeared a moment later.

Thanks for entering! Finalists will be notified via email on February 1.

Tate looked at his calendar. That was just over two weeks away. Was it really mid-January already? He shook his head. Time had been fleeing him lately. Days would go by in a blur. He couldn't remember what he ate or where he went. It was like he was running on autopilot. His mother said that it was a symptom of grief. She was a holistic doctor who loved to diagnose her son and then cure his ailments with a slew of natural remedies. Tate had tried them all, and they usually worked, but not this time. Unfortunately, no vitamin, mineral, or supplement could heal a broken heart.

From her bedroom, Ophelia heard the chime of her computer. "An email!" she squealed. It was the first of February, and she'd been pacing around her apartment eagerly awaiting a message from the Charming Chocolate Company. She ran to her makeshift office, which was really just a corner of her living room, and opened her inbox.

Congratulations! You have been selected as one of two finalists in Charming Chocolate's Valentine's Day contest! On February 12, you will be flying to Brussels, Belgium, to participate in the Sweet Showdown, which will take place on February 14 at the Charming Chocolate headquarters, where our tasting panel will select one winner to take home the grand prize of $25,000!

"We did it, Teddy!" Ophelia sang, picking up the cat and twirling him around the room until he hissed and jumped out of her arms.

Eleven days later, Ophelia stood in Brussels Airport with a small suitcase and a pet carrier. Her hosts were gracious enough to let her bring Teddy, who had recently been registered as an emotional support animal. She did rely on her feline friend for comfort and companionship, plus, with no one to watch him in her absence, she really had no other choice.

Near the exit of the terminal, Ophelia spotted a well-dressed man holding a sign that had her name on it.

"Ms. Watson?" he asked as she approached him.

Ophelia nodded.

"I'm Jasper. I'll be bringing you to the Charming Chocolate Company's headquarters. You'll be lodging in a quaint cabin on the property during your stay. I have a car out front to bring you to your destination. Come, come. The other finalist is already there."

Jasper led Ophelia outside to a shiny black sedan. He took her carry-on bag and put it in the trunk, then he opened the door and ushered her inside.

"I can't believe we're really here," Ophelia whispered to Teddy as they drove out of the airport and into Belgium's capital city.

The Charming Chocolate headquarters was located about an hour outside the Brussels metropolis, in a picturesque country town. Despite the rural setting, the property was sprawling with a large industrial building, two storefronts, and several small cottages, all of which sat on a perfectly manicured lawn.

Ophelia was completely awestruck.

"Your cabin is just up there to the left." Jasper pointed. "But before you get settled in, I'm going to bring you to the factory. Ms. Charming is eager to meet you."

Charming Chocolate Company was a family-owned business founded by Bert Charming in the late 1800s. Since then, several Charmings have served as CEO, with the current being Delilah Charming, Bert's great-great-granddaughter.

Delilah had inherited the company at just thirty years old, and in her short five-year career, she'd built an impressive résumé: several viral marketing campaigns, a spot on *Forbes* 40 under 40, countless philanthropic pursuits, the list went on.

Ophelia was excited—and a little nervous—to meet her. Ophelia was just a couple of years younger than Delilah, but her accomplishments were significantly fewer. Aside from a dead-end work from home job, Ophelia didn't have much going for her. She'd be lying if she said that she wasn't a little embarrassed by her own lack of achievements.

Jasper escorted Ophelia into the industrial building. Inside, she saw a man and a woman examining a large mural of the Charming Chocolate Factory back when it first opened. The pair had their backs turned to Ophelia, but she assumed that the woman was Ms. Charming; the man must've been the other finalist.

As she approached, they turned to greet her. Ophelia's mouth fell open.

Tate couldn't believe his eyes. He gaped at Ophelia in disbelief. He hadn't seen her since she left him, without explanation, at the altar.

"What are you doing here?" he asked, stunned.

"I-I could ask you the same thing," she stammered.

Tate swallowed hard. Not long ago, there wasn't anyone who knew him better than Ophelia—they were best friends, lovers, family—but now, standing here, face to face with his runaway bride, it felt like they were total strangers.

Tate. The man who Ophelia had been prepared to marry. He looked different. Weathered. She hoped that that wasn't her fault.

Ophelia hadn't wanted to hurt him, even though she knew it was inevitable. She'd stood him up on their wedding day, but she had no other choice. She was protecting him from a future heartache that would have been far worse.

A few weeks before their wedding, Ophelia felt a lump in her breast. Out of precaution, she went to the doctor. Just days before the ceremony, she heard the words: "You have cancer. Stage four."

She wanted to tell Tate about her diagnosis, but he was so excited for their big day. She was, too. As it neared, though, she realized that she couldn't put him through that kind of pain. She couldn't marry him when she had so little time left.

If Ophelia had told him, she knew that Tate would have loved her until her last dying breath, but she didn't want that for him. She didn't want him to wed a woman with an expiration date.

Tate and Ophelia continued to stare at each other, neither knowing what to do about this very unexpected encounter.

Finally, their host, Ms. Charming, spoke up. "Hello, Ms. Watson," she said to Ophelia. "I was just showing Mr. Ripley, our other finalist, around the facility. Do you two know each other?" she asked, opening the question up to the both of them.

Tate cleared his throat. "We do," he said. "Ophelia is my, um . . . ex-fiancée."

Ophelia gave Ms. Charming a tight-lipped smile.

"Oh," Ms. Charming said. She looked surprised, confused, and a bit uncomfortable. "Was this . . . planned?"

Tate let out a sardonic laugh. "Planned? No. Not planned at all. In fact, I haven't seen or spoken to Ophelia since the night before our wedding. I waited at the altar, but she never showed."

Ophelia felt a bead of sweat drip down her forehead. She knew that she owed Tate an explanation, and now she felt like she owed Ms. Charming one, too. This was not how this was supposed to go.

"I have late-stage breast cancer," she blurted out. "That's why I bailed on you and our wedding, Tate, and it's why I decided to do this contest, Ms. Charming. I'm just trying to live while I still have time, but without burdening anyone else with my problems."

Tate's throat tightened. He looked at Ophelia and felt as if the cancer was suddenly screaming at him. How did he not notice it when he first saw her? She was considerably more frail, her face was gaunt, and her hair was completely different. *Because it's a wig.*

"O," he choked. "Why didn't you tell me?"

Ophelia looked down. "Because I didn't want you to put your life on hold for me. I'm not getting better."

Ms. Charming shifted her weight from one foot to the other. "I'm going to leave you two alone for a bit," she said, quietly excusing herself. "I am so sorry to hear of your diagnosis, Ms. Watson."

Ophelia nodded and Ms. Charming scurried off with Jasper trailing behind her.

It was just Tate and Ophelia now, and neither one of them knew what to do next.

Tate had so many questions. *When did she find out? Is she getting treatment? How long does she have left?* But instead of asking them, he just stood there, taking in every inch of the woman he once loved; the woman he still loved.

Ophelia caught him staring and frowned. "I know. . . . I look different."

"You look beautiful."

"No, I don't."

"Yes, you do."

Silence fell over them.

"What made you decide to go through this alone?" Tate asked, his voice shaky.

Ophelia didn't want to get emotional. She didn't want to have this conversation. "What made you decide to enter a recipe contest? You usually scoff at this sort of thing."

"Neil thought it'd be good for me," Tate answered earnestly. "He thought it might take my mind off what happened . . . take my mind off you."

Ophelia didn't want to acknowledge that either. "It was the bacon, wasn't it?" she offered instead.

Tate smiled, taking the bait. "It was. And for the record, I did scoff."

Ms. Charming returned a few minutes later. Jasper was behind her, clutching the pet carrier.

"Your friend was calling for you, Ms. Watson," Jasper explained. "I hope you don't mind that I've brought him inside."

"You got a cat?" Tate asked with an eyebrow raised.

"His name is Teddy," Ophelia said to Tate. She looked at Jasper. "Thank you for bringing him to me. He gets separation anxiety."

Jasper nodded and then stepped away so that Ms. Charming could go over the schedule. When she finished, and with nothing else planned for the remainder of the day, Tate and Ophelia went outside to the car that was waiting to bring them to the cozy cabin where they'd be lodging during their stay—a cozy cabin they would be sharing.

Later that evening, after two much-needed naps, Tate and Ophelia sat around the fireplace in the den of their cabin.

Tate still had questions, and Ophelia still didn't want to talk. So instead, they watched a movie and sipped on hot chocolate.

Stealing glimpses of his ex-fiancée whenever he could, Tate was certain that this was a sign from the universe that he and Ophelia were meant to be together. Why else would they have both ended up here? *It can't be a coincidence.*

The next morning, before heading out for his daily jog, Tate made Ophelia an almond milk latte with a hefty serving of cinnamon, exactly how she liked it.

They had a busy day ahead of them. The Sweet Showdown was just over twenty-four hours away and they needed to perfect their recipes, which they'd be doing with the help of the Charming chocolatiers.

If Tate was being honest, he didn't really care about winning the competition, not anymore at least. His only focus now was winning back Ophelia. He wanted to ensure that the rest of her days, regardless of how many, were magical and meaningful. He could be the one to do that for her. He would love her—he already *did* love her. He could take care of her.

When Ophelia awoke, she was enveloped with the scent of coffee. She went to the kitchen to find a mug and a note on the counter.

Almond milk latte, extra extra cinnamon. Tate.

Ophelia tried and failed to fight the smile tugging at her lips. Tate was notorious for his sweet little gestures and falling back into their old rhythm, even if only momentarily, felt really nice. She hadn't realized how much she missed these simple acts of kindness.

She shook her head. *You can't*, she thought.

She had noticed the way that Tate kept looking at her the night before, and she was certain that them being together at this competition, in this cabin, was a sign from the universe that they shouldn't be together. She knew that she had hurt Tate when she left him at the altar, but that would not hurt him nearly as much as it would to watch her die.

You have to protect him. Ophelia felt an ache in her chest. Sometimes loving someone meant letting them go. Even if it broke your heart, too.

At the factory, Ophelia was quickly swept away by a group of chocolatiers eager to begin working with her on her truffle recipe. She was grateful for the distraction; she needed to keep her mind off Tate and the desire that was growing for him, regardless of how hard she tried to suppress it.

Ophelia wasn't surprised that she'd felt this way after being around him again. They'd been like magnets since the day that they met at a dive bar in Portland, Oregon, ten years earlier. They were both fresh out of college, broke, and blissfully optimistic.

Their chemistry was instantaneous, and after a few too many beers, they'd gone back to Tate's dingy apartment. Ophelia assumed that it was going to be just another drunken hook up, but Tate stuck around, and so did Ophelia. The two were practically inseparable . . . until their wedding day, when Ophelia ran away to New York.

That magnetic pull was exactly why Ophelia had had to put so much distance between her and Tate, because she knew that as long as they were near each other, she wouldn't be able to stay away from him.

Like Ophelia, Tate spent the majority of his day in the chocolate factory. Unlike Ophelia, he didn't preoccupy himself with his recipe or with the contest. How could he when the only woman that he had ever loved—the woman he was supposed to marry, whom he'd thought he would never see again—was working in the same building as him . . . staying in the same house as him? The caveat was that this was only temporary, and time was not his ally. They'd be returning to their respective sides of the United States in forty-eight hours. Tate had to get his girl back before then.

With Jasper's help, he planned a romantic dinner for the two of them later that night. Tate had given Jasper a grocery list and Jasper had picked up and delivered all of the requested supplies by the time they returned to the cabin.

Tate waited until Ophelia retired to her room for a nap, and then he began his preparations. Equipped with her favorite food, wine, and flowers, plus candles to set the mood, Tate was confident he'd be able to remind Ophelia of what they had. It was a once in a lifetime love, after all, and deep down, she knew that, too. He was certain of it.

Ophelia awoke to the sound of a 1950s ballad and the smell of roasted garlic. She knew what it meant: Tate was cooking her favorite dinner. She didn't want to engage; she wanted to keep her distance, to maintain the wall that she had erected, but it'd been so long since she had Tate's vegetable lasagna and her mouth was already salivating at the thought. *It's just one shared meal,* she thought in an attempt to justify her inevitable surrender.

She decided to freshen up, reapplying her makeup and putting on the wig that she had removed before her nap. She even changed out of her lounge clothes and into a cashmere sweater and wide-leg trousers. *What are you doing?* she asked herself as she examined her reflection in a full-length mirror. She had to admit, she liked how she looked, and she knew that Tate would, too, but she wasn't supposed to be doing this. It just felt so good to be around him again—to feel seen, to feel beautiful, to feel loved.

"Maybe I was wrong," she said to Teddy, who was sprawled out on her bed. Her furry companion seemed to be thoroughly enjoying his time in Europe. "Maybe I'm causing more heartache by not being with Tate than I would be if we were together. Maybe I should let him decide if he wants to love someone who's dying."

Ophelia felt a tear fall down her cheek. The past few months had been so hard for her. She'd isolated herself from friends and family in an attempt to protect them, too. As a result, she'd gone through everything alone: doctors' appointments, chemotherapy, hospital stays. Maybe it wouldn't be so bad to have someone alongside her.

Tate was setting the table when Ophelia emerged from her room. He had prepared an impressive spread: roasted vegetable lasagna, crusty garlic bread, and a creamy Caesar salad. In the center of it all was a vase full of rainbow tulips and several tall vanilla-scented candles. All of Ophelia's favorite things.

He turned around when he heard her soft footsteps padding across the floor. He was surprised to see that she was wearing a nice outfit. Tate had expected pajamas, and while that would have been more than okay with him because he'd always thought Ophelia looked beautiful in everything, he couldn't fight the flutter in his chest. *Did she dress up for me?*

"O," he said, trying to catch his breath. "You look incredible."

Ophelia's eyes danced. "It smells *incredible,*" she said, "and that," she pointed toward the table, "looks absolutely amazing. You didn't have to do all this."

"I know, but I wanted to," Tate smiled. He pulled out a chair. "Here, have a seat."

Once Ophelia was seated, Tate poured her a glass of wine, made her a plate large enough to feed two, and ensured that she was comfortable and content before joining her at the table.

Ophelia took a bite of lasagna and let out a deep, satisfied sigh. "Oh my gosh, it's even better than I remember," she said with a hand over her mouth to conceal her chewing.

Tate grinned proudly. He was going to respond, to start a much-needed conversation—there was so much to be said—but he held his tongue. Tonight, he just wanted to enjoy Ophelia's company. He wanted to remind her of what they had, of how good and easy and effortless it was.

So they ate and drank and talked about everything and nothing all at the same time. It was perfect—they were perfect. Surely, Ophelia realized that, too.

When Tate awoke the next morning, he was still buzzing from the night before, things truly could not have gone any better.

After he and Ophelia had finished eating, they sat together outside looking up at the stars with a large blanket wrapped around them. They stayed out there until their eyelids got heavy and they couldn't fight sleep any longer. Before Ophelia went to her room, she had pulled Tate in close and gave him a kiss on the cheek. "Thank you," she had whispered in his ear. He could still feel the tickle of her breath on his skin.

Tate looked at the alarm clock beside his bed: 6 a.m. He and Ophelia didn't have to be at the chocolate factory for the Sweet Showdown until ten. He rolled over and tried to go back to sleep, but it was no use. He'd always been an early riser. So he decided to go for his jog and when he returned, he'd make Ophelia a special Valentine's Day breakfast.

An hour later, Tate strolled back into the cabin, expecting to see Ophelia, but she wasn't in the kitchen or in the den. He assumed that she was still asleep, but her bedroom door was open, and when he peeked inside, she wasn't in there.

"O?" he called. No response. "Ophelia?"

He looked around, searching for a clue to where she could have gone. Her bed wasn't made, and her belongings were scattered on the floor. Her suitcase was still there, along with the pet carrier, but he saw no sign of Teddy. From the disheveled state of the room, it appeared as though she'd left in a hurry.

What the hell is going on?

"Ms. Watson, my name is Doctor Martens. You're at the Brussels University Hospital. I'm going to be taking care of you today."

Ophelia looked at the doctor, trying to piece it all together, but the last thing she remembered was kissing Tate goodnight and going to bed.

Doctor Martens must've sensed her confusion. In a gentle voice, he explained, "You called for an ambulance this morning. When the paramedics arrived, you were unconscious. It appears you had a seizure. Fortunately, your vitals were quickly restored and you're in stable condition now. We'd like to hold you for a few hours for observation, though. Is there anyone you'd like to call and notify?"

"Tate," Ophelia choked, her throat dry and her voice hoarse.

Moments later, or what felt like moments later, Tate came barreling into the emergency room. "Ophelia," he gasped, rushing toward her. "Are you okay?" He cupped her cheeks. "What happened?"

The lines of his face were etched with fear, panic, and worry. This had been exactly what Ophelia was trying to avoid all of this time.

"I'm okay," she assured him before explaining how she wound up in the hospital. Well, according to the doctor, at least. Ophelia still didn't remember anything.

After the initial shock, Tate seemed to pull himself together. "I'm so glad you're okay," he sighed. Ophelia could see the relief in his eyes.

Tate sat down beside her. After a few minutes, he asked, "Where's Teddy?"

"He wasn't in my room?"

"I didn't see him," Tate replied.

Ophelia considered where her furry friend could have gone. "I bet he's under the bed," she concluded. "He gets spooked when I'm not around and has a tendency to hide until I return."

"Ah," Tate nodded. "I didn't even think to look. Poor guy."

Ophelia smiled. It made her happy that Tate cared about Teddy, but then again, she wouldn't expect anything else from him.

For the remainder of the morning, Tate stayed by Ophelia's bedside, unless asked to leave by doctors or a well-meaning nurse. She was finally discharged at noon.

"I guess this means we missed the Sweet Showdown." She sulked as they exited the hospital. Jasper was waiting for them outside.

"Woah, woah, woah. What makes you say that?" Tate asked.

"It was supposed to start at ten. We're two hours late," Ophelia pointed out.

"I called Ms. Charming when the doctors asked me to step out of the room, and I told her what happened. She postponed the Showdown to this afternoon. It starts at three." He grinned.

Ophelia's face lit up. "Really?"

"Yeah, she actually just texted me to confirm the new time. I didn't want to say anything until the plans were finalized, just in case they fell through."

"Thank you." Ophelia clapped her hands, beaming. "Now I'm going to feel even worse when I beat you," she teased.

Tate gave her a crooked smile. "Your truffles don't stand a chance against my bacon." He was happy to play along, even though the only prize he was interested in winning was Ophelia.

The chocolate factory was busier than a beehive when Tate and Ophelia arrived. Apparently, the Sweet Showdown was a bigger deal than either of them had anticipated. They followed Jasper to the center of the main room where Ms. Charming was standing.

"My finalists!" she chirped, greeting them warmly. "Ms. Watson, I am so glad to see you. How are you feeling?"

"I'm much better now. Thank you for asking," Ophelia replied with a polite smile.

"Are you two ready for the Showdown?" Ms. Charming asked. "We're going to be live-streaming it! Last year, we had almost five thousand viewers. This year, we expect even more!"

"We're finally getting our fifteen minutes of fame, O," Tate whispered, bumping his hip into hers.

"I'm so excited!" Ophelia squealed, practically bouncing up and down. Tate was thrilled to see her acting like herself again, she used to love to be the center of attention. He hated that cancer made her feel like she needed to hide, to isolate herself. Ophelia was meant to be a star.

Tate, on the other hand, couldn't care less about the spotlight. Normally, he would loathe a production like this, but seeing Ophelia so happy actually made him excited for it, too. Hopefully her recipe would end up winning. Had he known that he'd be pinned against his ex-fiancée, whom he was still very much in love with, he would have made something less impressive.

"Happy Valentine's Day, chocolate lovers!" Ms. Charming roared into a microphone as a man with a camera rotated around her. "And welcome to our fourth annual Sweet Showdown! You're in for a real treat this year because our two finalists, Mr. Tate Ripley and Ms. Ophelia Watson, brought recipes that are sure to make this our closest competition to date, and one of them will be leaving with $25,000! Who will the winner be? You'll have to stay tuned to find out!"

The camera panned to Tate and Ophelia, who were now wearing white chef's jackets embroidered with the Charming Chocolate Company logo. Tate flashed a meek smile as he lifted a hand. Ophelia, on the contrary, wore an exuberant expression while waving enthusiastically.

After greeting the viewers, the two went their separate ways. They were each assigned a kitchen station on either side of the room where they began to prepare their recipes. As they worked, Tate was pleased to catch Ophelia sneaking glances at him, almost as many times as he snuck glances at her. Every time their eyes met, they'd share a smile before returning to their respective tasks.

Thirty minutes later, after both Tate and Ophelia had finished making their recipes, it was time for the panel of judges to choose a winner. Tate watched as they tasted Ophelia's chocolate balsamic fig truffles, smiling and nodding to each other while they chewed. Then they moved on to Tate's chocolate-peanut-butter-covered bacon, looking equally enamored with his offering. When they were done eating, they huddled together to deliberate. Ophelia grabbed Tate's hand and squeezed it tight, and he could tell she was nervous. *Please let her be the winner.*

The judges released from their huddle, waved Ms. Charming over, and then passed her an envelope. Ophelia squeezed Tate's hand again.

"The judges have made a decision," Ms. Charming boomed. "Inside this envelope is the name of the Sweet Showdown winner and the recipient of $25,000!"

Ophelia squealed. "I don't even care about the money," she said just loud enough for Tate to hear. "I just really want to win the contest. I've never won anything before."

Tate's chest ached. "It doesn't matter whose name they call," he whispered. "You're the winner to me."

Ophelia looked at him, her irises dancing with gratitude, affection . . . love.

And in that moment, Tate knew that he was never going to lose her again.

"I can't believe I won!" Ophelia cried, clutching the giant check for $25,000. She was so excited. The last time she had been awarded something was a participation trophy back in middle school. All her life, she was always good enough but never the best. Today, though, she'd come out on top, even after the tumultuous start.

"You deserve it," Tate said earnestly. "I'm so happy for you, O." He wrapped his arms around her and kissed her forehead.

Ophelia leaned into his embrace. She put her ear against his chest and listened to his heartbeat, steady and strong. Maybe this is what she'd needed all along.

"Do you want to try this again?" she asked quietly. "Us?"

Tate took her face in his hands and looked her directly in the eyes. "You know I do."

"And you don't care that I'm sick? That I could . . . die? Soon?"

"I'm with you until the very end," Tate replied, unwavering. "It's you and me, O. Forever. Whether that's a day, a month, a year, or a decade."

Ophelia's eyes filled with tears. The emotion, so raw and honest. She felt his love fill every inch of her body. "So, we're really going to do this another time?"

Tate grinned, exuberant. "The first time was fun," he said, "but this second time is going to be even sweeter."

About the Author

Melissa Mastro was born and raised in New York but now calls North Carolina home. A lifelong lover of words, she has a bachelor of arts degree in English from Stony Brook University, where she graduated with honors. When she's not reading or writing, you can find her working one of her two marketing jobs or enjoying a night in with her favorite takeout and a glass of wine. Her debut novel, *One Week of July*, is releasing July 1, 2025.

You can find Melissa on:

Instagram: @authormelissamastro

You can visit her website at:

melissamastro.com

MISERY ON THE BOUNTY

Misery on the Bounty

Elizabeth Baizel

IT WAS THE PERFECT PLAN—a foolproof way to save her failing company from bankruptcy. Kim had come up with the marketing and even Gretchen had seemed to think it was a good idea. *Sea Magic Sorcery: Find your soulmate. Guaranteed.* Five days of companions and cabins with the final day ending in a spectacular Valentine's Day masque and celebration of love. Kim had promised her algorithm was perfect, and they had devised a matchmaking scheme where the promise was love and the product was a soulmate. Dorothea just prayed they were right, otherwise the little inheritance she had recently received would be lost.

Two days before they were set to sail, Dorothea was sitting in her small office going over her checklist and jotting down reminders to herself to make duplicates of the filing cabinet keys, make sure the decorations for the final dance were ready, check the weather reports and verify with the captain that it was clear enough, and check with the florist to see if there was any way to cut the cost even a little bit. Her meager savings were already so depleted, she worried the bank might shut down her account.

She had just started to go over the menus again when a short, blonde-haired woman walked in looking distressed, mascara streams distorting her otherwise perfectly applied makeup. "Is this the office for the Sea Magic Sorcery cruise?"

Dorothea stood up, walked the few steps to the door, and extended her hand. "Yes, I'm Dorothea Engles, the owner. How can I help you?" she said, wishing she had thought to have her nails done or at least painted over the chipped polish. Her hands were rough from the hard work she had put into the ship, and looking at this young lady, the contrast was staggering. She motioned for her to sit down near her cluttered desk.

"Anabelle Runtler. I was hoping you still had a few spots available on board your ship. All my plans have fallen through for Valentine's Day, and my friends were counting on me to make the arrangements."

Dorothea looked a little taken aback. Almost all the reservations she had received were from singles; that was the entire premise of the cruise. She knew of two or three friends who had signed up together in a show of solidarity, but nearly everyone else would be traveling alone.

"That depends, Miss Runtler, on how many people?"

"There are eight of us, four girls including myself and four guys. Oh, please, you have to help me. Everything everywhere is booked and has been for months. The little bed-and-breakfast down the street actually laughed at me when I asked. But it's not my fault. I had arrangements at this lovely plantation. There was going to be horseback riding, a masque and dancing, and a Southern-style barbeque. I booked it months ago. Well, I thought I booked it. It turns out it was a scam. I only found out two weeks ago. I was able to get the money back but now everything is ruined!"

She looked as if she were going to cry again. In fact, more mascara was trickling down her cheeks already. Dorothea was torn. On the one hand, it would bring her to a near full complement, and she could use the money. On the other, a spring break–esque cruise wasn't the kind of cruise she was hosting. This was a cruise to find love, not a party, and some of the other activities she had planned weren't exactly geared toward the college crowd. Anabelle and her friends might get bored and leave a bad review; she couldn't afford that. In the end, she decided to be perfectly honest and let the young lady decide.

"Miss Runtler, I'm not sure I'm what you're looking for. This is more of a singles cruise, and many of my other passengers are in their thirties or older. I'm not sure you and your friends would genuinely enjoy this type of event. It is a smaller ship, and you may find yourselves somewhat unenthused with our planned events and entertainment."

"That's perfect, though. None of us are in serious relationships, except for maybe Madysen and Devin, or maybe it's Brenten this month, it's a little hard to keep up sometimes, but we can mingle with anyone, I promise. We're just a really close group of friends most of the time. And Maddie is the sweetest girl you've ever met along with Tristanne and Allysen. I promise we won't be bored, I promise. I still have a paper to write, and so does Tristanne for English, and the guys are really good at entertaining themselves. Please let us join you."

Dorothea still wasn't sure. "Wouldn't you rather go to Florida or something like that? Isn't that where the college kids go? Or home and see your families?" She didn't want to be rude, but a bad review could kill her business, and she didn't want to risk it from this group or her already booked passengers who may not appreciate college kids aboard the boat with them.

"We can't afford the airfare or hotel prices now even if we wanted to go somewhere farther south. We're all seniors and wanted a last hurrah before we graduate."

She spoke in such a pleading tone that Dorothea had to relent despite a gut feeling telling her it was a bad idea.

"Okay." Dorothea tried to hold in the exasperated sigh she felt wanting to escape. "Okay, just scan the QR code. You'll all have to complete the profile paperwork, and I'll need the full payment by tonight. You can pay now or fill out the forms online. Don't forget to select your meal preferences."

Anabelle jumped up and hugged Dorothea tight around the neck. Dorothea could smell her perfume, something floral, not something she thought a young lady would wear, and she spotted a tiny gold cross dangling around her neck, too. She managed to disentangle herself from the enthusiastic Anabelle and gave her some paperwork that also contained the QR code.

"We set sail in two days promptly at three p.m. Make sure you and your friends are ready." She tried to sound stern to make sure the young lady knew that there would be no refunds if they missed the boat.

Anabelle smiled, agreed, and promised to have everything filled out that night and the payments made. Dorothea just hoped she had made the right choice and that they were going to be all paid up before they set sail.

Dorothea spent the rest of the afternoon going over her paperwork, meal confirmation, orders for decorations including the giant mermaid and sea creatures, alcohol quantities, a weather check, and making sure they had enough crew to manage everything, but not so much as to overdraft the bank account. With eight additional passengers, she may just be able to survive this and come out ahead.

She pulled up the website and checked her reservations. Kim had promised her that there was an automatic lockout and that no one would be able to register for the cruise after midnight tonight, ensuring they could have everything they needed on board before leaving port. Dorothea had wanted to make the cutoff earlier, but Kim had argued that they were a new company and that in today's world of instant gratification, some people didn't make plans until the last minute, so they should keep the window up as long as possible.

Kim had been right. Dorothea looked and saw that not only had Miss Runtler and her friends registered and paid in full already, but there were three more guests: a Miss Anderson, a Mr. Duckers, and a Mr. McAdams. She waited and watched until one in the morning to make sure there were no additional reservations and that the registration link had, in fact, closed. She shut off her laptop and went to bed.

The next day was filled with confirmation calls with the caterers, florist, and other vendors in the morning followed by loading the ship and making sure that each room was set up exactly as she had planned it. Gretchen joined her shortly after lunch with a fresh coffee in hand and a turkey and Swiss on rye.

"How did you know?" Dorothea asked, gratefully taking the sandwich and coffee and quickly digging in. She had even remembered the spicy mustard.

Gretchen just chuckled. "Because you're a control freak and worried sick about this. Everything is going to go great. This is going to work out perfectly, you'll see."

Dorothea shook her head. "I've already had two crew members call and cancel today. No reason given, just a text that said 'I can't do it,' and the other called and left a voicemail, 'Hey, can't come in tomorrow but be there Friday.' It's a boat! No, you won't! Also, the seashell chocolates for the rooms haven't been delivered yet, and the florist says the cost is almost double what they quoted. Something about a frost affecting the flowers! Gretchen, I don't know how I'm going to get through this!" She knew she sounded on the verge of a nervous breakdown. Because she was.

Gretchen gave another little chuckle. "Dotto. *Stop freaking out!*" she commanded as she grabbed Dorothea by the shoulders and gave her a firm shake, knocking the ballcap she was wearing off her head and onto the gangplank. "This is going to work! You will do this! This will work! Now tell me what you need me to do."

Dorothea looked at her friend and right-hand woman. Where would she be without Gretchen? She had kept her sane during this entire endeavor. From the crazy notion to turn her great-uncle's super yacht into a small, private cruise vessel to getting the business loans and working up the nerve to follow through with all of this. She had always wanted to do something like run a bed-and-breakfast or a small hotel but never had the funds. But after Great-Uncle Alfred died, she'd inherited this huge boat. She had tried to sell it, but given its age, anyone with the money to buy it wanted something new, and anyone who wanted to buy it as-is couldn't afford it. It was while she was lamenting all this to Gretchen one day over coffee that she had been struck with the idea of turning it into a boutique cruise ship.

They spent two months cleaning it up and working to create a website with a variety of cruise packages. It had been Gretchen's idea to launch a magical singles cruise after her cousin Kim had claimed she had developed an algorithm for matchmaking.

Dorothea took a deep breath and counted to ten. She met Gretchen's eyes. "We need to check all the cabins and make sure they're perfect so that when the chocolates do get here, all we have to do is put them on the pillows. Then we need to double- and triple-check the stores to make sure we have more than enough for everyone. Also, do you know anyone we can get on such short notice to help with the crew?" It always helped to talk to Gretchen. She made things make sense.

The two of them spent the rest of the afternoon making sure everything was perfect, the seashell décor tasteful and understated but with a touch of whimsy. Gretchen had even managed to rope her cousin Mark into helping out as part of the crew. Mark normally worked in hospitality during the summer months, but he was willing to sign on for a short stint. The stores were checked and triple-checked. She printed out the passengers' love profiles and locked them in the cabinet in her office on board the ship just to make sure she had them in case anything happened to her laptop. The chocolates finally arrived, and Dorothea was able to pay off the florist without dipping into her savings. Everything looked ready for the launch of the *Amore* and the first Sea Magic Sorcery cruise, a cruise to find love and your soulmate over the Valentine's Day weekend.

Dorothea had a restless night's sleep, convinced she had forgotten something. She went over checklists in her head. She had read all of the guests' profiles and learned their particular wants and needs by heart. She had memorized their faces and room numbers. She knew her crew and trusted the captain, and the weather report was positive for their first cruise down the southern coast of South Carolina and Georgia. She was as ready as she could be.

She woke up early the next day and rushed around finishing all the little incidentals that popped up when no one was looking. She managed to get her hair to cooperate into a somewhat flattering style and her makeup looked, if not perfect, at least neat and clean. She had even been able to apply a fresh coat of nail polish to freshen up her look. She was at the dock at 9 a.m. to finish everything and start checking in guests. Gretchen and Kim were waiting for her at the dock. They had agreed that Dorothea would be the face, as it was her boat, and Gretchen and Kim would help show guests to their suites. By 10:30, the rest of the crew had arrived, and Gretchen showed them their quarters and went over their duties one last time. She also made sure their uniforms, tan khakis with a navy polo, were clean and pressed.

A little after 11:30, Kim approached Dorothea nervously. "Dorothea," she started, "I think there's been a mix-up."

Dorothea looked at her. "A mix-up? What kind of mix-up?"

But before Kim could answer, Dorothea's phone went off. It was the caterer, and Dorothea asked Kim to take charge of check-in while she dealt with a potential crisis.

The day continued much in that fashion. Dorothea would just be settling a guest in, and Kim would ask to talk to her, and just before she could continue, someone else would need something. First, the caterer had mixed up one of the hors d'oeuvres and so the mini puff pastries set to go out that night for the vegans would not be vegan. They could whip up something else, but they wouldn't have time for puff pastry.

Next, Miss Anderson arrived but didn't want a port-side room. Something about not being able to sleep on the left. Gretchen had tried to explain that the ship moves and that all the rooms were nearly identical, but she just wouldn't have it and demanded to speak with the owner. Dorothea was able to calm and soothe her by switching her room with Mr. Duckers, who still hadn't arrived and wouldn't know about the change.

Then Anabelle Runtler and her group arrived, and while most of them seemed happy with the arrangements—Tristanne was over the moon about the starfish and seashells in the tiny bathroom—Madysen seemed determined not only to be unhappy but to make everyone miserable. First, she complained that her room was too small, and then she didn't like the color of her sheets and claimed her room smelled of fish from the shells. She stated she was vegan and couldn't have the chocolates, even though she hadn't checked that box on the questionnaire, and finally, her room was too far from Brenten's and she needed to switch with Devin. Dorothea walked away from Kim to help calm all of Madysen's concerns and was eventually able to satisfy the girl for the time being, having switched out the offending chocolates with a bottle of champagne and rearranged the rooming situation so that Brenten's room was next to hers.

Anabelle had tried to keep the peace with her friends, promising that once they set sail, Madysen wouldn't be any trouble. Though Dorothea doubted it, she thanked her and made sure that the rest of the party were satisfied with their rooms. Devin insinuated the change to be closer to Madysen was a vast improvement and the other two gentlemen, Rhett and Brett, twin brothers, appeared to be happy just to be there.

The last to arrive was Mr. McAdams at a very close two-thirty. He was a tall, lean man in his early fifties with gray hair and tired-looking, deep-blue eyes. He greeted Dorothea cordially and followed Gretchen to his room without any incident.

When the *Amore* set sail off the coast of Charleston, she had a nearly full complement and an almost equal ratio of men to women . . . almost. Dorothea had managed to book forty-nine of the fifty cabins and now that they were out to sea, she realized they were one female short. She prayed that Kim's computer would work its magic with odd numbers, and if not, maybe one of her guests would fall in love with the sea—or themselves and realize they didn't need a soulmate.

Dorothea shouldn't have been surprised. After all, before leaving port, Kim had tried numerous times to get her attention, but she had been so busy with guests and last-minute details she hadn't had time to stop. She wished she had made the time, or that Kim had been more persistent or had sought out Gretchen. Gretchen always knew how to fix everything. Now, thirty minutes before the sunset Mingle Magic was set to begin, a frantic Kim was in her office having a near panic attack.

"What do you mean none of the keys work?" repeated Dorothea, who felt she might join Kim in her meltdown.

"I mean, I can't open the filing cabinet with all the profiles! Namoi dropped the laptop and none of the keys you gave me work on the filing cabinet," she replied, exasperated, blowing stray strands of reddish hair out of her eyes.

Kim had questioned all of this before they left: Who still used paper files anyway? Why hadn't they backed things up on the cloud? Dorothea, while not a total Luddite, didn't trust the cloud and always wanted things where she could reach them, hence printing out the profiles.

"What about the flash drive or another backup?" Dorothea asked, hopeful she'd remembered she had saved everything to a thumb drive.

"You wouldn't let me use the cloud. I can't find any thumb drives—no one can—and unless you have a backup computer where this information is, we don't have it," Kim replied, her voice rising with her panic.

Dorothea took a deep breath, her stomach doing flip-flops. "So, what you're saying is the laptop's smashed, the flash drive is missing, there are no backup electronic files anywhere, and the nearest locksmith is miles away? The entire premise of this cruise is locked in an un-openable cabinet, and I have forty-nine people ready to find true love with no discernable way of establishing compatibility."

"That's about it," replied Kim.

"Did you try to open the filing cabinet without a key? A crowbar, screwdriver, hammer? Anything?" Dorothea asked impatiently.

"Yes!" was all Kim said through gritted teeth. She went on to explain that she had tried everything, including YouTube clips, and had even asked Jerome, one of the ship's hands who had a bit of a shady past, to pry the thing open. Nothing worked. Whatever thrift store or curb sale Dorothea had picked this thing up at, it was built to withstand anything short of a bomb.

Dorothea let out a long sigh and ran her chewed fingernails through her dark hair. She *needed* this cruise to work. She was already in too much debt. She had spent much of what she had made on the reservations to cover provisions and payroll already. What would happen if this flopped?

"Send in Gretchen," was all Dorothea said, trying to seem calm while silently screaming at the unfairness of the universe.

Kim exited, and a minute later, the tall, imposing figure of her blonde friend entered the room, perfectly quaffed in a deep-green cocktail dress and dark-red lipstick. "You have twenty minutes before the shit hits the fan," Gretchen stated matter-of-factly.

Dorothea gave Gretchen a forlorn look. "The computer has been destroyed and the profiles are locked up. I have forty-nine people out there expecting to be matched with their soulmate, and no way of doing it."

Gretchen thought for a moment, then let out a slow, unbothered sigh, as if finding someone's true love was the easiest thing in the world. "Sure you do. Match them by room numbers or eye color. You have a copy of everyone's driver's license, so check their social media pages."

"What?!" exclaimed Dorothea, astonished at Gretchen's blasé attitude toward finding someone's sweetheart, not to mention the invasion of personal privacy. "Is that even legal?"

"If they put it out there on Facebook or TikTok or Instagram, it's not illegal to check them out. In fact, most people want more likes and that kind of crap. Everyone's always taking those 'What Kind of Car Are You?' type quizzes online. Everyone is dying to be the next big influencer or viral sensation. It's all there. Just look at their profiles and match Caddies with BMWs, and Volkswagens with Teslas. They won't notice the difference," Gretchen said, pulling out her phone to offer proof.

Dorothea thought to herself, debating the ethical and possible legal ramifications. She took a deep breath. Assuming it was all out there in cyberspace just floating around like personal information flotsam, what did it hurt to look? It wasn't like she was hacking into bank accounts or anything. They'd just be scrolling through what was already there for all the world to see. Her mind whirled. It just might work, but she needed more time.

Kim came back in. "Ten minutes to showtime, boss. What do you want me to do about the Mingle?" she asked hesitantly.

Then inspiration struck.

"Do you have everyone's drink orders?" Dorothea asked Kim hurriedly.

Kim nodded and held up her tablet. Dorothea greatly regretted not taking Kim's advice to put all of this on the cloud and made a mental note to do this for the next cruise, assuming there was a next cruise.

"What about their second? They have to be on seconds by now."

Again, Kim nodded, confused. Dorothea figured a first drink would be for show, something to demonstrate to others the drinker was fun or sophisticated or daring, but a second would be more true to personal taste.

A smile spread across Dorothea's face. "Okay, ladies, here's what we're going to do."

That night, they matched people by drinks. Scotch with Appletinis, rosés with bourbon, sodas with Jägermeister, and beer with champagne. There were a few oddities, but for the most part, everyone seemed happy with their companion, and somehow there was an even number.

That bought her sixteen hours before the next mingle event and twenty-four before the next cocktails mingle. Dorothea, Kim, and Gretchen scrolled through profiles all night, matching "What Kind of Shoes Are You?" with "What Kind of Bird Are You?" They combed the "Have You Ever?" quizzes and surveys about First Jobs and To-Be-Read lists, Crazy Dance challenges, and the top 100 Things You May/May Not Have Done. "Have You Ever Skydived?" with "What's Your Favorite Color?" Sometimes they argued over whether a classical book vermillion went better with a pulp crime series blue or a fantasy raspberry. Finally, they seemed to have come up with enough for the rest of the cruise. All Dorothea could do now was cross her fingers and pray they were right.

The morning came and they hadn't received any complaints from the guests, except for Madysen, who felt her vegan eggs were cold and the vegan butter wasn't salty enough. The coffee bar had people mixing and talking, and Namoi had pulled people out onto the deck for whale watching. Dorothea was happy to see people on deck enjoying the sunshine and taking pictures together and posting them online; the large banner advertising the cruise line with a magical-looking mermaid holding a heart-shaped wand in the corner seemed to be a popular spot for a selfie. She inhaled the warm salt air deeply and let herself enjoy this fleeting moment of peace.

The brunch mingle went off without a hitch. They watched as their matches of TikTok challenges matched with Viral Dance Crazes had people putting down phones and enjoying the warm February sunshine while sipping coffee or mimosas. Even Madysen Wilcox could be seen talking and mingling with a guest, not from her party, a Mr. Cayden Cooperman, and Dorothea was happy to see that Runtler's group seemed to be having fun overall.

That night, the cruisegoers were even happier with their matches than before, and quite a few Sandals ended up in the beds of Stilettos, even when Gretchen had been sure that they would go better with Hiking Boots. They were just congratulating themselves over coffee the following morning when a defeated-looking businessman in a sharp suit showed up in Dorothea's office.

"I have no soulmate. You can't match me," he said brokenly. Kim and Gretchen looked at each other, exhausted, and excused themselves hurriedly. They had to help organize the afternoon mingles and activities and wanted to continue to enjoy the buzz of success a little longer.

"Mr. McAdams, I'm so sorry. What seems to be the problem?" Dorothea said with a smile she didn't feel. He was the only one without any kind of social media presence they could find. The only one they couldn't scroll through—and they had really looked. If he had an online profile, it was very well hidden.

"The problem is I don't have a soulmate. It's not your fault, Ms. Engles. I told my friend this was a silly idea. The likelihood of finding love on a ship with fifty people is astronomical. Do you know what the odds are of finding that kind of love, Ms. Engles? I do. I have better odds of winning the lottery or getting bitten by a shark. No, it was foolish of me to come. But my friend insisted this was what I needed."

Dorothea looked taken aback. She had expected him to be angry, or upset, maybe yell or threaten a bad review. But instead, he just seemed resigned and disappointed, like a child waking up on Christmas morning to discover Santa had brought him socks instead of a skateboard.

"Mr. McAdams, I'm sure we can find you your match. In fact, I have a special lady in mind that I think might be perfect for you," Dorothea started.

"Really? Why haven't I met her yet? Where is this mythical creature?" he asked, a tinge of hope in his voice.

"You haven't had a chance to meet yet because she has been unavoidably detained."

"We're on a ship!" he snorted. "Where has she been detained?"

Dorothea had to think on her feet. "She . . . has had a touch of seasickness. Though I believe she'll be fully recovered soon. Hopefully by tomorrow."

He seemed to brighten, but only for a moment before he adjusted his face to a sterner, businesslike manner. "Well, please make sure she's not like the last one. I like a woman who can appreciate good beer and enjoys a hamburger with real beef, not some bean concoction. Someone with meat on her bones. Some of these stick girls look like they'll fall over in a strong wind."

Dorothea winced at his referring to the women on the cruise as *girls*, a pet peeve of hers. "Anything else?" she said, mentally going through eligible bachelorettes in her head.

"My perfect mate would enjoy fishing, be a good cook, make beautiful pies, and follow the Mets."

"Syracuse or NYC?" she replied automatically, a bit bolstered by the question. She had followed baseball since she was ten years old.

He looked impressed. "I prefer Syracuse. Fewer crowds, more heart. I look forward to tomorrow and your unicorn."

She smiled approvingly and silently agreed.

Night three passed with a small storm and lightning matching the witchy lighting designed to be reminiscent of an underwater sea cave, setting a slightly darker tone with louder music that encouraged the guests to get closer to talk. Namoi called out matches based on books, challenges completed, and TV show characters the guests most resembled. It was a massive success for the guests if posts online and a recent review was any way to judge. A great success for all except for Mr. McAdams.

The young lady matched with him that night, Miss Rebeccah Johnstone, who was a strict teetotaler and didn't know which sport the Mets were associated with. He was not impressed with her, nor was Miss Johnstone with him. Before the end of the second drink, she had wandered off to spend the rest of the evening with Mr. Duckers, the gentleman she had been matched with the evening before. Mr. McAdams finished his beer and retired to his room early.

Where am I going to find his match? Dorothea thought to herself. If she were to stereotype, he presented himself like a man who loved nothing better than to write damning reviews based on the slightest inconvenience in service, and she couldn't risk a single bad review. But where could she come up with another woman?

Inspiration struck, and for the brunch on the fourth day, Dorothea had convinced Kim to play the part of Ms. Right. "It's one date," she pleaded. "I can't afford bad reviews. You don't have to fall in love with him. You just have to have him not hate you."

Kim reluctantly agreed. They both hoped he hadn't gotten a good look at her before she had left the office the other day so she could play the part of the mystery woman convincingly. It was a disaster. Kim may have been the only female McAdams hadn't remembered seeing, but her strict veganism and dry drinking habits made for a miserable afternoon for them both. She tried to steer the conversations to popular television or the newest movies coming out, but he only looked at her blankly. He talked about his love of smoking his own meats and his latest hunting trip in Montana, which had Kim nearly sick to her stomach. She tried to power through the date, but thankfully she was able to excuse herself pleading illness, and since that had been the cause of her initial absence, Mr. McAdams didn't question her.

McAdams was back in Dorothea's office before dinner, bemoaning the blight of the loveless. "Is it so hard to find a woman who likes good beer and ballgames? You had said love was guaranteed! Is it so hard to find that one special someone who enjoys comics over trash TV? This is hopeless. I know you tried, Ms. Engles, but love is never a guarantee."

"DC, Marvel, or Indie?" she interjected.

"I-I'm sorry?" he stuttered, a little stunned at the question.

"Do you prefer DC, Marvel, or Independents?" she asked again.

"Silver Age DC. Or New—" he started.

"New Era Indie or Marvel!" she finished.

His eyebrow raised. "Alan Moore or Frank Miller?"

"Unfair," she replied. "You can't compare such different master storytellers."

He nodded, a slight smile forming on his lips. Clearly, she had passed some sort of test he used to judge comic connoisseurs. They talked comics for another hour before he left, feeling a little better about the upcoming evening.

That evening was the fourth night, the night before the feast, and the last of the mingles. Most of the guests had broken off into couples already, but a few were still looking into their options. Anabelle Runtler had coupled with the same Brenten who Madysen had been so eager to be close to. But

Madysen seemed happy with her conquest of Cayden. In fact, all the guests seemed happy except for Mr. McAdams. Dorothea threw on her nicest jeans and a Nirvana T-shirt and joined the mingle.

"I'm sorry, Mr. McAdams, I had tried to match you with someone for this evening, but she wasn't able to make it," she lied. There was no one to match him with. She had thought about Gretchen or Namoi, but after the disaster with Kim, she didn't want to risk another disappointment.

He nodded glumly. "Ms. Engles, I understand. Please don't worry, I won't write a bad review. It's not your fault I am fated to be lonely. I missed my chance years ago with a young lady back in college."

"Really?" she asked, intrigued, and grateful he didn't seem to want to tear down her new business. "Why don't you tell me a bit about her?"

He sighed and went a little misty-eyed, remembering his youth and a lost love. "We were young and stupid in love. We met in chemistry class. She said she wanted to be a teacher, get married, have four kids, travel, and so many things. I was majoring in business and had accidentally signed up for the class by transposing some numbers. But it was a lucky accident. She tutored me, and I got an A. At the end of the semester, I asked her out. By the end of our sophomore year, we were engaged. But graduation came around and I wanted to go on for my MBA, and she wanted to settle down. We started fighting more, I wasn't sure about kids, and that was something she desperately wanted before she was thirty. In the end, we split up. She's married now and her oldest just started college a year ago, I think."

"And you?" Dorothea asked.

"I made a lot of money. I traveled the world. I dated off and on, nothing really serious. I spoil my nieces and nephews, I have everything I could want, then two years ago, I had a heart attack."

Dorothea gasped. He looked too healthy to have had a heart attack.

"It was minor, barely even counts, really. But it got me thinking. I have everything. Money, family, and the ability to go wherever I want, whenever I want. But at the end of the day, I come home to Snickers—that's my dog—and an empty house. There's no one there. When I travel, there's no one in the picture with me, and I would like that to change. So, my friends saw this online and told me to try it. And here I am."

As tragic tales went, his was barely on the pity meter; he had chosen his life, and for the most part, it had turned out remarkably well, if lonely. He had friends and family who cared for him, a good job, and a stable life. He had so much more than so many others, but he was lonely. Dorothea felt for this sad, lonely man who loved the same comics and teams as she.

"Do you have a picture of Snickers?" she asked.

He pulled out his phone and started to scroll through photos. There was the pup, a portly basset-poodle mix of some kind with a goofy grin and soulful eyes. He showed her pictures of his nieces and nephews. The baseball game where his nephew Darrin had hit his first home run, and a clip of his niece Fiona dancing at a recital. There were pictures of his latest vacation, his hunting trip to Montana where he had successfully got two deer with his friend Adam.

"And what about you, Miss Dorothea Engles, what made you open this type of floating bed-and-breakfast?" he asked.

"It's Dotto. At least, that's what my friends call me. Dorothea was my grandmother," she said with a smile.

He smiled back the first real smile she had seen, the kind that comes from within and lights up your whole face. She liked his smile.

"I inherited the boat from my Great Uncle Alfred, though no one is sure how he got it. I couldn't sell it, so I had to do something with it. I had always wanted to have a bed-and-breakfast, but this is better. It floats on the water, and I can always decide to move to another location if I want."

He nodded.

"You've met Gretchen; she's been my best friend since forever, and she's the one who convinced me to do this. So here we are, floating on the ocean breathing in fresh sea air, enjoying life, and trying to find love." She continued: "I guess I'm like you in that respect. I have always been so busy working or taking care of my parents, or my siblings, or their children. I never really went looking to see what was out there for me. But unlike you, I don't have a Snickers. I have a Leo, my cat. Well, sort of my cat. He's more like the neighborhood cat. He just likes my apartment best, I think."

"Do you have a picture of this community cat?" he asked, taking a real interest in his amiable companion.

She dutifully pulled out her phone, and they spent the rest of the night looking at each other's pictures and talking about their families and friends. At a quarter past eleven, Gretchen interrupted them to inform Dorothea that there had been an incident in the kitchen that needed to be addressed.

"I had fun talking to you, Dotto," Mr. McAdams said cheerfully.

"I had a good time, too, Mr. McAdams," she replied with genuine warmth in her smile.

"My friends call me Sean," he replied.

"I had fun, Sean," she said before walking away with Gretchen.

Dorothea was worried that something had happened to some of the food for the feast the next day. "Is everything all right?" she asked Gretchen as they approached the kitchen. "They didn't mix up any more of the vegan items or the gluten-free foods, did they?"

Gretchen wore a look that was half somber and half mischievous. "No, the food is perfectly fine. No, the problem in the kitchen is a bit more . . . messy."

"Messy? I can't handle messy. What do you mean *messy*? What is it?"

They were almost to the kitchen at this point, and Dorothea could hear giggling, laughing, and several shrieks. She opened the door, scared of what she might find. There, sitting on the counter, was a very intoxicated Madysen drinking champagne straight out of the bottle and half covered in chocolate. On a chair beside her was Cayden Cooperman, painting her with chocolate while drinking from his own bottle of champagne. The two of them were giggling at their own jokes, taking turns painting each other with chocolate, licking it off, and then shrieking with laughter before repeating the process. It would have been sweet if Dorothea wasn't going to have to clean up the mess.

Gretchen giggled behind her. "It's like two children making mud pies."

Dorothea didn't think it was funny. "It's two adult children making a mess, and that's not even vegan chocolate." She was annoyed that, after everything, Madysen wasn't even using the vegan chocolate she insisted on.

"What do you want to do?" Gretchen asked.

"I'm going to ask them to go back to their rooms, nicely, of course. And then I'm going to clean up this mess before I go to bed." She was too tired for all this.

Gretchen and Dorothea entered the room, and Cayden and Madysen looked up and froze for a moment. Cayden had chocolate on his hands, and it slipped from his fingers before falling to the floor with a *plop*. The sound made both of them burst out into more giggles.

"Madysen and Cayden, while I am delighted to see you two so happy, this is a kitchen, and that is a food-prep area."

"Yup and 'm preppin' the chocolate for dessert," interjected Cayden, sending the two young people into more fits of drunken giggles.

"Yes, I can see that, and you've done a very good job, I might add," Dorothea said, trying not to lose her cool. For all she knew, they were filming this and planning to upload it later as part of some new trend she wasn't aware of. "But since neither of you are wearing gloves, I am going to have to ask you to leave and maybe continue this food prep in your room. You can, of course, take the champagne with you, with my compliments." She wanted to remain the picture of a gracious host just in case the cameras were rolling.

Madysen and Cayden looked a little confused, but Gretchen came up behind them and helped Cayden to his feet before assisting Madysen down off the counter. "I can help you find your rooms if you need," offered Gretchen with a grin, finding the whole situation rather amusing.

They both giggled and grabbed their bottles before leaving the kitchen. Dorothea sighed, wondering if she had ever been that young and carefree. Maybe, but those days were long gone.

"Gretchen, can you return Miss Madysen's shoes to her? Just leave them outside her door for her to find in the morning, if you don't mind. I want to get started cleaning up this mess."

Gretchen nodded. "Let me help. It's late, and tomorrow is the feast, which will be a lot of work."

Dorothea wanted to argue, but she was too tired, and Gretchen had a point. Tomorrow was the grand finale, and she had an idea to make it extra special. "Okay, please get the mop."

The two worked until almost three in the morning cleaning the mess and sterilizing the area after the two lovebirds had flown away to their nests. Dorothea wasn't quite done, though. She sent Gretchen off to bed but stayed behind to finish up one last thing. It was almost dawn when she had finished and finally returned to her room to catch a bit of sleep before the grand finale.

Kim approached Dorothea's bed a few hours later. "Dotto, Dotto. It's almost nine and you told us we had to get started by ten if everything was going to be ready in time."

Dorothea jumped awake. It was Valentine's Day, and they had to start setting up for the magical sea masque and feast. It had been Gretchen's idea to hold a masque at the end. It seemed a little old-fashioned but also new in an old way. They had advertised that there would be a masked dance and that would end with the feast and that everyone could bring a costume if they wanted, but that masks would be available, as well.

There were no other activities planned for the day since everyone on the crew had to help set up. Dorothea saw Cayden and Madysen up on the deck around one in the afternoon snuggled in a lounge chair, though both avoided direct eye contact with her. Dorothea smiled to herself at that.

By five in the evening, everything was ready, and the dance was scheduled to start at six. To save money, they had planned a DJ, but he too had canceled before leaving shore. Luckily, Gretchen's cousin Mark, who had joined the crew last-minute, had also proved to be a very good DJ throughout the week, providing a balancing tone for the mingles and meals for the evenings. For the masque, he had even shown Dorothea the playlist he had compiled, and it was just the right mix of fast and slow, spanning several decades. She was impressed and made a note to ask him if he'd like to place his business cards on a table before they disembarked.

She got back to her room in time to take a quick shower and rummage through the clothes she'd brought. She settled on a classic little black dress that she didn't remember packing but found at the bottom of her suitcase. She did her hair up simply, but for once, it decided it would cooperate, and she applied a little makeup to complete the look. She tied a green-and-blue-sequined mask that looked a little like fish scales loosely around her face before heading up the stairs to the party.

Mark was setting up and adjusting the speakers he had rearranged as well as some of their lighting. They had decorated the space to give the feeling of being in an underwater castle and had gratefully avoided looking like a tacky Under the Sea prom. Several of the support crew were stationed throughout with trays of canapes and hors d'oeuvres for everyone, and some tables had been set up on deck and under the stars for dinner later in the evening for those who were less bothered by the cooler February night air.

The guests started to arrive all in couples, and all seemed to be very happy. Even Miss Anderson had found someone to put a smile on her face. Mark started the music and people milled around, dancing and enjoying the evening. Lights glimmered and reflected off the decorations, giving the room a wave-like feeling. Gretchen came up to Dorothea. "You look great. Where did you get the dress?" she asked, appraising Dorothea's appearance.

"I found it at the bottom of my suitcase. I don't even remember packing it, but it works, don't you think?" Gretchen nodded and then walked over to Anabelle and Brenten in matching clownfish-inspired masks to make sure they were having a good time.

Dorothea knew she should be doing the same, but she kept looking for Mr. McAdams—Sean, she corrected herself. It was a small enough space, but she hadn't seen him yet. She moved about, greeting people in colorful masks and receiving congratulations on a job well done and sincere appreciation for all her hard work. Even Madysen didn't have one negative thing to say;

instead, she thanked Dorothea for giving her the opportunity to meet Cayden before they returned to the dance floor.

Finally, Dorothea saw Sean standing in a corner drinking a beer and watching all the happy couples. She retreated downstairs to retrieve something from the kitchen before coming back and sidling up next to him at the bar.

"I believe you've been waiting for me."

A broad smile cracked his face, followed by a chortle. "Was I now?"

"The only thing missing on your list is I don't make beautiful pies," she said honestly before handing him a box with a lumpy cherry pie in it. The filling leaked out the sides and the slits she had cut, and the crust was crumbling at the edges while the center seemed to be collapsing in on itself.

He laughed and broke off a piece. It was mostly a congealed, soupy, crumbling mess, which only made him laugh harder. He tried a bite. "You're right. You don't make pies."

"I said I don't make *beautiful* pies," she countered.

He broke off another piece and offered it to her, but she shook her head. "Okay, okay, I don't make pies, but I *can* cook."

They spent the night talking, laughing, and dancing. At dawn, as the ship came into port, he bent down and kissed her—the first of many.

Matches made. Happiness guaranteed.

About the Author

Elizabeth Baizel is an excited new writer from upstate New York. She enjoys creating stories in her head while running and hoping they will still be there when she gets back to her coffee. She lives in the Adirondacks, where she loves the mountains (unless they are at Mile 10 of any race) and the outdoors, as well as her career, her family, and her dog, Watson.

You can find Elizabeth on:

Instagram: @elizabethbaizelwriter

MJ'S JERSEY

MJ's Jersey

Mitchell S. Elrick

FEBRUARY 14, 1990. THE CHICAGO Bulls traveled south to face off against the Orlando Magic. Prior to the game, Michael Jordan's jersey was stolen. The cause is up for speculation. Some say it was a custodian. Some say it was rival players. Nothing has been confirmed. Even though the Bulls lost, MJ poured in 47 points.

This is how that happened.

"Jesus Christ, no one knows how to drive down here." Tate's annoyance fills the car as he and Sarah inch their way down the Orlando freeway.

She raises her eyebrows in response to his tone. "It's no worse than it was back in Denver," Sarah says, defending her hometown.

As a firefighter back in Colorado, Tate loved his job; he was a real-life hero. He'd met Sarah in college. He'd already been part of the Denver Fire Department for a couple years then, but Sarah had been a junior at Denver University. They met like most young people in the 1980s—at a party. Normally, Tate wasn't a big partier, but he'd just finished a seventy-two-hour shift up the mountain and one of his mates had mentioned free beer and food. So he'd showered, fluffed his mullet, threw on his favorite jean jacket, and was out the door.

He'd just finished his second beer when he found the tasty treats. With Rick Astley blaring from the Sony speakers, Tate decided to try his first cake ball. The first one was nothing short of ecstasy. Red velvet with a burst of cream cheese filling. Somehow, the second one was better. When he'd clutched the third, a voice next to him said, "I'm glad you like them."

With his mouth full of cake and hands full of beers, Tate had turned and damn near choked. Just seeing her forced a smile. He cupped the cake ball in his cheek, causing cream cheese to somewhat seep through his lips. She'd laughed and he almost fainted.

"You look like Nellie Fox," she said.

"Who's that?" Tate responded, trying not to lose more cake ball as he spoke.

"You don't know who Nellie Fox is? Next thing you're going to tell me is you're a Cubs fan. You're not a Cubs fan, are you?"

The conversation started with sports, but eventually Sarah spent the rest of the night telling him she was studying to be a teacher and wanted to open up her own bake shop. Cookies, cakes, cake balls, everything! She spoke like a dreamer, and he listened like someone falling in love. That's how it had started back in Colorado.

But, a few years, a college degree, and a teaching job later, when the person Tate loved more than anything else in the world said she missed her family and wanted to move back to Florida, he didn't hesitate. All the stuff was boxed. Taped shut. In the truck. Seatbelts latched. Off they went.

Tate had a few offers to continue his career, but it wouldn't be the same as it was back home. So, he was offered and took a facilities manager position at one of the middle schools just outside Orlando. He'd always been a Mr. Fix It at the station in Denver. And, while waiting for his interview, he'd fixed the fire alarm in the secretary's office, very much winning Dorris's approval. To top it all off, Sarah got a job at an elementary school right across the street. Third grade.

Tate had admitted he didn't hate the slight pay raise and happy girlfriend, but . . . he missed the adrenaline rush of the Colorado fires. That's why he's been so irritable lately. He misses home. That's what Sarah thinks, at least. She can understand that. Hell, she told him she missed her hometown almost two years ago and he moved across the damn country for her. So the least she could do now was something nice for him. And what better night than this one?

After all, it *is* Valentine's Day. But even with their planned date, doing something she knew *he* wanted to, he still seemed to be on edge. Couldn't he just enjoy tonight? They were going to see his favorite basketball player (and pretty much everyone else's in the eighties and nineties) in the world: Michael Jordan. MJ.

Sarah didn't know much about basketball, and really, she couldn't care less. She was raised as a baseball kid. No, she didn't play softball. Never one to play. She just loved to watch baseball—infatuated by all the stats and numbers involved. Plus, it didn't hurt that the person she'd loved most (at the time), loved the game more than life itself, loved the Chicago White Sox, to be specific. Florida didn't have a pro team, at least when Sarah's grandpa was growing up. And in his day, it was either be a stuck-up Cubs fan, or be a hardworking, nose-to-the-grindstone White Sox fan. The choice was simple for a poor kid in Orlando in the 1950s. So, he and his friends did what everyone else did: pretended they were Nellie Fox. When they'd play in the field behind the school, every single one of them wanted to play second base, which is where Nellie played. They'd wear their hats just like Nellie. They'd bat lefthanded, choked up as much as could be, just like Nellie. In their jaws, they'd stick the biggest "chaw" (bubble gum) they could, just like Nellie. Stories of this nature and more swirled around Sarah's youth as Grandpa told each tale with as much vigor as the last. The only time Sarah saw her grandpa without his brownie-stained White Sox T-shirt and his White Sox hat was at Christmas. At Christmas, Grandpa would actually dress up. By dressing up, that meant he'd wear his White Sox polo (that also had brownie stains). And of course, the collar was smashed and uneven—but he didn't care. Nellie wouldn't have, so why should he?

Growing up in central Florida never stopped Sarah and her grandpa from sitting down to watch games. He kept his own scorebook for every game and paid for extra cable services to "watch my damn Sox!" as he would so eloquently put it. He was the first in the family to get a color TV just so he could "feel like he was at the park." Never missed a single pitch. In fact, Sarah has core memories of Grandpa calling the announcers "dipshit idiots" whenever they were wrong about the pitch count or that two innings ago the third baseman flew out to center, or something else that wasn't really a big deal. But it was a big deal. After all, IT'S THE DAMN SOX.

When she turned ten, Grandpa gave Sarah her first scorebook. And that might have been the first time she fell in love. The scorebook tracked everything. It had all the necessary information you needed to keep track of a good game, much like a good recipe has all the necessary information needed to keep track of a masterpiece. Every number counted for something. Every amount amounted to something. So, every summer from then on, Sarah made a trip to Grandpa's to watch their damn Sox, always showing up with a pan of treats. Something she'd concocted the day before. Something Grandpa always said he'd only have "one" of, but by the fifth inning, half the pan was bare.

Oftentimes they'd hardly talk. They'd sit, eat, watch, and keep score, every so often checking each other's work. These were some of the best times of Sarah's life.

Though she didn't understand how anyone could really like any sport other than baseball, Sarah could definitely understand people and their love for sports. Because it's not the sport that's loved. It's never the damn sport. The sport is merely the binder.

Which is why Sarah splurged on these tickets. Michael Jordan only came to Orlando once a year. It was a little pricey, yeah. But it was all worth it when Tate wrangled her in for a hug that said more than words could.

And here we are. The couple finally squeezes into their parking space and speedwalk to Amway arena.

Sarah's first worry is about crushing them. Smashing them if she hurries too much. And that can't happen. Not her cake balls. Not tonight. Not on Valentine's Day. They're Tate's favorite—red velvet with cream cheese. Not her best batch, but Tate would love them all the same. He always does. She figures they'll be a sweet treat before the game starts. A nostalgic staple of their love.

The couple makes their way through the lines and crowds, their perforated tickets clutched in their hands. When they finally make it to their seats, Sarah notices something.

"Where is everyone?" she asks.

"We still have an hour before the game starts," Tate says. "Some of the players will be coming out to shoot for warmups."

Sarah considers this, and immediately, an idea, THE BEST idea, pops into her head. "I'm going to get a soda and use the bathroom," she says to her boyfriend. "Want anything?"

"No, thanks," Tate says, looking at his watch. "Hurry though. The pregame stuff is pretty cool! I don't want you to miss it!"

Sarah's a little annoyed at Tate's tone, rushing her everywhere. But this is his thing, and even though she thinks it's absolutely ridiculous that grown men idolize other grown men who chase each other with an orange ball, trying to put it through a hoop, she tries to keep a positive attitude. And besides, Sarah now has a mission. She doesn't really want a soda, and she used the bathroom before they left.

As she and Tate were walking into the arena, she did see a ton of people wearing jerseys. More so, she'd noticed Tate noticing them. And she couldn't help but think how cute her boyfriend would look in his very own Michael Jordan jersey. Even better, she saw a sales shop as they were walking in. They must have jerseys there—maybe scorebooks, as well? Most baseball shops had scorebooks. Surely basketball shops had them, too. So, out the row, up the aisle, and into the abyss of the sports arena she goes.

With each step she takes, more and more people are milling through the vending area of the arena. She's seen more than a handful of people with a funnel cake, everyone is carrying a Pepsi logo'd cup, and there's already a line for the women's room. Every thirty or so steps, there's a vendor trying to sell, "Programs! Get your programs for tonight's game! Watch your Magic beat up on Michael Jordan and the Bulls! Get your program!"

One of the vendors tries to shove a program at her. "Program, only two bucks! Great souvenir!" Sarah asks if the program contains a scorebook.

The man's mustache moves when he talks. "A scorebook?"

"Yes. A scorebook," Sarah says, not sure how else to describe a noun that is self-describing.

"A scorebook?" the man repeats.

"Yes," She's starting to get annoyed.

"No. I have programs. I just said that. Two dollars. It's a great deal. Great souvenir."

Sarah's shoulders drop along with her hope. "Yes. I'm sor—" Sarah begins to apologize and walk away. Clearly, the answer is no.

The man snorts. "Why would a program have a scorebook? It's a program, not a scorebook."

"I'm sor—" She tries to apologize again with another step backward.

The man's mustache turns angry. "Are you making fun of me? Is that what you're doing here? Programs don't have scorebooks. Why would you need a scorebook if the score is on the scoreboard?"

"You're right, I'm sorry," Sarah finally gets out her entire apology before being a full three steps away, washing into the crowd.

This is why she sticks to baseball.

Though the arena is busier, she still has her bearings and can see the outline of the shop.

She's solicited by a couple more program-not-scorebook sellers and a few beer salesmen, but finally makes her way to the store. The sign at the top in black and blue lettering says *Orlando Magic Team Shop*.

Right away, she sees the jerseys. A whole wall of them. The only problem is they are all black and blue and say *Magic*. Sarah may not know much about basketball, but even she knows Michael Jordan plays for the Chicago Bulls. But still. She browses a little while longer before giving up in the sea of black and blue and of course there isn't a single scorebook to be found. Which isn't a big deal, but it would have been nice to have something to do during the game. Finally, after more than a few minutes searching, Sarah asks an attendant. He looks like he could be in high school, but Sarah is desperate and she doesn't exactly have a ton of time.

"Excuse me, where are the Michael Jordan jerseys?"

The attendant looks at Sarah like she just asked if the programs had scorebooks inside them. He waves down an older, but only *slightly* older, attendant and leans to his friend. "Hey, where do we keep the MJ jerseys?"

At first, the older attendant seems to be confused, but then a smile creeps across his face like he's just had a revelation. "Oh, the MJ jerseys? Yes, we keep those on the main floor in our visitors' merchandise shop!"

"What about scorebooks?" Sarah asks.

"Scorebooks?" the first attendant asks back to Sarah as if he didn't hear her correctly.

"Yes, scorebooks." Sarah says flatly.

The two attendants look at each other. The one that asked the first question looks back at Sarah. "Like the books you keep score in?"

"That would be the one." *Christ, here we go again.*

"Like players' names, their position, their number, and stuff like that?" the high schooler asks, sounding like he knows exactly where this might be.

"Yes," Sarah says with a smile.

The kid keeps going. "The ones with the number of fouls, number of points and their differentiations, number of total points, number of points by quarter, number of timeouts, and possession?"

Sarah was impressed by the high schooler's ability to ramble all of that off, and honestly, it sounded exciting. All that to keep track of? Awesome!

"Yes!" Sarah all but shouts in excitement.

"No, I'm sorry, we don't have those," the high schooler says flatly.

Sarah takes a deep breath and closes her eyes. "Okay, w—"

"Oh," the younger of the high schooler's interrupts. "I do have one idea," Sarah's hopes rise again.

"Have you asked a program seller?"

Sarah walks past the *Restricted Personnel Only (RPO)* sign. The attendant told her this would happen. Apparently, the usual visitor merchandise shop was being renovated so the temporary shop was set up on the main floor. "Only a five-minute walk if you hurry!" the attendant said as he sent her on a path of twists and turns. At every turn, Sarah sees fewer and fewer people, until, eventually, she is on her own.

Map-learning is a third-grade standard in the state of Florida, and Sarah thought of herself as an expert. How hard could this be? In the eighth minute of her adventure, she begins to get nervous. Passing the RPO sign a few minutes ago, more than twice Sarah is certain she is exactly where the attendant said the store would be. And more than twice, she comes up empty. She followed the directions of the attendant, and she was definitely hustling. It takes a minute before Sarah begins to ponder the possibility that she was duped by a couple of assholes.

Upset with her results, she decides to rush back to her seats. To her Valentine. To Tate. She pushes on the brass handle of one of the doors she came through, but there's a problem. It's locked. She pushes a couple more times, each time harder than the last. It doesn't budge. Not too concerned yet, she heads down a hallway in search of another set of stairs, making many turns in the process. It doesn't take more than two minutes for Sarah to feel like a mouse trapped in a maze.

Tonight was supposed to be special for Tate. Cake balls and the jersey of his favorite player. And now, he's not going to get either. She looks down at her watch. Gone more than twenty minutes. Now it hits her. Fear. She doesn't know how to get back. She knows eventually she will. Of course she will. But, right now, all she can think about is Tate. All he should have to worry about is enjoying the game and those pregames or whatever he called them. But instead, he's probably wondering where his daft girlfriend is. Sarah's not scared; she's mad at herself. It all becomes too much. With her face in her hands, the tears begin to fall as Sarah stands in the middle of the hallway area.

When she tells this story years later, Sarah isn't exactly sure how many seconds she stands there before she gets a tap on her shoulder and hears a man's voice.

"Ma'am. Are you okay?"

Sarah wipes her face as she turns and immediately sees buttons and a tie. Being five-foot-seven, Sarah is tall for a woman, but this man is closer to being a giant than an actual man. She looks up and sees his tufts of graying hair, glasses, fluffy mustache, and soft face. He wasn't old-old. But definitely old enough to be her dad. And tall. Dear god, did she mention he was tall?

"Are you okay?" the man asks again.

Sarah begins to respond, "I-I," but she can't. She doesn't know what to say.

How does she say she was duped by a couple of teenagers while en route for a Michael Jordan jersey that clearly isn't sold here, and now she doesn't know how to get back to her seat? How do you say that? Especially to someone who could pass as Gandalf the Grey.

This man, whomever he is, must be someone important. Probably with security. He looks like he could run security for President Bush—he's that big, that official. He's probably going to call the cops. That's what he should do. That's what Sarah would do if some crazy person was crying hysterically on the playground while her students were trying to enjoy recess. She feels the cake balls in her purse and realizes just how much more ridiculous she will seem to the cops when they inevitably search her. So, in the end, she decides on the truth.

"I'm lost."

"Ha!" the man laughs, jovially. "Easy to do around here! Maybe I can help! I work here. Come with me!"

As she follows, the man's calming voice brings a Zen to Sarah she didn't know existed. She wonders if he makes everyone feel like that. He leads her to a room that looks more like a small jazz lounge than anything. Dark lighting and light music from above. At the end of the room is a bar with a bartender—bow tie and all. There are scattered seats with a few people in suits. Mostly men, a couple women. In another section is a group of women, most of them dressed scantily in Chicago Bulls cloth. The man leads Sarah to the bar and pulls out a seat.

"Phil! How are you!" The bartender reaches out and shakes hands with the tall man and nods at Sarah. "What can I get you two to drink?"

"Just a couple waters. Thanks, Dave," Phil says before turning to Sarah.

"What brings you here tonight?" Phil asks Sarah. "Are you a big Magic fan?"

Sarah wipes her face, trying to salvage the unsalvageable. "No, not exactly. I don't even like basketball."

Phil does one of those old-man laughs. The kind that lets you know he's not laughing at you, but more so at life. He doesn't even ask why. "Yeah, fair. So how'd you get down here?"

Sarah goes on to tell Phil all about Tate and how much she loves him and how much he loves Michael Jordan and how she got these tickets and how she made the cake balls from the night they met and how he always tells her to follow her dreams and how she loves Tate so much (did she mention that?) and she wanted to get him a jersey and how she got lost and then lost, again. She said *and* a lot.

In the end, after all that, Phil says, "Cake balls? Can't say I've ever had one."

At this, Sarah reaches into her purse and pulls one out and hands it to Phil. Someone might as well enjoy them before they melt. As he pops the whole thing into his mouth, Phil's eyes roll back.

"Oh my goodness. That is quite possibly the best thing I've ever tasted. Absolutely blissful."

Phil's moment of heaven is cut short by a loud sound.

"Dave! Need my oranges!" a voice boasts from the back of the room.

"Pip!" Phil smiles at the man demanding oranges.

The bartender fetches a couple of oranges for a tall man in a suit while Phil and the man embrace. Sarah decides this must be another security guard, this Pip guy. He's a lot younger. Even under his suit, you can tell he's in incredible shape. Must have to be well-conditioned to protect those ball player guys. After all, Tate said one of them makes more than $4 million a year now. Can't imagine that much money! In only one year!

Phil motions to Sarah. "Pip, this is Sarah." Sarah loses her hand in Pip's humongous but kind hand. Phil continues, prying Pip. "You gotta try these cake balls. It's like a bite of bliss!"

Sarah blushes and pulls one out of her bag. *Bite of bliss.* She likes the way that sounds.

"I wish, but I can't," Pip says, taking the cake ball anyway. "My girl's got me on a diet. But I'll take it to Mike. He loves this shit."

Phil, Pip, and Mike.

Wait, he couldn't mean Mike as in THE Mike, right? Like, Michael JORDAN?! Of course not. There are millions of Mikes all over the world. Probably hundreds of them here tonight!

Sarah's silly, whimsical thought is cut short when Pip extends his hand and says, "It was nice to meet you."

And just like that, with his orange slices, Scottie Pippen walks off to deliver one of Sarah's cake balls to Michael Jordan while Phil Jackson sits across from Sarah. If only Tate could see her now.

Sarah looks at her watch. The security guards have been nice and the water has been refreshing, but she needs to get back to Tate. As if reading her thoughts, Phil says, "Well, we better get ya back. But hold tight for a minute."

Phil gets up and walks out of the lounge as if he has no plans to return. Sarah only checks her watch ten times. But, within a couple minutes, Phil is back with a black plastic bag.

"Let's get you back to your date."

Sarah and Phil walk down a hallway, up a random staircase, out another hallway, and make a bunch of turns before Phil stops and points. "Just go up those stairs and you'll be right outside your gate. Oh, and don't forget this." Phil hands her the black bag.

Sarah leans over and peaks in. The red mesh with the stitched letters "OR" could be seen. She can't believe it. Is this real? How did he find a Michael Jordan jersey? She grabs the jersey and begins to take it out, but Phil puts his hand over hers. "No, just wait until you give it to Tate."

She asks the only logical thing she can think of. "How did you . . . how did you get this?"

Phil simply shrugs and says, "Michael Jordan gave it to me."

Sarah scoffs and rolls her eyes. Phil is so silly.

Phil smiles. "It's an extra one we had laying around the merchandise closet."

Sarah begins to take out her wallet, but it's Phil's turn to scoff. He's not as good at it as she is. "After those cake balls, how dare you try to pay me. Just do me a favor and get that business going. It'll be big. At the very least, you'll have a customer every time I'm in town."

"How long have you been doing security for the team?" Sarah asks.

Phil gets a weird look on his face, "Security?"

Sarah starts to panic. He'd said he was part of security. Right? He had to have said that.

Right?

"Yeah," Sarah says, a wave of embarrassment begins to wash over her. "You're not part of security?"

"Oh, no, not exactly." Phil begins to do another Phil laugh.

"Then what do you do?"

"Not much!" Phil laughs at his own joke, then continues. "I just help out here and there. Definitely not as important as security. That's for sure."

Sarah's not sure what to say to that so she just says, "Well, thanks. For, well, everything. You really are good at helping. You're like a Zen Master or something." She chuckles at her joke.

"It was nice to meet you, Sarah."

And just like that, Phil Jackson walks back downstairs to get his Chicago Bulls ready to face off against the Orlando Magic, savoring one last cake ball from Sarah as he does so.

By the time Sarah gets back to her aisle, she has to awkwardly scoot past people before she finally makes it to her seat.

"You're back!" Tate says, hugging Sarah tighter than normal. She thought he'd be mad, and he'd have every right to be, but he seems to be relieved more than anything.

"Yes, sorry. I got you something." Sarah pulls the Michael Jordan jersey out of the bag and hands it to Tate.

His jaw is on the floor. He can't believe it. Elated, he takes off his jean jacket and puts on his new Michael Jordan jersey. The first thing Sarah notices is that it's way too big. Like, way too big. Like, so big it would only fit someone that's six feet, six inches tall. Or so big it would only fit someone who plays shooting guard for the Chicago Bulls.

Tate doesn't ask why it's too big, or how she got one that's incredibly authentic. Almost like the ones the actual players wear. He doesn't care, though, how she got it. He loves it. He also doesn't ask how she got a Michael Jordan jersey at an Orlando Magic arena. Because again, he doesn't care. He loves it. And, besides, his mind is elsewhere. It has been for weeks.

As Tate hugs his girlfriend the announcer comes over the intercom and says, "Ladies and gentleman, we have a special announcement on this Valentine's Day of love. Please bring your attention to section 182."

That's odd, Sarah thinks. That's the same section she and Tate are sitting in. She looks up at the jumbotron and she sees it. Her name, along with Tate's. It says words, but she never reads them because there's a tug at her sleeve.

She looks down. On one knee is some idiot who didn't know who Nellie Fox was, her former boyfriend, her about-to-be fiancé, and her future husband. With thousands of fans watching the couple from their seats and TVs, they see a man in an oversized Jordan jersey proposing to his girlfriend.

"Get a jersey that fits, ya bum!" many of them will say.

"Is that a jersey or a dress?!" others will sneer.

The tears have been wiped, the cake balls have been enjoyed. Tate got a little cream cheese on his jersey, but that's okay. He decides to never wash it. You know, to celebrate the occasion. To add icing to the cake, Tate pulls something from under his seat.

A program.

Sarah can't help but smile.

"I bought this," Tate says. "Go to page 18."

Sarah shakes her head and flips to the pages 18 and 19—where a scorebook covers from corner to corner. Tate pulls a Sharpie out of his pocket (something every firefighter and facilities manager has on them at all times) and hands it to his future wife.

All Sarah can do is laugh as she takes the marker from her future husband.

Clearly nervous that it had been a stupid idea, Tate laughs and says, "What? I thought you could send it to your grandpa. Like a souvenir."

Sarah's eyes well up and she begins to say the three magical words but is drowned out by the dipshit announcers.

"Starting at shooting guard for the Chicago Bulls, number 12, Michael Jordan!"

"Oh no, did I get the wrong one?" Sarah asks, now panicked. "I thought he was number 23!"

"Oh," Tate says, "you didn't hear? Someone stole his jersey before the game. How crazy is that?"

That's too bad, Sarah thinks. And that's as far as that thought goes. Because she's got bigger things to think about right now. Like a big fat rock on her finger. She checks it for the seventh time that minute. It's perfect. Her bite of bliss.

About the Author

Mitchell S. Elrick lives near Denver, Colorado, with his wife and pets. When he isn't teaching English or coaching basketball, he's tip-tapping at his computer, usually cursing that he can't find the right words. His short story "Polka Dots" was published in *Another Chance to Get It Right: A New Year's Eve Anthology* released from And You Press in 2024. When he isn't teaching, coaching, or computer-cursing, he's definitely losing to his wife at *Mario Kart*.

You can find Mitchell on:

Instagram: @mitchellselrick.author

WE ALREADY HAVE

We Already Have

Desi Stowe

THE COOL, DAMP BREEZE BLOWS across my face as I walk the roads of the French Quarter in New Orleans to say goodbye. The winter never makes much of a fuss this far south, but the day is chilly enough for my favorite fuzzy pink sweater. It's a fitting, festive look for today. The inescapable holiday for lovers.

My steps cover the familiar cobblestone streets that have been part of my home for the past few years. The music. The art. The food. The memories. Everything about this city used to make me feel so alive.

Until it didn't.

Now it feels rife with memories and mistakes. Not major, life-altering mistakes. But those pesky little ones. The mistakes you look back on and think, *Hmmm . . . that could've gone better. I wish I could try that again.* A few of those mistakes here and there are no big deal—just life lessons common to all of us. Recently, however, all my little mistakes, all these pesky life lessons, converged into a pile of nonsense I'd rather leave behind. I need to leave it behind.

I need to leave him behind.

With a heavy sigh, I shake my head, trying to dislodge any thoughts of Ethan. Instead, I redirect my thoughts to my job, something else I need to leave behind. For the past four years, I've been a nurse manager at a hospital in downtown New Orleans. I can assure you that the crazy things I've seen working in healthcare in this city are greater than anything an over-active imagination can conjure. I spent my days fighting with patients, with families, with staff, and even with fellow managers who looked down on me and questioned my drive. Everything every day has been a fight. I've been known to enjoy a good fight, but this one is over. Knowing when to walk away is as important as the fight. Maybe more.

It's time to move on. Throwing down roots has never been my strong suit, anyway. A bit of a traveler's heart directs the path of my soul and my life. I'm not typically restless or unhappy, but I am a wanderer. It was time to wander on.

I wander, quite intentionally, into my favorite candy store in New Orleans. The smell of decadence is nearly overwhelming, but my senses welcome the strong presence. The quaint little shop is packed today with long lines at the registers and people crowding every aisle. Not unexpected for Valentine's Day. The procrastination in the air is almost as strong as the delicious scents.

I've never been without a date on Valentine's day. Not since my first middle school boyfriend. I fall in and out of love rather easily. I wouldn't say I'm promiscuous. Rather, inundated with the need to have a person, a partner, a *someone* in my life. But that stops now. After numerous therapy sessions and more than a few nights of soul searching, I've realized that no one can make me happy if I'm not happy on my own.

No *one* can make me happy. Not to be confused with no *thing*. The very reason I'm in this bustling establishment is to pick up my cherished dark chocolate mint truffles. They are worth the wait among all the holiday procrastinators. A gift to me from me, in honor of my first solo Valentine's Day. A Valentine's Day without Ethan, without anyone. Time to discover who I am and what I need, beyond the chocolate. I purchase my delicious treat and trepidation sneaks in as I walk outside to the busy city streets. This is uncharted territory; I don't know how to do life on my own.

The buzz of my phone interrupts these intrusive thoughts. I've had enough self-reflection and could use the distraction. I answer the call from my next place of employment. An obnoxiously professional voice comes across the line. "This is Vivian Ashmead, here to confirm the dates for your orientation—" The conversation dissolves into giggles from both of us, as many of ours do.

The call from my recently acquired gal pal pulls me out of my funk. We met when she was a consultant and came to improve my hospital's employee acquisition and retainment. We hit it off immediately and became fast friends. She's now in Charleston and has offered me a job I can't refuse. The greatest benefits? It's not here, and it's near my new bestie. "The director of human resources is calling me about orientation dates. Really?"

Vivian laughs. She's happy now. She's well respected in her new job and plans to marry her beau, Eugene. A guy who softens her edges and balances her perfectly. Not to mention, he should be gracing the covers of romance novels instead of working as a physical therapist. He really did miss his calling there. "I just wanted to hear your voice."

I grin. "Same here, love. I'm out walking, thinking about how my wandering soul needs something new."

"It's time for a new chapter." She's alluding to just a few months ago when I told her she could write the next chapter of her life and she didn't have to let her idiot boss call all the shots. She did, too. Walked away from a high-paying consultant career to a still successful but simpler life where she isn't used but appreciated.

Here's the thing. It's easy for me to help others find their paths. I can't seem to turn that skill inward. I've always been a bit lost. Not in a doom-or-gloom sense, just . . . lacking in foundation or direction.

Vivian continues. "You know I'd love to have you in Charleston, but is that what you need? Are you sure? It's not too late to back out."

I don't miss the kindness of this offer—it's her job to fill positions. Giving me an out is all kinds of counterproductive, and this woman is productive on a superhero level. Vivian has this cross-me-and-regret-it presence, but she also has a heart. Color me amazed. Who knew both traits could coexist in the same person?

"I have no idea what I need, other than something new. Have you ever felt like you're on the autocorrect text of life? Like, life is making choices for you, just like autocorrect does, but they're wrong and don't make any sense?"

I turn on the street that leads me toward home. All this walking has led to an overdose of deep thoughts.

My friend chuckles again. Our conversations are like that—fun, full of laughs but also real. No pretense. I'm a mess sometimes. So is she. That's why we click. It's the most honest friendship I've ever had.

"Do you remember any of my last year?"

I pick up my pace after scanning the darkening clouds of the sky. Vivian is in a good place now, but she went through a lot to get there. "You've got a point."

"So, Charleston? Is that the correct path or a bad autocorrect? I mean, *I'm* in Charleston, which has to count for something."

I chuckle. "It totally counts. I need my thrift store shopping buddy back." The reprieve of laughter didn't last long, and I find myself sighing. I'm not sure of anything and that's so unlike me. "Yeah. I need something new."

She brings up the source of my melancholy. "You tell Ethan yet?"

Not bothering to hide the level of irritation this topic causes, I answer, "No, I'm still trying to avoid Ethan the Ex, ever since he decided he wasn't on board with our break-up. I thought we'd achieved an understanding."

Ethan and I were casual friends for quite some time, but we hooked up about a year or so into the pandemic. Working as a nurse manager during the single most disruptive event of our generation wore me down, and Ethan's charming and fun. He made me forget the horrors of my workday. But that's all we ever were. Just a good time. The relationship itself lacked any kind of substance. We broke things off right before Vivian left New Orleans. Then we got back together. Then we broke up again. We both almost fit each other. Just enough to keep trying, not enough to stay. That's the hardest part. The *almost*.

Vivian laughs. "He could win a gold medal for persistence. If that was a thing."

I roll my eyes, though she can't see it. I bet she can sense it. "You say persistence, I say annoyance. I'm gonna have to tell him I'm moving or he's gonna assemble a search party when he and his stalker-like tendencies can't find me."

For the record, he's not a stalker. He just shows up unannounced. Maybe that's worse? That might be worse.

Vivian's voice turns a bit more serious. "Henrietta, it does seem like Ethan isn't good for you."

I take a deep breath. "We're not good for each other."

Ethan and I had developed this somewhat toxic codependency. We bring out the worst in each other—really, we do. But it was so easy to stay together. Neither of us wants to put in the effort to find someone new. So we return to our bad habits.

"Anyway. It's Valentine's Day. Are you and Eugene doing anything?"

"We have a favorite, low-key BBQ place that we like. We'll eat there and walk along the Charleston Bay. Ever since I left consulting, I can't do fancy dinners anymore. Besides, I'm not really one for greeting card holidays."

I snort. "Listen, love, I know you. I'm guessing Eugene had to even tell you Valentine's was coming up?"

She hedges. "Yeah, maybe. What are your plans tonight?"

My plans. Ha! Right. Leaving this city and moving to the next. "Just packing. I don't need a greeting card holiday either, especially not this year."

Inwardly, I reaffirm to myself that it's time to take an intentional hiatus from relationship drama.

We hang up after promises of thrift store shopping and coffee runs as soon as I make it to Charleston.

I head home only to find annoying Ethan there, sitting on the steps to my apartment. My walk slows, and I groan. I don't want to do this now, but he's gonna force my hand.

Ethan and I were together for a couple of years. We started out spending our late nights together, drinking and dancing and other debauchery that New Orleans has to offer. It was fun. We were fun. I can't do the party lifestyle for the long-term. It isn't me, not anymore. We always had an expiration date, something he's yet to come to terms with. Hence the flowers and chocolate. He's a romantic. I am not. Maybe I could be given the right circumstances. But not in these circumstances.

I approach the handsome rogue and notice he did not come empty-handed: a bouquet of flowers and the same dark chocolate mint truffles I just bought myself complete his look. Should've known he wouldn't bypass this opportunity for a last-ditch grand gesture, Valentine's Day style.

My heart squeezes just for a second. He does know me; he knows exactly what I like. Wildflowers instead of traditional roses and my favorite chocolates.

I'm taking the chocolate, even if I do have a new, unopened box in my hands. That's payment for dealing with whatever nonsense he's about to throw my way.

"Ethan, Love, there are these nifty little devices called phones. You can call, text, email, or even slide right into someone's DMs. Contact someone to make plans." He's grinning too much at my words, so I go for a dig. "Or to see if someone is even interested in plans."

Nonplussed, he moves on. "We need to talk."

I stop just a few steps in front of him, mentally fortifying myself for this conversation. Trying to, anyway. I'm so irritated that he's shown up out of the blue—again. Irritation wins over calm logic.

"Why can't you stalk me like a normal ex-boyfriend? Lurking quietly in the shadows while I'm unaware of your presence?"

He stands up and holds out the flowers for me. I don't take them, thus adding to the awkwardness of this encounter.

"Etta—"

No one else calls me Etta, and I don't like him doing it. Not anymore.

"Emphasis on the 'I'm unaware of your presence' part."

Ignoring my obvious disdain for this evening's turn of events, he continues. "Can we please talk?"

The last time he pulled this sort of shenanigan, I drug him, quite literally, to his car, ran back to my apartment, and deadbolted my door. Vivian's right: this level of persistence is award-winning. If only he'd put this kind of effort into solving world hunger. I get that I'm a catch, I do. But we've done this song and dance several times over the past few months, and it always ends the same.

I nod and tilt my head, indicating that he can follow me inside. "Ethan, I'm doing the talking."

"You're so bossy." He smirks at me after delivering the tease. An attempt to get under my skin. Further under my skin.

It's true, but I ignore his words. He loves to fight. Loves to make up. Loves the drama. I've grown so very weary of all of it. Working in healthcare during a pandemic forced me to grow up to some extent. I'm just not in a place to deal with this nonsense anymore.

"Ethan."

"Etta."

My lungs fill with air and the determination I need to cut this stubborn string for good. "We're done. For real this time. I'm moving to Charleston in a couple of days."

He looks like someone just sucker-punched him in the stomach, and I almost feel bad. He looks around at the mix of boxes and packing materials scattered around my space. It's evidence that confirms my words.

"South Carolina?"

"Yeah." I shrug. What else is there to say? We've hashed things out countless times now. But me relocating? That makes this moment real for him. For both of us.

He seems to be having difficulty processing this new information. "No. No, you're not."

Cupping my hand over my mouth, I use my best intercom voice. "Welcome, passengers. We've arrived at the gate of denial. Please gather all your belongings."

He gives me some serious side-eye. "You're not funny."

I snort. "That was funny. I should be a comedian."

He ignores my comment. "New Orleans is your home. Why would you leave this? Why would you leave me? I know we've had a rough patch, but we work."

"Ethan, no. No, we don't."

I'm sticking to my boundaries this time. We've broken up maybe forty times now. Okay, slight exaggeration. But only slight. It feels like forty times.

I continue. "This isn't a 'rough patch.'"

Ethan's brother was tragically diagnosed with terminal cancer recently. He has months to live, if that. Not surprisingly, this threw Ethan into a tailspin. He decided he needed to start ticking off the to-do list of life and proposed to me this past fall.

Marriage.

I'm not sure I'm even marriage material. I know *we* aren't marriage material. Ethan sees me as a chance to forego his playboy persona and show his family he's capable of stability. His father never approved of Ethan's lack of commitment to any one person. Until we got together, he had a string of women in and out of his life, which fit his lifestyle. It wasn't intentional, not on my end anyway, but I bridged that gap. Not only was I willing to party into the wee hours of the morning, but I also offered a semblance of stability. Bottom line, he had the best of both worlds and now he doesn't want to let it go.

Ethan's pacing around, erratic and unsettled. He's having to dodge boxes and piles of packing materials as he moves around. "Do you care so little for me that you would move? Several states away without even discussing it with me?"

He's missed the memo that the world doesn't revolve around him. *Again.* My teeth clench and I try to dampen the anger of my response. It's a struggle.

"This isn't about you."

He gestures to the chaos around us. "How is all of this not about me?"

I can't read his emotion; it's oscillating somewhere between fury and sadness.

Every minute of this conversation drains me more. How much longer until there's nothing left?

"We're over. Done. Finished. I don't have to check in with you. I didn't have to tell you I was moving."

The mood between us suddenly shifts. Our mutual anger and frustration dissolving into sadness. His voice is like a soft breeze. I don't doubt its sincerity.

"I care for you, Etta."

I know he cares for me. It's not that the feeling isn't mutual; it's just that it doesn't matter. I shake my head no. This conversation has been replayed several times now, but this time things feel different. He looks into my eyes and he knows. *He knows.* He knows this time I'm gone for good. Achieving finality cracks my heart enough for a wave of sadness to rush in.

He pulls me into a tight embrace mixed with fond memories and desperation. He whispers into my ear, "I don't want us to end."

On this day, this Valentine's Day in the year of my need for a change, I cut the ties between us for good. *Almost right* isn't enough for me. I need more. It's a beautiful, painful and necessary gift to both of us to kill the codependency. The air surrounding us is bittersweet. Though today he'd deny it, deep down, I think Ethan knows this is for the best, too.

I lean back so my eyes, which are inexplicably tear-filled, meet his. "We already have."

"We Already Have" is a standalone short story that exists in the Charleston Harbor Series by Desi Stowe. The events in "We Already Have" occur following the end of Shadows. *The Charleston Harbor Series can be found on Kindle Unlimited, Amazon ebook, and via paperback at most major retailers and independent bookstores.*

About the Author

Desi Stowe officially started writing in early 2022. However, she'd been developing her scaffolding as a writer for many years. She had a way with words and a love of stories, so writing was a natural next step. She also found that writing was a wonderful escape into a fictional world, even if that world mirrors real life.

She worked to combine her experience in healthcare and her love of writing into her first novel. In February of 2024, she published *Done*, her first novel of the Charleston Harbor series. In 2024, her second novel *Shadows* and a short story "Seeking Sanctuary" were new additions to the Charleston Harbor world.

She lives in Raleigh, North Carolina, with her husband and two children. During the day, she works as a physical therapist. Her writing occurs in sporadic spurts while juggling other responsibilities. Desi often finds herself daydreaming about plot progression and character arcs while working out or washing dishes. The characters of her novels have a special place in her heart and hopefully yours, as well.

You can find Desi on:

Instagram: @desistowe

You can visit her website at:

authordesistowe.weebly.com

LOVE THROUGH A COOKIE

Love Through a Cookie

Heather Culler

"MOMMY, MOMMY, MOMMY!" SEVEN-YEAR-OLD PATRICK yelled as soon as he was off the school bus. "Guess what? We have a Valentine's Day party coming up!"

"Really? That's exciting!" I giggled. His joy tickled my heart.

Patrick's two older brothers, Paul and Michael, were not as thrilled about the upcoming holiday, and they didn't try to hide their distaste for it.

"What's so exciting about Valentine's Day?" eleven-year-old Michael sneered, rolling his eyes as he followed Patrick up the walk, kicking loose bits of snow that had rolled back into our previously painstakingly shoveled driveway.

"We get candy and there are parties! Duh!" Patrick shouted, red in the face from the apparent argument they'd had on the bus ride.

Paul, my twelve-year-old, was quiet. I tried to catch his eye, but he kept his trained on the ground. Finally, I bumped his shoulder with mine.

He sighed. "Mom, they argued all the way home about this ridiculous holiday."

"Sounds exhausting," I said, knowing there was more. They were brothers; they were constantly bickering. This was nothing new. "Is there something else?"

"I have a party, too. And my teacher is making us do something nice for someone else, and I got paired up with a girl," he mumbled.

I worked to hide the smile on my face. Paul was shy when it came to girls and mostly kept to himself. I swallowed hard. "I see."

"It's not funny, Mom," he groaned, throwing up his hands before walking through the back door.

"Haha, Paul has a girlfriend!" Michael teased.

"No, I don't!" Paul hissed.

"Yes, you do, and you've kept her a secret this whole time!" Michael badgered.

"Michael, that's enough. Do you have a party as well?" I interrupted, cooling down the conversation a little.

"Wellll, yeeeah, but it's just a little class thing like Patrick's. No big deal."

Paul stormed past me up the stairs. "I hate Valentine's Day. It's so embarrassing," he grunted, a stomp per step punctuating each word he spoke. I heard his heavy footsteps thud across the bedroom floor above me. The angry zip of his backpack preceded the groan of springs as he threw himself down on the bed.

I decided to leave Paul to sort his thoughts and feelings and turned my attention to the warm kitchen.

Patrick and Michael sat at the table stuffing their faces with popcorn, washing it down with hot chocolate, and working to get their homework done. Stew simmered on the stovetop, and the timer dinged. Donning my oven mitts, I carefully pulled fresh-baked bread from the oven. What comfort it brought on a cold, snowy day; however, I didn't sit long in its coziness. My thoughts wandered to whether, and then how, I should explain the importance of Valentine's Day to my sons. I decided to wait until supper to bring it up. Perhaps I could come up with a fun and simple way to celebrate what I had always felt was a truly wonderful holiday.

While washing the baking bowls and measuring cups, elbow-deep in warm, sudsy water, I was hit with an epiphany. I knew what we'd do! I dried my hands, sliced the moist, warm bread, and called for Paul to come down to dinner.

Michael and Patrick moved their completed homework and helped set the walnut dining room table. Paul trudged down the stairs and plopped down in his seat, still pouting. He stared at his bowl of beef stew. I glanced at him and offered a smile as I handed him a glass of milk.

He rolled his eyes, still miffed about Valentine's Day.

I took my spot at the end of the table, we all joined hands, and we thanked God for the the warm meal, good health, and other continued blessings. At the end of the prayer, I added: "And bless those who do not feel love tonight and put us into a position to show them your love, in Jesus's precious and holy name, Amen."

I then watched my boys savor the beef stew and buttered bread sweetened with honey. The cold winter wind howled outside the window; I noticed the snow wisping magically about as I got up to close the thick curtains for the night.

"Boys, I've been thinking about Valentine's Day."

Paul groaned and slid down in his seat a bit while Michael smirked and Patrick leaned forward eagerly. I raised my eyebrows, signaling them to adjust their attitudes, and I continued.

"What do you think Valentine's Day is all about?"

They stopped, pondering its meaning, and I braced myself for a slew of different responses, from ridiculously silly to hopefully realistic.

Michael spoke up first, puffed like a peacock. "It's all about the candy, Mom!"

Patrick bolted upright in his chair. "No no no, you have it all wrong, Michael! It's about the parties, duh!" I wasn't surprised. Those two could not agree on anything, ever. Even if Michael had been excited about the parties earlier and Patrick had been over the moon for candy just five minutes ago, they'd have disagreed right then.

Paul stared into his bowl. "It's all about girls and what *they* want," he mumbled, shoving himself away from the table.

"Hm, okay." I nodded. "Let's think about this for a minute," I added as I gathered my own thoughts on Valentine's Day.

The candles flickered, casting a warm glow on the wall. With a mouthful of soup, Patrick stared at me, in thought, and then swallowed. "Actually, what's so wrong with candy?" he asked, agreeing with Michael for once.

I smiled. "Nothing. Lots of people give and receive candy on Valentine's Day. Let me tell you a story," I said, meeting eyes with each of my precious sons. Even Paul finally looked up from his stew.

They each sat up straight and eagerly leaned in. Though they were growing up, this had not yet changed: They still loved any story that spilled from my mouth.

"Once upon a time, there was a young girl who was, oh, sixteen years old, and she lived right outside of town by the old railroad tracks."

"You mean over where the houses are falling apart?" Paul interrupted.

"Mmhmm." I nodded. "Her whole life, she lived in poverty, and she did not have many friends or nice clothes. Her father, no matter how hard he worked, seemed to never have enough money.

"The house she grew up in was brown and raggedy. Missing shingles, falling siding, and a crack in her bedroom window. A breeze always blew through her room. She made her room look beautiful, though, with all of her artwork; everyone thought she was talented. Even though she lived in a run-down, two-story farmhouse, she made the most of it. But she had dreams of her own. Dreams of living well, having money, and most of all, being loved by a prince who would come and take her away from her hardships."

"Ohhhh great, I can see where this is going." Paul sat back in his chair, rolling his eyes again and folding his arms.

"Just let Mom finish the story!" Michael insisted.

Paul sneered at him, but luckily Michael didn't notice.

I cleared my throat and continued:

"This sweet girl tried to make the most of her life. She loved her family, but despite her best efforts, she felt alone and out of place. Holidays came and went, and she noticed that the other kids at school and around the village all had someone special, so why couldn't she? Valentine's Day was a dreadful holiday for her. Though they had little money, her parents always went on a special date. Her friends all had their special plans, too. As for her, the attention she desperately desired did not come. She didn't get any cards or flowers. No candy at all."

"Well that's just sad! She didn't get anything at all? Not even a little candy?" Patrick whined in concern.

"Unfortunately, no. Can you imagine how she felt?" I asked.

"Sad and disappointed," Michael said, his voice soft.

"That sucks," Paul mumbled.

"No one likes to feel alone or forgotten, right?" I asked my sons. Again, I looked at all three of them. The candles flickered in their big, bright eyes.

"So what happened next, Mommy?" Patrick asked.

"Well, she had a brilliant idea. Instead of waiting around for someone to show her love, she decided to show love to others by making cookies. On each cookie, she would write a special message. She decided that it would mean more to spread love than to yearn to be loved."

"Heeey, hang on. That's like what St. Valentine did. He showed love to others by setting himself aside. We talked about that in school. I completely forgot about it, Mom, until just now," Paul stated confidently.

I put my finger to my nose, signifying he was spot-on, and winked at him. The pride he felt in that moment appeared through the grin on his face.

"And that's why we celebrate Valentine's Day, to show love to others."

Paul fiddled with his soup spoon.

"Well, Mom, since you put it that way, I guess it wouldn't be *so* weird to do something nice for someone else, even a girl."

Michael gasped. "Ahhhhh! I have an idea! Why don't we make special cookies, for everyone, just like the girl in the story?"

"Heeeyy, that's a good idea! Can we decorate them with sprinkles and food glitter and write cool stuff on them?" Patrick looked to me for approval, and I snuck a glance at Paul, who was not only agreeable, but also seemingly into the idea.

I grabbed a piece of paper while they cleared the table, and we collaborated on a shopping list.

"Tomorrow is Friday. We have three days before the Valentine's Day parties on Monday. That should give us plenty of time to get our cookies done. We can put the cookies in the freezer so that they last longer."

"Or we could put them in the cooler outside in the snow!" Michael laughed.

"No no! The raccoons would find them and eat them!" Patrick chuckled.

"Hey, the raccoons need a little love, too, is all." Paul grinned.

I couldn't help but laugh as the boys almost fell out of their chairs from laughing so hard at their own jokes.

The next day, Paul, Patrick, and Michael rushed off the bus and threw their backpacks in the mudroom by the cobalt-blue back door. They jumped into the warmed car, snow from their boots melting onto the thick plastic mats as we drove to the store.

In the store, they were ecstatic to see the barrels full of different hard candies and a stand of special cookie icing on display alongside them.

We went to the baking aisle and carefully selected the appropriate ingredients we needed for our project.

"Mom, we need special boxes or bags to put the cookies in for delivery," Michael suggested as shiny ribbons caught his eye.

"What a great idea, Michael! I always put them in small bags when I did this as a kid." That tiny detail didn't make it past Paul. "Mom, were you the sixteen-year-old girl in the story?"

All the boys stopped in their tracks, awaiting my answer.

"Well, the cat's out of the bag!" I giggled.

Their jaws hit the floor.

"What?! That was you?! How did you end up with Dad if you didn't have a Valentine?" Patrick asked, his big eyes holding the innocence of his seven years.

"Well, why don't you ask him when you get home?"

Now a mystery, the unanswered question had added suspense to the story. The boys rushed to get their special ribbons and little boxes of red, gold, and pink. At the candy barrels and colored icing stations, they eagerly placed their selections into the cart.

At checkout, Mr. Joe, a man in his mid-fifties or so, grinned at the sight of my sons. Mr. Joe was a familiar sight at our store, and the kids knew him well. In his Southern accent, he asked, "My now, what are y'all up to?"

"We're making special cookies for people for Valentine's Day," Michael chirped.

"Oh now, special cookies, are they?"

"Yes, sir," Paul replied.

"And we get to decorate them, too! With candy!" Patrick nearly shouted

"Well now, how 'bout that?" Mr. Joe grinned, clearly amused by my sons' excitement.

"That'll be $45.57, ma'am." I dug in my purse, pulling out my debit card from my new leather wallet.

"Y'all have fun making cookies now, all right?"

"We will!" the boys hollered, waving at Mr. Joe as we left the store.

It was nearing dinnertime, so I decided on three meat lovers' pizzas, two orders of breadsticks, and cheese dip for dinner. It would be a pizza and movie night in our house. My husband was off from work from the factory, and this would be the perfect opportunity for the boys to ask him about our story.

The boys were excited for pizza night, and they were even more excited about a long baking day tomorrow. They talked about different cookie cutter shapes: hearts, circles, an arrow, maybe a Cupid if they could find one in the bag. How were they going to decorate their cookies, and how many would they need? There were twenty-four students in each of their classes, totaling seventy-two cookies for the students and a few more for the teachers and anyone else they thought would love a special cookie. We would possibly need a grand total of eighty cookies.

As we pulled into our driveway, which was now covered with a fresh coat of snow, the plan for the night fell into place in my head. To ensure the best Valentine's Day cookies, we'd make the dough tonight, let it chill overnight, and roll it out in the morning. I figured we'd make the dough after dinner but before the movie. Then in the morning the real work would begin.

The boys helped carry in their goodies while I followed with dinner. My husband, Lee, opened the door for us wearing a relieved smile, grateful we were all home safely. We found a fire crackling in the fireplace and coffee brewing in the pot. He'd even meticulously prepared the kids mugs of hot chocolate, which sat cooling on the counter.

Another smile, a kiss for me, and hugs for the kids—his eyes lit up when he saw the cookie supplies. This was a special time of year for us, and he fondly remembered the fun that we'd had together some twenty years ago.

"Whatcha got there, Liz?" he teased.

"We're making cookies, Dad!" Michael and Patrick yelled together.

"Oh yeah, that reminds me. Dad, how did you and Mom meet?" Paul asked.

"Well, get your plates fixed, and I'll tell you the story."

The boys rushed to get their food and their soda pop and then gathered around their father, waiting for part two of our Valentine's Day story.

My husband started: "A long time ago, I was almost seventeen years old, and I was helping my grandma in her cookie bakery in town. Your momma came into our shop one day wanting to talk to my grandma about her cookie recipe, because she couldn't get her cookies to turn out quite right. Well, Grandma—she'd be Great-Grandma to you—asked her to bring her cookies to the bakery so she could see what the problem was, so your mom did. Mom's cookies were good, but not great. Great-Grandma nearly chipped a tooth on a cookie that was meant to be soft!"

The boys tried to hide their laughter from me. "But Mom's cookies have always been soooo soft," Patrick interrupted, licking his lips.

My husband chuckled and shot me a look. "Eh, not always," he grinned.

I waved him off.

"So, Mom, Great-Grandma, and I worked together to make her cookies better. Every day for two weeks, your mom came into the store to learn the proper way to make cookies. With enough practice and love from me and your great-grandma, a perfect sugar cookie was formed!"

"And that's how you fell in love with Mom?" Paul asked.

"Oh no, that was just the beginning. Great-Grandma needed extra help in the bakery, so she hired Mom. I spent every day with your momma, and despite our differences, I was falling in love with her. She would smile at me and I would sneak glances at her. It wasn't until Valentine's Day morning that I found a very special cookie in my locker!"

"Daddy, what did it look like?!" Michael smiled excitedly.

My husband looked at me, beaming, remembering the sweet moment.

"It was a heart-shaped sugar cookie with smooth, pink icing and gold glitter sprinkles, wrapped neatly in a little red bag. There was a message on it that said, *You are special to me!* After that, your mom and I had a romantic, candlelit dinner on Valentine's Day. I had every intention of showing her my love first by getting her a single red rose. However, she beat me to it with her cookie!"

"But, Dad, you showed Mom love first!" Paul stated.

"How so?" Dad asked.

"By growing to love me during our cookie-baking days at the bakery. By helping perfect my cookies, so I could spread love throughout our community," I said, moving over and kissing my sweet husband.

The boys chuckled and *ooh*-ed and *aww*-ed over us kissing, making a huge deal. I turned to them and said, "Now we can continue showing others love through a cookie." Later that evening, the boys thoroughly enjoyed taking turns putting in the ingredients, running the mixer at the appropriate times, and picking out which cookie cutter shapes they were going to use to cut the dough the next day.

With my sleepy-eyed sons seated anxiously at the table, I took a long sip of my warm coffee and then floured the clean surface and my rolling pin. Through grace and strength, I showed each child hand-over-hand how to roll out the dough, which had chilled well overnight, to a perfectly even thickness, measuring the thickness of the dough with a ruler.

I explained how important it was for each cookie to be perfect; you're not just giving someone a baked good—you're presenting someone with a symbol that you love or care for them. "You should give it your all," I told my children.

The cookies' sweet, buttery aroma filled the house as they baked, and the boys took turns peering into the oven's front glass to watch them grow. Impatient but somewhat understanding, they waited for the cookies to cool so the icing wouldn't melt right off. Then, with flour handprints on their aprons and icing on their cheeks and hands, they carefully iced all eighty cookies. Completing ten at a time, the boys decorated their cookies according to their personalities, adding their own touches to them.

I'm pretty sure Michael and Patrick ate more decorations than they placed on the cookies themselves, but that couldn't have been avoided. Their love for sugar won them over; they could not resist the temptation.

With my help, they were able to write messages with edible writing ink. I found this to be easier—and *way* less messy—and I loved watching them come up with the words and phrases they wanted to feature. Michael held his tongue just so in his mouth, careful not to break his focus. Patrick silently stared intently as he wrote on his cookies, and Paul steadied his shaking hand the best he could.

I was amazed at the transformation before me. My boys had taken their desires for mountains of candy and parties, not to mention their harrumphs over having to gift girls, and turned them into an eagerness to celebrate Valentine's Day selflessly by creating something to share with others. I was proud of them. The life lessons I tried to share with them didn't always work out this way, so I was happy to sit in this moment for as long as they'd let me. My husband joined our festivities, using his skills to help us organize a system of efficiency. The boys wrote their classmates' and teachers' names on the boxes and then took their time deliberating which cookies should be placed in which boxes. We stacked them neatly in a large tote and placed padding around them, securing them tight so they wouldn't tumble and break.

Snow fell yet again on that beautiful Valentine's Day morning. Large, glistening flakes landed in my hair, teasing my cheeks, which were certainly red. The air was cold and crisp, but I was warmed by the memories of my teenage years, which had always lived in my heart and which I was so happy to have shared with my sons on this holiday.

All bundled up in their coats, knitted hats and scarfs, and woolen mittens, the boys shuffled to the car, excited to skip the morning bus ride and deliver their baked goods. Anticipation filled their bellies as they wondered aloud what sort of reaction each person would have when they received their special cookies. Would some be speechless? Sad? Happy? How different love could be when shown through a cookie!

In my experience, gifting a cookie on Valentine's Day had started my new life, which had led to a lifelong relationship with my wonderful husband—someone who had chosen a life with me despite the battles of overcoming my fears and insecurities. I was curious as to what life had in store for our sons. Is it possible that their futures would be influenced by a simple cookie?

As I turned into the parking lot of their school, a brisk wind blew the American flag, and its colors shining proudly in the sunlight caught my eye and reminded me of how grateful I was to live in a free country where I had the freedom to express love and gratitude, to be happy. One by one, the boys stepped out of the car. Careful of the mixture of the ice, slush, and snow underfoot, we brought the cookies inside and delivered them to each of the boys' classrooms. Proudly my sons placed a small box on each student's desk and one on each of their teachers' desks. I was moved as I watched them receive hugs, smiles, and even tears as each child or adult thanked them for their special treat.

"Mom, Mom!" Paul caught up to me before I left his classroom. He called for another student to come over to him, and she rushed over as I smiled at her. "Mom, this is Abigail. She was who I had to make something for. She had to have surgery to help her spine. She has been feeling down, because she couldn't do the things that she once could do."

Abigail shook my hand. "My cookie said, *You are strong!* and that gave me so much encouragement not to give up. To have friends like Paul and my other friend Katie, they help me get through the day."

My sensitive son was overjoyed, and I could see he was trying to hide his happy tears as he was realizing that love is what his friend needed to heal and become even stronger.

I smiled at Paul and winked at him. He grinned back at me and returned to his classroom festivities with Abigail.

Clouds soon came. Another potentially heavy snowstorm was brewing. Bright yellow and red lights flashed as the bus pulled to a stop at the curb. Michael, Paul, and Patrick ran up the driveway and in the cluster of winter gear, slush, and snow, one of them thrust a letter into my hand.

> *Dear Mr. and Mrs. Baker,*
> *Your sons are a wonderful addition to our classrooms, and the beautiful cookies they handed out today had a positive impact on our classes. Some of our children do not have much and struggle with feeling important, and we strive to show them love here to the very best of our ability. Your children added to that effort today, showing love and extending grace and support, especially to those who have low self-esteem and need a little extra love.*

We encourage your sons to continue with that and not to change that quality for anything or anyone. That they stay true to themselves.

Boys, keep up the good work and continue to be you!

Happy Valentine's Day!

Mrs. Cook

Mr. Pearson

Ms. Milner

Tears welled in my eyes, and my heart filled with pride. Care that *our* children had shown was a light to a dark world! A hope burned inside of me, a prayer that our sons would never lose that light.

I held the letter close to my heart and inhaled deeply, basking in the moment, but a shout interrupted my moment of peace.

"Mom! We have one cookie left! Let's take it to the grocery store and give it to Mr. Joe!" Michael suggested. Before I could process the idea, the boys had agreed with this plan and were already in the car with the doors shut.

Quickly but carefully, we traveled the five miles up the road. Inside the grocery store, Mr. Joe waved at us, welcoming us warmly. The boys moseyed over to him and waited patiently as he finished scanning a customer's items.

"My, my, what are you boys up to today, huh?" He cracked a smile, his salt-and-pepper beard following the contour of it. His eyes glimmered as he waited for their responses.

"Mr. Joe, we brought this for you." Michael handed him the small box, placed his hands back in his pockets, and watched as Mr. Joe opened it.

"Ah, now. That's somethin' special right there." He pulled out a pink, heart-shaped cookie with silver letters and red sprinkles. "It says, *A Kind Friend*. Thank you, boys." He grew solemn. "I needed a friend, and in order to get friends, you have to be one."

"You are special to us, Mr. Joe. You make us laugh with your jokes, and you help us in the store when we need it." Paul spoke sincerely.

"Yeah, and you're an all-around good guy who needs love, too, like everyone else," Patrick whispered.

Mr. Joe hugged all of the boys and then his eyes met mine. "My best friend just passed away recently, and well, I've been feeling a little blue. But not anymore." He returned his attention to the kids. "And that's all because of you. This little cookie, through its shape and pink color and message . . . what a brilliant way to show a lot of love today."

Paul, Michael, and Patrick ate their treats of choice on the way home. We didn't talk much as I drove. We just listened to music as their little minds whirled with deep thoughts and I concentrated on the snowy road.

"Mom, can we do this every year?" Paul asked.

"Yeah, we should!" Michael and Patrick agreed.

I pulled the car over, turned around in my seat, and looked at each one of my boys' hopeful faces. "I think that would be a wonderful idea, a tradition to be carried on."

The boys were delighted with this, and I grew hopeful that they would teach their own children one day to show love through a cookie.

About the Author

Heather Culler resides on a farm in rural Indiana. She enjoys working with children in an educational setting and in agriculture programs. Many hobbies she loves include gardening and raising poultry and rabbits, but her favorite is writing stories. She writes for her children and for others, and she also has a passion for art. She loves God and her family. She strives to perfect the arts, fulfilling a deep desire to pass on a legacy of writing and art to others.

THE MISSING CUPCAKE

The Missing Cupcake

Megan D. Wood

I HAD JUST HUNG UP my coat and purse and plopped myself down at my desk, nearly prepared to start another day in marketing, my not-quite-dream job, when I heard Miriam call out to me.

"Lucy! Lucy! Did you see the memo I sent you yet?"

I turned in my chair to see my coworker, Miriam, come to a full stop in front of my desk and immediately begin running frantic fingers through the ends of her hair. She was staring at me with the widest eyes I had ever seen.

Something in my chest dropped to my stomach and then squeezed. "N-no? What's wrong?"

"The caterer dropped out from the promo event on Saturday," she half-whispered, half-whined. "We may be able to find someone else to make the bulk of the main food at the last minute, but we're having trouble finding someone to bake the desserts."

Miriam and I have been in charge of planning this event for our prospective clients. I'd thought everything had been well taken care of by this point, given that we were only two days out. If this event failed, our reputations would be irrevocably tarnished at this company. The promotion that had been within my grasp at the start of this year would surely slip right through my fingers. In fact, I might even lose my job if this event failed. And starting over at a new job is the last thing I wanted. My short-term goals included a promotion, a pay raise, and saving up enough money to go into business for myself. To open the small bakery I'd always envisioned.

I couldn't let this event fall apart. I couldn't lose this job or my spot on this promotion track.

My thoughts were interrupted by Mr. Edwards, our boss, bellowing down the hallway. "Miriam! Lucy! Can I see you in my office?"

I locked panicked eyes with Miriam and then we turned in unison to go toward his office.

"What's the plan, ladies? How are you going to address this catering situation? I cannot emphasize enough how important this event is for the company," he paused, gesturing at us to take our seats in front of his desk. "If we do not get a new client on board, we are in danger of every one of us losing our jobs."

I hadn't realized it was that serious. Sure, I was concerned about *my* job and my future plans, but I didn't know everyone else's were at risk, too. This news shocked me, and I sat frozen for way too long, hoping that Miriam would quickly come up with an idea. Though determined to save the day a few minutes ago, I had nothing.

After a few more seconds of Mr. Edwards looking increasingly irritated, Miriam spoke. "Well, I'm confident we can find someone to cover the dinner, and we may have an unconventional idea that would solve the rest of our issues."

"Yes?" Mr. Edwards said.

"Well, Lucy here . . ."

I shot a quick glance at her, wondering where she was going with this.

She cleared her throat, and her anxious hands were in her hair again. "Lucy is actually an incredibly talented baker. She can make the dessert—the cupcakes—we need for the event."

I held back the incredulous face I wanted to make at her. What was she thinking, volunteering me for this? We needed at least a hundred cupcakes for all the people expected to attend on Saturday. When would I find the time to make, decorate, and transport all of those?

I sat on my hands and kept my face as neutral as possible, even though my heart was in my throat and my back was starting to sweat. As much as I doubted I could pull this off, I couldn't let Mr. Edwards know I didn't have the same sort of faith in my abilities that Miriam apparently did.

I wasn't sure what prompted Miriam to think about my hobby, to think I could pull this off. Sure, I talked about baking—a lot—and I shared a lot of the recipes I tried on social media. And I brought my treats in for her to sample countless times. . . . Okay, so maybe she knew I really liked to bake, but it still amazed (and confused) me that she thought about *me* as the answer to our problem during this time of crisis.

"Well then." He clapped his hands together. "That is an excellent idea. I suppose the desserts you've brought into the office in the past were delicious, Lucy. What all do you need from us to make this happen?"

"Oh. Uh." This was hard to think up on the spot. It would've been nice to have had time to make a detailed plan of what this project would require. Ingredient lists, an oven schedule, an idea for decorations.

"We will, of course, pay you like any other caterer, but if you need a stipend for the ingredients, or to take a half day tomorrow, paid, to start baking—"

"That would be great, actually," I interrupted. "I can have nine dozen cupcakes made by Saturday afternoon. It will be no problem, really."

Oof, that was a big, fat lie. It was a little bit of a problem. I had no idea if I was capable of baking that many cupcakes at a professional quality with this short of notice.

However, I had to admit this would be a great opportunity for me. I did need more experience with baking for a large group of people, and the extra money was nothing to scoff at. Plus, saving the day would put me in Mr. Edwards's good graces. He wouldn't forget this anytime soon. I'd stay on the promotion track, and I could already envision myself using the pay raise for my bakery. My goals would still be within reach.

"Great! I'll just go ahead and send an email to HR and accounting to explain that you're leaving early tomorrow, the fourteenth." He waved his hand at us in dismissal, and we got up to go back to our desks.

Once I got to mine, though, I saw the framed picture of my boyfriend, Ian, and it hit me. The fourteenth. Valentine's Day. That's tomorrow. We had a romantic dinner plan. Instead, I would be spending my Friday night, my Valentine's Day date night, baking in my little kitchen—not for myself, and not even for Ian, but for a corporate work event.

I had to cancel our date. Ian would be so disappointed. I immediately felt terrible. He had mentioned a few times how much he was looking forward to our date, and even though we had technically been dating for over a year, this had felt like the first Valentine's Day we were going to celebrate as an "official" couple.

Still, I just could not give up this opportunity.

I hoped he would understand and not end up hating me after I broke the news to him.

"Hey, honey! How was your day?" I greeted Ian with a giant hug and kiss on the cheek, hoping to distract him from the thoughts plaguing my mind with my outward excessive joyfulness. He had come over for our Thursday night dinner. That was usually one of the highlights of my week and just the push I needed to get through the last day of the workweek.

He regaled me with the events of his day as he walked through the doorway of my apartment and placed his bag on the floor and his hat and jacket on the back of the couch.

"And how was your day, sweetie?"

I stopped midstride. Even though I had been trying to figure out how to tell him that I had to break our Valentine's Day date all afternoon, I still didn't know what to say. I felt so guilty, and I wanted to word it in a way that didn't make it sound like I was choosing work over him, over us. This was a huge opportunity that could have big implications for my future—a future I hoped he'd be involved in. But it was also so easy for him to argue that I was choosing work over him on Valentine's Day.

I'd been nervous about this for hours, and now this gorgeous man was standing right in front of me. And I had to crush him. His dark-brown hair was slightly tousled from the hat he'd worn on the chilly, snowy walk over, and it was ever so slightly sweaty from the pickleball game I knew he had come from, but it was still perfect to me. And his equally dark-brown eyes were staring at me, as they always did, in a way that made me want to forget anything else going on in my life.

Oh, how I wished that I could.

But I had a hundred cupcakes to bake!

So . . .

"I actually have some bad news," I started.

He cocked his head at me in a loving but questioning way. There was no point in stalling.

I proceeded to share everything that had happened at the office that day as I set the table and brought dinner out of the kitchen, simultaneously saying a silent prayer that my kitchen had ample space for my cupcake challenge, considering I lived in a one bedroom apartment in Boston.

"Oh," was all he said in reply when I'd reached the end of my ramblings.

"I am so sorry, Ian. I was so looking forward to our Valentine's plans. I just couldn't say no when Miriam sort of threw me under the bus like that." I took a step closer to him and put my hand on his arm. I always felt calmer when there was no physical distance between us.

He frowned and looked lost in thought for a few seconds before he returned his gaze to me. "No, I understand. I guess if there's no way out of it, there's no way out of it. I just wish we could have had more warning that this would happen."

I dropped my hand, but he reached up and tucked a strand of hair behind my ear. I loved it when he did that, but it didn't fix what was happening. True, we could reschedule. Lots of couples celebrated Valentine's Day on days other than the fourteenth to accommodate work schedules and other events; it wasn't the biggest deal in the world. But Ian had been very obviously excited about this year's celebration. I knew he'd wanted to make it extra romantic. I knew he'd made reservations that he now had to cancel. I knew he'd had plans for us.

We still tried to have a pleasant dinner together, trying to make up for what we were going to miss out on the next night. But my simple baked pasta dish would never compare to the five-star meal he had planned for us at the hottest restaurant in town. He never revealed where he'd made the reservation, but I had some ideas. And I sure hoped there wasn't a cancellation fee.

After we cleaned up dinner, I grabbed the remote for the television and took my place on the couch—we always watched whatever new movie was streaming after dinner on Thursdays—but he stopped me. He placed a tender kiss on the forehead and said, "I actually have to go, Lucy. I need to cancel the reservation and stuff. . . . But I was thinking I could come over for dinner tomorrow night. To give you a break from all that you have to do?"

I nodded in agreement. I couldn't exactly argue, after all. But still, I was sort of upset that he was in such a rush to leave. Sure, he had seemed off during dinner—he didn't crack any jokes or mention anything that happened during his game. But those things didn't give me any reason to believe that he was actually upset about the change of plans. I mean, we saw each other almost every day, so was Valentine's really so different?

The upset transformed a bit into anger as I settled on a movie to watch by myself. All I knew was that he better get over it soon. It was just one night. One canceled date. And he was going to come over anyway. We couldn't let this little incident cause any issues in our relationship. We were in a really good place.

Or at least, we had been.

Friday afternoon could not come fast enough. After a restless night of sleep, I was ready to get the whole ordeal over with. Bake the cupcakes, deliver the cupcakes, make up with Ian (Were we fighting? He hadn't texted me all morning. What was going on?), and then resume life as normal on Sunday.

Once lunch hour hit, I was out of the office and on my way home to start my baking marathon.

Even if I was stressed out over all that I had to do that afternoon and evening, I couldn't say that I wasn't looking forward to being alone in my kitchen and in my element. Baking was something that took all my focus. If I made one mistake measuring, who knows what might become of my creation? If I overmixed the cake batter, I'd have a tough and displeasing result. If I undermixed, I'd have globs of unappetizing flour. It required precision and a keen eye—and lots of practice. Thankfully, I had a lot of experience with a spatula.

Still, I had to admit there was still a part of me that was worried I couldn't handle this big of a task by myself. What would that say about my ability to one day run a bakery of my own?

Thankfully, I had a system to ensure I succeeded. I had gathered all the ingredients yesterday that I believed I would need. Then, I triple-checked that I had everything last night after Ian left so that I could get the remaining ingredients today if I needed them. So at least I was feeling confident about having all the necessary tools at my disposal. I even borrowed some cupcake tins from some coworkers so that I could constantly have a batch in the oven.

As I was putting the second batch in to bake, I felt really good about my system. All of my tools were laid out in a neat row and all of my ingredients arranged in the order I needed them. I almost had the recipe memorized from baking it before, and every move I made felt like second nature. That is, until I managed to knock over a bowl with my elbow that I had just started mixing ingredients in. All of the wet ingredients were spilling out onto my laminate floors and the anti-fatigue mat that I needed under my feet.

"Crap!" I exclaimed to the rows of cupcakes cooling on the rack nearby. Not only was this a mess that would impact the timing that I had planned for how to bake everything in one day, but I didn't have the extra eggs required to remake this batch.

I would have had a couple left over as backup; however, in a moment of stupidity, I'd thought scrambled eggs and toast would make a good, protein-rich lunch to fuel my afternoon of baking. So, I ate those last two eggs.

I thought I had done *so well* with my planning, but I'd forgotten about crazy, freak accidents. Each of the five batches needed two eggs. Five batches would give me 120 cupcakes, more than enough for what the event required, but it was just easier to do five whole batches and have extra cupcakes than it would have been to try to halve a recipe.

I now had no choice. I needed to hurry and clean up my mess while the current batch was cooking in the oven, and then I had to go to the store for more eggs. The closest one was only a block away and shouldn't cause me that much of a delay, I figured.

As I was making sure that my keys and purse were ready, I heard the faint sound of my phone vibrating on the counter. A quick glance at my smartwatch showed it was Ian calling. I had almost forgotten that he still hadn't talked to me today. My heart leapt, and I hoped he was calling to confirm our Valentine's Night In plans rather than cancel them.

"Hey, Ian," I said as I tried to hold the phone in between my ear and my shoulder.

"Hey, Lucy! Is six o'clock all right for me to head over? You can just text me your takeout order whenever."

"Sure, that's fine. I'll look up the menu once I get back home and get the next batch going."

"Huh? Where are you going? Don't you have, like, a bazillion cupcakes to make?"

I let out a small, quiet sigh mixed with laughter. "Yeah. I had an accident and need to go grab another dozen eggs really quick."

I heard a lot of shuffling on the other side of the phone before Ian spoke. "No, no, let me grab those for you. It will take just a few minutes. The store is on the way to your place. We can just get the food delivered."

"Are you sure? The batch in the oven right now is almost done, and then I could go."

"Yes. Please let me do this small favor for you, Luce. It's the least I can do after how distant I've been."

"All right, if you really want to . . . and don't worry about it. You know I don't like having my plans changed at the last minute, either."

"Thank you," he paused, and I could hear him moving around to lock the front door of his apartment. "Also, did you know I used to bake with my grandma a lot growing up? I might be able to be of some help."

"Really? Are you sure you want to?" I asked.

"Yes, as long as you're sure that you can forgive me for leaving last night and not checking in with you today."

"Of course I can, Ian."

"Great. See you in a few minutes."

Once Ian arrived, I was able to get back into the rhythm of baking without a hitch. Apparently, he had never told me about baking with his grandma because he felt intimidated by my skills. He really did have a surprising amount of experience in the kitchen. This was a relief to me, because it meant I could enjoy his company without stressing over whether he was going to make any horrible mistakes. Then again, I was the one who had already made the crazy mistake during this baking process. So, I shouldn't have worried about him.

As we were putting the fourth batch in, he happily exclaimed, "Almost there, Lucy!"

I breathed a sigh of relief. The end was in sight. So far, things looked promising. Everything was baking uniformly, and the cupcakes looked delicious. I almost wanted one to be messed up, so I could sneak a taste. With Ian here, I switched my focus to making all the frosting that we would use to decorate the cupcakes. The first round would be cool enough for me to start icing once I got all the piping bags and tips together.

Thankfully, I planned to do a simple swirl on the top of each cupcake, which would be beautiful, but it would not require too much effort. The hardest part of the icing process was just making it and filling the bags.

I snuck a glance over at Ian and saw him stirring the batter for the next batch. He stopped stirring to go measure out the flour, and I noticed that his hands were shaking while pouring it into the bowl on the kitchen scale we were using to accurately measure the ingredients. Baking does require some exact measurements, which can be daunting, but it's not like the amount of flour can't be adjusted in the bowl before mixing it in with the rest of the batter. I took a closer look and noticed a few beads of sweat on his forehead. Even with the oven running constantly almost all afternoon, it wasn't that hot in here. I made sure to turn on the air-conditioning, and I'd even brought in a fan to help keep cool air blowing on us. I was adamant about this when baking for multiple hours because I wanted the cupcakes to be able to cool as quickly as possible.

"How's it going over there?" I asked.

He looked up at once when he heard me speak, but he seemed to regain his composure. "Fine. The batter should be done soon. I should have a few extra minutes before the oven is open again." He made eye contact with me for a brief moment, and his cheeks were tinged a light shade of pink.

Is he getting sick? I wondered. Maybe it was a good thing we ended up canceling our dinner plans. If he were possibly coming down with something, it'd be better for him to be at my apartment than all dressed up and miserable at a gourmet restaurant.

"Okay," I said. "I think I'm going to run to the restroom. Don't let the place catch fire while I am gone." I laughed.

"Sure thing, sweetie."

When I returned, he seemed to have composed himself. He was less shaky, less sweaty, no longer flushed. I settled back into my workstation, hoping that he had gotten over whatever was troubling him. I wanted to ask him about it, but despite things feeling better between us, he didn't seem to be in a very talkative mood, so I wasn't going to force it.

As I reached for my tools, I noticed that the piping bag and tips were not in the positions I had left them in, and some frosting was now smeared on the outside of the bag that I had to wipe up. "Did you taste test some of the frosting while I was gone?" I asked innocently, trying to make conversation. He could have just asked to taste test it.

"Oh, yeah," he said, pausing before continuing. "That's not a problem, is it? It was good." One of his eyebrows was raised, but he was smiling, and his face seemed undisturbed.

"Of course not." I waved my one clean hand dismissively and started frosting the first round of cupcakes.

With the few minutes he had before the next batch could go in, he wandered off down the hallway without a word. What on Earth was up with him? Whatever. He would tell me when he was ready.

"That's strange," I said a little while later. "I could have sworn I had a full two dozen cupcakes in that first batch. But I seem to have lost one."

"Oh? Are you sure you had that many when you started?" he said, without looking over at my workstation.

"Yes, I was pretty particular about measuring out twenty-four somewhat evenly sized cupcakes."

"Weird."

"It is not like they can just disappear. . . ." I counted the cupcakes again. And then again. But I kept coming up one shy.

"You made extra, right?" Ian reminded me.

"Well, yeah. But—"

"It'll be okay, Luce. You probably just counted wrong the first time."

One cupcake didn't really matter, so I went back to my task. I doubt I'd counted wrong, but maybe when I was cleaning up the mess from earlier,

I'd misplaced one. Or perhaps someone had sampled one and didn't want to tell me, for some reason.

I looked up to tease and accuse Ian of stealing not just a taste of frosting, but an entire cupcake, just in time to see him walk off toward the hallway again. I was starting to get really worried about what he was up to, now that he had finished mixing all of the batter that we needed. Why did he have to keep leaving the room? Hundreds of heartbreaking reasons flashed through my mind, and I tried my best to shake them off. I just needed to concentrate on my own stuff.

This time when he returned, he wore a strange look on his face and had one hand behind his back.

"Are you okay?" I asked.

"Never better," he replied. Then, he did the last thing I had expected.

He dropped down on one knee and revealed a fully decorated cupcake, which he held out toward me.

Sticking out of the very top of the uneven, small mound of icing was a bright, shining ring.

My hands shot up to cover up my mouth, which had dropped open at the sight. I didn't even care that this meant that I had smeared frosting all over my chin.

"I know I've been acting strange these past couple of days, but honestly, it was just because I was planning to propose at the restaurant tonight. I know it's cliché—and I started to just move things around and plan another date for us, but then I figured that there was no point in putting it off. It doesn't matter where we are, as long as we're together and happy and in love." He paused. "Lucy, will you do me the honor of becoming my wife?"

I bent over to pull on his arm, making him stand back up in front of me. "Yes! Of course, Ian. I love you!"

In response, he pulled me into the sweetest kiss we had ever shared, careful not to smush the cupcake and knock away the ring in the process.

"I suppose I should clean off this ring, so you can try it on," he chuckled after he broke away.

I laughed and waited until he was ready for me to stick out my hand for him. It was just the style that I had always dreamed about and, of course, was even better than any of my dreams because of the man who had given it to me.

"So, that's what happened to my missing cupcake, huh?" I asked with a jovial tilt of my head.

He shrugged. "I thought I had a good decoration to add to it."

I laughed. "I just figured you ate it."

I placed the cupcake down on the counter before pulling him into an embrace. Our moment of revelry was only interrupted by the sound of the timer going off. He rushed over to check the cupcakes, but I didn't care whether they were underbaked or burnt at this point. Nothing could ruin this night.

Everyone at the corporate event ended up enjoying our cupcakes the next afternoon, though the true star of the show was my new accessory. It was all most of my coworkers could talk about when they were not busy interacting with potential clients. My boss even went out of his way to congratulate me on a job well done and hinted that I was on their radar for future opportunities at the company—of the marketing and catering kinds. The event was a great success. I was confident it wouldn't be too much longer before I would be able to afford the down payment on a bakery space.

For now, though, I wanted to think only of wedding planning.

Did Ian and I dare attempt making the wedding cake ourselves?

No, definitely not.

But at least we knew that we could do it if we needed to.

About the Author

Megan D. Wood is a romance writer creating captivating stories that transport her readers. She fell in love with reading at age six and started writing for herself soon after.

She lives near Wake Forest, North Carolina, and enjoys spending time with her family, especially her niece and nephew. She attended UNC–Chapel Hill, where she studied history and religions. Inspired by these studies, she is currently working on a historical romance novel.

When she is not writing, you can often find her baking, playing cozy video games, or working on whatever craft she is obsessing over.

You can find Megan on:

Instagram: @megan_studios_

A NOTE TO REMEMBER

A Note to Remember

Bjarne Borresen

A BITTER, COLD WIND BLUSTERED through the streets and alleys of Chicago, causing Charlie Nunley to lose his balance, slip on the parking lot's frozen blacktop, and fall to the ground. He lay there for a second, cursing the ice and the weather and the city and his life, for that matter, then glanced down and saw a newly formed hole in the knee of his pants. *Perfect*, he thought. He staggered to his feet, his butt now cold from the icy wetness, and pulled the collar of his jacket tighter around his neck against the wind.

"What a freakin' day," he muttered.

One week from today was Valentine's Day. He saw the preparations of his coworkers in the office, their smiles like kids at Christmas in anticipation of the holiday. He had watched as Chrissy hustled off to the nail salon and had sat mute as Jim showed off a pair of diamond earrings. Charlie had no such plans, felt no excitement. This would be his second Valentine's without Janice, a day he was *not* looking forward to. The first had been sheer torture. Watching friends and coworkers talk about their plans, giddy with excitement and the knowledge of what the night would lead to.

As painful as it was, Charlie couldn't blame them—he and Janice had been just as goofy in love. They had met purely by chance. He had been late for work, rushing into the parking lot, not paying attention. She was backing up slightly to make sure her car was straight in the parking space. His car hit hers with a *crunch*, not hard, but enough to scare them both. When they'd both gotten out of their vehicles and their eyes met, somehow, they'd both just known.

He'd apologized profusely, promised to pay for the damage, but each time he did she'd simply shrug it off, saying, "It's no big deal, it was barely a scratch."

She'd been tall, nearly as tall as Charlie, with medium-length, dark hair. Her olive complexion wasn't as pale as his in the Chicago winter, suggesting a little Mediterranean blood in her ancestry. Her eyes were large and light brown with streaks of yellow that held intelligence and a spark of mischief. Charlie had been spellbound.

Before he'd even known what he was doing—very unlike Charlie—he'd started a little small talk, asking her what type of business she'd had in the building. She said she'd been working on the fourth floor at Cinch for three years in marketing. *How in the world had he missed her? He was only one floor below that! Surely, they'd passed each other on the stairs or waiting for an elevator.* They'd walked into the building together and unbelievably, tongue-twisted as he was, he'd asked her to dinner.

That was four years ago. They had spent nearly every waking minute together from that day forward. They could talk for hours about nearly any subject under the sun. They both enjoyed the same cuisines, read the same books, and liked the same movies. And the sex? Words could not describe. They married before the end of that year in a small ceremony with just a few friends. Everything was perfect. She was perfect. Life was perfect. Until . . .

Valentine's Day two years ago. Janice had just left a nail salon in anticipation of their dinner when a truck swerved across the center line. Drunk, the policeman had said. Janice never had a chance. "She never felt a thing," they'd told him, as if that were some consolation prize. Charlie had never realized how pitifully hollow and condescending that had sounded. Sure, he was glad for the possibility of a pain-free death, but *his* pain was all-encompassing and absolute. The emergency room doctor said that they'd tried everything but knew as soon as they'd seen her that there was no hope. She was simply too far gone. They'd offered no details beyond that, and he couldn't bring himself to ask more.

Charlie had stood alone in the hospital's hallway holding a plastic bag of her belongings that felt pitifully light in his hands. It should have weighed a million pounds with the weight of that beautiful soul. He had peered into the room. She was covered with a sheet, her body still. The monitors above her were dark and silent, no longer needed. There was a distinct smell of disinfectant in the air. He saw several nurses walk by, going out of their way to walk around him and what lay inside that room—possibly out of respect, possibly choosing not to think about what they were unable to do for her. He prayed that this would not be how he remembered her.

Charlie had never been the same after that day. He'd been moving through life in a daze, going through the motions. One day blurred into another, which blurred into weeks, which blurred into months. To be honest, he'd considered ending it all many times, but he couldn't bring himself to do it, knowing she wouldn't want such an end for him.

So, there he was, walking along the frozen streets of Chicago with a cold, wet butt and limping on a sore knee across the parking lot with a hole in his pants one week from the happiest day of the year for lovers.

"Janice, God how I miss you," he mumbled to the chilly wind.

He got to his car, a beautiful Tesla sedan that had been Janice's dream car. He turned on the heater full blast, but intensely cold air streamed out of the vents. He suddenly realized he was starving. *Had he even eaten today?* He thought about what he had in the refrigerator at home. Nothing. He hadn't been shopping in weeks. He pulled out his phone and looked up the information for Gino's. It had been their favorite restaurant and somehow seemed appropriate with thoughts of Janice running through his head.

Gino's was a local establishment run by Gino himself, an immigrant from Italy who'd arrived in America nearly thirty years earlier. He was a caring soul who would come to each table as the patrons were finishing up their meals to make sure the food had been just as they liked it. The restaurant was decorated with whitewashed brick walls, white tablecloths, and fancy napkin holders in the shape of a fleur-de-lis, and soft music echoed through hidden speakers. Janice had always ordered the chicken parmesan and Charlie the lasagna with meatballs. It had been the site of their first date and was every bit as important a memory as their first kiss.

He called and placed an order, thought about ordering the chicken parm since he was feeling so sentimental, but settled for the lasagna. He'd just run in, grab the bag, and run back out into the cold. No looking around, no hellos. Just grab the bag and get out.

As he'd expected, the parking lot was packed. Gino's was by no means their little secret on the South Side of Chicago. It was always busy. He had to park next door at the abandoned gas station and tiptoe across the parking lot, slipping and sliding, grabbing onto parked cars as he went. Hot air and conversation hit him as he pulled the door open. The heavenly smell of garlic and parmesan felt like a hug from an old friend.

He smiled at the hostesses, two of Gino's daughters, each with long hair so dark, hints of blue shone through in the soft light.

He pointed at the bar and said, "To-go order."

He'd been doing that a lot in the past two years, not wanting to see the happy couples enjoying their dinners together, imagining them staring and whispering questions like, "Wonder what happened to him?" and "Why do you think he's always alone?" He was not ready for that, even after all this time.

The hostesses smiled and nodded as one as he passed. The bar area was as packed as the parking lot had been: Every table was full and the bar was busy, except for a lone chair at the end near the wall. He wound his way through the tables and sat heavily. The bartender, Gabe, whom he and Janice had shared a drink or two with many times, raised his head once he noticed him and pointed at him.

Charlie mouthed: "To-go."

Gabe nodded back and went through a door at the opposite end of the bar that led to the kitchen, returning a minute later empty-handed. "Sorry, Charlie. Food's delayed." He nodded toward the main restaurant. "Crazy busy, as you can tell. What can I get you to drink? It's on the house for the wait."

Charlie nodded. Hard to turn down a free drink. "How 'bout a beer?"

Gabe tapped the bar with a knuckle and went to the taps, pouring a tall glass of Peroni. He set the beer and a shot glass half full with amber liquid in front of Charlie and smiled sadly. Charlie lifted the shot glass and sipped as Gabe went down the bar to take another order. Amaretto, the kind Janice drank. There was nobody like Gabe in all of Chicago.

Charlie smiled and took a sip of beer, feeling the cool liquid slide down his throat, and stared into the mirror behind the bar. He barely recognized the stranger staring back at him. His hair was thinner, his cheeks sunken. And his eyes: Even to him they looked sad and lonely. He shook his head slowly and went back to his beer.

As he was nearing the end of the Peroni, the shot of Amaretto finished, Gabe stepped out from the door carrying a brown bag and headed straight for Charlie. He set the bag on the bar, then leaned forward, pushing a napkin toward him and whispered, "I know you're going to want to say no—trust me, I know—but if I were you, I'd think long and hard about accepting."

Charlie's eyebrows scrunched together. "Huh? Accept what?"

Gabe tapped the napkin. "Oh, and it's $19.74 for the food."

Charlie reached into his back pocket, pulled a credit card from his wallet, and slid it toward Gabe, who picked it up and tapped it on the napkin. "Seriously, man. Just think about it. That's all I'm asking."

He turned and crossed to the register. Charlie looked down at the napkin. What the hell was Gabe up to?

The napkin was folded in half. *Gino's* was written in a elaborate script. Charlie pulled it closer and opened it up. The handwriting was equally as elegant as the *Gino's* on the other side, with big, loopy letters, clearly a woman's handwriting. It read: *I know this is sappy and way overdone in the movies. But I'd love to have dinner with you. Valentine's is next Tuesday. What better day for a first date? 7 p.m.*

Charlie stared at it for several long seconds, not quite believing the words even as he stared down at them. He looked around the bar for the first time. Nearly all of the patrons at the small tables were couples: holding hands, their heads pressed together in whispered conversations. There were a few business-types at the far end of the bar, two were women, but neither so much as glanced in his direction. They were both dark-haired, like Janice. Before falling for Janice, he'd tended to prefer blondes, if he was being honest, probably because of his high school crush, Jennifer Thompson. She'd been petite and funny and *way* out of his league, but the memory of her had stuck. She'd been forever attached to Chad Johnson. Had they gotten married? He couldn't remember. He could still picture her long, blonde hair in class. But once he looked into Janice's eyes, he was done and her dark hair became his new favorite.

He turned back to the bar and found Gabe standing in front of him, placing his check and credit card back in front of him.

Gabe wiggled his eyebrows and smiled. "Seriously, man. I'd do it." He leaned on his elbows. "I know it's been hard, Charlie. Look, I'd see the two of you in here all the time. I know what you and Janice had, Charlie. I do." He tapped the napkin yet again. "But this, this is here and this is now, and I gotta say, she's worth the risk."

"Who is it?" Charlie asked.

Gabe pressed a finger to his lips. "Nope. Not from me, dude. You'll have to be here to see. Me? I'd cut off my left leg for a chance."

Charlie laughed at that. He hadn't seen anyone that could have gotten Gabe all giddy, but then again, he'd been consciously *not* trying to see anyone. He looked around the bar area again, knowing the mystery woman wouldn't still be there.

Then Charlie had a thought. *What would Janice think?*

The week passed quickly. He had purposely avoided going to Gino's since receiving the note. He had to admit he was tempted to go, however. Sure, he'd been lonely these last two years, but he never really realized just how lonely he was until Gabe had passed him that napkin. His house now felt like a prison; its empty rooms mocking him when he'd enter. He heard every creak and groan as if the house itself was urging him to go on the date.

But then again, there was Janice. Everywhere he went in the house, Janice. On every wall, on every bookcase, Janice. Their wedding photos hung on the wall in the den. Their trip to Hawaii in a three-frame set on the mantle. Hundreds of photo magnets stuck to the refrigerator with friends and family in all manner of places. God how he loved that woman.

Suddenly, it was the night before Valentine's. The week had passed as if it had only been a day. He'd laid out a pair of khaki slacks and a nice button-down shirt just in case he'd made up his mind and decided to go. He'd fussed over the shirt: picking one out, then putting it back and grabbing another. All in all, it had taken nearly an hour to pick out a pair of pants and a shirt. He chuckled as he stared down at them. Should he iron it? He hadn't ironed a shirt in two years! Maybe he'd wear it to work just in case, so he'd be ready. Or would it wrinkle too badly throughout the day? Maybe he'd just bring it in a bag. Should he'd bring his Dopp Kit? Freshen up in the restroom before leaving work, or would he have time to come home after? Maybe he'd just forget the clothes and if he *did* decide to go, he'd be forced to come back home first, giving him time to think if that's what he really wanted to do.

As he was trying to decide what to do, he sat heavily on the couch and switched the TV on but kept it muted. He pulled out their wedding album and set it in his lap. A lone tear slid down his cheek. He absently wiped it away as he opened the cover. Janice had been radiant that day: her hair pulled up in an intricate braid, her gown making her look like a princess. He smiled as he remembered how many bobby pins they'd pulled out of her hair after the reception. Him counting as he pulled them out, one by one, and her laughing and swatting at his hands. He couldn't wait to get her out of that dress, as much as he loved to see her in it. She was an amazing lover: patient, always thinking of him and his needs. Didn't she know that all he'd ever wanted, all he'd ever *needed*, was her? He turned the page and saw the picture of the two of them slicing the wedding cake. He had set a drink down on the table on their one-year anniversary and accidentally set it on the picture. The water had left a stain on the photo, making Charlie's tux look half black/half white. She had been so mad at him that night . . . until they made up.

He wiped another tear and rested his head against the back of the couch. Two years. How could it be two years?

He grabbed a photo from the end table. Janice in Cozumel. Or was it Cancun? Her cheeks rosy from the sun. She was seated on a bench, the beach and Caribbean in the background. She wore a colorful sundress that gave hints to the beautiful figure that lay beneath.

"What do you want me to do, sweet pea?" he asked. "Is it okay to move on?"

He was still a young man, just thirty-four last September. He shouldn't have to go through life alone, should he? Till death do we part. . . . Did that mean it was okay? He'd done the "for better or worse" part, though it was pretty much all better, very little worse. Did her untimely death mean it was okay?

What would his friends think? Well, what friends he had left. He'd pretty much turned into a hermit these past two years. Work, eat, sleep, repeat. He couldn't even remember the last time he'd seen anyone socially. Work was just him and his car with occasional breaks to see clients. Zero chitchat. And the fairer sex? Ha! Never even crossed his mind.

Until last week.

He shifted a bit and reached into his jeans pocket, pulling out the note Gabe had handed him. He held it up to his nose and sniffed, hoping to get a hint of her perfume for the hundredth time and failing. For some reason, he'd been carrying it in his pocket all week. He stared at the handwriting of the note then turned to the wedding album again and stared at his wife.

"Please tell me what to do, Janice, 'cause I really don't know what to do."

That night's sleep was a complete waste of time. He'd tossed and turned in the bed, reading page after page in a crappy book, watching infomercials with no hints at sleep. He'd pictured Janice in so many different places and times and thought of the women at the office. Could it be one of them? Surely not. He'd have picked up on some sort of sign. Maybe a flirty smile or a hand absently worrying a strand of loose hair. But he couldn't remember seeing anything like that. He had to admit, the mystery of it was both exciting and frustrating as hell. He turned on his belly and covered his head and grumbled as the alarm sounded.

Work was the same. He'd been a zombie, driving through town on autopilot, his mind miles away from the task of driving. When he was in a meeting, or waiting in reception, he'd look at each and every woman he saw and wonder if she could be his mystery woman. The clock on his dashboard seemed to have a mind of its own, zipping along like a speedometer, racing toward the deadline. Before he knew what hit him, it was 6:35. He looked at the small suitcase he'd set on the passenger seat. His button-down shirt and khakis, Dopp Kit with deodorant and cologne. If he was going to go, he needed to go.

A horn honked behind him, and he realized he'd been sitting at a stoplight, the light long since changed to green. He realized that he'd been somewhere far away, anywhere but here, and decided that he had to make a change. He couldn't simply keep going through life like he had been—in a daze, just going through the motions. As scary as it was, he was going to give happiness a second chance.

He waved a hand in the air in apology to the driver behind him, pulled into a Wendy's on the next block, and grabbed his Dopp Kit. Feeling like a fool, he bypassed the counter and went straight to the bathroom, trying his best to hide the little bag with his toiletries from the counter workers. He brushed his teeth, applied some deodorant, and spritzed a bit of cologne on his neck. He was back in his car before the pimply kid behind the counter could yell, "Hey, you gotta buy something!" at his back. He pulled around to the back of the parking lot and changed into the khakis and button-down. Luckily, nobody pulled through the drive-thru line and called the cops on him.

When he got to Gino's, just before seven, the parking lot was packed like it had been the week before. He went next door to the abandoned gas station and once again did the shimmy across the frozen parking lot. He stopped when he reached Gino's front door. He almost, *almost*, turned around and went back to his car, but he took a deep breath and pulled the door open and stepped in.

It suddenly dawned on him that he had no idea what to do now. Was he supposed to give his name to the hostess, but how would the mystery woman know what his name was? Perhaps Gabe told her? Maybe he should just go to the bar and ask Gabe if she'd arrived yet?

He looked past the hostess desk and peeked into the bar and immediately spotted Gabe. He stood behind the bar as always, but his face broke into a huge Cheshire Cat grin when he spotted Charlie. Well, apparently he was supposed to go to the bar. He walked in, looking around, but all of the tables held couples leaning toward each other, holding hands and snickering. Gabe gestured to the end of the bar with a hand, where he'd sat last time. He walked that way, Gabe mirroring his steps behind the bar.

"Charlie Nunley," a voice said as he neared.

A blonde turned on her stool and Charlie couldn't believe his eyes.

"Jennifer Thompson?" He laughed out loud. "Is that really you?"

Her face broke into a huge smile that lit up the room. She stood. She wore a form-fitting red dress that came to just below her knees. She was still slender but curvy in all the right places. The passage of years since high school had left a few subtle hints of lines at the edges of her blue eyes, but they only seemed to add to the beauty he remembered.

She took a step forward and held her hands out. "I've waited nearly twenty years to go on a date with you, Charlie Nunley. Twenty long years."

"But how? Why?" he stammered, taking her hands in his.

She laughed and pulled him into a hug.

He suddenly leaned his head back a little, looking at her with a sideways glance. "Wait. *You* waited twenty years?"

She smiled again and nodded. "You weren't the only one that had a crush in high school, Charlie Nunley. You don't think I noticed you were sneaking glances at me during cheerleading practice? Or the way you'd always be near my locker after history class?" She laughed. "You were the nicest, funniest, sweetest guy in school. But for some reason, I could *not* get you to ask me on a date!"

Charlie laughed. "How could I? Stupid Chad was always two steps away!"

Her smile suddenly faltered and slid from her face as she lowered her eyes for a moment. It dawned on Charlie that he had very little idea what had happened to her after high school. She had gone to Northwestern for nursing school, he remembered that, but did she and Chad . . .?

He pulled her close. "Oh no, Jennifer. I'm so sorry. Did something—I think I remember you and Chad getting married? Did something happen?"

She nodded slowly, sadness passing over her like a shadow. "We did. It was . . ." She shook her head quickly and straightened up, pulling her shoulders back. "Let's just say it wasn't what I had dreamed a marriage would be and leave it at that."

He waved a hand at the two stools at the bar and they both sat.

She said, "But, not to be too forward, I always had one eye on you, the one that got away, so to speak. I'd hear from friends about your work and where you were, what you were doing through the years. And when you got married . . . Well, that was hard, but I was just some high school friend, right? What did I have to be upset about?"

She laughed self-consciously.

She reached a hand out and took his in hers. "But then I read in the paper about your wife." She swallowed hard. "I am so, so sorry, Charlie. From everything I'd heard, from what people had said, I know she meant the world to you. I wanted so bad to call you or to write or something but it just never seemed right. But then I saw you in here last week." She nodded at the bar. "And I saw this as a chance, a small little ray of hope in my miserable life after finally getting away from Chad. I just had to take a chance."

Charlie smiled and mumbled, "Jennifer Thompson."

She smiled back, true happiness now. "Charlie Nunley."

Charlie laughed, then had a thought. Gabe was at the other end of the bar, wiping the bar top absently, keeping one eye on them. He waved him over.

"So?" Gabe asked.

"You got a napkin and a pen?"

Gabe's brow furrowed as he looked back and forth between them. He reached down and grabbed a napkin and plucked the pen from his pocket, laying them down in front of Charlie.

Charlie grabbed the pen, turned the napkin and scribbled quickly, then folded it neatly and slid it over to Jennifer.

She smiled coyly as she picked up the napkin. She read it quickly and laughed, holding it up for Gabe to see. She read, "'Will you go out with me? Yes or No.'"

With a giggle, Jennifer grabbed the pen and hastily circled *Yes* several times.

Gabe threw his head back and laughed, clapping his hands as he walked back to the other end of the bar.

About the Author

Bjarne Borresen is the author of several children's books, including The Hansen Clan series, *How Mila and Audrey Saved Christmas*, *Freya and the Valley of Obershire*, and *Wyatt Beasley and the Evil King*. He currently works full-time as a nurse anesthetist and writes whenever possible.

Bjarne lives in Jasper, Tennessee, with his wife, Rachel, and their two dogs. They have two grown children who have provided them with a lifetime of stories and adventures from which to draw inspiration.

You can find Bjarne on:

Instagram: @bboresen5150

You can visit his website at:

bjarneborresen.com

SWEET AS PIE

Sweet As Pie

Krista Renee

EVERYTHING IN LIFE HAS ITS own recipe. Even the bad times could be turned into something sweet. My daughter, Lulu, had continued to prove that. But there'd been one thing I'd been unable to nail down. No matter how many times I tried, this one thing failed me. I couldn't put my finger on it. It remained clawing at the back of my brain, festering like a boil.

That night's outdoor temperature sat at fifty degrees. In Texas, that was almost snow-day territory. Fifty degrees should've meant I slept like a baby. Instead, every night for the past three months, I'd woken up soaked in sweat. Before you suggest menopause, don't. I went through that years ago. Now, I was a sixty-something woman who just couldn't sleep.

I threw the covers off my sweaty body. After a shower that could've turned water to ice, I put on a pair of high-waisted jeans and a hoodie well past its expiration date. At five a.m., I didn't care what I looked like—not that I did any other time. My daughter had moved out, and my customers never seemed to care if I was done up as long as the pie was edible.

I needed to get to the diner. Days like these, the only thing that could soothe my soul was coming up with a pie. With it being Valentine's Day, everyone would be expecting berries and chocolate. Heck, most every year, that's what I did. Give the people what they want, right? But that wasn't going to cut it this year. If I was going to get out of whatever this funk was, I needed something different. Something new.

By the time I pulled into the diner's lot, oranges, pinks, and yellows painted the sky. My daughter would say otherwise, but you couldn't get a sunrise like that in a big city. I may not have originally moved to Sulphur Bluff by choice, but I couldn't imagine my roots being planted anywhere else.

My ex-husband's daddy, Pop, waved at me from across the feed store parking lot. I smiled and waved back. His hands shoved in the pockets of his jeans as he walked across the grassy area separating our businesses.

"Mornin', Georgiabelle."

My smile widened as I shook my head. "Mornin', Pop."

He nudged me with his elbow. "It's five-thirty. What in heaven are you doin' here so early?"

As if on cue, I yawned. I tried my best to shake it away before it turned into a whole-body thing, but it didn't work. That seemed to be the theme for my life lately.

"The early bird gets the worm, or somethin' like that. Besides, it's Valentine's Day. Somebody's gotta make the pie for all the couples making the babies tonight." As someone whose daughter was conceived on Valentine's Day, I knew this fact all too well. "What are you and Lolli doing for Valentine's?"

"I would say nothing, but even at eighty-five years old, she'd kick my butt. So, I'll say we're going to the movies and dinner."

"Sounds like a plan. I gotta get bakin'."

He smiled and pressed his lips to my forehead. "You're my favorite daughter."

"You're my favorite Pop. Tell Loll I love her."

He nodded and I turned to head inside. It sounded silly, but raising a kid takes a village. Lu wouldn't have turned out half as well as she did if it wasn't for Lolli and Pop. They'd been my rock when Eddie was at his worst, and they stood by me even though he tried to turn them against me. Divorcing him thirty-three years ago was the best and scariest decision I'd ever made, I wouldn't have made it through my divorce or pregnancy without Pop and Loll.

The second my foot was on the pavement, I was drawn in by a pair of sapphire eyes. Eyes that were so blue they were almost clear. Eyes that I probably should've avoided staring at for any length of time. Up till that moment, I'd taken my own advice. Ever since my daughter and her girlfriend, Ella, hosted Thanksgiving, those eyes had haunted me. I saw them every time I closed my eyes. I didn't need them following me when I was awake, too.

I pulled my gaze from hers and tried to focus on the car she was driving, or the color of the trashcan to her right. "Focus, Georgia. They're just a pair of eyes. Go inside and start making pies. She can't haunt you inside. Not to mention, she's your daughter's girlfriend's mom. That's enough reason to avoid her."

But no matter what I told myself, my feet remained locked in place. My heart pounded in my chest and ears when she parked beside my old Jeep and got out. Sugar and gardenia invaded my bubble when she stepped beside me.

"We don't open till eight," I said quickly before darting in the direction of the front door. In thirty years, I had never had a problem getting the key in the door. Naturally, the one day I needed that to apply would be the day my keys decided not to work.

"We need to talk, peaches," she said, her voice a whisper. My breath caught in my chest when I realized our proximity. If I turned around, our skin would brush. "That pie you made for Thanksgiving—it was out-of-this-world delicious. I haven't been able to think of anything since. The way you married the peaches with the strawberries and cinnamon. Oh, my god. Heaven. That's the only word that captures what happened in that moment."

My face flushed. I closed my eyes and forced myself to breathe like a normal human and not someone who had a schoolgirl crush. "Thank you, Jill."

Once I was certain I could function, I turned to face her. "I can show you how to make it, if you'd like. It's not a complicated pie, and I need something to put out."

I saw her daughter in her eyes when the corners of her lips curved up. "Are you sure? I'd bet you have better things to do and I wouldn't want to put you out."

I shook my head. "You're not. Like I said, I gotta get something in the case." After unlocking the door, I held it open for her. "You will need to wear an apron and a hair net."

"Is it hard?" she asked while I prepped the table. "Obviously you're going to say no because you do this for a living, but for someone with no experience, is it hard?"

I chuckled softly. I reached across the table and gave her hand a squeeze. "You're a doctor. Compared to that, this is a slice of pie."

My insides felt like melted sugar when she laughed. It was a warm, light laugh, the kind of laugh that wraps around you like a warm blanket. She wiped tears from her cheeks while she caught her breath. "You're funny, peaches."

"My name's Georgia, not Peaches."

She took a step forward and tucked rogue locks of hair behind my ear. I pulled my gaze from hers when she continued to linger. "I know, peaches.

Every time I see or smell peaches, I think of you. You can't imagine how many times I've thought of you since Thanksgiving."

I cleared my throat and put some distance between us. "A good pie starts with crust."

"Right," she said, wiping her hands on her jeans. "Can't have pie without a crust."

After I made the dough ball, I handed her the rolling pin. Her brow cocked. "You want me to roll out the dough?"

"Would you like some help?"

She nodded with wide eyes. "Yes, please."

I came behind her and wrapped my arms around her. Electricity shot through me when our fingers brushed. "Gently roll it out. It's Valentine's Day. You want people to think it's made with love."

"It always is. Isn't it? You make sure of it."

I nodded. I rose on my tiptoes and held out a piece of dough. "Taste the difference that love makes." Heat rushed to my core when she moaned in approval. I should've taken that as a sign to go start the filling, but I couldn't get my feet to move. They were stuck in cement.

"No wonder our daughters like each other. You probably bribed them with pie."

Every breath I tried to take ended up catching in my chest. Why didn't I move? I wasn't a young girl anymore. A pie needed to go out and I couldn't move.

A smile played across her face when she turned to face me. "You did. Didn't you, peaches?"

She was too dang close. I tried pushing her away, but my hand betrayed me and began tracing her exposed collarbones. All my life I knew I should like men, but none of them gave me the rush she did. "I haven't thought of much anything else but you since Thanksgiving, Jill."

Why, oh, why did I say that? She didn't need to know that. She shouldn't know that. There were things in life best kept for yourself. That was the one thing that was fact right then. If only my hormones would get the memo.

Because I apparently had the hormones of a teenager, I was going to have to force things to work; my feet being first. I backed into the opposite counter and took a long, slow breath.

That was good. See? I could function like a grown woman. "Pie. Let's make the pie."

She gave me a nod while she played with the strings on her apron. "We're two adults. We can make a pie."

"Right." I began making the filling and prayed she didn't notice the squeak in my voice. If she did, she didn't say anything. Thank heavens.

She approached as I was carefully finishing the filling for the pie. I handed her the hot pan and helped her guide it into the crust. She inhaled sharply when some of it got on her finger. Without much thought, I cradled her hand in mine, brought it close to my lips, and blew softly on the red skin to ease the pain.

"There," I said after a minute had passed and dropped her hand. She held her hand against her heart. "All better."

She gave me a small smile. After a few seconds, it turned into something that spread across her whole face. Something warmed inside me when she smiled—not my core, but something. For all the talk her daughter gave about her being an awful person, I had a feeling she wasn't as bad as she wanted people to believe.

"You're a million times better at this mom thing than I ever thought about. Hell, I wasn't even around my daughter."

There was a sadness in her voice that shattered my heart. I wrapped my arms around her and held her close. I didn't say anything. I just held her. Sometimes all people needed was a hug. She didn't push me away. Her cheek rested on the crown of my head, while a hand moved up my back.

"I'm sure I'm ruining your Valentine's Day."

I looked at her and cupped her cheek. "Our daughters have each other. Every couple has each other. For the first time in years, I have someone to spend this day with—even if it's a tad out of the norm." I hiked my shoulders. "Having company is better than no company. Trust me, Jill, you haven't ruined anything."

While we waited on the pie to bake, we sat on the floor drinking coffee. "I tried to make this day special for Charlotte, my ex-wife. But no matter what I tried, she resisted. It was as if my very presence put her off. Then I wrote a book and gained recognition and she despised me more. Nothing I did was good enough. Peaches, you're the first person I'm spending time with that hasn't used me for anything."

"What's there to use? Our daughters are gonna get married eventually, so we might as well make the best of what we've got. And right now, that's each other."

Her soft chuckle heated my core and made my entire body tingle. "You know, if you weren't my daughter's girlfriend's mom, I'd kiss you right now."

"What's stopping you?"

My face flushed at the realization that I'd said what I was thinking out loud. Her gaze locked on mine, and it was as if time was ticking in my ears.

I was in my sixties, sitting on the floor of my diner before opening hours, hoping my daughter's future in-law would kiss me.

Yup. This was the strangest Valentine's Day of my life.

"Because if I kiss you, I'm worried I won't be able to stop. For everyone's sake, I need to control myself."

"Makes sense," I said with a nod.

I should've listened to her words. I had every intention to. But then I leaned into her and pressed my lips to hers.

Shiiiit.

This was a bad idea. Maybe the worst idea of all time. I needed to pull away, to stop it. Why wasn't she pushing me away? This would've been so much easier if she would've. Instead of doing anything we should be doing, her hand cupped my cheek, then tangled in my hair. It had been too long since I'd been kissed. That was the only explanation I could come up with.

To make things worse, she smiled. "Peaches, I was going to maintain the control of a wet noodle. Thank you for having even less than me."

I snorted. After taking her cup, I put them in the sink, then set the pie on the cooling rack. She appeared behind me and kissed the curve of my neck.

"God, I forgot what it feels like to be kissed there."

Shut. Up. Georgia Lynn. Don't keep talking. This is going to get you in trouble.

Hands rested on my hips. "I knew your pies were out-of-this-world unbelievable. Somehow you taste better than the pie."

I swallowed as her hands moved up. They were slow. Too slow. Even through my hoodie, her fingers left a trail of fire.

"You know," I started as she moved to the other side of my neck. "We should stop. What if someone walks in?"

I giggled when her breath tickled my skin. "Well, we'll just have to say we're rehearsing a play."

"I don't normally do this."

"What is *this* exactly?"

I turned to face her. After gesturing between us, my arms wrapped around her neck. "Kiss people I've known less than twenty-four hours."

"Technically," she said, lifting me on the counter. "We've known each other three months. In the lesbian world, that's practically a century."

"You're a lesbian. I'm—" I actually didn't know how to finish that. "I don't know what I am, but I do like kissing you. I shouldn't. But I do."

The pad of her thumb traced my bottom lip. "I like kissing you, too. Not sure our daughters would approve, but I do."

I crossed my feet at the ankles when she put a slice of pie on a plate and topped it with whipped cream. She brought it back and held it to my lips. "Kissing you is my new favorite thing. This pie is a close second."

The flavors exploded on my tongue when I accepted the bite. That was the good thing about pie; it'd never judge you or make you feel awful about yourself. I've never made a pie that didn't make me feel warm and cozy after eating it.

"And I'd like to continue kissing you for as long as you'll let me."

I pressed my lips to hers. A throaty whimper bubbled to the surface when she parted my lips with her tongue. My face was red hot. Her tongue was teasing mine while one hand rested on the small of my back and the other tugged on the strings of my hoodie.

"I'd like to continue kissing you, too," I whispered. We were the only two people in the room, but the way my voice resounded in my ears made it sound like I was yelling. "But I know certain things need to be taken into consideration before we go all in with us."

"I'm not going to rush whatever we've got going on. Why don't we agree to take it slow and just spend some time together?"

I nodded. She helped me off the counter and pulled me against her. For a while, we just swayed. It was the closest thing to perfect that I'd had in a long, long time.

"Slow is good."

My teeth sank into my bottom lip when fingers tilted my chin and our eyes met. "With you, slow is everything. I feel something with you that I haven't in years. I'm not a spring chicken anymore. I'm not into playing games. What I say, I mean. And right now, I want to spend time with you."

I knew the risks that came with getting involved. My brain screamed them at me. But up till that moment, I lived my life how you were supposed. I got married at seventeen. By thirty, I was pregnant. For thirty-four years, she was my life. I didn't date because I never wanted to upset her. But she had her own life now. It was possible that this was one of those times where the rewards outweighed the risks. If it blew up in my face, I'd accept the consequences.

I grabbed her hand and led her to the cooler. Once we had semi privacy, I pressed her against the shelves. My hands explored her body until they stopped at her ribs.

"My daughter was conceived on that table, but I've never kissed anyone here. May I kiss you again?"

She framed my face with a smile. "Peaches, with you, the answer will always be yes."

I leaned in and pressed my lips to hers. The smile against me as she pressed her hands to the small of my back made my insides turn to goo. It was addictive. But not the kind that makes you do something stupid that you'll regret. No. This was the kind of addictive that brought peace and clarity. I couldn't explain it, but kissing her was what I was meant to do. Things felt right, like I could breathe for the first time.

"Happy Valentine's Day, Jill," I said in between kisses.

She smiled. "Happy Valentine's Day, peaches."

She followed me into the kitchen. While I was getting ingredients together for another pie, she wrapped her arms around me. "What kind of pie are you making now?"

"It's called She's Worth It Dark Chocolate and Strawberry."

Georgia and Jill first appeared in Krista Renee's debut novel, Bad Idea Lane, *which released in 2024. To read more about them and their stories, and to meet their daughters, Ella and Lulu, pick up a copy today! Available in print and ebook on Amazon and other retailers.*

About the Author

When Krista Renee isn't writing, she's obsessing over Broadway and hanging out with her four munchkins. She's from East Texas and is currently writing a horror *Wizard of Oz* retelling.

You can find Krista on:

Instagram: @kristareneeauthor

BROWNIE POINTS

Brownie Points

Aimee Moineaux

CORDELIA'S BAG BROKE WHILE SHE was fumbling for her dorm keycard. The carton of eggs crashed to the ground with a sickening crunch.

Perfect. A fitting end to this crappy day. She sighed and looked at her phone. Not even 7:30 p.m. yet. There was still plenty of time for it to get even worse.

She shoved her phone back in the pocket of her anorak and knelt to salvage as much of her groceries as she could. She only needed two eggs, anyway. The fat bottle of vegetable oil was still intact, the plastic barely dented. She glared at it, as if it were the real culprit. Never mind that choosing paper bags over plastic had resulted in this exact scenario more than once before; the Earth would thank her for her sacrifice.

She managed to scoop the other items back into the remains of the bag, ignoring the grotesque ooze coating the bottom of her egg carton, just as the doors to Amato Hall slowly swung open by themselves. She glanced at the front desk and cursed under her breath.

David Herz was on duty tonight. The sexy senior—well, if you were into the reserved, nerdy sort of guy—was always somehow a witness to her worst moments. He had been the one on desk duty the night she accidentally put her cup of noodles in the microwave for three hours instead of three minutes. He'd watched impassively as she was scolded by the firemen for her carelessness and by the other girls on her floor for her dietary habits. He'd been there the morning she'd tried to nip out for a quick coffee while still in her PJs, which became a whole ordeal when she accidentally dropped her keys down a storm drain and had to beg him to let her up to her room wearing a Rainbow Dash onesie. Somehow, he'd kept a straight face that time, too.

If it weren't for all the moments she'd seen him laughing with his girlfriend—a cute, perky little blonde who barely came to eye level when she perched on his desk—she would have thought he was incapable of showing any kind of emotion at all.

The bottle of vegetable oil nearly slipped through the hole in the bag again. Cordelia caught it between her hip and her elbow and waddled through the open doors, desperately trying to keep hold of everything.

David arched an eyebrow at her, the barest flicker of emotion on his impassive face. "Need a hand with that?"

"Nah, I'm good," she said through gritted teeth. "Please, don't get up."

He took her sarcasm at face value and turned his attention back to the open textbook in front of him. *Schmuck.*

She scuttled sideways into the small communal kitchen, grateful that she didn't have to go much farther. She lost her battle with the vegetable oil and aimed a kick at it as it slid from under her elbow, but she missed and it clattered to the floor, unharmed. She couldn't say the same about the eggs. She set the dripping carton on the counter, trying not to think about the salmonella outbreak she would probably be held responsible for, and shrugged off her coat before unpacking the rest of her bag.

"What's going on in here?"

She screeched and whirled around just in time to see David's eyes go wide with surprise before that cool mask slipped right back into place.

Cordelia clutched her heart. "Don't sneak up on me like that!"

"Sorry." He gave a fair impression of a normal human man expressing contrition on his robot face, and Cordelia turned back to her groceries. "I just wanted to check on you. Are you qualified to do . . . whatever this is?"

"Ha, ha." She opened the carton of eggs and did a mental fist pump. Three of the eggs were smashed to hell, but the other nine seemed to be unharmed. This was the best thing that had happened to her all day. "Aren't you supposed to be sitting at the front desk? Protecting the dorm from stranger danger?"

"It's Valentine's Day." She saw his shrug from the corner of her eye as she laid out the foil baking dish and measuring cups she'd just bought. "It's completely dead out there."

"I know it's Valentine's Day. Why else do you think I'm here, on a hot date with Duncan Hines?" She turned to him, hugging the box of brownie mix to her chest, and batted her eyes at him as cartoonishly as she could.

He only blinked. Her comedic talents were wasted on him.

Disgusted, she turned back to her brownies. "Preheat oven to 325," she read aloud and turned on the oven.

"That's Fahrenheit, right? You haven't put it in Celsius by mistake?"

Cordelia glared at him over her shoulder. "Don't be ridiculous," she snapped but surreptitiously checked that she hadn't. Nope, 325°F. *Nobody will be calling the fire department tonight.* It was honestly sad how proud that thought made her.

"Stir together brownie mix, eggs, oil, and water," she continued and frowned. The one thing she hadn't picked up on her grocery run tonight was a mixing bowl. She could probably just stir it all together in the pan she'd bake it in, right? Although, come to think of it, she didn't have a proper mixing spoon, either. She rummaged through the drawers and cabinets in the communal kitchen, but the closest thing she found was an individually wrapped plastic knife and three wooden coffee stirrers at the bottom of a drawer. It would have to do.

"Wow, you're really good at this," David said as she broke an egg yolk with her coffee stirrer. *Was that . . . sarcasm?*

"Don't you have anything better to do with your Valentine's Day than watch me make depression brownies?"

He paused as if he was seriously considering her question. "Nope."

She glanced back at him. He was leaning against the kitchen door, arms crossed over his chest in a way that made his biceps pop under his spotless, plain white T-shirt. His light-brown hair was pushed back, impeccably held in place like a Ken doll's plastic coiffure. His black-frame glasses only added to his Clark Kent allure. She resisted the urge to smear oily brownie goop across his sharp cheekbones and square jaw. She'd give anything just to see him get a little messy.

"Really? No hot date waiting after your shift?" The oven beeped and she frowned at the mess in the tin pan before her. It would probably taste better than it looked. Probably.

"Sarah and I broke up."

That got her full attention. She turned to him, ignoring one mess she'd made to apologize for another. "That sucks. I'm sorry. I shouldn't have said anything."

He shrugged. *Classic robot move.* "It was a long time coming."

"Yeah, she seemed terrible. All that smiling and perky adorableness." She winced and clapped her hand over her mouth. "I'm sorry again. I will stop talking now, for real this time."

He laughed. David Herz, the man, the robot, actually *laughed.* "Something like that. I guess we were just too much alike."

"You? I wouldn't exactly call you perky or adorable, you know."

"Fair enough. I think she was just tired of dating another engineer."

"Oh. You mean she wasn't captivated by all your robotic charms."

He blinked again. "You think I'm robotic?"

"David. Bubbeleh. Listen to yourself." She waved a batter-smeared coffee stirrer in the air for dramatic emphasis. "You're a judgmental engineer who has triple-checked the temperature settings on this oven—don't deny it, I saw you—and has said maybe fifteen words to me the entire time I've lived here, ten of which you've said tonight." She smirked and crossed her arms over her chest, mirroring his stance. "English majors know a thing or two about word count, you know. You can't fool me."

He looked thoughtful, as if actually considering her points. She thought he would argue with her, explain how he'd been wronged by Sarah, but he surprised her by asking instead: "So what's with the depression brownies?"

She snorted and shoved the pan into the oven. "Seriously? You want to know?"

"You haven't set the timer."

She scowled. "I was *about* to." She hadn't been. She punched in thirty-five minutes and fidgeted with her coffee stirrer while turning back to him.

"Fine. So, first, obviously, it's Valentine's Day. Not really a great day for the chronically single. But then there was that pop quiz in my biological anthropology class and *excuse me* for not knowing the names of all the different types of hominids that ever walked the Earth. And then my mother somehow found me at lunch and made a big production out of asking me how my semester was going and how I was feeling about midterms and all that crap—I have no idea if she was asking me as her daughter or as one of the new students in her department. Turns out nobody wants to be your faculty mentor when your mom is the chair, but I digress."

She snapped the coffee stirrer in half.

"*Then* in my afternoon class we got our first term papers back, and let's just say Dr. Williamson was fundamentally unimpressed with my hot takes on Holden Caulfield's emotional immaturity or the alleged ad hominem attacks I threw in there. But I'm sorry, when you assign a book about a whiny man-child, you have to know that I'm going to assume you're a whiny man-child, too."

She made a face to show her own emotional immaturity; this was a topic she knew plenty about.

"Then when I got back to the dorm, my roommate had a scrunchie on the doorknob and was making gross animal noises with her boyfriend. Yay, Valentine's Day! So I thought I'd have an early dinner down at the student union, only I lost my meal card for the third time this week—probably threw it away at lunch when I was trying to escape from my mother—at which point I said screw it, I'm having depression brownies for dinner instead." She gestured toward the mess on the countertop. "You saw the rest."

He rubbed his chin. "Your mom's the chair of the English department?"

She threw her hands up in exasperation. "*That's* what you took away from this story?!"

His chuckle was a low, rumbling sound, like the purr of a big cat. It was . . . *nice*, she decided. Not a word she employed often as an English major, but the safest option she had right now. She definitely wasn't in the mood to interrogate the full extent of her feelings about his chuckle or the reasons she wanted to hear him do it more often.

"You're an English major and your mom's the chair of the English department."

She sighed, nodded, and ran a hand through her hair, hoping that any batter she might be smearing through her curls would disappear into her hair's overall brownness. "Yep. Third-generation English major. I know they're all hoping I'll be the third generation of English professors, too, but the next time my mom ambushes me like today, I'm going to tell her that my dream in life is to write technical manuals for the software industry." She jabbed the broken end of the coffee stirrer toward him. "Maybe I can write the instruction manual for you and similar robot-boy prototypes."

"Your services would be much appreciated," he said, touching his palm to his heart. He paused and then asked, "Is that why you're called Cordelia? From the play?"

"I'm impressed—an engineer who knows his Shakespeare?" She pretended to fan herself. "People act like my name's so weird but, like, Cordelia was the *good* daughter, all honest and caring and stuff. Do you know how many Regans I had in my kindergarten class? *Three*. Three different families decided to name their babies after one of the evil, backstabbing daughters in *King Lear*, but I've never even met another Cordelia." She paused. "Though after lunch today, my mom is probably regretting not naming me Goneril instead."

"I'm sure it wasn't that bad." The barest hint of a smile twitched on his face; if she hadn't been staring at him so closely, she never would have seen it.

She just pointed to the oven. "Depression. Brownies."

His smile twitched wider, and he ducked his head to hide it, looking at his watch instead. "I should probably get back to the desk. My shift's about to end, and I don't want them thinking I was slacking off." He nodded toward the oven. "You sure you're okay here? You're not going to accidentally explode anything? Set your hair on fire? I'd really like to make it through today without calling 9-1-1. Again."

"That was *one time*," she groused. "Fine. Go. But come back for brownies when your shift is over. I owe you one after trauma-dumping on you for the last twenty minutes."

"I like listening to your stories."

A small shiver ran up her spine at his quiet words. She raised her eyes to meet his and was surprised by the gentleness she saw in their hazel depths.

"They're very . . . energetic."

"Energetic?" She wrinkled her nose. "I guess that's nicer than what I usually get. Mostly people just tell me I'm a hot mess."

He laughed, surprising her. "You're not a mess."

But I am *hot . . . ?* Her throat was doing something weird that blocked her airflow. *Stop trying to read between the lines. You're talking to an engineer; he's got the emotional range of a Roomba. There's no subtext here.*

"I'll come back for a brownie," he promised, and then he was gone.

She was still standing there, half-stunned, wondering if the strange tingly sensation across her skin and the lurching twisting of her stomach were signs of serious illness or if she could wait to visit the campus health clinic when it opened tomorrow. Maybe brownies for dinner was a bad idea when she was already getting sick. Maybe it was a great one. It's what she would have wanted for her final meal anyway.

The timer beeped, breaking through the fog of her hypochondria, and she realized another crucial baking tool she lacked: oven mitts. She looked wildly around the empty kitchen but saw nothing except the paper towels hanging in a metal bin over the sink. She pulled down a half dozen and stacked them in her hand. That would work, right? She opened the oven door and pulled out the brownies.

The edge of the foil tray burned surprisingly hot through the paper towels, and she yelped and let go, sending the pan somersaulting through the air until it landed, bottom-down, on the tile floor.

She stuck her burning fingers into her mouth and knelt next to the pan, considering her options. The brownies still *looked* edible, at least—but certainly not appetizing, sitting on the floor, edges slightly charred. She could wait until they cooled off enough and then eat them from the dish. If it left scorch marks on the tile of the dorm kitchen, well, so be it. Nobody would ever have to know.

"Are you okay? I heard a scream."

She screamed again and nearly toppled over. "Honestly, David, you can't keep doing that to me. You're shaving years off my life every time you pop out of nowhere like that."

"I was worried. What are you doing on the floor?"

Before she could answer, he was striding into the room and crouching beside her. Concern warred with amusement in his eyes as he said, "Mind telling me what's going on here?"

"They were hot." She raised her hand to show the rosy tips of her fingers. The burning feeling was already subsiding. *One less thing to chat with the doctor about tomorrow.* Too bad that strange arrhythmia in her heart seemed to be back.

He reached for her hand, cupping his own around it as he inspected her fingers. His palms were cool and smooth, big enough to swallow hers. Her heart pounded faster in its new rhythm, and she felt almost dizzy until he said, "Yes, things that come out of the oven tend to be hot."

"I *know* that," she snapped, snatching her hand back from him. "But I didn't have an oven mitt and paper towels definitely do *not* work." She pointed to the brownies. "Good thing they landed the right way up."

He followed her finger with his gaze. Two small frown lines appeared between his brows once he realized the implication of her words. "You're not eating brownies off the floor."

"Honestly, I think it's genius. I've managed to make the most depressing depression brownies ever made. I'm ready to accept my Michelin star."

He shook his head. "No. These have gone way past depression brownies. I'm sorry, Cordelia, you can't eat these." He gingerly picked up the pan off the floor by its still-warm edges and dropped it into the trash can, ignoring her squawks of protest.

"My brownies . . ." The emotion in her own voice surprised her. Was she going to cry in front of David Herz? Over the most disastrous pan of brownies ever made?

He reached for her hand, his strong fingers sliding down to grip her wrist as he pulled her to her feet. "Forget those brownies." A faint blush spread across those chiseled cheekbones, and he dropped her hand. "I'll make you some that are even better."

Logically, the words made sense—subject, verb, defining relative clause—but she wrestled with the meaning as they echoed through her tired brain. "Huh?"

"Grab your coat." He swiped the mess off the countertop straight into the bin, cheap measuring cups and all, before dampening another paper towel and wiping the surface clean. She wanted to point out the salmonella risk, but her tongue appeared to be glued to the roof of her mouth. "I'm taking you to my place and showing you how to make brownies the right way."

"What?" It was marginally better than *huh?* She shook her head, trying to get control of her mouth again. "Wait—stop. Going to *your place?* Absolutely not. Rule number one is never go to a second location."

He gave her an incredulous side-eye as he continued to wipe down the countertop. "That's for serial killers. Not me."

"How do I know that? You've always given off big serial-killer energy to me." His side-eye was even fiercer now. For a robot, he had certainly mastered these little micro-expressions.

"Only because you've always been so ridiculous. Do you want depression brownies or not?"

"Of course I do. Weren't you paying attention? Or do you want me to tell you *again* how awful my day was?"

"If you do that, I really might serial kill you."

The playful glimmer in his eyes made her stomach do that weird swoopy thing again, which frankly made no sense. She should be *less* nervous knowing that he didn't plan to murder her, not *more* nervous.

"Look. I live just off campus. I have a fully stocked kitchen with oven mitts and everything. I've been background-checked and vetted by campus housing for my job here. I promise you, I'm not a serial killer or ax murderer or whatever else you're thinking in that wild brain of yours."

She didn't like the way his smile made her skin go all tingly, so she covered it up by jabbing a finger at him. "A background check just means you've never been *caught*," she argued. "Who knows how much evidence you've destroyed in your very grown-up, professional-quality kitchen?"

"Professional quality? Because I own oven mitts?" His smile twitched wider. "Wait till you find out that I bake my brownies from scratch."

"Someone get this man a cooking show." That faint blush returned to his cheeks, and she grabbed her wrist, physically restraining herself from reaching out to stroke the light pink feathering across his smooth cheekbones. She didn't need to do anything else to make him think she was patently insane. "Fine. I will come with you to an undisclosed secondary location for made-from-scratch brownies. Sheesh, I'd be easy to kidnap."

"Noted. Now, put your coat on."

Chastened, she did as he said, shrugging into her heavy, black anorak and patting her pockets to check that she hadn't managed to lose her keys in the minutes since entering the dorm. With her luck, they would be buried at the bottom of the trash can, under her burnt brownies and smashed egg yolks and a metric ton of paper towels. So much for her carbon footprint.

She was explaining how much energy went into the production of plastic bags and why she always favored paper while they walked through the cold night, her breath clouding her vision with little puffs of steam as she talked. David listened quietly, occasionally interrupting her monologue with a question or comment of his own. His companionship felt comfortable, steady, safe. Not very serial killer-ish.

They paused in front of an old brownstone, just two blocks from the steady glow of campus. "This is me," he said, gesturing with his keys. Cordelia shivered in anticipation. He misinterpreted the movement and added, "Come on, let's get you inside where it's warmer."

She followed him in, suddenly mute as she passed a row of dented silver mailboxes, a bicycle propped beneath it. It was strangely intimate, being with him in his space when he had worked in hers for so long. He inserted his key into the door at the end of the hall and gestured for her to come through.

She didn't know what she had been expecting. Movie posters, maybe: Al Pacino gnawing on a cigar and glaring at her. Scattered Solo cups and the faint whiff of beer pong games past. Whatever it was, she certainly didn't expect the neat, cozy, little apartment. Plants filled all the window ledges, trailing greenery to the hardwood floors. A small, gray sofa—midcentury modern or Nordic minimalist—took up the center of the room, a braided rug in neutral colors in front of it with a matching afghan draped across the back.

"Can I get you anything to drink? Beer, wine, tea?"

"Tea is good," she murmured, still looking around. She imagined sinking into the little sofa and wrapping herself in the afghan, a cup of tea in one hand and a book in the other. She would never want to leave.

"Great. Come into the kitchen with me and pick one out."

She followed him into an equally tidy kitchen, all chrome appliances and whitewashed cabinets without so much as a spill or stain marring their surface. He opened one of the cabinets. "I've got jasmine, Earl Grey, or chamomile. Any of those catch your fancy?"

"Chamomile, please." Something about this place made her suddenly want to be on her best behavior, but she couldn't stop herself from blurting, "You're kind of a neat freak, aren't you?"

He chuckled as he filled the kettle. "I don't know about that." His eyes slid to her, that teasing, sideways glance that she was starting to recognize. "Maybe you're just extremely messy."

"Oh, that is absolutely true," she agreed. "My roommate keeps complaining about it, but I really feel like if *she* just paid a little more attention, she'd stop stepping in the half-empty bowls of cereal I've left on the floor."

He blinked. "There's . . . a lot to unpack there." He poured hot water into two mugs and handed one to her. She tried not to notice the way his long fingers cupped the curved edge of the mug, or the parting of his lips as he blew cool air across the surface of the mug. Her body, though, definitely noticed, and she clenched her thighs against the sudden rush of heat. *Stop it. There's no reason to get all worked up over a cup of tea.*

Thankfully, David turned away from her to pull more things out of the cabinets—mixing bowls and spatulas and measuring cups—and place them neatly on the small, gray countertop. She watched him move confidently through the kitchen with something like amazement. "Wow. You really cook, huh?"

"And bake. It's not so hard," he said, shrugging. "It's actually kind of relaxing. And it definitely beats eating crap on campus every single day for the last four years."

"You're talking to the girl who started a fire trying to make a cup of instant noodles. None of what you just said makes any sense."

"Fair point. Think you're up for buttering this pan? Or is that outside your skill set?"

She took the pan and the stick of butter he held out to her, ignoring the way the corners of his eyes crinkled when he smiled. She'd seen more expression from him in the past hour than she'd seen in the six months she'd lived on campus. It was hard to remember that she had once found him so robotic and aloof when he was so lively and friendly here in his kitchen.

By the time she had finished greasing the pan, he was whisking together the dry ingredients. The smell of cocoa powder, bitter and rich, filled the air.

He put the mixing bowl down and held up two bags for her to inspect. "Chocolate chips or walnuts?"

"Yes to chocolate chips, no to walnuts." She made a face. "I know people like the crunchy texture, but putting fruit and nuts in desserts is a bait-and-switch I will not tolerate. If these brownies aren't the unhealthiest thing I can stuff into my face, then what is even the point of them?"

"Valid reasoning," he agreed, a whisper of a smile on his face. He dumped a handful of chocolate chips into the mixing bowl and held a larger bowl out to her. "I need two eggs. Do you want to do the honors of cracking them, or should I?"

"Ooohh, me!" She winced at her overenthusiastic response. "Sorry. I just love that satisfying feeling."

"Is that why you dropped a dozen outside the dorm tonight?"

He was teasing her again. She glared and took an egg from the carton, giving it a solid whack against the edge of the bowl before pulling the ends apart. She peered into the bowl. "Boom! Not a single piece of shell either."

He stepped closer to look, and she was suddenly intensely aware of how much space his body filled in the small kitchen. Heat radiated off him and spread through her, a slowly cresting wave that burned her cheeks.

"Nice job." His voice was a low purr. Cordelia's knees went weak. "Let's see you do it again."

"Trust me, I'm a professional." She cracked the second egg into the bowl as neatly as the first.

"I hear it's pretty lucrative, being a professional egg cracker."

"Probably just as lucrative as being an English major."

His laughter in such tight quarters surprised her, bursting from his chest and ringing into the small kitchen. She *really* liked that sound. She bit her lip to keep from blurting that out and watched him mix together the last of the wet and dry ingredients before pouring it into the square pan she'd greased. He smoothed the surface with the spatula, poking batter into the corners of the pan, and slid it into the oven before setting a timer.

"Now we wait." His eyes sparkled, friendly, kind, those little crinkles so kissable and cute. *Nope.*

"I hate waiting."

"I'm not at all surprised." He smiled down at her, still too close in the small kitchen. "Come on. I'll make you another cup of tea and we can go watch something on TV."

She followed him back to the living room like an obedient little terrier. He settled onto the couch, long legs splayed out in front of him, one arm draped over the back. She wiped her free hand on her jeans, almost afraid to touch anything. He'd throw her out the second any of her mess rubbed off on his pristine place. It didn't feel safe to settle in on the sofa beside him, though she wasn't sure whose safety was most at risk.

He didn't seem to notice her hesitation as he grabbed the remote and began flicking through channels. She slid gingerly onto the opposite end of the sofa, doing her best to limit the amount of contact between her body and the dove-gray upholstery. If only she'd tried harder at Pilates.

"Tell me when to stop," he said, and it took her a full minute to figure out that he was referring to the channels. She swallowed and tried to focus on the TV.

He paused on each channel for a few seconds, just long enough to catch glimpses of limpid eyes and breathless kisses and saccharine Valentine's Day sweetness. She wedged herself deeper into the corner of the couch.

"You'd think the networks would have a little more self-awareness," she grumbled as the hot brunette couple on the screen changed to a hot blonde couple on the next channel. "If you're sad enough to be sitting around at home on Valentine's Day watching TV, you probably don't want to be reminded of it over and over."

"I don't know what you're complaining about," he remarked in that dry, almost sarcastic tone. "I'm the only one sitting around at home watching TV on Valentine's Day. You've somehow finagled your way into an upperclassman's house, where he has dutifully supplied you with tea and—soon—brownies." He snuck a look at her under thick, golden lashes. "Seems like your Valentine's Day is going pretty well, if you ask me."

"It's my womanly wiles." She took a small sip of the hot drink, hoping she could hide her burning cheeks behind the mug. He did have a point—her Valentine's Day was suddenly going *much* better than she had expected. "Nobody can resist the sight of a chaotic damsel in distress."

"I see. It's all part of your master plan. The late-night calls from the fire department and countless lock-outs and God knows how many near-death situations you've put yourself into—all just a ploy to get in my pants."

She choked on her tea. Embarrassed, she leaned forward to set down the mug, still spluttering. His hands were on her a second later, patting her back with firm, heavy beats.

"Sorry, I'm so sorry—"

She recovered just enough to wheeze: "So you *were* trying to serial kill me!"

He laughed, his pats slowing as her breathing returned to normal. "It's the perfect crime."

His hand stilled on her back, the steady pressure lighting up her nerve endings and sending prickles of anticipation skittering across her skin. She met his eyes, tawny-brown flecked with green, his large pupils burning into hers. Her lips parted as her brain scrambled for something, anything to say—anything to diffuse this heart-stopping tension, to bring them back to the comfortable teasing from moments earlier. He leaned toward her and her heart gave another desperate little lurch, climbing into her throat as he filled her senses, his touch and his face and the crisp, clean scent of him coming closer and closer—

She wrenched herself back when the timer went off, her already-weakened heart nearly giving out completely at the shrill noise. David leaned back, as well, snatching his hand from her like she had burned him. He gave her a tentative little smile—*my God, was he* shy*?!*—and stood, offering her a hand and pulling her to her feet.

"Your brownies await, milady."

He was already in the kitchen, slipping his hand into a blue-and-white-striped oven mitt, when she finally got her legs to work and followed him. Although she stood back while he opened the oven door, the heat from it still washed over her, fanning the flames in her cheeks. She probably looked crazy, all wild-eyed and disheveled. Her curly hair barely contained itself at the best of times, and now she was flushed and nearly fainting in this poor man's apartment, too. Maybe this was what salmonella felt like. How long after infection did the first symptoms usually appear?

Her thoughts were interrupted by the sight of the most beautiful pan of brownies she had ever seen being pulled from the oven. David's sinewy forearms flexed under the weight of all that chocolatey goodness, and her mouth began to water. She didn't want to probe whether it was the man or the brownies causing that particular reaction.

He set the pan on the stovetop and turned back to her with a smile. "They look pretty good, but the real test will be when we taste them. We've probably got another fifteen minutes until they're cool enough to cut."

"Who said anything about cutting them? Just get me a spoon and I'll eat them now."

"You're a greedy little thing, aren't you?" He laughed but pulled a spoon from the drawer by the sink and held it out to her. "Don't let me hold you back."

Her fingers brushed his as she took the spoon and stepped closer to the stove. He leaned against the countertop, arms crossed, watching her watch the pan. She felt a moment of hesitation; she'd been fully intending to eat her depression brownies straight out of the pan like some animal, but here in David's well-appointed living space, with his live plants and kitchen utensils and other trappings of adulthood, she suddenly felt timid. But the look on his face when she peeked at him was bemused, not disgusted, and she'd decided that if he didn't mind watching her stuff her face, she wouldn't mind it either.

Her spoon cracked the crisp surface of the brownies before sliding through the warm, gooey center. Steam rose from the end of it, and she blew a long, steady stream of air until the brownie was cool enough to eat. She tried her best to ignore the feel of his eyes on her as she raised the spoon to her lips and let the first taste of chocolate explode onto her tongue.

It was orgasmic, and she released the kind of throaty moan that said so. Cordelia shut her eyes, wantonly licking the end of the spoon, relishing the way the chocolate filled her mouth with its sweet bitterness. *This* was no depression brownie. *This* was perfection, ambrosia, the food of the gods. She wanted more.

She only remembered David was there when she opened her eyes to take a second bite and caught him staring. She immediately blushed and lowered her spoon. "What?"

He shook his head, as if to erase his own dazed expression. "Erm, y-you have chocolate on your face."

She licked her lips, searching for that rogue bit of chocolate. His eyes fluttered shut and he slowly flexed the hand at his side. She yanked her tongue back into her mouth, feeling ridiculous.

"Did I get it?"

"No."

She tried again. "How about now?"

He exhaled heavily, the sigh of a man suffering deeply. "It's still there."

"Well, jeez, David, help a girl out here."

His Adam's apple bobbed a few times before he gave a curt nod and stepped closer to her.

The feel of his thumb against her cheek was electrifying, and she jolted backward as if she had been shocked. He made soothing, gentling noises, like she was a skittish colt and not a nineteen-year-old woman, and approached her again.

This time, his fingers cupped her chin, the gentle pressure holding her in place as he swiped at the chocolate with his thumb. He held it up for her to inspect. "There. All better."

She didn't know why she did it. She could have chalked it up to her spontaneous, unorthodox nature, but even she knew there were boundaries that shouldn't be crossed. The only excuse that made any sense to her later was that she was somehow so intoxicated by the rich chocolate of the brownie, so captivated by the depth of flavor that she had been anticipating for hours, so starved for something delicious after a day of disappointments, that she leaned forward without thinking and sucked the soft pad of his chocolate-covered thumb into her mouth.

His eyes flew wide, the pupils expanding like starbursts as her teeth scraped over his skin, her tongue curling around the fleshy tip, tasting salt and chocolate and *him*. She released him with a gasp and then his hand was in her hair, cupping the back of her head, tilting her mouth up to his.

Her lips opened for him, and he pressed himself to her, all hard planes and rough stubble and solid, tender warmth. She threw her arms around his neck as he deepened the kiss, his tongue probing the corners of her mouth, stroking over her, each little lick sending thrills of pleasure cascading down her spine.

He broke the kiss abruptly, pulling back from her with a soft curse. "I'm sorry. I shouldn't have—"

"Less talking, more kissing."

She *was* greedy, she realized distantly, as his lips met hers again. His hands slid around her waist, spanning her lower back, and she sighed against him. She stroked her hands over the hard ridges of his shoulders, collarbone, biceps, down and back up, as he pressed her against the kitchen counter.

"We should slow down." His breath came in adorable little pants. She took in the flush on his cheeks, a dark-brown cowlick pointing to the ceiling, his crooked collar and wrinkled shirt, not to mention the liquid heat that filled her belly. She'd done that to him. She'd cracked that flawless outer shell and revealed the delicious mess inside. She wanted to lap him up.

"Hear me out." She reached for him, hands resting lightly on his hips. "We should speed up."

He gave a strangled little laugh and ran his hand through his hair, making his cowlick stick up even more. Concern marred his perfect, chiseled features and a sudden realization doused her lust like ice water on a flame.

"Oh no. I messed up, didn't I?" She yanked her hands back from his body and buried her face in them. "Is it Sarah? Are you still pining for her? You just wanted to make some platonic brownies and then I threw myself at you. God, I'm so embarrassed."

"What? No! Nothing like that." He grasped her wrists, gently pulling her hands away from her face, smiling when she met his eyes. "No. Cordelia, listen." He took a deep breath. "I really like you. I've liked you for a long time, in fact. You've always been so vivacious, so full of life—"

"That is *quite* the euphemism for 'most likely to burn down the dorm with a bag of popcorn.'"

"—and you're stunning." He reached for one of her curls, twisting it around his finger, then pulling it straight and releasing it to bounce back into its natural corkscrew. "Every time you came to the desk while I was working, I couldn't keep my eyes off you."

"A natural reaction to a girl in a unicorn onesie."

"Would you let me speak?" He was laughing when he kissed her again and she decided that this was the best kind of kiss, all teeth and stretched lips and the vibrating rumble of his amusement deep in his chest. How had she ever thought he was cold and distant, when he was so warm and funny?

"But I didn't want to make you uncomfortable or anything. I mean, not only are you a freshman and I'm a senior, but I had the keys to your dorm room, for crying out loud! And apparently you already thought I was a serial killer." He smiled as she winced. "So I tried to keep it professional." He rubbed his hand over the back of his neck. "I was legitimately concerned about you burning the place down tonight, but when you told me how crappy your day was . . . well, I figured you deserved the damn brownies."

"I definitely do." She beamed at him, polite, agreeable, compliant. "I also deserve make-out sessions with hot engineers in well-appointed kitchens. So, hop to it."

"You think I'm hot?"

"And your kitchen is well-appointed." She relented, dropping her joking tone with a sigh. "Fine. Yes. You are very hot, objectively speaking, and maybe also subjectively speaking, too."

She swept her eyes over his chiseled features, broad shoulders, trim waist, long legs. "Yep. Definitely subjectively hot."

His lips quirked in amusement, and she chewed her own, wondering how honest she should be.

"You're also wicked smart and surprisingly funny—for an engineer—and somehow patient and kind enough to save me from myself. And you feed me chocolate."

She hesitated again before deciding that hurtling headfirst into things had worked well enough for her tonight; there was no reason to change tactics now.

"I think . . . I think I could be really into you, if you wanted that sort of thing. If you were into me, too."

"Do you really mean that, or is this just your robot fetish talking?"

She moved to swat him, but he grabbed her wrist and pulled her close, his other arm snaking around her waist as he held her to him. He smiled tenderly and cupped her cheek with his hand, his eyes flicking across her face, drinking her in.

"I am really into you, Cordelia Lev, Amato Hall resident. You gorgeous, wild, wonderful girl."

He dropped another kiss to her lips, this one so sweet and full of promise that her insides threatened to melt, turning her every bit as gooey as the brownies left abandoned on the stovetop.

Her eyes shot open, and she wrenched herself away from him. "The brownies!"

"I bet they're cooled enough to cut now," he said with a smile.

He reached around her and pulled the pan closer, inspecting the hole she'd made with her spoon. He pulled a knife from a drawer and sliced the pan of brownies into four huge quarters before placing two of them on squares of paper towels.

Cordelia kept her mouth shut while she watched him work. There would be time for her to share her opinions on paper towels later.

He handed her one of the enormous brownies and tapped his against hers, as if toasting her with chocolate instead of champagne. "Cheers." His gaze dropped to her mouth. "Take a bite. Tell me how it is."

She did as he asked, screwing her face up in mock deliberation as she chewed. She swallowed, paused, smacked her lips.

"I don't taste any depression in these brownies." Her tone was regretful, as if she were delivering bad news.

He laughed and dropped a light kiss on her cheek. "That's because they weren't made with any depression."

"Oh yeah? So what were they made with, then? Love?"

"How about . . . excitement? Affection? New beginnings?" He gave her one of his beautiful, crinkle-eyed smiles. "Or is that too robotic for you?"

Her heart swelled, nearly bursting with feeling as she looked at this tender, adorable man who couldn't be robotic if he tried. Maybe it was too soon to call it love, but it certainly felt like it.

"I think those are some of my favorite ingredients."

About the Author

Aimee Moineaux's lifelong love affair with words was briefly derailed by a career in data science. She wrote her first romance novel in 2024 as part of RWA's Pen to Paper program and has not stopped writing since. Her favorite stories feature smart, spunky heroines and the men who admire them. Currently she lives in Louisville, Kentucky, with her husband, two daughters, and an inordinate number of pets.

You can find Aimee on:

Instagram: @aimeemoineaux

WELCOME HOME

Welcome Home

Melissa Cate

Chapter 1

ELLE FIDDLED WITH HER NAPKIN as she stole furtive glances around the restaurant, waiting for her date to arrive. "Why did I agree to this place again?" she muttered under her breath. She thought back to the last time she'd been at Fifth & Ivy. Had it really been seven years?

"I want a divorce."

Joshua blinked at her, blindsided by the statement. He gave his head a shake like he had misheard her. "What?"

"I want a divorce." She took another bite of her steak as he processed her words.

"I don't understand."

"Josh, I love you, but I don't think we should have gotten married."

His face flashed full of hurt, and she realized how that sounded.

"I mean, at least not right out of college. We are so young and have so much life to live. We need to experience that."

Joshua sucked in a breath. "I thought that's what we were going to do together."

"I think we need to do it apart."

"But, Dani..." he trailed off. He reached for her hand and she pulled it away. His touch alone would break her resolve.

"I really need the space. Losing the baby . . . I just need time on my own."

"We need to get through this together."

"I tried, but I can't do this with you. I need to figure out what I want from my life. I can't do that with you in it."

"Dani, please." He had never had a good poker face, and right now, she had to look away from the heartbreak she saw across it.

"Chris and Lexi are moving my things out of our apartment right now." She looked at her watch. "They should be nearly done. Don't worry—I'm only taking my clothes and personal items. Everything else will stay since I'm asking for the divorce."

"No, Dani, I can give you space, just please don't leave me."

Dani steeled herself. She'd been over it a million times, approached it from every angle. This was best for both of them.

"I've already decided, Josh. Please don't make this hard." She almost said harder, but she didn't want him to know how hard it actually was for her. If he knew she had any doubt or regret or guilt, it would be too easy for him to figure out how to get her to stay.

He pushed his plate away and waved down their server. "I'd like the check please."

"No, Josh, I'll get it."

"You can't let me have just one thing tonight?"

She put her head down. "I'm sorry," she whispered, though she made sure he didn't hear her.

Danielle stopped messing with her napkin and laid her hands in her lap. Over the past seven years, she had pursued a master's degree and began a new career. She had also lost weight—she had been depressed right after the divorce and couldn't eat much. Then she'd found a counselor and began making healthy choices for her body and spirit. One of those choices was to go by Elle instead of Dani. Josh had given her the nickname and she loved it, but it made her think of him, so she changed to Elle.

As her eyes roamed from table to table, taking in the couples and families dining around her, she wondered what Josh was doing now and if he had remarried. Her heart sank at the thought of it. She closed her eyes. *It was your decision to leave. Let's think about David.*

Danielle couldn't believe how nervous she was. Her sister, Lexi, who admittedly did not know the whole reason Danielle had left Josh, was always playing matchmaker, so Danielle had gone on quite a few dates, but none had made her nervous like this. Rarely did any make it past a first date, actually. This blind date, however, had been arranged by her coworker, John.

"David is the coolest guy. Liz and I met him at a young adults thing we hosted at our church about five years ago."

"You hosted a young adults' thing?" Elle giggled.

John raised his eyebrows. "What? You don't think I can hang with you young people?"

Elle laughed. "It's not that. It's just—umm, well—aren't young adult things for young adults?"

John winked. "I'm young at heart, and my Lizzie looks twenty years younger, so what are you trying to say?"

Elle pursed her lips and tried not to laugh again. She treasured this friendship with John. He may be thirty years older, but he was a good friend. She trusted his judgment—and his wife's, since she had, after all, chosen him. "So . . . tell me more about David."

"Well, he has brown hair and brown eyes."

Elle laughed. "Okay, okay, how does Liz describe him?"

"She knew you were gonna ask me that." John grinned and pulled out a piece of paper. He slid on his reading glasses. "It says, 'Now Elle, you know that we would not introduce you to someone that wasn't nice or kind. David is a really great guy.'"

He paused and Elle stared at him. "Really? The personality thing? I mean, that's good, but didn't she say anything else?"

He continued reading. "'And lest you think his personality is all he has going for him, he is a black belt in karate, so you will always feel safe. He is strong and will allow you to be strong, but will also be your backup when you're not feeling strong. He loves reading, walking, eating good food, and playing board games. He has a strong jawline and is slightly taller than my Johnny. He's not quite as handsome as him, though.'" John blushed.

Elle smiled. "Sounds good. You two tell me when and where. I'll be there."

Elle took a peek at her phone to check the time. Her eyes widened as she realized how early she'd arrived. *I still have ten minutes.* She called Lexi, who picked up right away.

"You will be *fine.*"

"How do you know that's why I'm calling?"

"Because I know you. We've been sisters for what, three decades now? I have a little insight."

Elle laughed. "John and Liz really like this guy. I would hate for this date to go badly and then be awkward around John at work."

"From what you've told me about John, I don't think you'll have to worry about that."

"Yeah, but still—"

"'But still' nothing. It will be fine. You will be fine. And it sounds like he will be *fine*. If you know what I mean." Lexi laughed.

"Oh, ha ha." Elle giggled. "But it does sound like it."

"I can't believe they picked Fifth & Ivy, though. What are the odds?"

"I know, right? I haven't been back here since that night. Seven years now? I'm sitting here living in memories while I wait."

"It is kind of weird."

"You think so?"

"Elle, did you even look at the calendar?"

"Not closely. Why?"

"It's the tenth."

"No, it's not. John told me to meet David on Tuesday. Today's Tuesday, and it should be the ninth."

"Sis, it's the tenth."

"Oh."

"Yeah, oh."

"Should I leave and call John to have him pick a different time, or at least a different place tonight?"

"I think it's late for that, Elle. He should be there in just a few minutes. I guess just put Joshua out of your mind and try to have fun."

"Thanks, Lexi. Love you."

"Love you, too, Elle."

Chapter 2

ELLE ENDED THE CALL AND tucked her phone into her purse. She was ready to focus on her date with David and see if there was any potential, even if she was missing her ex-husband a little more than normal tonight.

The hostess was approaching, a man trailing behind her. "Here you go, sir. Your server will be right with the two of you."

"Thank you, Maddie," replied David as he sat down.

Maddie blushed and hurried off.

"Nice to finally meet you, Dav—*Josh*?" Elle was speechless. David was her Josh? Well, not *her* Josh, not anymore. Not since she'd broken his heart seven years earlier. But what was he doing here? And looking *that* good? The nerve.

"Dani? I thought I was meeting Elle. I'm sorry, this must be a mistake. I'll get Maddie and see if she can help me find the right table." He started to stand.

"Wait." Elle reached out and grabbed his hand. Sparks sent shivers up her arm as she realized the electricity they'd always had together was still strong. He must have felt it, too, as he stilled and closed his eyes. "Please sit. I'm Elle."

He turned and regarded her. She could see the questions written all over his face. She'd always been able to read him so easily. She gave him the puppy-dog eyes he had never been able to say no to.

"Please?"

He sighed and ran his hand through his hair. "Okay." He took his seat and looked her over.

She could almost feel his eyes take her in. Yes, her weight had changed, but so had her hair, the shape of her face, and her sense of style. She gave him a tentative smile.

"You've changed quite a bit. Even your name." His voice held a question, but she wasn't quite sure what it was.

"You have, too, including your name. You decided to go by your middle name?"

"You remember." There was no question this time. When she nodded, he continued. "I couldn't stay Josh, or even Joshua, when all I could hear was your voice."

Elle bowed her head and closed her eyes. "I'm sorry," she whispered.

"Dani—"

Elle gasped. "I haven't been called Dani in nearly seven years."

"That bad of a memory, huh?"

She barked out a laugh. "If only." He searched her face questioningly and she continued. "All I could think of was how you would say my name when you were kissing me. How raspy your voice would sound when you'd walk in while I was getting dressed. How much I loved being *your* Dani."

David's face blanched. "Then why?"

"I don't think I can do this now." Her voice broke.

"If not now, then when, Dani?"

She noticed that he continued to use Dani, even after knowing the effect it had on her. She closed her eyes and memories flashed by. Their first kiss. His proposal. Their wedding night. She was blushing when she opened her eyes. She saw the look on his face and knew he was thinking of similar moments.

"Josh—" She stopped. "You want to be called David. I'll try to do better."

"You can call me Josh, Dani. Or would you prefer I call you Elle?" He raised an eyebrow.

"Dani is fine." Her voice was thick with emotion. "Josh, I want to tell you all the things. I really do. But I'm not sure I am emotionally prepared for it tonight. I-I didn't know you were going to be *you* tonight." She grew quiet. "Could we maybe talk about what we've done with ourselves the past few years tonight, and meet tomorrow for lunch to talk about what happened back then? I can take a long lunch. Or if you would prefer, we could meet for another dinner." She sped through the last bit, hoping he would be okay with it.

He took a deep breath and rubbed his hands over his face. For once, Dani didn't know what he was thinking.

"Okay."

Chapter 3

THIRTY MINUTES LATER, THEY WERE digging into their meals. Dani took a bite and closed her eyes. "This steak is just as good as I remember it."

Joshua admired her and chuckled. "You have always loved a good steak dinner. When was the last time you came here?"

"Seven years ago." When he seemed puzzled, she continued. "I couldn't come back after that night. It hurt too much."

When he reached for her hand, she didn't move it. His fingers touched hers and she felt heat with every fingertip. When he began making a circle on her palm with his thumb, goosebumps traveled up her arm and she hoped he didn't notice.

"So, umm." She was frazzled, and he knew it. She blinked a couple of times and shook her head. "Liz mentioned that you have a black belt in karate? That's new. How did that happen?"

"Lots of training," he deadpanned.

"Well, obviously." She giggled. "Seriously, though?"

"Seriously, though, I got into a dark place after you left. You remember Tyler?" When she nodded, he continued. "Well, Tyler had started training at the dojo and wanted a friend. He insisted that it would be good for me and would help me get my mind off all the things."

"*All* the things?"

He gave her hand a squeeze. "You were definitely a big part of the 'things,' but also the loss of our baby, the loss of the life I thought we'd live, the loss of my best friend. I had a lot of loss to grieve."

She squeezed back. "I'm so sorry for all of that, Josh. I hope you know that."

"I guess I'll know for sure tomorrow."

Dani nodded.

"Anyway, I started going to classes with Tyler a couple times a week. It was a lot of fun, and it seemed like the more I learned, the more I wanted to learn. So, here I am now, a Shodan—which means I'm a first-degree black belt. I enjoy it and am continuing to work toward my Nidan, or second degree."

"That's so awesome, Josh! I'm so proud of you."

"Thank you, Dani."

He pulled his hand away to take a drink of water. Dani instantly missed his touch and instinctively started to reach for his other hand. She stopped with her hand halfway across the table and stole a glance at him. He had an amused expression on his face. She grabbed her water and took a sip.

"So, what about you? What's something new and exciting you've done the past seven years?"

The server came then to clear their plates and offer dessert. They asked for a few minutes and turned back to each other as the server hurried off.

"Well, I got my master's in social work. I am a hospice social worker. Something I never thought I would do, but I sincerely love being able to help families at a time when they truly don't know what all kinds of help they need."

"That's amazing. I bet you're very good at it."

"I'm not sure about that, but I do love people and helping them however I can."

"That suits you well." Josh smiled. "Anything else you want to tell me about?"

Dani thought for a moment. He hadn't seen her tattoo, so that couldn't be it. Was he really asking about her weight? "Well . . . I lost some weight."

"Okay? How do you feel about that?"

Dani blinked as she realized that wasn't what he had been asking about. "Well, it wasn't good at first. I was depressed and quit eating much of anything after the divorce. I was in a bad place, but Chris and Lexi pushed me to a counselor, who was absolutely the *best*. She helped me process a lot of things, including the unhealthy relationship with food I'd had for years. I learned better, so I do better. I feel good about my physical health now, which is what's important."

"That's wonderful. I know that's something you really struggled with since before we were ever together. I'm glad you feel better now."

She grinned. "I look better now, too."

"I thought you always looked good."

"I know, but—"

"Don't get me wrong, Dani." She noticed the look in his eyes then, a flash of desire. He took her hand again. "You are glowing from that confidence you have now, and you are simply gorgeous."

She blushed. "Thank you."

"I'm not really in the mood for dessert tonight, are you?"

He was making circles on her palm again and she couldn't think. It was a small thing he'd always done that used to get her flustered, and she wasn't sure if he was doing it on purpose or if it was simply out of habit.

Her face heated as she replied, "Not at the moment, no."

Joshua waved down the server and paid quickly as they headed out the door together. She linked her hand through his arm, and it felt like no time had passed between them. She knew, though, that she needed to tell him about what had happened that caused her to file for divorce. She wondered how he would feel about her once it was all on the table.

"Dani?"

"Yes?"

"Did you hear me?"

"I'm sorry, my mind is scattered. What did you say?"

Joshua gave her a small smile. "I think I need to let you get home. Where are you parked?"

Dani felt her heart sink. She thought they could maybe take a walk. She had even been contemplating telling him tonight since it had gone so well. "I'm over a couple of streets. I guess I'll see you tomorrow. Where do you want to have lunch and what time?"

Joshua stared at her blankly. "Over a couple of streets? Do you think I'm going to let you walk over there by yourself? I'll walk you to your car, Dani. Just because we're not married anymore doesn't mean I don't care about you."

Dani wondered about that for a moment. *Does that mean he* does *care about me, despite the heartache I put him through?* She remembered that he hadn't even fought the divorce.

"Thanks, Josh. You've always been a good man, even when I don't deserve it."

He mumbled something that sounded like "you deserve the world," but she was too afraid to ask what he meant and let it go.

Chapter 4

DANI DIDN'T HAVE ANY CURRENT families needing her on Wednesday, so she called in to work so she could prepare for her lunch with Joshua. She didn't talk to John when she called, so she figured she'd fill him in when she got back in on Thursday.

She thought about her lunch date. *Wait, not a date.* This was a lunch with her ex-husband to talk about why she'd wanted a divorce in the first place. Last night, though—that *was* a date. At least, it was once they'd decided to put off the hard talk until the next day. Now, she was feeling like she should have just ripped off the Band-Aid then. But, she realized, she wouldn't have spotted glimpses of the feelings she felt he still had. After seeing him again, she knew she couldn't deny that she still had strong feelings for him. Every single time he touched her, and when he whispered near her ear back at her car, she felt each nerve ending light up like a switch had been flipped. She thought about the time they'd spent at her car all morning.

"Here I am," Dani said as they approached her car. Between the good, healthy, and occasionally very flirty conversation they'd shared all night and while walking to her car, she wondered if he would kiss her. And she wondered if she wanted him to. She slid her hand out of the crook of his arm and turned to face him.

"Here you are." He reached out and pulled her into his arms for a hug. She reached her arms around him and breathed in his masculine, woodsy scent.

That was new—and she liked it. She closed her eyes as he rubbed her back. It was unseasonably warm this February, and at the moment, she was glad. Joshua wasn't wearing a coat, and she could feel his strength through his button-up shirt.

She was feeling bold, so she lifted her head up to tempt him. "Thank you for walking me to my car." Her eyes found his lips, and she wondered if they would still ignite fireworks for her. She glanced back up to his eyes and saw his gaze flutter to her lips as she licked them. He sucked in a breath and closed his eyes. She closed hers in anticipation.

He leaned down and whispered in her ear: "I have learned a lot of self-discipline over the past seven years, and it is taking every bit of it right now not to continue with you where we left off. You have no idea."

She opened her eyes and looked at him, seeing unmistakable desire in his eyes. "Then—"

"Dani." His voice was raspy, and she knew it was because of her. "Not yet. I need to know why, and you need to know more about what I've been up to, before we can return to all of this." He ran his hands down her back and brought them to her waist. "We need to know it's more than just habit or physical attraction."

"Please?" She brought out the puppy-dog look for the second time tonight.

He groaned and gripped her waist tighter. "Dani, please get in your car so I can walk away before we do something we might regret."

She knew then that he was serious; he had never turned down that look from her for anything before. She pushed up on her toes and kissed him on the cheek. "I'll see you tomorrow at eleven-thirty at Mack's Diner." She hurried around the car and got in. He was still watching her as she turned the corner.

"UGH! What do I wear?" Lexi had just answered Dani's Facetime call.

"You know, it's a good thing there were a couple of cancelations this morning. I can't normally Facetime at work about clothing choices." Lexi's grin told Dani she was teasing.

"But you *know* I need help."

"I've said that for a while now, sister dear."

"Okay, I'm calling Chris. Bye!"

"Because big brother can help with your fashion decisions?"

"Okay, fine." Dani stuck out her bottom lip in a pout.

"That doesn't work for me."

"Okay, fine!" Dani laughed.

"It's so good to see you like this again. I still can't believe David was Joshua! Or Joshua was David? Which way does that go? Anyway, what a story!"

"*You* can't believe it? I about died when he sat down and I realized it was him. I'm so glad it went better than I expected."

"I'm glad it did. What are you thinking of wearing for your lunch date?"

"This is not a date."

"With everything you told me about last night, there is no way this isn't a date."

"Nope. I told you we're talking about why I filed for divorce."

"Still—"

"No 'still.' This has to be about that and only that. I can't think about anything beyond that."

"Fair enough. Are you going dressy or casual?"

"As much as I'd love to dress up and make him ogle me," she grinned, "I think I'm going casual, as I'm quite sure there will be some tears, at least on my part. Blue jeans and a T-shirt?"

"Sounds good. Didn't you tell me once that one of his favorite looks on you for going out was blue jeans and a white tee?"

"Yes?"

"So do that. Show him you remember. That you still care. If you do, and I think you do."

"Um, hello? Were you not listening last night? Of course I do."

"Well, you didn't come right out and say it, so I wanted to be sure."

"I appreciate that, sis."

"No problem." Lexi grinned on her end of the phone. "I have to go, though. Can't wait to hear about it—tonight—when I'm not at the office." She winked at Dani.

"Bye, sis!"

Dani grabbed her favorite jeans out of the dresser and pulled them on, then went to her closet to find a T-shirt. She grabbed a V-neck and put it on. She glanced in the mirror and decided she needed something else. She remembered a dainty necklace Joshua had given her on their first anniversary, so she dug out her jewelry bag from the drawer it was in and found the necklace—a thin chain with a pearl in a gold teardrop. She fastened it around her neck and decided to do something with her hair. When they'd gotten divorced, she'd had short, dark brown hair with red highlights. She wore it strawberry blonde now with icy blonde highlights. It was different and fun for her. Even though it was longer now, it felt lighter, as though the dark color she was born with had been weighing her down for years.

She gave herself some beachy waves and appraised her look in the mirror. She would love to put on some makeup, but she was expecting this hard conversation to be emotional, so she decided to forgo everything but her moisturizer. Her phone buzzed and she shut off the alarm telling her it was time to leave. *Here goes nothing.*

Chapter 5

DANI WALKED INTO MACK'S DINER, humming whatever had just been playing on the radio in her car. She didn't even remember what it was, just something upbeat and happy sounding. Even though she knew this wasn't going to be the lightest of discussions, she hoped it would bring some closure to the past and help them move toward a new future.

She inspected the restaurant, trying to decide where to sit, when she saw Joshua seated in the back of the diner at a corner booth. She walked over to him and raised her eyebrows. "How long have you been waiting?"

He smiled at her. "Not long."

"This is another change, huh? Being early?"

"Yep."

"How did that happen?" she asked as she slid into the booth across from him. Dani couldn't believe it. When they'd been married, it had been like pulling teeth to get him anywhere on time, let alone early.

"Karate."

"I see." She picked up the menu and flipped through it. "Do you know what you're having?"

"Yep."

"You're awfully full of words today."

"Sorry." He grinned. "I've just been in this kind of daze since last night."

She offered him a small smile. "I know what you mean." She perused her menu and made a decision just as the server walked up.

"Hi. My name's Jen. I'll be your server. What can I get you to drink?"

"I'll have an ice water, please, and I think we're ready to order." He looked to Dani, who nodded. "I'll have the Frisco melt with fries, please. Could I have some Thousand Island dressing on the side for the fries, too, please?"

"Sure thing." Jen turned to Dani. "For you, miss?"

"I'll also have an ice water to drink. Could I get a bowl of vegetable beef soup and a small salad please?"

"No problem. Would you like the house dressing with your salad or something different?"

"I'll try the house, thank you. Please bring out my soup with his meal. I'll take the salad sooner, though."

"Sure thing."

Dani turned her attention back to Joshua as Jen walked away. "Well," she said, feeling nervous.

"It's a pretty deep subject."

She smiled in spite of herself. "Yes, it is." She grabbed her napkin and started twisting it. "Josh, I need you to know that I really am sorry for ending our marriage. It was the hardest thing I've ever done, and I've regretted it ever since."

Joshua leaned forward and gazed into her eyes. "Then why did you do it?" His voice held the pain that she knew she had inflicted.

She looked out the window, trying to gather her strength as she moved forward with the conversation. "Do you ever think about her?"

Joshua blinked. Confusion was written all over his face. Then realization hit. "Our baby?"

Dani looked at him and nodded.

"Yes. I wonder if she would have looked like you. I wonder if she would have been into princesses or if she'd rather be on a skateboard. Or both. I wonder what we would have named her." He bowed his head. "That's one thing that has bothered me. We never gave her a name."

"Charlotte."

"What?"

"I called her Charlotte in my mind. I never said it out loud because I didn't think you wanted to name her."

"I was afraid to ask you. You were hurting so much, and I was afraid of making it worse. Charlotte is a beautiful name, though. It was a good choice."

"Thank you." A tear traveled down her cheek as she remembered holding their tiny stillborn daughter in her arms and silently whispering her name.

Jen appeared then with Dani's salad and their drinks. Joshua thanked her and turned his attention back to Dani, who had started picking at her salad. "You okay?"

"Yeah. I've worked through a lot of this already, just not with you."

"It's okay."

"So, here's the thing. After we lost Charlotte, the doctor told me it was my fault." She grimaced recalling how hurtful the doctor's words had been.

Joshua's eyes widened. "H-he said *what*?!"

"Well, not exactly in those words, but basically there was something wrong with my body that would not allow me to carry a baby to term. My weight only complicated the problem."

Joshua's eyes flashed and his face fell.

"It's okay. I've come to terms with the fact that I might never have children, at least not biologically."

"You never told me."

"I couldn't."

"You could tell me anything."

"Not this." She shook her head. "I know how badly you wanted to be a father, to hold your babies in your arms, to watch first steps and see first teeth, to teach your daughter to throw a football and how to expect to be treated, to teach your son to fix a car and how to treat women." She sobbed. "No, Josh, I couldn't tell you."

A look of understanding crossed his face. He moved to the other side of the booth and slid his arm around her. "So you did what you thought would be best for me." It wasn't a question. He knew her well enough to know that she would feel like she could never be the wife he needed if she couldn't bear his children.

Dani nodded. Jen walked up with their meals and set the dishes in front of them. She pulled an unopened tissue package from her apron and handed it to Dani. "These are a little softer than the napkins."

Dani gave her a watery smile. "Thank you."

"You're welcome, hon. I don't want to interrupt anymore, so just give me a little wave if you need anything." She walked back to the servers' station.

Joshua let out a breath. "Dani." She wouldn't look at him. "Danielle." She shook her head. "Please." She regarded him. "You have to know that you were always more important to me than any child that did not yet exist." She sniffled and shook her head. He pulled her close. "I promise, Dani, you were my everything. I didn't need to be a father as much as I needed to be with you."

"B-but you always wanted to have kids. I couldn't give that to you anymore."

"Dani, there are ways to be parents that don't involve biological children."

She peered up at him through wet lashes. "I just never thought that was an option for you."

He shrugged. "It wasn't something I thought much about then, but it was definitely something I was open to."

She slid out from under his arm and picked up her spoon. "I suppose we should eat while our food is still at least a *little* warm."

Joshua nodded. "Okay. I'm going to sit on the other side—"

"So you can see me while we talk," she finished for him.

He grinned and slipped back to the other side. "Exactly." He gawked at his Frisco melt as she started on her soup. "This looks so good. Are you sure you don't want to try some?"

"Normally, yes, but I just want a light lunch today. This soup is delish. Do you want a bite?" She offered up a spoonful.

He eyed it and leaned forward. Her eyes widened as he took the offered bite. "Mmm. This *is* good." Dani raised an eyebrow as Joshua smirked at her. "What?"

"That's new, too," she said.

"You mean eating after you?"

"Eating after anyone!" It had been a longstanding joke between them that he wouldn't eat after anyone else. She'd always thought it was weird, since they spent a lot of time with their mouths together, but he wouldn't take a bite of food from her fork.

"Well . . ." He took a bite of his sandwich.

Dani shook her head, laughing to herself as she waited.

He swallowed. "Do you remember me saying you needed to know what I've been up to?"

Oh yes, she remembered. His hands on her waist, his breath warm on her ear, his woodsy scent filling the air. She felt her face heat as she remembered how tingly she'd gotten all over. She bit her lip and nodded.

Joshua took a deep breath and jumped in. "You know I started karate a few months after our conversation at Fifth & Ivy. That has really helped me in self-discipline and self-awareness the past seven years. I even added a self-defense session to my P.E. classes."

"Wow, that's great." She took another bite of soup. "Mmm. So good. What else has been going on in your life?"

"As I mentioned earlier, there are ways of becoming a parent without a biological connection."

Dani could tell he was hesitant to tell her, even shy about sharing this part of his life with her. He had never had a problem sharing parts of his life with her before, and it made her sad to know that she'd broken that between them. "Yes, you did say that."

"I'm a foster parent, Dani. I have been for three years now."

"That's great, Josh! You are probably an amazing foster parent." He had always amazed her with his compassion and generosity toward others, and this was no different. She softened a little more toward this man with the huge heart.

"Thank you." He gave her a small smile. "Right now, I have two kids: a five-year-old girl and fourteen-year-old boy. Siblings, if you can believe it."

"Oh wow. That's quite the age difference."

"It is. They're very close, though. They've been through a lot, losing their parents and two siblings."

"That's so sad. I'm glad you're able to be there for them."

"It's more than that, Dani." He ran his hand through his hair. "Oh, boy."

Dani reached for his hand. "What is it?"

"I've had them a little over two years now. Children's Services has been trying to find a relative willing and able to take them in." He sighed. "They haven't had much success, and these two kids are becoming available to be adopted. I've asked to be their dad."

Dani's jaw dropped as she took in the news. "Oh, my goodness, Josh! That's so awesome for you! You really are the good guy I remember." She angled her head toward the servers' station but didn't see Jen.

"Are you okay, Dani?" The confused expression on his face was one she'd only rarely seen Her heart broke as she realized he was building his family without her.

"Yeah," Dani shook her head. "I guess I just misread things last night." She noticed Jen walking toward the servers' station and waved to get her attention.

"Wait, what?" Joshua reached for Dani's hand, but she pulled it away.

"It just seemed like you were interested in trying to rekindle something with me, depending on how today went. I didn't realize you were just trying to let me down gently."

Jen came over. "Did you want dessert? Refills? Or—?"

"Just the check, please."

"Refills would be great. I might like dessert, too." They shared a glance, and Dani quickly bowed her head.

"How about I give you a few minutes?" She went to clear a table that had just emptied.

"Dani, will you wait a minute, please?"

She brought her head up, tears in her eyes. "What?" she whispered.

"You read things just fine last night."

She exhaled and felt her shoulders relax a bit. "I did?"

"Oh, Dani, you have been the one for me since we met. I didn't hate you for the divorce. I didn't understand it, but I never hated you. I don't think I ever stopped loving you."

She gasped.

"I didn't know we were going to meet again. I talked to Children's Services about adopting Ellie and Luca a month ago." He reached for her hand again, and this time she let him take it. "I want to see what we have, but we can't just pick up from where we left off. I have two kids now who need me, too. You need to know that and figure out if that's something you'd be okay with."

Dani let out another haggard breath. That was so much more than she'd been expecting. She fingered her necklace mindlessly for a moment, then remembered what she'd put on.

Joshua's gaze drifted to her neck and the pearl hanging just below. Tears threatened to spill as his eyes met hers. "You still have it."

Dani nodded. "Of course I do. I never stopped loving you either. I just didn't realize it until I saw you last night. I tried so hard to forget the past, but the moment I saw you, I knew I needed you back in my life."

Jen stopped by again. "Did we make a decision?"

This time, it was Joshua who asked for the check. Dani noticed the glint in his eye and nodded in agreement.

Chapter 6

DANI TUCKED HER HAND INTO the crook of Joshua's arm again. This time, she couldn't resist giving his bicep a little squeeze. He grinned down at her. "Yes, that's new, too. Well, not new-new. I've had it a few years now." He gave her a wink.

"I like it. I'm guessing your biceps aren't the only muscles you've developed the past few years." She blushed and turned away.

Joshua laughed. "That would be correct. I bet you'd love to get your hands on them, too." He gave her a wolfish grin.

"If you only knew," she mumbled.

"What was that?"

"Oh, nothing."

"You know what I'd like to know?"

"I couldn't begin to guess at this point."

"Fair enough." They stopped at her car, and he moved to hold her hands in his. He lifted her left wrist and slid her jacket sleeve back. He bent his head down and touched his lips to her bare wrist. She gasped as every nerve ending in her wrist lit up. "When did you get this?"

She worked to steady her breathing and contemplated the small tattoo. "About five years ago." She stared up at him and bit her bottom lip. He focused on her mouth, and she fought to keep her train of thought. "Um . . . I was missing you. Like, a lot. I went and got it done." She studied the tiny lovebirds and the anniversary date she'd put under it. She gazed back up at him and whispered, "I could never let go of us."

Joshua pulled her into a hug and took a deep breath. "If you knew how badly I want—"

"So do it." Dani watched as he swallowed hard. She leaned up and placed a soft kiss on his Adam's apple, feeling him growl in response. That drove her to put another just below it. "I mean, I'm okay with it."

His arms tightened around her. "Dani, you are going to be the death of me." He took a step back and sighed. "How about this: you take the next few days to think about what it would mean to be in my life again. If you're in, I'm all in. And if you're in, I come with two kids: one grumpy teenager who is mad at the world and one little girl who can't remember any parent except me. We can have more—if you want to try—or can take more in if you want. If you're in, then that means those decisions will be made together. We can get together Saturday night to celebrate." He sighed. "Or to say goodbye."

"Valentine's Day?"

He nodded. "I'm hopeful we'll be celebrating."

"Will the kids be joining us?"

"No. My mom loves them and will be happy to watch them that night, just like last night."

"Even if she knows it's for a date with me?"

Joshua nodded and grinned. "So, it's a date then?"

"I think it's a good idea for me to take some time. I want to say yes right now—that I am all in, ready to be a mom and ready to live life with you—but I think taking a few days apart for me to think about it is a good idea. Because I cannot think with you next to me."

"How about I pick you up at six? I want a real date with you again. It's been too long, and I don't want to chance walking you to your car with an audience seeing a good night kiss."

Her insides warmed as she remembered his kisses and how her body used to respond to them. "I think that's a good idea. I'll text you my address."

"Thanks." He kissed her forehead and stepped back. "I'll see you Saturday."

Chapter 7

DANI TEXTED LEXI. THEN CALLED her. "Alexis Katherine Richards! You call me back ASAP! I mean it! We need to talk!" She laid her phone on her dining table and began to pace the room.

She wondered why John hadn't mentioned that "David" had kids, even if he only knew them as foster kids. *No time to dwell on that*, she thought. She was grateful she'd taken the whole day off and was on-call the next two days because she was a bag of nerves. Joshua had given her a lot to think about, and she didn't want to tread lightly moving forward. She couldn't. Not with kids involved.

"Sisters. Sisters. There were never such devoted sisters," played her phone's ringtone. She accepted the call on her earbuds. "Lexi! You will never believe this."

"Well, hello to you, too."

"Hello. Now honestly—Joshua has kids." Silence. "Lexi?" Dani picked up her phone and made sure they were still connected. "Lexi, did you hear me?"

"Yes."

"Can you say something?"

"He has kids?"

"Well, foster kids. But he's adopting them soon."

"How wonderful for all of them!"

"Why don't you sound surprised?"

"What do you mean? I was very surprised."

Dani closed her eyes. Of course Lexi already knew. "When?"

"When what?" Lexi sounded puzzled.

"When were you surprised?"

"When I found out that Josh has kids."

"Yes, when did you find that out?"

"When did I find that out?" Lexi's voice squeaked as she repeated the question. For being a brainiac who graduated early and top of her class from *everything*, she was not good at hiding things from her sister.

"Doctor Lexi, is there something you should be telling me?"

"Absolutely not. Doctor Lexi has nothing she should be telling you."

"What about Sister Lexi?"

"Sister Lexi would love to be able to tell you, but sometimes Doctor trumps Sister."

"What are you—just a second." She picked up her phone and texted Joshua, grateful that he'd put his number in her phone Tuesday night on the way to her car. Her phone buzzed moments later and she had her answer.

"So, Doctor Lexi, pediatrician to Luca and Ellie, has known for a while now."

"I can't really say, Dani. You know that."

"Ugh!" Dani could feel her frustration mounting when she realized something. "Wait, can you tell me nonmedical stuff about them?"

"I can't give you anything, Dani, I'm sorry."

"What if he tells you that you can?"

"Why would he do that? Unless . . ." she trailed off.

"Unless what?" Dani was texting Joshua again.

"Are the two of you getting back together?" Her voice held hope.

"Maybe, but I need to—wait, why are you so invested?"

"So many reasons, Dani. A big one being that you never should have left him. I'm quite sure you still love him. Another big one being that he has never stopped loving you."

Dani dropped to a chair. "Why do you think that?" she whispered.

"Because each and every time he has seen me anywhere, he asks about *you*. He still shops at the same places he did when you were married. Eats at the same restaurants. He still works at the same school, Dani. He wanted to be where you could find him in case you ever changed your mind."

Dani closed her eyes as she processed what Lexi was saying. "And you know this because?"

"Because even though you might have decided to stop going to those places that had been your favorites, I still went. I see him at the school sometimes when I go to do vision tests or show up for presidential fitness testing.

He asks how you're doing. I tell him minor things, because I know better than telling major news for you, and we move on to a different topic."

"What are the kids like? He tells me the fourteen-year-old is grumpy and the five-year-old doesn't remember her parents, but I don't know anything about them! What are their personalities like? What do they love to do? How are they coping?"

"Dani. Pause for a moment and take a deep breath."

"How is it that I'm the big sister, but you're the one calming me down?"

Lexi giggled. "It's just the way it is, I guess."

"I guess so."

"Here's what I want you to think about: I know you want to know all about the kids in Josh's life before you make a decision. That's not uncommon. What is also normal is that most parents don't know any of that information about their children before they have them. Josh didn't get to know them or their personalities before taking them in. He just made a decision to love them, no matter what, and he's done exactly that. The real question here is can *you* love them without knowing anything?"

"I don't know, Lex." Her voice was a whisper, and a tear trickled down her cheek.

"Dani. You loved Charlotte completely not knowing who she would be, how long she would live, or any of the things that you're worried about."

Dani nodded, then realized Lexi couldn't see her. "Yes," she whimpered.

"This is not unlike that. They're just older." Dani heard a knock at Lexi's door. "I have to get to my patients. I love you, Dani."

"I love you, too, Lex. Thank you."

Chapter 8

DANI COULDN'T BELIEVE THAT SHE was getting another chance at a Valentine's Day with Joshua. She had thought long and hard about what Lexi had told her. Other than confirming with Joshua that Lexi was his kids' pediatrician, she hadn't been in contact with him since their lunch on Wednesday. She wanted to focus on what Lexi had said and examine her heart to see if she could do it. She was thankful she'd only been needed for work twice—once at the hospital and the other at a local assisted-living facility. She'd been able to concentrate fully on what she needed to do there and return home to contemplate her future.

Saturday arrived and she found that she couldn't wait to tell Joshua about her conversation with Lexi and the decision it had led her to. He was supposed to pick her up at six, and at five thirty she'd finished her makeup and hair and just needed to choose between two looks she was torn between for the evening.

She walked to her closet and found the little black dress and the red bodycon dress, trying to decide which Joshua would fully appreciate. She reached for the red dress when she noticed a men's pink dress shirt in the back. She'd forgotten she had snuck that from Joshua when they were married. Back then, she'd worn it over a tank and left it unbuttoned to run errands in, as it was a bit snug on her, but now . . . *hmmm, I wonder if this would work as a dress now.*

She slipped it on and inspected herself in the mirror. *Definitely not snug anymore.* She grabbed a thin belt to add to it. It was like a shirtdress now, and it hit her mid-thigh. A little shorter than she normally wore, but this was a special occasion. She added her teardrop necklace. She grabbed her highest black heels from her closet and put them on and checked the clock again. *Five-forty. I must be super anxious to get this date started*, she thought.

Her phone started buzzing in her clutch. She pulled it out and glanced at the screen. *Josh.*

"Hey there."

"Hey. Um, I have a problem."

"Don't tell me you're calling to cancel our Valentine's date twenty minutes before you're supposed to pick me up." She kept her tone light since the Joshua she knew would never do something like that.

"Well . . ."

"Joshua David, you are not." She switched to a video call with him. She needed to see him.

"Not on purpose." He appeared defeated. "You look beautiful."

"You should see me in person." She winked at him, and he blushed.

"You have no idea how badly I want that," he whispered, his voice husky.

"Not on purpose? What does that mean?" She did a double take and realized he was wearing a suit and tie. He was still at home—the home they'd once begun building together. "Wait . . . is everything okay? Is every*one* okay?"

"I guess that depends on your definition of okay."

"Does anyone need to go to the hospital? Are the kids okay? Are you okay? What's going on?"

"No one needs to go to the hospital. Ellie was sick Thursday and Friday, so my mom didn't think she should watch her tonight. Luca said he'd watch her, but about five minutes ago, he started puking his guts out."

"Oh no. Poor Luca."

"Yeah, he's not doing well. I can't leave him here like this, and I can't get a sitter at this point . . ." He trailed off, his voice heavy with disappointment. He didn't even notice that Dani was no longer standing in her apartment but climbing into her car.

"It's okay, Josh. Things happen when you're a parent." She shrugged to show him she was okay with it.

"Could we make it up next week?"

"No."

"Oh good." He stopped. "Wait, did you say no?"

"Yes, I said no." Dani couldn't help the grin spreading across her face.

"I really am sorry."

"It's okay, Josh."

"Can I Uber you some dinner to make up for missing you tonight?"

"No, it's okay. I can find something around here somewhere." She gave him a soft smile. "I need to go, though. Can I call you later tonight?"

"Oh—um, yeah, that should be fine." He seemed flustered. "I should probably clean up Luca's mess anyway."

"Ick. Yeah, you don't want that around for long. I'll talk to you later, okay?" She ended the call when he nodded. She didn't want him to see where she was.

Chapter 9

FIFTEEN MINUTES LATER, DANI'S NERVES were starting to overtake her. She picked up the bags from her front seat and walked up the sidewalk to Joshua's front door. She closed her eyes and took a deep breath before knocking. She looked down and groaned; she was still dressed to go out. She had just started to turn around, figuring she could run back home to change, when the door opened.

"Dani? What are you doing here?" Josh had taken off his suit jacket and tie but was still wearing the dress shirt, his sleeves rolled up his forearms. His hair was mussed, as though he'd run his hand through it a few times.

Oh. My. How did I ever divorce this man? She stumbled over a response. "Bags. Food. Quick."

She watched his face as he took in her appearance. His jaw dropped when he got to the bottom of her "dress." He swallowed hard as his gaze made its way back to her lips and back down to linger on her dress. He smiled. "Is that my shirt?"

Her face heated as she noticed the hungry look in his eye. She didn't trust herself to speak. "Mm-hmm."

He took the bags from her hands and peeked inside. "Chicken soup, crackers, Sprite, coloring book, crayons, and—is that frozen pizza?" He looked up at her. "This is very thoughtful, Dani. Thank you."

"You're welcome." She bit her lip and closed her eyes. "I needed to see you tonight. To tell you what I decided."

"Oh." Joshua set the bags on the ground and pulled his front door closed behind him. "When you said no to getting together next week, I thought that was clear, but then you showed up. Here. With 'get better' food." He took her hands and intertwined his fingers with hers, setting her nerve endings on fire. "What did you decide?"

Dani nodded, her eyes flittering to his lips and back to his eyes. "I'm all in, Josh. I had a talk with Lex—"

She was cut off when he kissed her. He let go of her hands and brought a hand to her back, pulling her closer to him. She ran her fingers along his back, remembering how much he loved that. He moaned and deepened their kiss. She turned and pulled him to her as she backed against the door. He brought his hand up to her hair, lifting it away from her neck as he traced kisses along her jawline and down her neck.

"Ohhh," she breathed.

That seemed to remind him of where they were. He stepped back. "I'm sorry."

"Oh no you don't. No sorry for kisses."

She pulled him back to her and placed a small kiss just below his earlobe. When he shivered, she continued down his jawline. Her hands slid to the buttons on his shirt, where she undid the first one. He lifted his head up as she kissed where the button had been.

"Dani, you have no idea what you do to me." His voice was thick with desire.

She pulled away. "We better stop." She noticed he was breathing as hard as she was, and she took the moment to try to steal another kiss.

He stepped back again. "Dani—I shouldn't have kissed you."

"I said you can't say sorry."

"It's not that. It's just that, well, we're a house of sickos right now, and you're standing there, all gorgeous and looking like you've been very thoroughly kissed."

"Which I have been, and which I wouldn't mind repeating." She winked at him.

His gaze heated. "Same." He gave his head a shake. "What I'm trying to say is that now you're probably going to get sick, too. I didn't think it would be a good idea to invite you in, but since you now have *all* my germs, which are pretty much all their—" He pointed inside. "—germs, you might as well come inside."

"Wait. I want you to know. Lexi asked me if I could love these children completely, without knowing anything before making that decision. My decision was yes. It was made before you called tonight, and then when you called because Ellie and Luca are sick, I was worried. Not just about you, but about them. I felt like I needed to be here tonight, because this is where my family is. It's where I belong."

"You always have." Joshua laced his fingers through Dani's and kissed her knuckles. He reached around her, twisted the knob, and pushed opened the front door. "Welcome home."

About the Author

Melissa Cate has always been a storyteller—her mom would record the bedtime stories Melissa would tell at night and type them up for her. After thirty years of mostly academic, devotional, or biographical writing, she jumped headfirst back into fiction in October 2023 and was a Write on the River winner in the spring of 2024. She has finished two women's fiction novels that she is starting to query. Melissa currently lives in the Pacific Northwest with her family but is a Midwesterner through and through.

You can find Melissa on:

Instagram: @melissacatewrites

BAKED IN LOVE

Baked in Love

J.E. Smith

Chapter 1: Katie

You're invited to join us in
celebrating the marriage of
Julia Nash and Jacob White
on the true day of love
Friday, February 14, 2025, at The Lakes Country Club.
In lieu of gifts, the bride and groom are asking for
donations to the American Liver Cancer Institute
in honor of Julia's brother, Jeff,
who was a shining light of joy and optimism

I STARE AT MY YOUNGER sister's wedding invitation as I wait for my turn to leave the plane. I swore I would never come back to my hometown of Lakes, Arizona, but I can't abandon my sister on the most important day of her life. Especially since my brother isn't here to see it.

Julia had just graduated high school, and I was wrapping up an internship with Pascal Mirao, the best baker and cake decorator in Arizona, when Jeff took a turn for the worse.

After his death, I tucked tail and ran away to Hudsonville, Michigan, and swore never to return to the place that reminded me of him.

Stepping foot in my hometown will inevitably bring unwelcome memories and feelings to the surface, but there is one person I really hope to avoid: Travis Hardy. My brother's best friend and the one man I always wanted but could never have. I don't think I can face him, even after all these years.

"Finally, our turn," the lady in the seat mutters next to me, pulling me from my thoughts.

I put my long blond hair into a ponytail and fix my glasses before standing to deplane.

The wedding is only three days away, and I am booked to fly out the day after. From what I understand, the itinerary is simple. Today, family brunch. Tomorrow, rehearsal dinner. Friday, wedding. Saturday, I'm out of here.

As I walk through the airport, I spot my younger sister bouncing and waving as soon as she spots me. When I am off the escalator, she wraps me in the tightest hug. As much as I hate coming back here, it's great to see her again.

"Oh, Katie! It's so good to see you." She beams, still not letting me go. "I've missed you so much!"

"I've missed you, too, Jules," I say with a smile as she finally releases me. I fill my voice with enthusiasm that I don't really feel simply because she deserves to hear it. "So . . . are you ready for the wedding festivities to begin?"

"Yes!" she squeals but then turns all business like a switch flipped in her. "Speaking of which, we have to go, or we won't be able to pick up the pastries and coffee bar stuff from the bakery before the family brunch!"

In an instant, she turns and drags me through the airport toward her car.

It's only a fifteen-minute drive to the small town of Lakes, but my sister is driving like the world will end if we get even one minute off schedule. I never pegged Jules to be the Bridezilla type, but I guess when it's the biggest day of your life, you're allowed to go a little crazy.

Lakes is the same as I remember. All the stores are on the main road through town with the church at the end before the road climbs the small mountain. The townsfolk are walking around carrying various bags and I recognize everyone. A perk and downfall of a small town.

Jules pulls up in front of the bakery, which has received both a makeover and a name change since I left. Butter Your Buns Bakery is a small shop with two tables out front and a huge glass window showing the modern interior with blue and gray tones throughout.

"Oh crap, I forgot to call the caterer with the setup time for the rehearsal dinner!" Jules scowls at her phone. "Katie, can you go in and grab the stuff while I handle this?" She looks up at me with pleading eyes.

"Really? Can't you call the caterer later?" I drone, not wanting to leave the car.

"No, I don't want to forget again. It's just a few things, please?" She gives me her best pleading expression, which she's perfected as the baby of the family.

My heart clenches as my eyes shift back to the bakery. Travis's mom used to own it, and we all spent a lot of time here. When things were hard, Jeff and I would come here to work out our problems over coffee and sweets.

"I guess if I must," I concede to her, simply because that is what Jeff would have done for me. She deserves the same older-sibling love.

"Thank you! You're the best! The order is under my name and should already be paid for." A beaming smile spreads across her face and she immediately starts dialing the caterer's number.

I climb out of the car and make my way into the cute, little bakery where people are eating and drinking coffees at tiny tables throughout. As I approach the counter, I freeze in my tracks when I realize who the man working the register is. Travis.

In five years, he has managed to become even better-looking. He has gone from tall and lean to somehow possessing muscles that now strain his T-shirt. Tattoos cover his left arm, and his once short, chocolate-brown hair has grown out and he has tied it up in a sexy manbun.

The last time I saw him . . . I blew him off at Jeff's funeral.

Steeling myself, I approach as he builds a latte on the back counter. "Be with you in a moment," he tosses over his shoulder.

He turns around and pauses as he looks over my face, and I swallow hard as butterflies erupt in my belly.

"Becky, here is your latte," he shouts without taking his eyes off me, and I can only stand frozen. "It's been a long time, Katie." His voice is flat and monotonous.

"Yeah, it has."

Why is this so awkward? He was constantly around growing up, but I never talked to him again after the funeral. He called and texted me multiple times, but I didn't want to talk to him, because it meant remembering my brother was gone. I pushed Travis away, just like I had everyone else.

"You're in town for the wedding?" he asks.

"Yeah, that's why I'm here. I need to pick up Jules's order."

"Sure thing." He smiles at me like I'm just another customer to please and I hate it. "Max, can you get Julia Nash's order from the back and carry it to her car? It's the white Chevy out there."

"Absolutely," Max yells back from behind the kitchen door.

Travis turns to me now and punches a few keys on the register.

"I thought you were working construction with your dad. Why are you in the bakery?" I ask, unable to resist my curiosity.

"Dad retired and I decided to take over this place from my mom instead. I didn't want to work construction without Jeff by my side."

"Oh . . . I guess that's understandable."

"What have you been doing with yourself up in Michigan?"

"I work as a freelance cake decorator for various bakeries. It's fun. Pays the bills." I shrug.

"That seems like a good fit for you."

I feel heat flood my cheeks as his eyes lock on to mine. I still feel like the high school girl who was head over heels for him, except now I'm twenty-five and a grown adult! Goodness, I need to get a grip on myself.

Someone clears their throat behind me, and I realize I'm holding up a line that has now formed.

"Oh, my bad. I guess I better go or Jules will start freaking out about being late." I laugh awkwardly and turn for the door, walking away.

"Katie!" he shouts, and I turn to look at him. "You um . . . you look great."

I nod and smile, feeling my blush deepen as I head out the door to the car.

Chapter 2: Katie

"SERIOUSLY, JULES, YOU COULD HAVE given me a heads-up that Travis owned the bakery," I scold my sister as we set up brunch on my parents' back patio.

"I didn't think it was a big deal. He's been around forever and still helps around here with bigger things that need to be done." She shrugs as she arranges the muffins on a platter.

"I was just shocked to see him was all." I try my best to sound nonchalant, but inside I am screaming.

He was the only person I hadn't wanted to see on this trip home.

All it took was one look into his honey-colored eyes and a smile, for the feelings I had locked away in a deep part of me to rush back to the surface.

"Well, you should get used to it because he's one of Jacob's groomsmen and making the wedding cake."

Of course he is. I wouldn't be home if I wasn't drooling over my brother's best friend. I take a deep breath and carry the plates to the table. *It's only three days and then you won't have to talk to or see him. You can do this.*

Jacob and his parents are the first to arrive and Jules basically jumps into his arms when she spots him. She has been infatuated with him since the day they met, and I wonder if in five years from now, she will still be leaping into his embrace when he enters a room.

It's sweet to see her so in love. My love life is a mess, so at least one of us has it figured out. I've dated off and on again since moving to Michigan, but in the end, I called them all off because I couldn't shake the feeling that they would never win my brother's approval.

No, only one man would have ever had a shot at winning my brother's approval.

The same one who invades my dreams . . . and whom I will never actually be with.

Other guests arrive and I am berated with the never-ending questions. Just when I am ready to shout, *Yes, I am single, and I don't plan to move home!* to the third aunt to ask, I excuse myself and go to the coffee bar. Coffee always makes everything better; even family members who are a bit too nosy become more tolerable.

"Ahem." A deep, smooth voice clears their throat, and I jump and whip around.

Travis is here.

"I'd like to get some coffee if you don't mind."

Why did we have to stop at the bakery if he was coming anyway?

"Umm, why are you here?" I whisper with an aggravated bite.

He raises his eyebrows at me and crosses his huge arms like I have offended him. "Because I was invited."

"Today is for family only. You're not family."

A smirk plasters his face, and he wets his bottom lip, making all my focus go to how bad I've always wanted to kiss him.

"Travis is family!" My dad comes up behind him and slaps a hand on his shoulder. "He basically lived here when he and your brother were in high school."

I roll my eyes, and Travis wears a smug grin.

"Dad, we need you over here for some pictures!" Jules yells.

"Excuse me, Katie-Bear. I'll be back soon." He leans over, kisses my cheek, and whisks off to attend to the demanding bride-to-be.

"Aww, it's sweet your dad still calls you Katie-Bear," Travis teases as he fills a cup of coffee. "Though I much prefer Gummy Bear."

I whirl to fully face him at the sound of the old nickname he and my brother used to tease me with. He doesn't get to use that anymore. Not without Jeff.

I seethe at him and start toward my seat. "Screw you, Travis!" I throw over my shoulder.

"Bet you wish you could!" he yells after me, and I know his perverse joke has me turning redder than a cherry, especially since there's an edge of truth to it.

As I take my seat, I notice all the eyes on me. Over half the party probably heard that exchange between us and thankfully there is no pyre, because this place would burst into flames from the level of my embarrassment.

As everyone resumes their conversations, my father takes a seat in the chair next to me.

"Are you okay, Katie-Bear? That looked intense over there." He glances to the coffee station and then back to me.

"Yeah, just a misunderstanding, Dad." I place my hand on his arm, trying to reassure him. Dad cares with his whole heart, and I can't have him pressing me. Jules's wedding weekend can't become about my messy life.

"Okay, as long as you're sure?" He raises an eyebrow at me, and I roll my eyes as I smile at my overprotective father.

"Yes, I'm sure." As soon as the words leave my mouth, Jules stands, clanking her mimosa glass with a fork.

"Thank you all for coming. Everything is set up and ready for us to enjoy some food. Let's eat and then we can cover details for the upcoming events." She smiles at all of us and then turns to Jacob, who wraps his arm around her waist.

"Let's get some food. But know I'm always here for you, sweetheart." Dad stands from his chair and kisses my forehead before heading over to grab some coffee. Luckily, the rest of brunch moves forward without a hiccup and we're able to celebrate Jules and Jacob as a family. They drill each of us with the schedules. Jules is excited, to say the least, but she is also stressed beyond measure. I am worried about her; a stroke would be less than ideal while trying to keep everything perfect and on time.

Carrying the leftover muffins into the house, Jules is in the kitchen micromanaging Travis. As I stay hidden just on the other side of the wall, I experience a certain sense of pleasure overhearing their exchange.

"Okay, so the cake and cupcakes are done and the desserts for the reception will be ready for tomorrow?" Jules inquires.

"Yes. Trust me, Julia, I have everything under control on my end. Relax and try to enjoy this. You only get married once." He soothes her with a comforting voice that makes the butterflies erupt again. Why the hell does he have to be so sweet? It makes being upset with him difficult.

"TRAVIS!" Jacob's panicked voice fills the house as he blows in off the porch.

Crap, hopefully he didn't notice me eavesdropping.

"Dispatch just called me in. There's a fire at the bakery!"

Chapter 3: Travis

THE BAKERY IS MY WHOLE life. I've poured every ounce of blood, sweat, and tears into this place and even built an apartment above it where I live.

And I watched as it burned.

The last of the fire is out now, and the firefighters are starting to clean up, but I just stand, frozen, staring at the rubble of my life.

Anything of real importance in my life always seems to leave. First, Jeff. I never wanted to imagine he would leave me, and I miss him daily.

Then, Katie. She was my closest friend after Jeff. I told Katie everything, and her carefree spirit was a joy to be in the presence of. As we got older, I often found myself wishing I could hold her close, kiss her lips, and make her mine, but that was never going to happen because Jeff was my best friend. And then she up and moved to Michigan.

Now the sanctuary I created is in shambles, too. *What the hell do I do now?* I don't even have a place to sleep tonight. My parents sold the family house and are currently traveling the country in an RV, so going home isn't a possibility anymore.

"Oh, Travis, I'm so sorry!" Mrs. Nash approaches and wraps me in her warm embrace.

She has always been like a second mom to me.

Looking behind her, I see the whole crew came with her. Julia is talking to Jacob, Mr. Nash is scowling at the bakery like he's as upset as I am, and Katie is staring right at me.

I wish hers were the arms wrapped around me right now. She has no idea how much I've missed her over the years. Jeff made it more than clear she was off-limits in high school, and I respected his boundaries because that's what you do for a person who's more like a brother than a friend, but I can't help but wonder what would've happened if I hadn't. Maybe Katie would be mine.

Mrs. Nash releases me and takes my face in her hands. "Tell me what you need."

"I don't even know where to begin. My apartment above the bakery needs repairs, along with part of the kitchen. On top of that, all the food that has been prepped for the wedding has to be thrown out due to smoke damage."

"Oh, sweet boy, I know this is a big hit for you, but let us help you." Her voice is desperate, and her eyes well with tears. "You can come stay in the guesthouse with Katie. There's an extra bedroom and a huge kitchen that you can work out of for now."

"What? Mom, no! Why can't he stay in Jeff's old room or something?" Katie chimes in from behind her mother, clearly annoyed.

I knew after Jeff died everything changed between us, but for her to want to avoid my company completely is ridiculous.

"Jeff's room is Jeff's room, Katie." Her mom pins her eyes at her and holds a warning tone to her voice. "He can stay in the guesthouse with you."

My first thought is to decline, but with Katie's reaction, I can't pass up an opportunity to get under her skin even more. I want to work this out with her, but if she won't let me, then she leaves me no choice. She's ignored every attempt I've made to try and connect with her, to be there for her, but now that she's back, I won't let her get away so easily.

"Thank you for the offer. Staying at the guesthouse would be a huge help, plus the kitchen is big enough for me to redo the cake." I smile at Katie the whole time I speak, and her little attitude is on full display with a silent scoff, her arms folded over her chest.

Oh, this is going to be so much fun.

"Perfect!" Her mom claps her hands together. "It's settled then. Just come over whenever you're ready."

"Will do. Thank you again."

"Of course, dear, that's what family is for." She smiles at me and heads off to go talk to her husband, leaving me alone with a thoroughly irritated Katie.

"What's wrong, Gummy Bear? Can't handle sharing a house for the next few days?"

"Stop with the Gummy Bear thing!" she shouts at me and moves toward me, stepping into my space.

"Sorry." I hold up my hands in surrender. "I just love seeing you look like a tiny Hulk with all that pent-up rage, when we both know you're just so sweet and soft." I lower my face next to her ear, and I don't miss her breath hitching as I do. Keeping my voice at a whisper, I add, "Like a gummy bear."

She shoves me back, but I don't budge.

"You're a real jerk, you know that?" she yells at me. "I cannot wait to get out of this town and away from you!" She turns on her heels and walks away, her hips swaying.

Oh, I am definitely under her skin, and I can't wait to push her until she cracks. We both know that she's shoving me away on purpose, but if her shaky breathing is any indication, there's something more going on here than just hatred for me.

Chapter 4: Katie

TWO DAYS. ONLY TWO MORE days and then I can go back to Michigan and leave everything in this tiny town behind, including him.

Deep breaths, Katie. Deep breaths.

Last night was a complete mess. He kept walking around this tiny house like he owns it!

I have not had any relief in the annoyance I feel toward him, and I'm about ready to kill him. It's seven in the morning, and he's running the huge mixer in the kitchen! How can anyone sleep through that?

I groan into my pillow and, in a fit of fury, I climb out of bed, throw on my glittery, red slippers, and stomp my way to the kitchen.

He is completely oblivious to my arrival. The mixer is turning, and he's looking at a recipe card while sipping a cup of coffee like this is his everyday routine.

"SERIOUSLY, TRAVIS!" I yell over the mixer, getting his attention.

He moves to the machine and shuts it off. Then he meets my gaze, and a smug smirk plasters his face. God, I would really love to knock it right off.

"It's seven in the morning! Some people actually like to sleep, you know." I cross my arms over my chest.

He sighs deep before setting down his coffee and walking over to stand in front of me.

His eyes trail down my body and then back up. Seriously, is he checking me out right now? I roll my eyes in annoyance.

"I couldn't sleep last night, and some of us have work to do. I have to have the cake made by this afternoon so my decorator can come this evening because he can't come tomorrow." He places a hand on his hip and sighs. "I would do it myself, but most of my supplies were destroyed last night, " he snaps.

Guilt pangs in my chest at my lack of empathy, and I take a minute to really look at him.

He looks like hell. His eyes have dark circles beneath them and they're slightly puffy and red. The normal light energy he carries is still there, but it's almost like it's been dowsed in water.

I soften toward him and sigh. "Just give me until nine, noise-free, and I'll decorate the cake, okay?"

He wets his bottom lip, contemplating my offer. "All right, you've got yourself a deal."

God, I wonder how those lips would feel on mine.

Stuffing the thought down, I give him a victorious smile. "Thank you!" I turn toward my room, ready for more sleep.

"No problem. Nice messy bun and slippers, by the way. It's a good look for you," he teases, but I'm too tired to play his games right now, so I slam my bedroom door closed in response.

I am awoken by the blaring noise of the mixer once more. Groaning, I look at my phone and it's nine on the dot. *Well, no one will ever say he's late,* I sneer to myself.

Tonight is the rehearsal dinner, and Jules is probably an anxious mess. I need to head up to the big house to make sure she doesn't need anything extra from me. At the very least, I want to give her a hug and assure her that her wedding will be perfect. My poor mother doesn't need to be dealing with Bridezilla all alone this morning.

I hop in the shower and then dress in my favorite Red Wings hockey T-shirt and skinny jeans that make my butt look amazing before heading to the kitchen.

Of course, Travis is still slaving away. He pauses before adding ingredients to a bowl and stares at me with a twinkle in his eye. Or maybe I'm wishing there's a twinkle there, but either way, under his gaze my pulse quickens, and butterflies erupt in my stomach.

I shove the unwelcome feelings down. "I'm going up to the big house. Let me know when you're ready for me to decorate."

"Okay, tell everyone I said hi." He nods and takes another sip from his coffee mug. I wonder if the man drinks coffee all day. It's the only thing I've actually seen him drink since I've been home.

Shoes on, I rush out the front door and come face-to-face with Jules.

"Well, good morning." She eyes me curiously. "What has you rushing out the door so fast?"

"Oh, nothing, just coming to see if you needed anything for tonight." I start walking toward the main house and my sister hurries after me.

"Oh, nothing? Right. So, you rushing out of there had nothing to do with your new housemate?" she eagerly asks.

"What? No. If anything, he's annoying to have around!"

She jogs in front of me, forcing me to stop, and raises her eyebrows at me.

"Katie, I know when you're holding back, and you're definitely holding back! Did something happen between you two that I don't know about?"

I feel my cheeks heat at her words. Why does my body always betray me?

"Nothing happened. He's Jeff's best friend and that's that."

"Yeah, and you're blushing. Do you have feelings for him?"

"Really, Jules?" I drone, begging her to drop something for once in her life.

"Ha! You do! How did I not know about this?" She throws her hands on her hips like she has been wronged in some way.

"Okay, we're done here. We're not going to talk about any feelings I may or may not have for Travis. Do *you* need anything?"

"Nope, I'm all set." She gives me a knowing smile, and I narrow my eyes.

"Okay, well, goodbye then. I'll see you this evening."

I can feel my sister's eyes burn into the back of my head the whole way back to the guesthouse. Once inside, I shut the door and lean on it, letting the relief of escaping my sister's questioning wash over me. Travis and I will never happen, and that is exactly why I keep those feelings strictly to myself.

I push off the door and start toward the living room.

"That was a fast visit." Travis's voice flutters in from the kitchen. Of course he's spotted me. It must be written into this wedding weekend's agenda that I be forbidden to ever get a moment of peace!

I work up the best fake smile I can muster to hide the stress I feel. "Yeah, they were set for the day. So, I'm going to chill here until setup this afternoon."

He walks in from the kitchen, wiping his hands on a towel. "Actually, if you're free, would you be able to help me for a few? Julia really wanted strawberry heart thumbprint cookies for the dinner tonight, and if I remember right, yours were always the best." A soft smile graces his face as he speaks. *Is he flirting with me?*

"They *are* the best. I make them for some local bakers here and there and the townsfolk in Michigan always love them."

He laughs and I smile at the sound. "Wow, are you always so humble?" he jests, and I smack his chest playfully. He throws his hands up as if to block another attack. "And so violent."

I laugh at his feigned injury and then sigh. "All right, I guess I'll help." I groan like I'm so inconvenienced, but really, the idea of sharing the kitchen with him and having the opportunity to bake for my sister's wedding is enticing. "Now, move it! I've got cookies to make."

Chapter 5: Travis

SHE'S A BEAUTY TO WATCH in the kitchen. My four round cakes are in the oven now, so I'm just leaning against the wall and watching her magic unfold. She glides through the kitchen, adding various ingredients to different bowls, preparing the dry mixture, the wet, and the filling.

I remember watching her practice when she was doing her internship with Pascal Mirao. The kitchen was her happy place, where she always had this light and joyful energy. Her focus on the meticulous details, the pride she would exude when she had Jeff and I taste-test her newest creations. She has that light energy to her now, and I haven't seen it since before her brother died. She belongs in the kitchen, baking and creating masterpieces. She's meant to be doing this.

Pushing off the wall, I walk up next to her, wanting to be a part of her magic and not simply observing it from the sideline. Lost in her own world, she turns and runs squarely into my chest, the small bowl of flour in her hands jostling enough for flour to fly everywhere, covering both of us.

"Oh, goodness!" she exclaims. "I didn't realize you were standing there."

"I gathered that." I gesture to my floured shirt. "It looked like you needed some help."

"I'm good actually." She turns back to the flour container to refill the bowl she was taking to the mixer.

"No, Gummy Bear," I tease, following close behind her until I've trapped her against the counter. "You do need help. You're not messy enough to call yourself a baker."

Before she knows what's happening, I gracefully scoop a handful of flour into my hand and drop it right on the top of her head. Then I immediately retreat.

"Ahh! Travis!" she squeals. "My hair!"

I take another step back, laughing at her powdered hair and face. She's biting her bottom lip in a suppressed giggle and my chest warms at the sight.

She saunters over to me, a mischievous glint in her eyes. "You think this is funny, do you?"

"Oh, this is the funniest thing I've seen all week."

Quick as a whip, she swipes an egg off the counter and cracks it over my shoulder. Then she dashes for the corner of the kitchen and laughs at me.

"Sweetheart, you just started something you can't finish."

I playfully growl and dart toward her. I wrap one arm around her waist, and she squeals as I drag her over to the counter. I grab the sugar—"You need some of *this*"—and laugh as I dump some on her.

She wiggles against my hold but manages to get the spoon from the jam jar. She smears it across my cheek. "Ha! Gotcha!"

I grab the bag of flour and drop it forcefully onto the counter, sending a white cloud into the air that sprinkles down on both of us. She turns to face me, with a lightness to her that makes my heart stop. Both of our chests are heaving, and the laughter dies out.

"There, you're definitely a baker now," I say, holding her icy-blue eyes with mine. She bites her bottom lip and longing pulls in my chest. She has always been more to me than just my best friend's sister, and now I don't want to hold back anymore. Jeff is gone, and we're adults. I can't say goodbye to her again without even trying.

She steps closer to me and tips her chin. Daring me to take what I want. Cupping her cheek, I slide my thumb over her lips wiping away the flour remnants. Her eyes flutter at my touch and her lips part. She desires for me to kiss her just as much as I want to.

I lean down and kiss her pillow-soft lips. Every nerve ending lights up inside me as she deepens our kiss and laces her fingers into my hair.

Every doubt I ever had about what I have felt all these years disappeared as soon as her lips hit mine. This is what I've been wanting, needing. This is *right*. Katie is the missing piece in my life.

A knock on the door sounds, and she pulls away from me. "Travis, the door."

"Forget them. We're busy right now." My voice is deep and husky. I don't want to leave this moment with her. I lean in to kiss her again, but she places a hand on my chest, stopping me.

"Travis, we can't. This can never happen between us, and you know it." She turns and heads straight for the bathroom with barely a hesitation.

Irritation engulfs me. Jeff would have been upset with me and Katie if he were here today, but I know in time he would have approved. He would have known I would take care of her the way she deserves. But she's so stuck in what *she* thinks her brother would think to even give us a chance.

Another knock sounds on the door, and I walk to it still covered in our baking mess.

I yank it open and find Jacob. His eyes scan me, and a knowing smirk forms. He's holding a stack of clothes I can only assume are meant for me.

"What the hell happened to you?"

"Nothing, just working on making the cake and dessert for dinner tonight." I open the door, and he strides into the house, setting the clothes on the table.

"You know, I've been to the bakery many times while you were working, and I can't recall even once when you had more than a little flour on an apron."

"Shut up, man. Did you need something or are you just here to harass me?" I scowl at him.

The shower starts in the bathroom, grabbing Jacob's attention before returning to me. "Were you baking with Katie?"

"Does it matter if I was?" I feel defensive, worried he's going to tell me to stay away just like Jeff had.

"Yeah, it does!" he exclaims. "You two have been pining after each other forever. You're the only ones who never noticed, and maybe Jules, but she never picks up on those sorts of things." He laughs as he slaps me on the back.

There's no way he's right. If Katie had been interested in me all this time, she would have never pushed me away.

I scoff at the notion. "If she were interested in me all these years, Jeff would have said something. The only thing he ever told me was to leave her be or he would knock my teeth in."

"Why do you think he told you that, man? Probably because he knew she liked you and didn't want to see you break her heart. He would've had to break your kneecaps for that." He crosses his arms and smiles at me like I'm a blind idiot to this whole thing. And maybe I am. . . .

"It's time you shoot your shot with her, Travis."

"I can't, okay? I kissed her in the kitchen, and she shut me down because of Jeff. She's never going to be open to anything between us. I know her well enough to know that she would rather spend the rest of her life alone than dishonor any of her brother's wishes." The words are bitter as I speak, but they are the truth and completely unavoidable.

"Look, my best advice is to go to the big house and get cleaned up. Take some time to think, and I know you'll figure this out." He winks at me and the timer for my cakes goes off. They'll need time to cool, so doing as he suggests is possible.

I move to the kitchen and pull the cakes out, setting them gently on the glass stovetop and on the counter with hot pads.

I guess cleaning up and taking time to think this through isn't a bad idea. "You're probably right. Let me clean up here and then I'll take some time for me."

Lord knows that girl in there is stubborn and loyal to her core, so if I'm to get through to her, I'm going to need a miracle or something.

Chapter 6: Katie

DID HELL FREEZE OVER? I mean, it's almost Valentine's Day, so I guess the better question is, did Cupid lose a fletching on his arrow? Because Travis just kissed me. I know it was real because I'm still scrubbing the sugar from my scalp!

This cannot be happening right now. It's both my literal dream come true and my worst nightmare! That kiss made my heart melt, made fire ignite in my veins, made the whole blasted world stop turning. For the first time since Jeff died, I felt . . . whole. But it can't happen. None of this can happen.

Jeff was the only one who ever suspected my crush on Travis, and he told me never to go there. That Travis was his best friend and was a playboy to his core. Which he was in high school, but not after Jeff got sick. Regardless, I'd promised him that he never had to worry, that I wouldn't. I gave him my word before he was ever sick, so how can I break that?

Travis may be a changed man, and if my brother were alive, maybe we could reason with him, but I can't betray him now that he's gone.

Ugh. Life sucks sometimes.

With the last of the sugar and flour washed away, I climb out of the shower and throw on my bathrobe. Exiting the bathroom, I figure Travis will still be in the kitchen, but he's gone and the kitchen is clean.

Did he go to the big house? Disappointment starts to creep in at the thought. Nope, I'm shutting that down right now. I am not his keeper, and I don't care whether he's here or not!

Maybe if I tell myself this enough, I'll start to believe it.

Once in my room, I dress in sweatpants and a tight tank top and toss my hair in a messy bun. I need grounding, and sometimes comfy clothes help a bit. My head is reeling, and I have cookies to make, along with a cake to decorate.

Grabbing the Bluetooth speaker out of the living room, I head to the kitchen. With the house empty, it's time to have a baking party. I connect my phone, blast my empowerment music, and get to work.

A while later, the cookies are done and packed for dinner tonight. I'll have to do the cake this evening since Travis failed to come back and never told me what it's supposed to look like.

Abandoning the kitchen, I head to my room and change into my dress for the rehearsal dinner.

It's dark green, form fitting, and stops at my knees. Next, I slide on gray heels and then add some silver earrings. To finish off my look, I add some loose curls to my hair and light makeup. This evening will be great, and I will avoid Travis like the plague to my heart he is.

With my small clutch in tow, I am off to meet the caterer.

Hopefully Travis and I can just forget that kiss ever happened. We are friends, and no matter how much I wish it could be different, it's never going to be.

Two days. . . . Two days and I will leave him and this town behind to nurse my aching heart in Michigan.

Again.

Chapter 7: Travis

MY SHOULDERS ARE TIGHT WITH tension that I can't seem to shake as the hot water beats my back. This shower was supposed to help clear my head, but I'm pretty sure it has only made it worse.

Katie is in the guesthouse locking away any feelings she ever had for me. She's going to run again. I can feel it. But can I stop it?

This shouldn't be this difficult. Kissing her felt so right, and it sealed my fate of never being able to let her go. If I could, I would punch Jeff right now. So instead, I curse him beyond the grave. He left me here to deal with life alone, and now I can't even have the woman I've wanted forever because he took any chance of that with him.

I climb out of the worthless shower, quickly dry off, and throw on the T-shirt and basketball shorts that Jacob brought me. What the hell do I do now? Women are strange creatures. My gut is screaming at me to go back to the guesthouse and work it out with her, but what if space is what she needs?

No, what she needs is her brother. I swallow hard, knowing what I must do.

When Jeff died, he left us all letters. Final words of sorts, but Katie was never given hers because she took off before anyone found them. Her letter should still be in the nightstand next to Jeff's bed.

I walk the hallway until I'm standing in front of his door. I've been in this room more times in my life than any other room in this house, but only twice since he passed. Nobody comes in here. Mrs. Nash has her cleaning lady clean it, because she can't come in here herself. None of us can, really.

I twist the doorknob and push the door open, revealing all the beautiful and painful memories within. His gray walls, covered in photos of all of us.

The three guitars on stands in the corner, even though he could hardly play. The baseball magazine on his dresser that really holds inappropriate photos of women. We thought we were so smart to disguise it like that.

My heart aches being in this room, but it's also where I feel my friend the most. God, I miss him. I miss the laughs, the advice, the sketchy crap we would get into, even the arguments. I would give so much for him to be here today. It's not fair he was taken from us so early.

I cross the room to the nightstand and pull open the drawer to reveal her letter still inside. I grab it, shut the drawer, and walk over to his dresser. This magazine should have been moved somewhere out of sight years ago, but I couldn't bring myself to touch it. It's only a matter of time before Mrs. Nash finds the contents, though, and what's inside should be a secret Jeff gets to keep even in death.

I chuckle to myself as I lift the magazine and look for a suitable spot to stash it.

The top shelf in the closet is probably the best spot, but as I move forward, an envelope hits the floor. My stomach drops as my name stares back at me. I already got my letter; he told me how much he loved my friendship. How I was the brother he never had, and to always live life to the fullest. But this is something else, and if it was in this magazine, he'd wanted to make sure I was the only one who saw it.

I pick up the envelope, quickly stash the magazine, and sit on the end of his bed. I swear if this letter tells me about a woman he knocked up or if there is a body decaying somewhere, I may bring him back to life just to kill him myself.

I blow out a breath and rip open the envelope, revealing the letter inside.

> ***Hey man, I see you found my letter. I knew I could trust you to hide that magazine, but did you ogle the pictures first? Don't lie, we both know you did.***
>
> ***In my last letter I told you all my sappy heartfelt crap, but in this one I need to take a serious tone. I am going to be gone soon and there is something I need from you.***
>
> ***I need you to look after Julia. She needs an older brother to look after her, and if she marries Jacob, help her with anything she needs. If she doesn't marry him, make sure whoever she is with is worthy of her, and if he's a tool, send him packing in a way that would make me proud.***

I laugh at his words as tears well up in my eyes. He felt the need to tell me to watch over his sister, but he never needed to. I have been here for all of them every day since he died and plan to be forever.

Now, we need to talk about Katie. She's going to take me leaving the hardest and don't be surprised if she disappears for a bit. Just don't give up on her. I know you're in love with her but stayed away for me. Well, Travis, if she's it for you, then go get her! Love her well, cherish her always, and make all her dreams come true.

And if I have to spell it out for you, let me tell you Katie loves you, too. So, don't be the idiot we both know you can be by letting her slip away.

I love you, brother. Take care of my girls. I'll see you on the other side.

—Jeff

My head is spinning. All this time he knew, for all this time I've had his blessing to be with her. I fold the letter and place it back into the envelope for safekeeping.

I have to find Katie.

I have to tell her that her brother knew.

I dash from his room with both of our letters and take off to the guesthouse, praying he was right and that she loves me, too.

"Katie!" I yell for her as soon as I burst through the front door. The hope and joy in my chest are threatening to internally combust. I actually have a shot here, but she doesn't answer.

"Katie!" I yell again, jogging to her door and knocking on it. No answer. The bathroom is open, the kitchen is mostly clean, and the cookies are gone.

The cookies are gone.

My gut sinks. She's already left for the rehearsal.

Chapter 8: Katie

THE WEDDING REHEARSAL IS IN full swing at the country club, and Julia is practically vibrating in excitement. I stand next to her in the line of bridesmaids, but I'm admittedly distracted.

Travis looks impeccable as he stands next to Jacob in the line of groomsmen. He kept it simple this evening with a white, button-up, long-sleeve shirt, loosely tucked into a pair of khaki dress pants. Thankfully, we were not paired together to walk down the aisle before the bride. So, my plan of avoidance is working perfectly thus far, even though all my heart wants is to kiss him again.

"All right!" Jules cheers. "That's a wrap on the rehearsal, and dinner will be in the reception area. The rest of our families should be arriving soon and then we will eat!" She clasps her hands together in front of her as she bounces on her toes.

"One last thing," Jacob continues. "I want to thank you all for being part of this special day." His eyes find mine and it's like he's speaking directly to me. "This day would not be the same without you here. Julia and I love and appreciate you all." He breaks eye contact with me after that. "Now, let's head to the reception area."

I have been so distant from my family for so long, his words feel like a gut punch. I'm not sure if I deserve the love and devotion that my sister and soon-to-be brother-in-law offer me so freely. For once, I find myself truly questioning if leaving was the right thing to do.

I spot Travis making his way through the rest of the bridal party heading straight toward me. He looks determined, yet there's a light in eyes that wasn't there before. Apparently, he's not going to forget about our kiss.

Hastily, I turn and begin moving toward the women's restroom. I won't be able to hide in here all night, but at least it will give me a moment to gather my thoughts, and with any luck, Travis will be pulled away by someone.

I make it to the bathroom before he reaches me, and I lean against the wall, letting the weight fall from my shoulders. Thankfully, no one else is in here now to see me in all my trainwreck glory.

At the bathroom counter, I'm looking over my makeup when two of the other bridesmaids, and Jules's close friends, Marie and Amy, walk into the bathroom. I never much cared for these two but always put up with them for Jules. They're a bit too snobbish for my liking.

"Did you see Travis this evening?" Marie says, fanning herself like an idiot.

"Um, of course. Those khakis he's wearing complement his backside real well," Amy teasingly jeers right before drowning her lips in more of her pinkish-colored gloss.

Something dark coils itself in my gut at their words. Travis may never be mine, but over my dead body will he be either of theirs. He's more than a piece of meat. He is funny, playful, and so caring he would put anyone else's needs above his own always. All these two know is how to take and use.

"What I wouldn't give to tie that man down." Marie smiles and something in me snaps.

"Sorry to say it, girls, but Travis is gay." I cross my arms over my chest and lean my backside against the vanity.

"What?" They both eye me skeptically. "No way—he was the biggest player back in the day!" Amy rolls her eyes

"No, really. He was just exploring back then. He is gay, and I would know since he was my brother's best friend and still close with my family." I do my best to stay casual, but worry coils in my gut. I should have come up with something better to say, but this was the first thing to pop into my mind.

"Ugh, whatever." Marie looks disappointed. "Why are the hottest ones always gay?"

"Well, either way. He is fine to look at," Amy jests to Marie. "You know my cousin Max is single. Maybe I can introduce them?"

I turn from them with a smile of victory on my face. I've been in here for a while now, so with any luck, Travis is gone.

I spot Travis in conversation with Jacob on the other side of the reception hall. Relief and slight guilt washes over me. I am successfully avoiding him, but something happened in that bathroom that I am not ready to face, and I just told the gossip queens of Lakes that he is undoubtedly gay.

Our eyes lock across the room, and I watch as he slaps Jacob on the back and heads my way. Crap. Why did I have to look over there? He probably wouldn't have even noticed me if I hadn't.

I move across the room to a slightly secluded corner, hoping to hide in the shadows, when Travis is stopped by Amy. This night could not be getting any worse. I see the moment she mentions something about him being gay, because his eyebrows raise in surprise, then he smirks, glancing to me.

He politely moves away from her and heads straight for me. If I wanted to be forgettable to this man, I'm doing a horrible job at it. Within moments, he's in front of me.

"I finally found you, Gummy Bear."

"What do you want, Travis? I need to check in with the caterer." It's a load of bull and he knows it.

"We need to talk abo—"

"We have nothing to talk about. You kissed me and nothing more. Just let it go, and we can pretend it never happened. Now, I have things to attend to and then a cake to finish decorating. Please text me with details about how Jules wants it done." I say it all matter-of-fact-like, but I feel like I want to vomit as soon as the words leave my mouth.

Trying to move past him, he blocks me in, and his light demeanor shifts as his shoulders tense and his mouth presses into a flat line. "Right, it meant nothing and that's why you told Amy I'm gay."

My cheeks heat with embarrassment being caught lying to keep them away from him. I really should've come up with something better to say.

"They were just . . . they, um." I stumble over my words, but I can't come up with an excuse that doesn't give credit to the green monster living in my gut.

"Whatever, Katie. You know, if you could let go of the past and admit to yourself for just a second that we have something here, we may actually have a shot. I went to Jeff's room and got this for you."

He pulls an envelope from his back pocket and pushes it into my hand.

"He left us all letters, but you took off before you could be given yours. Have a good evening." He shoves away from me and leaves me in the corner, shell-shocked.

My body begins to shake, and tears start to well in my eyes. I no longer need to avoid Travis, since I have successfully pushed him away, and now I must face something even more daunting. I'm holding my brother's final words to me.

Down the hall, I find a lounge area that has a door I can shut behind me. I sit in a giant, overstuffed armchair and stare at the envelope in my hand. *Katie* is scribbled on the front in my brother's handwriting. Will he tell me he loves me one last time, tell me to chase after my dreams? He was my rock, and now I have to face these feelings of loss all over again.

Slowly, I open it and pull the paper out.

Hey there, Gummy Bear. If you're reading this then I am gone and there are a few things I need you to know.

I pause and a sob pours out of me. Of course he would call me Gummy Bear in his goodbye letter.

First, I need you to know how much I love you. Little sis, even beyond the grave I will be loving you. Something as small as death couldn't stop me from watching over you.

I laugh slightly, only Jeff would imply death being a small inconvenience.

Second, I know you well enough to know that you're going to hide. You would rather outrun the pain than face it, but Katie, that is no way to live your life. Me being gone will hurt forever, but I promise it will get easier over time.

Lastly, and this is the most important, chase your dreams as a baker but don't forget to find love. I won't be there to see it, but I know you're in love with Travis. You promised me you would stay away from him, but I know beyond a shadow of a doubt that he will protect you, support you, and provide for you till his dying breath if you'll have him. Sweet sister, go build a life with him, if that is what you want.

The only thing I want for you, little Gummy Bear, is to find happiness and to know how honored I am that I got to be your big brother.

Love you always and forever,

—Jeff

My heart feels so full and so racked with grief that all I can do is stare at the letter as the tears stream down my face. I cry until I feel so devoid of emotion that I slowly pull myself from the chair and head back to my parents' house, leaving the party and Travis behind. I have a cake to decorate and maybe, just maybe in that space, I will find my next step.

Chapter 9: Travis

THE REST OF THE EVENING went by in a blur. I knew that letter would be hard for her and a primal need to be with her has been gnawing at my insides ever since my frustration dissipated. She never came back to the reception hall, and I know she holed up somewhere just out of my reach to cry her eyes out.

I played the part for the evening for Jacob and Julia, but as soon as I could get away, I searched that building high and low for her. Finally, when I ran out of places to look, I checked the parking lot, and the car she borrowed from her parents was gone.

I'm almost back to the guesthouse now, and anxiety is coursing through my veins with the fear that Jeff's letter might have sent her running to Michigan again, but this time, I will do what I should have done then. I'll follow her. I'm done letting her run away.

From her feelings. From us. From me.

Relief fills me when I enter the guesthouse and her clutch is lying on the table and her shoes are by the door. To my surprise, the cake is completely done. Covered in white fondant and topped with beautiful flowers of various shapes and colors. Katie sure did make a masterpiece this evening.

While knocking on her closed bedroom door, I brace myself for the possibility of her being angry with me, but there is no answer. I have to put my mind to rest, so I slowly peek inside. She's asleep with her letter clutched to her chest like she can feel her brother's warmth through it.

I should have been there for her when she read that letter, but I can't focus on that. I need a plan to win this girl—and fast. Tomorrow is Valentine's Day, and my last chance to finally be with the woman I've wanted for years.

Chapter 10: Katie

THE MORNING HAS BEEN NOTHING but a flurry between the hair, the makeup, the dresses. It's all one chaotic work of art. Julia looks like an absolute princess in her flowing, white gown, hair in a braided bun, topped with a veil hairpiece. My dress is a beautiful lavender purple with a long, flowing waist.

I know I should be focused on my sister today, but through the whole exchange of vows, my eyes are on Travis. Jeff knew, and now I have his blessing, but is this what I want? To be with him?

I think . . . I think I really do.

The crowd erupts with applause and pulls me from my thoughts.

"Now introducing Mr. and Mrs. Jacob White," the officiant declares, and I smile at my beaming sister. I'm so happy she got her happy ending.

The reception is in full swing, but I'm in nothing but a cloud. I want to talk to Travis, to tell him about the letter, to tell him I want to try this even though I have no idea how it will work.

"All right, folks, before we do the bride and groom's first dance, they have requested a dance for Julia's older brother," the DJ says above the crowd's noise. "Can I please have Travis Hardy and Katie Nash to the dance floor for the Jeffrey Nash dance?"

My stomach sinks as my eyes find Julia and Jacob. They are grinning with excitement, and I have no idea why, because this wasn't on the itinerary.

Moving to the dance floor, Travis takes my waist, and I place one hand on his shoulder and the other in his hand. The song "A Thousand Years" by Christina Perri drifts from the speakers as he begins leading me around the floor.

"Travis, what is this?" I look up at him and my heart swells as his eyes meet mine.

"This is me shooting my shot, Gummy Bear." He smiles at me softly, then dips me down and pulls me back closer to his chest. "Katie, I've wanted to be with you since we were teenagers, but I could never have you. When you left for Michigan, a piece of me left with you, and I didn't truly realize it until that day I kissed you in the kitchen. Sweetheart, I want this, and I want you."

A small tear streaks down my cheek at his words.

"How, Travis? I live in Michigan now. It can't work."

"Of course it can. I have nothing holding me here anymore. The bakery needs a decent number of repairs before it can open, and I'll have it fixed up before either selling or leasing it out. You're what matters to me. I can run a bakery anywhere, so I'll come to Michigan with you."

With that, I grab his face and kiss him. Pouring every ounce of my feelings into it. Letting the sparks fly through my body and savoring the feeling. Jeff was right about all of it.

Julia and Jacob start cheering, and the crowd joins in. I pull away from Travis, but he folds me into his arms.

"Looks like more love is blossoming on this day of love. Let's hear it for Travis Hardy and Katie Nash!" the DJ says.

Travis looks to me with a longing in his eyes that I'm sure matches mine. "So, are we doing this, sweetheart?"

"Yeah, I think we are." I smile up at him. "But if you think catching me was the hard part, you have no idea how needy of a girlfriend I'll be," I tease.

"Oh, I plan to spoil you rotten, Gummy Bear." He chuckles and kisses me softly on the forehead. "You're mine now, and I'll let everything crumble to pieces before I let you slip away again."

I am not sure what our future holds or what our life in Michigan will even look like, but it's time I stop running from things and start running toward them, starting with Travis Hardy.

About the Author

J.E. Smith is a romance enthusiast who loves to write sassy heroines and book boyfriends that make you swoon. Her short story "Cows & Kisses" was featured in *As the Snow Drifts: A Cozy Winter Anthology*, published by And You Press in 2024.

She resides in a small town outside of Grand Rapids, Michigan, where she enjoys country life with her family.

When she is not writing or lost in a new book, she loves to travel and explore the beauties of nature.

You can find Smith on:

Instagram: @author_j.e.smith

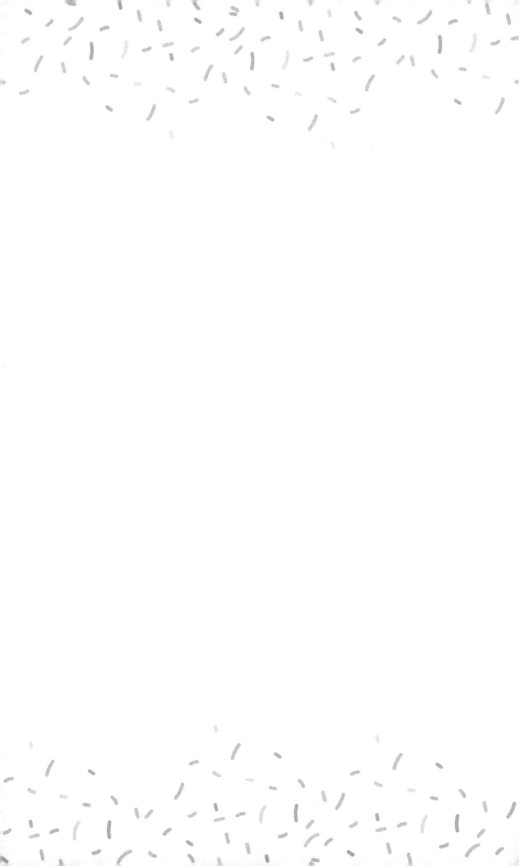

THE CHARRED GRAPE

The Charred Grape

Caroline Baccene

"SHOOT!" I MANAGE TO STOP any profanities from coming out of my mouth and look down at the cutting board to see a trickle of blood from my finger dripping onto Leo's blueberries. I turn on the water and run my hand under the cold liquid, ignoring the stinging and the sounds of my three-year-old screaming at me from the kitchen floor. Add to that the sudden blare of the smoke alarm as I remember the eggs on the stove, and I'm certain that this morning has been designed to truly test my sanity.

"Dang it!"

I trudge away from my spot at the sink, dodge my still-screaming son, and yank the pan off the hot eye.

"Can this morning get any worse?" I mutter to myself.

Of course the answer to this is yes.

Once Leo is clean, fed, and dressed, I throw on my black pants and white shirt, grateful I did laundry last night at the nearby laundromat. There's no time to do anything else except pull up my hair into a ponytail and grab our bags.

Leo cries the entire ride to his daycare as I struggle to see through the frost on the windshield, and even though I'm tempted to cry right there in the car, too, I know better. If I cry now, my face will become red and will remain splotchy for hours. Plus, I don't know if I'd ever stop.

Once Leo is safely in a large room with ten other kids to play with, I breathe a sigh of relief. It's not that I don't love my son unconditionally. It's just that being a single mom is almost more difficult than anything. Almost.

I pull my coat tighter around my waist, climb out my car, and head into my place of work: a modern brick building with huge black windows. All the exposed brick and beams and duct work is nice- looking, as is the huge, colorful artwork that covers much of the walls, but my favorite thing about where I work is behind the structure and the showpieces. There's a small patio with an herb garden on one side and some seating on the other. This area is for the employees. Someone even recently put a firepit out here. I've never seen anyone using it, but the burnt embers, already cold by the time I get to work in the morning, tell me that the space is appreciated. The entire thing is enclosed with a large, wooden privacy fence. This kind of backyard is something I could only dream of affording in a city this size. Of course, getting out of my tiny apartment at all is just a dream.

"Rachael, did you see the group chat last night?"

With a pat of my coat pockets, I realize I left my phone on my kitchen counter. Of course. I turn to my favorite coworker, Lisa, and a quick stab of envy comes and goes. She's wearing a similar outfit to mine, but her hair, three shades blonder, is curled and flows past her shoulders. And where I was just happy I managed to wash my face this morning, Lisa has had time to do her makeup in the most beautiful but natural way. Although, since it's safe to assume she didn't have to clean up spilled milk and soiled sheets this morning, I suppose she's got time for all that.

Shrugging off these thoughts, I shake my head in reply as I head toward the kitchen, but Lisa pulls me to a table in the back of the dining room where I see most of my coworkers have already taken seats.

"Well apparently the new owner and his staff are coming today. Like, officially taking over. There's a staff meeting before we open."

Her news startles me. Obviously, I knew the restaurant where I wait tables is undergoing new management. And we're all grateful it isn't closing completely. The Charred Grape won't close. It can't. The new owners would be idiots to even consider it since this is one of the most popular restaurants in town.

Seeing old Ms. Hoffby sitting at a table makes my heart hurt. She was always the nicest, and I'd miss her terribly. At least I know she got a pretty penny for the building and the name.

Ms. Hoffby stands up and clears her throat. "Alright, well, I'm not one for speeches, so I'll keep it short. As you know, I am no longer the owner of the Charred Grape. I'd like to introduce you to Robert Dunne, the new owner."

And with that, she exits the building. Not even a glance back at the business she ran for forty years. Not even a glance back at us, her employees. I mean, I know the turnover rate at restaurants is high, but I thought maybe I'd get a nod or a wave goodbye. I've been here for six years, and Lisa's been here for three. Not even a look back at *us.*

While I'm staring at the disappearing head of gray hair exiting the room in disbelief, I fail to notice the man standing where Ms. Hoffby was when she gave her "speech" until he begins speaking.

"Hello, everyone. I want to thank you in advance for your patience and flexibility as we begin this journey together. I know this whole process can seem difficult and scary to some, but I want you to know I will do everything in my power to help ease the transition."

The man talking, Robert Dunne, is probably in his late fifties and must be one of the most handsome and best dressed men I've ever seen. He's wearing a dark blue suit with a white button-up. No tie. And his salt-and-pepper hair is short and styled in a way that looks natural but surely must have taken a while to perfect. I'm positive if I were close enough to smell him, I'd inhale some fancy cologne that costs more than I make in a month.

"There's not much changing immediately, as I'd like to see how everything works before implementing drastic changes. There are just a few things: Gregory is going to be assisting in the kitchen as our new co-head chef. And Rebecca will be assisting in front-of-house as waitstaff."

I glance over in the direction where Robert extends a hand and I see a man and a woman around my age who must be related to Robert. Probably his kids, since they all have the same straight noses and are dressed nicely. The girl stands from her seat at the table and gives a wave. She's slim with a black dress that is a bit too revealing for waitstaff under the previous ownership. She has the same dark hair as her brother but hers is cut just above her shoulders. The man next to her doesn't stand, just lifts his hand in a casual wave. While Robert is wearing a suit, Gregory, his son, I suppose, is wearing a black button-up shirt. I can't see the lower half of his body, but even with his slightly slouched posture, he seems tall. As I survey him, watching as he runs a hand through his dark hair, which is just a touch too long, I change my mind. His dad is the *second* most handsome man I've ever seen.

Robert continues talking while he holds a clipboard to his chest, so I turn my attention away from his son.

"So, if everyone could just continue your normal day-to-day operations, I'd greatly appreciate it, and I look forward to working with each of you."

A bit unsure, the busboys glance around and slowly rise, heading back to the kitchen, while the waitstaff spreads out to prepare for opening. Our current head chef, old Mr. Jim, doesn't look happy as he walks toward Robert. I'm about to head to the kitchen to grab the silverware to place on the tables when Robert says, "Is there a Rachael here? Rachael Barr?"

I try to ignore everyone's heads turning toward me and feel my cheeks getting warm as I raise my hand, feeling like I'm in grade school. It only takes him a moment to spot me.

"If you could meet me in the back office in five?"

I knew this day could get worse.

I'm trying to stop the shaking of my right leg while I wait in what is now Robert Dunne's office. The notes taped up everywhere are gone, as is Ms. Hoffby's paintings of chihuahuas.

There's a new desk, chair, and sofa in here, which must have been moved in yesterday when the restaurant was closed. Since I work almost every other day of the week, I'd have seen them moving furniture otherwise. I don't love the black leather, but it's an improvement over the old threadbare loveseat and rusted desk that used to be in here.

There's a cell phone sitting on the desk, and either the owner is very popular or someone is desperately trying to reach them. Every time it dings, I'm tempted to lean forward and try to see the screen, but I'd never forgive myself if Robert chose that moment to come into the office and caught me snooping.

On the eleventh ding, Robert arrives with Rebecca following. He takes a seat behind his desk as Rebecca grabs the phone and sits on the other end of the couch, giving me a friendly smile before turning her attention to her phone. Robert extends his hand to me.

"Rachael, thank you for meeting with me."

As if I had a choice, but I nod and shake his hand, wishing I'd rubbed my hands on my pants before they entered. I'm not sure he notices my sweaty palms, but he has an excellent poker face either way. Rebecca seems to be in her own little world, staring down at her phone, while Robert continues.

"I'm sure you know you've been here a long time. Longer than most everyone here." I nod again. "Yes, except for the head chef, Mr. Jim."

"Unfortunately, Jim turned in his notice. Not happy with new management. He's agreed to stay for two weeks to show Gregory the menu."

Trying to hide my shock, I look at Rebecca as she types on her phone. Not happy with new management. . . . More likely he's not happy to have another head chef join him in his kitchen.

"I tell you this because, since you've been here longer than anyone else in the restaurant, I'd like you to be our new floor manager or front of house manager, whichever name you prefer. The previous owner highly recommended you."

"Ms. Hoffby?"

Such a dumb question, but I'm almost speechless. I expected to get fired or something, and now I find out I'm getting a promotion.

But Robert just smiles and nods.

"Yes, she had wonderful things to say about you. As our floor manager, you'd be in charge of the waitstaff, training and scheduling, and making sure they're doing what needs to be done. You'd also be the person brought to customers when there's a complaint or a private event, which we hope to do more of in the future."

He leans back in his chair, unbuttoning his jacket as he continues.

"Your hours would change. We'd need you here more days a week, especially when I'm not here. You'd be here a lot, but you'd get quite a large salary compared to what you're getting now."

As soon as the annual salary leaves his mouth, I accept the job.

Exiting the office, which I'm free to use any time I need to work on staff schedules, I tie my black apron around my waist and get to work. Lisa finds me just as I unlock the front doors for lunch.

"Oh my gosh, I thought you were getting fired!"

"Why would I get fired?" I ask her, even though it crossed my mind as well.

"Well, I don't know. I thought maybe they were letting everyone go. What happened?"

Debating what to say, I decide Robert didn't tell me to keep it a secret, and she would find out soon anyway.

"I got promoted to floor manager starting next week."

I try not to take offense to her surprised look. Why is it surprising to her I'd get promoted? I work practically every day and do a lot of the job already. She recovers quickly.

"Congratulations! We'll have to celebrate! Wait, does that mean you're my boss now?"

Shrugging, I pass her two menus and push her toward the customers who just walked in. "Not until next week."

Lunch passes quickly, which often happens when it's busy. In fact, I don't even notice Gregory, our new head chef, leaning against the counter in the kitchen watching Mr. Jim make our sautéed squash until I stretch my head over the counter to say, "Table 10 loved the pork. Told me to give my compliments to the chef."

As I turn, I realize I'm right in front of Gregory. He nods to me, and for reasons I can't explain, I do one of the more awkward things I have ever done and just pull my head back to my side of the counter. I grab my order and get out of there, feeling like an idiot.

My double shift ends without any drama, and besides the new waitress and owner and chef, everything seems just about the same. I go out to the patio and cover the herbs growing in the raised garden bed with a frost cloth, grateful the winter cold hasn't killed them yet. When I'd asked Ms. Hoffby why she didn't grow anything out here for her restaurant, she just laughed and replied, "Honey, if you want fresh herbs, *you* grow them."

So I did. And for the past three winters, I've managed to keep the plants alive in the cold, but it's not easy. Every time someone compliments the food, though, I smile, knowing I'm partially responsible.

I don't realize I'm not alone out here until I'm finished with the frost cloth and a deep voice behind me says, "You must be Rachael."

Turning, I see Gregory sitting on one of the patio chairs, leaning back while holding a beer bottle, wearing a light jacket.

"You must be Gregory."

He nods, even though he corrects me. "Greg. You grow the herbs we use. Jim told me."

Tightening my jacket around myself, I nod. He leans back in the chair but doesn't respond. Even in the dark with only one light next to the back door, I can see the hint of his stubble as he brings the beer to his lips.

Just as I'm about to go inside, he says, "Can I ask you a question?"

Shifting from one foot to another, I answer. "Sure."

"Don't you ever want to see stars living here?"

Looking up, there's just the black sky. I sigh and tell him, "The downside to living in the city."

He doesn't respond but holds out an unopened beer to me. I move closer and take it, twisting the top and taking a sip. "Thanks."

We stay out there for a minute and look toward the sky in silence. There are so many questions running through my mind. Where did he live before this? Why is he here? How much did his cologne cost? But I have to admit that his silence is refreshing. That's one thing I realize that's missing in my life. Silence.

Looking at him in the dim light, there's something that I actually can't stop myself from asking. "Aren't you cold?"

Greg stretches as he chuckles to himself.

"Freezing. I just moved here yesterday. Haven't had time to shop for winters in Philadelphia."

I nod like that doesn't make me wonder about him more. He turns to meet my eyes, and I notice the depth of his. It's like I'm looking into an oil slick in the ocean. Or possibly a deep cave where no light escapes. The way I feel when his eyes are on me causes my body to warm even in the cold.

"What do you think?"

Taking a moment to process his words, I finally reply, "About?"

"The beer. It's from Florida."

"Is that where you're from?"

He nods and drinks from his bottle.

Still meeting his gaze, I answer honestly. "It's good. But I'd say any dark beer is good beer."

He smiles in amusement, and I'm unsure of what joke I made. "So, nothing special?"

"Sorry."

"I didn't make it, but my dad would be disappointed."

"Your dad?"

"Yeah. His company."

I look down at the beer in my hand. *Dunne Industries.*

The name makes me snort before I can stop myself. Of course. "Sorry. Again." I'm sure he can hear my half-heartedness.

"No, you're not. That's okay. Honesty is refreshing." He says this like it has some deeper meaning that I can't decipher, then he stands and drains the last of his beer.

I silently follow him back inside.

After a quick stop at the market, I arrive at my sister's house to pick up Leo. I give her my thanks and load my sleeping son into my car. My routine is pretty consistent on the nights I work. If I don't need to run any errands, I head to my sister's apartment, which is about thirty minutes from the restaurant. On the way, I always call her (on days I don't leave my phone at home) and check in. It's usually so late that her kids have gone to bed, as well as Leo. If her husband minds her nightly calls with me, I've never heard anything about it.

One of the worst things about being a single mom is the guilt. There are so many days, like today, where I only get a couple of hours in the morning with Leo before I have to go to work. My sister is great and has three kids of her own, so I know my son is taken care of when I have to work. But on days like this, I know daycare and my sister raised my child just as much as I did, and there's nothing I can do about it.

Leo wakes just as I'm unlocking my apartment door, holding me tight as I try to put him down. So we curl on his bed and read bedtime stories until we both fall asleep.

The next day, I manage to get to work without cutting any fingers, and I even managed to put on the slightest bit of makeup before leaving. My hair is still up, today in a bun, but there's no hope for changing that any time soon. And Leo had a smile on his face when I dropped him off at daycare, which is all I wish for each morning.

When I get inside the restaurant, I set out a hat and gloves on the kitchen counter and attach a sticky note with *Greg* written on it in my scrawled handwriting.

I tell myself I would give anyone these things if they didn't have them, which is true. Although I do notice the blush on my cheeks in my reflection of the window as I set out silverware.

As I place a used wineglass in the dirty dishes bin on my way back to the kitchen to wait for my next order, Gregory's head pops up from the other side of the counter that divides us.

He smiles at me before saying, "You don't stop."

"Huh?"

"Moving. You don't stop moving. "

"I'm not moving right now. I'm waiting for my order."

He pointedly looks down at my foot, which is tapping ever so slightly. I immediately stop it and straighten my back.

Ignoring the cute way his eyes slightly crinkle in amusement, I ask, "Shouldn't you be cooking?"

"I'm watching."

"Me."

"Well, I was watching Jim cook onions, but you distracted me."

"Don't let me interrupt your learning. Please, continue."

He ignores my suggestion and instead rests his elbows on the counter, putting himself closer to me. I can smell just the hint of something familiar. Something like . . .

"Is that durian?" Wrinkling my nose, I lean a little closer as he leans back. "We don't sell anything with durian."

Greg lifts both his hands up and his cheeks turn slightly pink. "I may have decided to try something new on my way to work today. And I may have spilled the bubble tea on myself on my way here. And I may not have known how strong durian smells."

I can't stop the flabbergasted expression I'm sure is on my face when I ask, "You got a durian-flavored bubble tea on your way to work?"

"Seemed like a good idea at the time."

His expression, which I can only describe as sheepish, makes me laugh as I say, "I actually like the taste of durian."

"Well, since mine got all over me and the sidewalk, I never got a chance to try it. It has a very strong smell, though."

Still smiling, I say, "Such a shame." Using my apron, I wipe my eyes, which formed tears from laughing so hard.

"Question for you. Do most women who live here have men's hats and gloves? Or do you keep extra just in case you run into someone who isn't prepared for the weather?"

Feeling my cheeks heat, I lean further back as I reply, "Oh yes, we have drawers full."

I'm hoping he can't see on my face that when I stopped at the market last night on my way to my sister's and spotted a display of winter gear, I grabbed them specifically for him. It's not like I went there looking for them, though. They just happened to be near the checkout. From the knowing look in his eyes, I'm thinking I don't convince him.

"Well, thank you for thinking of me."

I grab my plate and head out, managing not to look back.

A new routine forms over the next two weeks. Being a floor manager is pretty similar to what I was already doing, except now I have to keep up with the waitress and hostess schedules. And I have the authority to tell my coworkers what to do. Thankfully, they are all pretty decent employees, so they don't require any micromanaging. And every night, after my shift ends, I go out to check on my herbs and Greg is there with two beers. He wears a warmer jacket after that first night, but he still wears the hat and gloves I gave him. I'm not sure how this nightly meeting started, but it's becoming one of my favorite parts of work, even if it is freezing outside.

"Favorite movie?"

I only take a moment to think, as this is part of the game we've started playing. We ask each other questions and respond with the first answer that comes to mind.

"*Batman*. The one with Jack Nicholson."

Greg thinks for a second before asking, "Is that the one with Christian Bale?"

"No, that one's good too. But it's the one from like, the eighties."

"Never seen it."

"It's a classic."

Taking another sip of my beer, I ask, "Favorite nonalcoholic drink?"

"Sweet tea."

"Like hot tea?"

He sighs disapprovingly, but from the twinkle in his eyes, I know he's more teasing than frustrated as he replies, "This is why I miss Florida. No, not hot tea. Iced tea."

Although I know what sweet tea is even if I didn't grow up in the south, I can't help but mess with him a moment longer.

"Iced tea that's sweetened? With like, honey?"

Greg runs his gloved hand through his hair, tousling it in the way I'd say is my favorite hairstyle on him.

"With sugar. Please tell me you're joking. I know restaurants don't serve it, but do people around here really not know what sweet tea is?"

"You're saying people make tea, put ice in it, and then mix sugar in it? How does the sugar dissolve? Or are there just crystals of sugar floating around in it?"

I suppose I may have played my ignorance up a bit too much, because he turns and stares into my eyes in that way of his that heats my cheeks. But I manage to ignore it and laugh at his confused expression.

"We may not drink it, but Philadelphians do know what sweet tea is."

He gives me a relieved look as he leans back in his chair and chuckles before asking, "Favorite sport?"

And this is how we spend a few minutes each night after work.

My sister has her own opinions about this when I mention the reason I have been arriving fifteen to thirty minutes later to pick up Leo each night.

"If you're hooking up with the guy, you can just tell me."

I manage to press the brakes before hitting the car in front of me as I stare at the phone resting in my cupholder.

"We are not hooking up. We just talk and have a beer."

"Every night."

Correcting her, I say, "Every night that we are both working."

"Which is almost every night that the restaurant is open."

"Maybe. But it's while I check on the herbs. And we're friends."

"Friends?"

I can hear the skeptical tone in her voice even through speakerphone and have to confess: "I bought him gloves!"

"Is that a euphemism for something?"

"No! But I bought him gloves. And a hat. I gave them to him the second day I met him. Does that mean something?"

She gasps. "You bought him *gloves*? You must be in love!"

"I'm not in love. I've known him for two weeks. But I probably shouldn't be hanging out with him."

"Why?"

"I have a kid. I shouldn't be dating."

"Says who?"

"Society? I don't know. I need to focus on Leo."

"Taking fifteen minutes after work to talk to someone is not damaging your son. And people with kids can date."

"Maybe."

"Definitely. Just be smart about it."

"Obviously."

Mr. Jim's last day is today, and even though he explained to me why he's leaving and I understand, it doesn't make me any happier.

He hugs me at the kitchen door.

"It's time for me to retire anyway. Been here since the place opened. Only stayed as long as I did for Ms. Hoffby."

"You could always stay longer. I'm sure Greg could use more tutoring. He doesn't know what he's doing back there."

Even though we're across the room, Greg's voice is clear when he calls out, "I heard that!"

"Quit eavesdropping."

Since Greg doesn't respond, I'm assuming he went back to whatever he was doing in the kitchen while Mr. Jim pats me on the back. "I'll miss you, too, kid."

Nodding, I give him one last hug before he leaves and make my way to the dining area where I see Lisa rolling silverware.

"Tomorrow night. After work. I already checked and neither of us works lunch on Saturday, so don't tell me you're busy."

"What's happening tomorrow?"

"Celebrating your promotion."

Groaning, I start rolling my silverware as I reply, "You know Friday is our busiest night of the week. We'll be exhausted. And Saturday is Valentine's Day, which is the busiest day of the year."

"Please, Rach. It's not every day the restaurant gets taken over and then gives you a raise. Besides, now you can afford to go out, so you can't use that as an excuse either, even though I know it wasn't true before. Let's party!"

"Who's partying?" Rebecca comes out with another bundle of clean silverware and begins rolling them into napkins.

"We are. To celebrate Rachael becoming my boss."

Nodding, Rebecca responds, "My boss, too."

Lisa and I exchange a glance. "What? You are?" I just nod, but Lisa had never been one to mince words. "Your dad owns the restaurant. I'm pretty sure he's your only boss."

Rebecca gives me a pointed look. "Maybe. But if Rachael rats me out to him, then I lose a lot more than this job."

"Like?"

"A monthly allowance that is much more than I make here."

Since Lisa and I don't have anything to say to that, we just keep folding napkins silently until there's enough for tomorrow's lunch shift. Greg and a couple of busboys come out of the kitchen to wipe down tables as we're folding menus.

Lisa winks at me as she says loudly, "So, tomorrow night. Who's in?"

"Me!"

Even though Rebecca's high-pitched voice puts a strain on my ear, I can't hate the girl for being excited. Moving here without knowing anyone except her dad and brother must be lonely.

Lisa pouts her lips at me. I wish I could tell her yes. I would love to go out with them, drink, and dance. But I'd rather spend that time with my son.

Shaking my head, I reply, "I don't think so. I have plans."

"With Leo? You know he'll be asleep by the time you get off work anyway."

At Lisa's words, I notice Greg turn to look at me, which I ignore. It's not that I'm embarrassed by my son. Most of my coworkers know I have a child. They've even met him a time or two. But it's the sort of thing I feel maybe I should be the one to tell others about, not Lisa.

I put my stack of menus away and turn as I say, "I'll think about it."

This topic comes up with my sister on our nightly phone conversation.

"Of course you should go! When's the last time you had some fun?"

"Um, three years ago."

"Exactly."

"Viv."

"I'm just saying, you deserve a night out. All you do is work and take care of Leo, which is admirable, but you need a night out. He'll be long asleep until you get back here to pick him up. Or let him stay the night with his cousins and pick him up in the morning."

"No, Viv. I hardly see him. What if he wakes up?"

"We both know he only wakes up when you move him. He'll sleep the entire night. If you don't go, I swear I'll set you up on another blind date."

Thinking about the awful date my sister arranged last year makes me shudder. "There's no way I'd go."

"Fine. Then I'll make sure he's here when you pick up Leo."

"You say that like you already have someone picked out for me."

"Oh yes, he's a banker. But not like a snooty or portly one. Like a super-cute one. Nice too. He lives with his mom still but—"

Exasperated by this entire conversation, I say, "Fine! I'll go out with my coworkers tomorrow. But I'm gonna be tired from working, and I won't have any fun."

"And if you decide to have fun, feel free to pick up Leo in the morning!"

I hang up on her and drive the last ten minutes to her house in blissful silence.

Lisa is thrilled the next day when I inform her of my decision to go out as we walk into work. I'm pretty sure she had given up hope for this night out.

"Yay! Gregory, are you coming?"

Turning to see him pulling off the gloves I gave him, I notice she doesn't call him by the name he gave me. But before I can give it much thought, Rebecca sighs loudly.

"No, he cannot come. He doesn't want to hang out with us anyway."

He smirks at his sister. "I might want to. Where are you going?"

"Celebrating Rachael's promotion. Tonight."

I glance away as our eyes meet, and I'm unsure why. I've worked with many hot guys. Maybe it's the fact that his dad owns the restaurant? Or that none of them have been a chef? Or maybe it's the way his eyes seem to study me, and I'm not sure what he sees?

"Well of course I'm coming to that."

And that's how, after my shift, I'm forced into the bathroom with Lisa as she fixes my makeup, putting more on me than I'd normally wear. She makes me pull my hair down and throws me a shirt, and I realize I was wrong about thinking she'd given up hope for our night out.

"I have a shirt on."

"Yes, and it's wrinkled and stained and looks like you're a waitress."

I look down at myself. "It is not stained."

"Fine, but just try this one on. For me."

As I go into a stall and pull it over my head, I tell her, "You won't even see it under my coat!"

"Once we get there, I'm assuming you'll want to take your coat off. And then maybe Gregory will give you the look."

"Whatever look you're referring to, I'm not interested in."

"Uh huh. I see the way you two talk to each other."

"We're friends."

"Sure. Except I don't blush every time I talk to my friends."

Once I'm out of the stall, I take a look in the mirror. I'm still wearing my black pants, which I refused to change. No matter what Lisa said, I refuse to walk even briefly outside in the cold in a short skirt. The top is dark blue, which makes my hair look lighter. It's a bit lower cut than I'd like, but the effect is attractive. And my hair is just a tad too wild to tame since it's been in a bun all day, but it doesn't look awful. The makeup is dark for me, but the bar will be darker, so it's okay. I've looked worse. I wrap myself in my coat and we head out since the others have already left.

Lisa was right. As soon as we enter the bar, I take off my coat and almost wish I'd worn her skirt. They must have the heat on, and with the packed bodies everywhere, I already start to sweat. We spot our coworkers at a round booth across the room. Greg and Rebecca are sitting between Dan and Jennifer. Dan is one of our busboys, and Jennifer is another of our newer waitresses. Dan looks torn between wanting to hit on Jennifer and Rebecca at the same time.

Greg is nursing a beer and looking at the crowd.

When we finally get to the booth, I notice Greg pause as he was about to take a sip of a drink.

Lisa whispers behind me, "That's the look I was talking about."

Ignoring her, I take a seat on Jennifer's other side as Lisa slides in beside me and find drinks already waiting for us.

"To Rachael, our new boss! May she always ignore our laziness and pick up our slack!"

"Here, here."

We all take a sip, and I'm glad that my drink is drinkable as long as I take small sips. "Thank you to whoever picked my drink."

Rebecca smiles. "That was me. Greg was going to get you a beer, but I told him beer was so disgusting, and you'd like my drink."

I ignore Greg completely and take another small sip of my overly sweetened drink as a waitress comes by and Lisa orders us a round of shots, which we take quickly.

Rebecca leans her head toward Dan, who is all too willing to give her his full attention. Or at least, her low-cut top.

"Dan, would you please dance with me?"

Dan seems to be fine with getting attention from anyone, so he follows Rebecca to the dance floor without a glance back at any of us. They are quickly lost in the large amount of people and flashing lights.

As Lisa starts telling Jennifer about a horrible customer we had today who didn't leave a tip after she spent twenty minutes explaining each item on our menu in great detail, I lean a little closer to Greg.

"Your sister seems happy to be here." I glance to where I think I see a glimpse of them move through the crowd dancing. "And determined."

"Poor Dan. The kid doesn't know what he's getting into."

I lose them in the crowd as the music changes to something more upbeat. Greg leans closer to be heard as he slides a beer across the table.

"I got you a beer if you'd rather have it."

"Rebecca's drink is good."

"From the way your lips purse after each sip, I'm guessing it's too sweet."

His words make me look down at his lips and then quickly glance away when I realize I've been staring at them a bit too long.

Giving him my thanks, I take the beer from his hand, pretending not to notice the warmth of his fingers as mine brush against his.

As Lisa and Jennifer swap waitress horror stories, I notice Greg's arm is close to mine, almost touching. I don't know if it's the alcohol or his body heat, but I feel like there's a slight electric current running through my body.

Drinking a bit more to gather my courage, I finally ask, "Want to dance?"

He seems to debate this for a moment before standing and taking my hand, leading me through the crowd. Even though it's been years since I've danced with someone, with the dark lights and pounding base, it's easy to lose myself in the music. I'm hyperaware of Greg's hands on my waist and his body against mine as we move to the music.

It could be the drinking or music or just Greg being so close, but I move closer to him, deciding that kissing a coworker wouldn't be the worst decision I've ever made. Just as my lips are about to touch his, a look of what I think is desire crosses his face before he visibly shakes it off.

"I can't do this."

Stunned enough to stop dancing, I meet his eyes. "What?"

"I have to go."

Surely, I'm not hearing him right, because if I am then I'd be completely mortified. Feeling my face burn from embarrassment, I ask, "Why?"

He gives me a knowing look but must see I'm dumbfounded because he says, "Come on, Rachael. Leo's at home waiting for you."

Understanding dawns and then I'm not just embarrassed for being rejected but furious. *Leo* is his problem? I wasn't asking him to marry me or help me raise my kid. I was just trying to kiss the guy. At least I *didn't* kiss him.

"Don't bother leaving because I am."

Grabbing my things from the booth and trying not to cry until I'm in a cab, I ignore Lisa's concerned questions and get out. I slam my hand on the back of the seat as we ride to my sister's apartment, not caring what the cab driver thinks of me.

Of course a rich, cute guy doesn't want to get involved with me. I have a kid, who will always be first with me. And I understand, and deep down maybe even respect, that he didn't make a move on me since he so clearly knows he doesn't want to be involved with someone with a child. But the rational part of me must be sleeping at this hour because all I can think about is his look of disapproval when I tried to kiss him, like he was judging me.

When I get to my sister's, she just manages to open the door before I burst into tears and explain everything.

"Screw him."

"I know."

She gives me a look that only sisters can as she says, "I thought you didn't even like him."

"I don't. I mean, not really. I almost liked him."

Seeming unsure, she finally says, "Well, I know he sucks, but at least he told you straight up. Better to do it now before you get invested."

"He just didn't seem like that type of guy."

"And this isn't some kind of crazy misunderstanding, right?"

"No way. He looked so disappointed in me. Like I should have been home with my son instead of in some bar and trying to kiss him. And he's right."

She shakes her head at me.

"That's totally unfair. All you do is work and take care of your kid. You've gone out, what? Like twice since he was born? Ridiculous."

Shrugging, I lie back on her sofa and close my eyes as she rinses out my water glass and turns off the lights. I think she asks if I need anything, but I'm too close to being unconscious to form a reply.

I forget what day it is until my sister's husband enters the living room the next morning with a dozen roses in his hand. Of course it's Valentine's Day. How perfect. They give each other googly eyes until I force them to go out for lunch. I spend the morning with my nieces, nephew, and son, and it's enough of a distraction that I don't have to think about it being Valentine's Day. It's almost enough to make me forget about the previous night until I have to go in for the dinner shift.

Lisa corners me in the entryway when I get there. "Tell me what happened last night. One minute you and Greg are groping each other on the dance floor, the next you look like you're about to have a mental breakdown. Or kill him."

"What did he say?"

"Nothing. He came to our booth and told his sister he was leaving. I asked him what happened, but he just shrugged and said I should ask you."

"I tried to kiss him."

Lisa's eyebrows go up. "And?"

"He wasn't interested in me because I have a child."

"For real?"

"Yeah."

"Wait until I get back into that kitchen."

"No, it's fine."

"It's definitely not fine."

"Yes, it is. I don't want to be with anyone who doesn't want me because I have a kid. Me and Leo are a package deal. When I find someone, he will love Leo like his own. Let's not waste our time with him."

She looks at me for a moment, scrutinizing me, as if trying to determine whether I'm telling her the truth. Deciding I must be, she responds, "Fine, but I don't have to be nice to him."

The dinner rush is filled with so many happy couples celebrating their relationships that I feel my mood plummet by the minute. The good thing about all the couples dining here is it's so busy that it's easy to ignore Greg. The brief times I call an order or correction, there's always something we're both doing, so there's no time to pause. And I can avoid eye contact from behind the counter.

"Table 5 wants to add another side salad."

"Right."

"Table 20 didn't want peppers."

"Sorry."

"Table 17 needs that extra melted butter ASAP."

"Working on it."

After I come back into the kitchen again to return a steak that is too rare, I finally look at Greg as I say, "Table 10 wanted their steak medium—"

The man is trying. I can see that from the sweat on his brow and the slight tremor in his hand as he pours crema over a pork chop.

"Are you okay?"

He glances up, ignoring my question and nodding toward my steak. "Not medium? Yeah, I thought that when I was plating it. Give me a minute."

Greg wipes his face with his apron, looks in the oven, and starts stirring a pot as I move around to the entrance to the chef's area. Even though I currently hate the guy, it's obvious he's struggling to keep up.

A quick glance around the kitchen tells me he's alone. "Do you need help?"

"Is it that obvious?"

"Where is Evan?"

"If you mean the sous chef, he quit about an hour ago."

Sighing, I pull on a kitchen apron over my own, wash my hands, and begin making salads and pouring soups. Lisa takes over my tables with a nod and a not-very-sympathetic look toward Greg. "Sure, I'll help you, Rachael. You are the nicest person here. Of course, I'll help you. Anyone who—"

Rolling my eyes at her, I thank her and shoo her out with a basket of bread.

The next hour passes in silence as I chop and mix and realize how much Greg really must have been struggling in here alone. And I can't help the compliment that comes from my lips. "I'm surprised you did so well in here by yourself."

He pulls out another pan of baked potatoes as he snorts. "Oh yes, I only got multiple orders wrong and managed not to burn the kitchen down."

"True. But at least the rush is over. And I'm sure your dad will find a replacement for Evan soon."

"Too bad you're our new floor manager. You make a great sous chef."

Shaking my head, I'm about to reply when Lisa comes into the kitchen. "Rach, Leo's here."

"What?"

Even though I asked the question, I don't wait for a reply before I'm out the door and in the dining room. My sister is holding a crying Leo near the entrance.

"What's wrong?"

I take Leo from her and notice his temperature before the words are out of her mouth.

"I'm sorry. I tried calling you, but it kept going to voicemail. He quit vomiting an hour ago, but he's been crying for you since. His temperature isn't so bad but he needed you."

Nodding, I carry him to the back into Robert's office and sit with him on the couch, where he quickly starts to doze off in my arms. Once I tell my sister she did the right thing, she goes home. After some internal debate, I decide to let him stay in the office to sleep. I check on him often, and I'm happy he doesn't wake up once.

When the dinner shift is over, I load Leo into my car. I have just shut the back door when I see Greg walking toward me.

"Leo is your son?"

"Who'd you think he was?"

He chuckles to himself as he runs his hand through his hair. "I thought Leo was your boyfriend or husband."

Suddenly understanding, I shove him. "I wouldn't have danced with you if I was—"

And before I can finish my sentence, he kisses me. And I forget what I was going to say.

Five Years Later

"I can't believe you didn't go on a honeymoon. You got married on Valentine's Day."

Shrugging, I reply, "It's not the best time. With Greg taking over the restaurant and Leo in school, we decided to wait and take a trip during summer break."

Lisa came in for a late lunch, which she does at least once a week ever since she left the Charred Grape to open her own clothing boutique. She takes a sip of her tea as she shrugs.

"When Dan pops the question, I'll say no if he tells me we can't go on a honeymoon."

Shaking my head at her, I turn as Greg sits in the booth next to me and kisses my cheek. He whispers, "Mrs. Dunne."

Shivering against the warmth of his breath on my skin I reply, "Mr. Dunne."

"I'm headed to pick up Leo. We have to make a quick stop. I've been promising him a trip to that new bookstore. We'll be back."

"See you soon."

My eyes follow him as he exits. We dated a year before I was comfortable enough to introduce Greg to Leo, and I was surprised by how well they got along. Then it took me another two years before I agreed to marry him. I was nervous about how my then six-year-old would react to this, but his response was to cock his head and say, "I thought you guys were already married?"

When he found out we'd be moving in with Greg, he was ecstatic and then disappointed to find out we were all moving to a new place. However, that disappointment evaporated when we showed him our new house, which is nothing fancy, but the small backyard is perfect. Watching them play soccer out there while I tend to my herb garden might be my favorite thing to do.

Or our camping trips where all three of us lay out and look up at the stars.

Or maybe when we all curl on the couch together and watch a movie.

Or maybe it's when Leo falls asleep in my arms, and Greg leans his head against mine and whispers, "I love you."

About the Author

Caroline Baccene is the author of the novels *Breathing in the Fog* and *A Beautiful Lily*. She grew up in the middle of nowhere, South Carolina, where she developed a love of reading, writing, acting, gardening, and caring for all types of animals. Caroline graduated from the University of South Carolina with a degree in Early Childhood Education and was a teacher for five years. She currently resides in South Carolina with her husband and son.

You can find Caroline on:

Instagram: @caroline_baccene

Visit her website at:

http://carolinebaccene.wixsite.com

CONTRIBUTORS' LIBRARY

Please also look for these titles, which were authored by, published by, or feature the authors in this anthology.

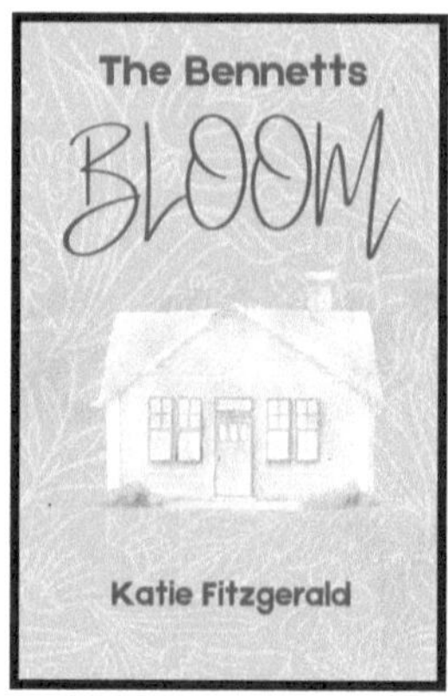

The Bennets Bloom
Katie Fitzgerald

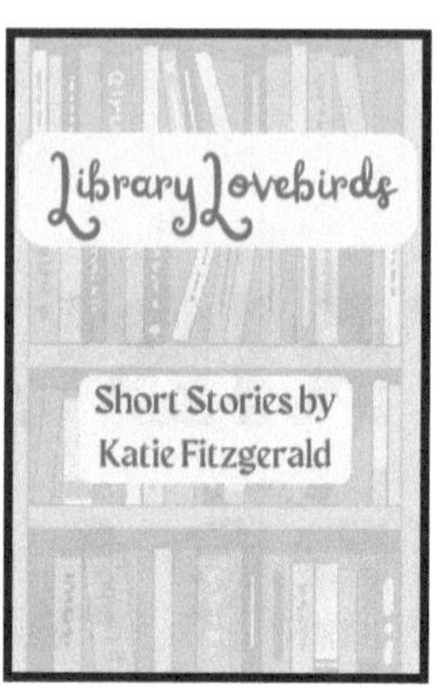

Library Lovebirds
Katie Fitzgerald

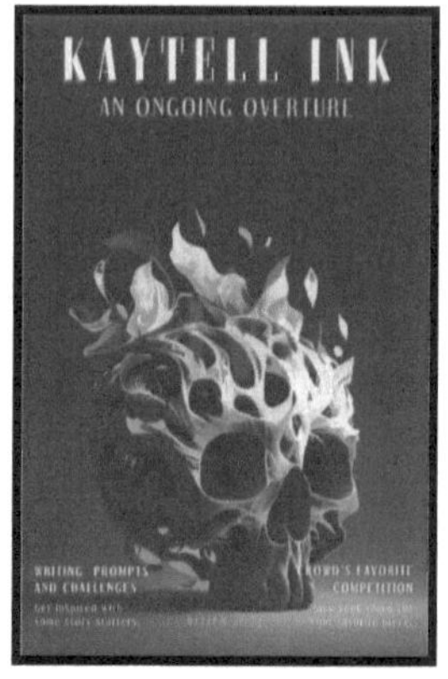

Includes "Dear Rose"
Jessica Daniliuk

Just Like Christmas
Annabel den Dekker

Purpose
Annabel den Dekker

One Week of July
Melissa Mastro

Done
Desi Stowe

Shadows
Desi Stowe

The Hansen Clan
Bjarne Borresen

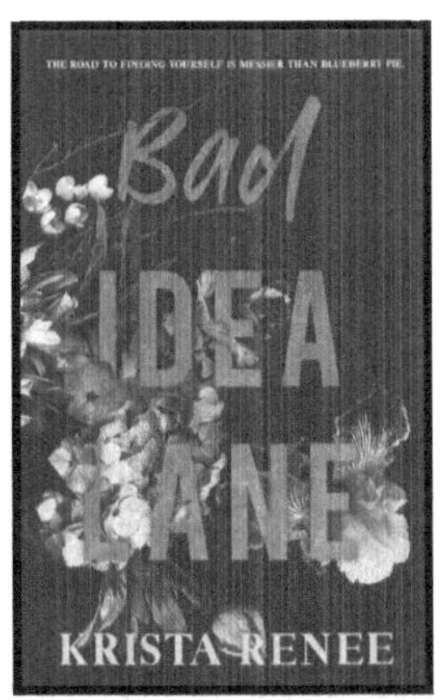

Bad Idea Lane
Krista Renee

A Beautiful Lily
Caroline Baccene

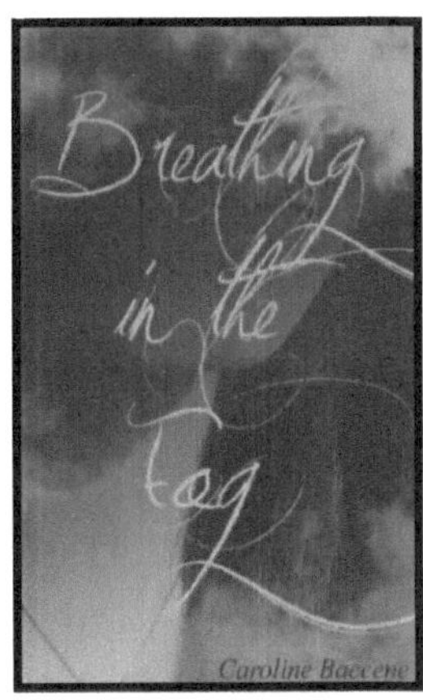

Breathing in the Fog
Caroline Baccene

About the Editor

Nicole Frail has been editing fiction and nonfiction books for adults and children for fifteen years. Between 2012 and 2024, she worked as an acquisitions and project editor for a traditional publisher based in New York City while simultaneously working with independent/self-publishing authors via her small business, Nicole Frail Edits.

In mid-2024, Nicole switched gears and decided to take her "side gig" full time, expanding the services offered through Nicole Frail Edits, LLC. Shortly after, she formed her own small press, Nicole Frail Books, LLC, to publish anthologies born out of short story contests as well as ebooks and other projects still to come.

Nicole lives just outside Scranton, Pennsylvania, with her husband, three little boys, and two Tuxedo cats.

You can find Nicole Frail on:

Instagram @nicolefrailedits & @nicolefrailbooks
Facebook @nicolefrailedits & @nicolefrailbooks

And visit her websites at:
www.nicolefrailedits.com
www.nicolefrailbooks.com

Acknowledgments

Writing is a solitary act, as is editing, but publishing a book correctly cannot be done alone—or at least, should not be done alone. Just because you *can* do it doesn't mean you *should* do it.

To all of the writers who submitted to the short story contests that led to the creation of *Recipes for Romance* and *Craving You*, thank you for your enthusiasm, your interest, and your support. Every time I put out a call for submissions, imposter syndrome creeps in, and I fear I won't have enough entries to release one anthology, let alone two. So the fact that we have two collections with thirty-one stories total is a true accomplishment!

To the nineteen authors who are included in this collection, thank you for hanging in there. Your patience and speed is much appreciated. I know my eleventh-hour style is not for everyone. Combine that with the holidays, cold and flu season, and winter weather, and production of this book was quite a roller coaster. But we did it!

To Courtney Umphress, I know your focus was on *Craving You*, but your excellent management of that anthology allowed me to concentrate on *Recipes for Romance* when I really needed to, and I appreciate that more than I can even describe. Thank you for being a dependable (and fun!) colleague and edi-buddy.

Thank you to the women who helped shape *Recipes* and *Craving*, inside and out—Kerri Odell, cover designer; Nicole Mele, proofreader; Constance Renfrow, proofreader; Sydney Ahrberg, editorial intern; and Sumbul Saleem, owner of Plunge Into Books Tours.

And, as always, I'm forever thankful for the men in my life, my forever Valentines: Matthew, Cooper, Travis, and Eli. Ily x4.

Looking for something a little . . . spicier?
Check out Craving You, the steamier selection in this anthology duo!
Available in ebook and paperback!

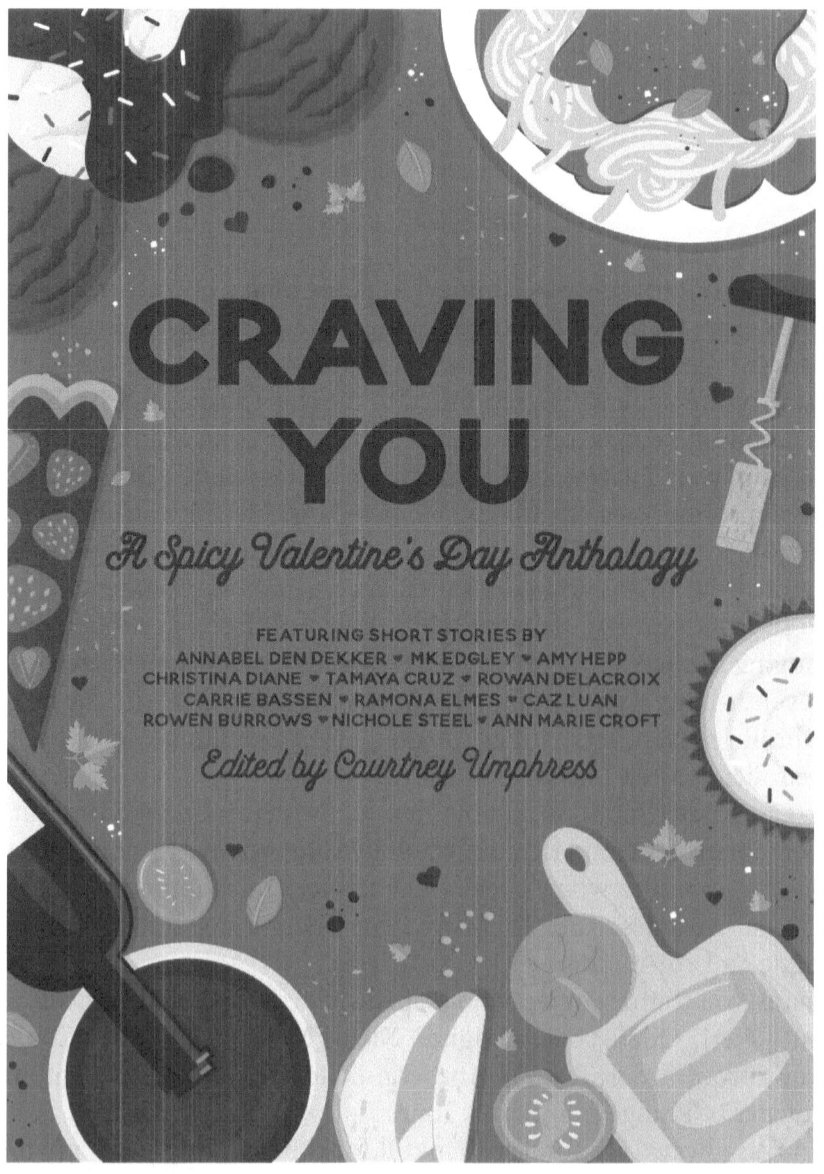

CRAVING
YOU
A Spicy Valentine's Day Anthology
FEATURING SHORT STORIES BY
ANNABEL DEN DEKKER ♥ MK EDGLEY ♥ AMY HEPP
CHRISTINA DIANE ♥ TAMAYA CRUZ ♥ ROWAN DELACROIX
CARRIE BASSEN ♥ RAMONA ELMES ♥ CAZ LUAN
ROWEN BURROWS ♥ NICHOLE STEEL ♥ ANN MARIE CROFT
Edited by Courtney Umphress

Made in United States
Troutdale, OR
02/03/2025

28602401R00224